Irresistible Greeks

Defiance & Desire

D1638683

Irresistible Greeks COLLECTION

May 2016

June 2016

July 2016

August 2016

September 2016

October 2016

Irresistible Greeks

Defiance & Desire

CAROLE MORTIMER CATHERINE GEORGE REBECCA WINTERS

First Published in Great Britain 2016
By Mills & Boon, an imprint of HarperCollins*Publishers*
1 London Bridge Street, London, SE1 9GF

Irresistible Greeks: Defiance & Desire © 2016 Harlequin Books S.A.

Defying Drakon © 2012 Carole Mortimer
The Enigmatic Greek © 2013 Catherine George
Baby Out of the Blue © 2013 Rebecca Winters

ISBN: 978-0-263-92214-1

24-0716

Harlequin (UK) Limited's policy is to use papers that are natural, renewable and recyclable products and made from wood grown in sustainable forests. The logging and manufacturing processes conform to the legal environmental regulations of the country of origin.

Printed and bound in Spain
by CPI, Barcelona

DEFYING DRAKON

CAROLE MORTIMER

Carole Mortimer was born and lives in the UK. She is married to Peter and they have six sons. She has been writing for Mills & Boon since 1978, and is the author of almost 200 books. She writes for both the Mills & Boon Historical and Modern lines. Carole is a *USA Today* bestselling author and in 2012 was recognised by Queen Elizabeth II for her 'outstanding contribution to literature'.

Visit Carole at www.carolemortimer.co.uk or on Facebook.

CHAPTER ONE

'Who is she?' Markos asked.

Drakon had telephoned down to his cousin Markos's office just a few minutes ago, and was now in one of the many rooms of the penthouse apartment on the thirtieth floor of the Lyonedes Tower building in Central London, where Drakon stayed whenever he was visiting from the company's New York offices. Markos, naturally, preferred to live away from the building where he worked every day.

Drakon's full attention was focused speculatively on one of several security monitors in front of him as he watched the young woman on the monochrome screen pacing restlessly up and down the room she had been escorted to several minutes ago by Max Stanford, his Head of Security, after causing something of a disturbance in the reception area situated on the ground floor of the building.

She was a tall and willowy young woman, the dark blouse she wore—possibly black or brown—clinging to the outline of small pert breasts, while slim-fitting low-rider jeans revealed a tantalising glimpse of the flatness of her abdomen before curving lovingly over her bottom and the length of her legs. She was probably aged somewhere in her mid to late twenties, with just below shoulder-length straight hair—blonde? Her face was arrestingly beautiful: delicately heart-shaped and dominated by light-coloured eyes. Damn this black and white screen! She had a small straight nose and sensuously full lips.

He glanced at Markos as his cousin came to stand beside him. The family resemblance and their Greek nationality were more than obvious in their harshly sculptured olive-skinned features. Both men were dark-haired and over six feet tall, although at thirty-four Markos was two years Drakon's junior.

'I'm not sure,' Drakon answered. 'Max telephoned a few minutes ago and asked me what I wished him to do with her,' he continued. 'Apparently when he removed her from Reception she refused to tell him anything other than that her name is Bartholomew and she has no intention of leaving the building until she has spoken either to you or me—but preferably me,' he added dryly.

Markos's eyes widened. 'Any relation to Miles Bartholomew, do you think?'

'Could be his daughter.' Drakon had met Miles Bartholomew several times before the other man's death in a car crash six months ago, and there was a definite facial resemblance between him and the young woman they could see on the screen now. Although at sixty-two Miles's hair had been silver, and his tall frame wiry rather than willowy and graceful.

'What do you suppose she wants?' Markos prompted curiously.

Drakon's dark eyes narrowed on the impatiently pacing woman, his mouth thinning to an uncompromising line. 'I have absolutely no idea. But I have every intention of finding out.'

Markos's brows rose. 'You intend talking to her yourself?'

Drakon gave a humourless smile at his cousin's obvious surprise. 'I have asked Max to bring her to me here in ten minutes' time. It is to be hoped she will not have worn a hole in a very expensive carpet before then.'

Markos looked thoughtful. 'Are you sure that's a good idea with our current connection to Bartholomew's young and beautiful widow?'

Drakon deliberately turned his back on the screen. 'Max's alternative was to have her arrested for trespassing and/or disturbing the peace. A move at best guaranteed to bring unnecessary and unwanted publicity to Lyonedes Enterprises,' he said, 'and at worst to have an adverse effect on our relationship with Angela Bartholomew.'

'True,' his cousin conceded. 'But isn't it setting something of a precedent to give in to this type of emotional blackmail?'

Drakon arched arrogant dark brows. 'You are expecting there to be more than one determined young woman in London at the moment who feels the need to stage a sit-in in the reception area of Lyonedes Enterprises until she has been allowed to talk to the company's president?'

Markos gave a rueful shake of his head. 'You've only been in England for two days—hardly long enough for you to have broken any female hearts as yet.'

Drakon's expression remained impassive. 'If, as you say, hearts have been broken in the past, then it has not been my doing; I have never made any secret of the fact that I have no interest in marrying at this time.'

'If ever!' His cousin snorted.

Drakon shrugged. 'No doubt there will come a time when an heir becomes necessary.'

'Just not yet?'

His mouth thinned. 'No.'

Markos eyed him teasingly. 'Miss Bartholomew seems to have piqued your interest…'

There were only two people in the world who would dare to speak to Drakon in this familiar way: his cousin and his widowed mother.

The two men had grown up together in the family home in Athens. Markos had come to live with his aunt and uncle and slightly older cousin after his parents were killed in a plane crash when he was eight years old. It was that closeness, and the fact that they were related by blood, which allowed the younger man certain freedoms of expression where Drakon was concerned. If anyone else but Markos had dared to make a comment on or question Drakon's private life like that, he would very quickly have found himself on the other side of the door. After being suitably and icily chastened, of course.

'I am…curious as to her reasons for coming here,' he acknowledged slowly.

His cousin glanced towards the screen. 'She's certainly beautiful…'

'Yes, she is,' Drakon acknowledged tersely.

Markos shot him another sideways glance. 'Maybe I could sit in on the meeting?'

'I think not, Markos,' he dismissed with dry humour. 'Whatever Miss Bartholomew wishes to talk to me about, she has gone about it in a very unorthodox manner. I do not think the Vice-Chairman of Lyonedes Enterprises showing an admiring interest in her is going to suitably convey our displeasure at her behaviour!'

Markos gave an unrepentant grin. 'Do you have to spoil *all* my fun?'

Drakon smiled in acknowledgement of his cousin's roguish reputation with the ladies even as he glanced down at the plain gold watch secured about his wrist. 'Thompson should be arriving shortly for his ten o'clock appointment. I will join the two of you in your office in ten minutes.'

The other man arched teasing brows. 'Are you sure that will be long enough with the lovely Miss Bartholomew?'

'Oh, yes.' He nodded.

Drakon gave one last glance at the young woman on the screen before striding through to the sitting room of the spacious apartment to stand in front of one of the huge picture windows that looked out over the London morning skyline, hearing his cousin leaving the penthouse a few seconds later as his own brooding thoughts continued to dwell on the impudent Miss Bartholomew.

He had taken over as head of the Lyonedes family business empire on the death of his father ten years ago, and now, aged thirty-six, Drakon knew he was rarely surprised by anything anyone did or said—and was certainly never intimidated by their actions. He was the one whose very presence invariably intimidated others; never the other way about.

And whatever reason Miss Bartholomew felt she had for her unacceptable behaviour, she would very shortly be made aware of that fact...

Gemini stopped pacing and turned to frown at the middle-aged man who had earlier introduced himself only as Head of Security for Lyonedes Enterprises as he finally returned to the elegantly furnished room he had made her prison fifteen minutes ago, before abandoning her there and locking the door behind him as he left.

No doubt he had gone off to take instruction from Markos Lyonedes as to what was the best thing to do with her—or maybe he hadn't bothered with that and had just telephoned the police to have her arrested! She doubted the visiting totally elusive Drakon Lyonedes, President of Lyonedes Enterprises, would even be informed of something so trivial as a young woman refusing to leave the building until she was allowed to speak to him.

Gemini had every reason to know just how elusive he was. She had desperately tried repeatedly to make an appointment to speak to the man since she'd learnt of his arrival in England two days ago. But as she had remained stubbornly unwilling to give her reasons as to why she wanted the appointment, her request had been politely but firmly refused by Markos Lyonedes's secretary.

Oh, she had been invited to send in her C.V. to the personnel manager—as if she would ever want to work for a circling shark like Drakon Lyonedes!—but had been refused an appointment with him *or* his cousin, who was Vice-Chairman of the company in charge of the London-based offices. Leaving her with no alternative, Gemini had finally decided determinedly, than to stage a sit-in in the ground floor reception area of Lyonedes Tower.

Only to be firmly removed within minutes of her arrival and locked in a room pending dispatch!

'Let's go.' The tough-looking Head of Security, dressed all in black, his grey hair shaved to a crewcut, stepped back in order to allow her to precede him out of the room. He was probably ex-military.

'I expected handcuffs at the very least!' she drawled as she strolled past him into the marble hallway.

He arched iron-grey brows. 'What exactly did you have in mind?'

Was that amusement she saw in those hard blue eyes? No, surely not! 'Nothing like that, I assure you,' Gemini said dryly.

'That's what I thought.' He nodded as he took a vice-like grip of her arm. 'And handcuffs wouldn't look good in front of the other visitors.'

That remark might have been funny if the man hadn't looked so deadly serious when he made it! 'Where are you taking me?' she prompted with a frown, having tried to resist that steely hold and only succeeded in bruising her arm as the now grim-faced man all but frogmarched her down a long and silent hallway towards the back of the building. 'I asked—'

'I heard you.' He came to a halt beside a lift before deftly punching a security code into the lit keypad.

He'd heard her, but obviously had no intention of satisfying her curiosity. 'I'm sure this building is far too modern to have a dungeon,' she commented.

'But it does have a basement.' He shot her a narrow-eyed glance as the lift doors opened, and he pulled her in beside him before pressing one of the buttons.

The movement was made altogether too fast for Gemini to be able to see which button he had pressed before the doors closed behind them and the lift began to move. Down? Or up? Whichever it was, the lift was moving so fast her stomach seemed literally to somersault! Or maybe that was just her slightly shredded nerves? She hadn't particularly enjoyed coming to Lyonedes Tower this morning and making such a nuisance of herself, and the dangerous-looking man standing so still and silent beside her certainly didn't inspire confidence as to her future wellbeing!

Maybe trying to force a meeting between herself and either Markos or Drakon Lyonedes hadn't been such a good idea after all?

It had seemed perfectly logical and straightforward when Gemini had considered her options earlier that morning, as she sat in the kitchen of her apartment. But here and now, on her way to goodness' knew where, with a hatchet-faced man who looked as if he was more than capable of killing with his bare hands, it seemed far less so.

It was all Drakon Lyonedes's fault, of course. If the man didn't make it so impossible for people to see or speak with him then there would be no reason for her to resort to such drastic measures as she had this morning. As it was…

Her chin rose defensively as she chanced a glance at the grimly silent man standing beside her. 'Kidnapping is a serious offence, you know.'

'So is making a public nuisance of yourself,' he came back remorselessly.

'Lyonedes Tower isn't exactly public!'

'Keep telling yourself that, love.' Once again she thought she caught a glimpse of humour in those steely blue eyes, before it quickly dissipated and only the steel remained.

'There's nowhere for me to escape to, stuck in this lift, so it's probably safe to let go of my arm now—' She broke off abruptly as the lift came to a gliding halt and the doors slid silently open in front of her.

Not into a basement. Or a dungeon. But into the unlikeliest-looking office Gemini had ever seen…

Probably because it *wasn't* an office, she realised

as Mr Grim pulled her with him into a huge and elegant sitting room. The thick-pile carpet beneath her booted feet was a rich cream colour, and several brown leather armchairs and a huge matching L-shaped sofa were placed near the marble fireplace. Occasional tables bore vases of cream roses, and a matching cream piano stood in one corner of the room, a bar area in another. She easily recognised some of the numerous paintings on the cream walls as being priceless works of art by long-dead artists, and the floor-to-ceiling windows that made up the wall directly in front of her displayed an amazing view of the London skyline.

So—definitely not the basement, then!

'I will ring you when it is time for Miss Bartholomew to leave, Max.'

'Sir.'

Gemini only vaguely registered the Head of Security as he stepped silently back into the lift and departed. She turned sharply to locate the owner of that deep and authoritative voice, her eyes widening in shock as she saw the man silhouetted in front of a second wall of windows, instantly knowing she was looking at the tall, powerful, olive-skinned Drakon Lyonedes himself.

It was perfectly obvious that he was far from pleased. The expression on his handsome face was even grimmer than the one on his Head of Security's.

Drakon Lyonedes was over six feet tall, with wide shoulders, a powerful chest, and long legs clearly defined in a tailored and obviously expensive charcoal-grey suit worn over a white silk shirt and pale grey tie. His dark hair was cut ruthlessly short, and piercing coal-black eyes were set in a face that looked as if it had been hewn from granite. None of the rare photographs of Drakon Lyonedes that had very occasionally appeared in the newspapers over the years had even begun to scratch the surface of the aura of power that surrounded him like an invisible cloak.

Not just power, Gemini realised as an icy shiver ran the length of her spine, but danger—like that of a deadly predator waiting to pounce on its prey.

A powerful and deadly predator who now had *her* firmly fixed in his sights!

Drakon's expression remained unreadable as he took in the colour version of the determined Miss Bartholomew. The straight, shoulder-length hair he had thought might be a pale blonde was in fact an unusual white-gold—the same colour as the long stretches of sandy beach that surrounded his private island off the coast of Greece. Her complexion was the palest ivory, and a perfect background for her eyes, which he could now see were the same deep aquamarine colour as the warm Aegean Sea, and shielded by thick dark lashes. Her full and sensuous lips were an unglossed and natural rose.

In fact she did not appear to be wearing any makeup at all, which was most unusual in his experience...

'Mr Lyonedes, I presume?' she enquired softly, moving with a natural grace as she stepped further into the private sitting room of the penthouse apartment.

'Miss Bartholomew.' Drakon remained unsmiling in response to what had obviously been an attempt at humour on her part. 'Max informs me that you have been most...insistent in your desire to speak with me.'

'Does he?' She continued to stare at him with those aquamarine eyes.

'Sitting on the floor of the reception area and refusing to move till you had either spoken to myself or my cousin *would* appear to be an act of determination, yes,' he pointed out.

'Oh, yes. That.' Gemini grimaced as she tried to gather her scrambled thoughts together—a situation she readily admitted had been brought about by this man's totally overpowering presence! 'Max soon took care of that for you, though,' she said, remembering the ease with which the security man had placed his hands beneath her elbows and just lifted her up from the floor and out of the reception area to that secure room.

Dark brows rose. 'You are on a first-name basis with my Head of Security?'

'I think it's fair to say I'm on an *only* name basis with him—he didn't introduce himself to me earlier, so I know him by the name you just called him.' She shrugged. 'And I wouldn't have needed to be quite so determined if you'd made yourself more accessible,' she said lightly. After all, she could afford to be a little more amenable now that she was actually in the presence of the man himself.

'And why would I wish to do that?' He seemed genuinely baffled by her statement.

'Because— Oh, never mind.' Gemini gave a dismissive shake of her head.

Drakon noticed how the movement caused that cascade of white-gold hair to be caught in the sun's rays, and found himself wondering if the colour was natural or from a bottle. Only to add an inner admonishment for allowing even that small personal interest to creep into this meeting. 'You do realise that causing a nuisance of yourself on private property is—'

'A serious offence,' she finished heavily. 'Yes, your Head of Security has already made it more than clear that you would have been quite within your rights to call the police and have me arrested rather than agree to see me.'

Drakon gave a hard and humourless smile. 'Oh, believe me, that possibility has not yet been dismissed.'

'Oh.' Uncertainty briefly flickered in her eyes as she drew herself up to her full height of possibly five feet ten inches in the two-inch-heeled boots she was wearing. The shirt that fitted so flatteringly over her breasts and the flatness of her abdomen was black in colour, the jeans that clung to that enticingly curvaceous bottom a light blue. 'I only did what I did because I so badly needed to talk to you—'

'Would you care for coffee?'

She blinked. 'What?'

'Coffee?' Drakon indicated the bar area, where a full pot of coffee had been brought up to him earlier and left on the black marble surface along with several black mugs.

'Is it decaf?'

He raised dark brows. 'I think possibly Brazilian, as that is my preferred blend...'

'Then, no, thank you,' she refused politely. 'Unless it's decaffeinated most coffees give me a migraine.'

'Would you like me to send down for some that *is* decaffeinated?'

'No, really. I'm fine.' She smiled.

Drakon had absolutely no idea why he had even made the offer; the sooner the two of them talked and she departed, the better! 'You do not mind if I do?' He didn't wait for her reply before walking over to the bar and pouring a cup of the steaming and aromatic brew, lifting the unsweetened liquid to his lips and slowly taking a sip as he used the respite in conversation to study her over the rim of the mug.

If, as he thought, this young woman *was* the daughter of Miles Bartholomew and the stepdaughter of Angela Bartholomew, then she did not appear or behave at all as one might have expected of the only child of a multimillionaire industrialist. Her clothing was as casual as that of any of the dozens of young women Drakon had seen as he was driven from the airport into central London two days ago, her unusually coloured hair was styled simply in straight layers and—as he had already noted—the fragile loveliness of her face appeared bare of make-up. Her fingernails were short and unvarnished on long and elegant hands, and she raised one to flick a wayward strand of that long white-gold hair over her shoulder.

The appearance of Miles Bartholomew's daughter— if this was she—was indeed unexpected. Her familiar manner towards Drakon—with a complete lack of the awe with which he was usually treated!—was even more so...

He placed the black mug carefully back on the bar beside him before walking softly, unhurriedly, across the room until he stood only inches away from her. Their gazes were almost on a level as she stood only three or four inches shorter than his own six feet and two inches in height.

'We appear to have omitted to introduce ourselves. As you have already guessed, I am Drakon Lyonedes. And you are...?'

'Gemini,' she blurted out. 'Er—Gemini Bartholomew. I'm Miles Bartholomew's daughter.' She thrust out a hand, her cheeks having become coloured the same beguiling rose as the fullness of her lips.

Gemini...

Drakon inwardly appreciated how well that name

suited her as he took the slenderness of her hand in his much larger one. The name was as unusual and beautiful as this young woman was herself...

'And what is it you believe that only I can do for you, Miss Bartholomew?'

Gemini felt a quiver of awareness travel the length of her spine as Drakon Lyonedes continued to hold her hand captive in his much stronger one. His skin was cool to the touch, but at the same time the huskiness of his voice seemed to wash over her senses with the warmth of a lingering caress.

Surely she must have imagined that *double entendre* in his question?

Even the thought that she might not have done was enough to make her aware of the fact that not only was she not prepared for the sheer physical presence of the head of Lyonedes Enterprises, but she hadn't even begun to guess—couldn't possibly have imagined!— the rawness of the overwhelming sexuality he exuded.

It was a raw sexuality Gemini would have preferred not to have even recognised, let alone responded to, when she had every reason to suspect that he was currently involved in an affair with the stepmother she disliked so intensely...

CHAPTER TWO

JUST the thought of her stepmother was enough to make Gemini pull her hand abruptly from Drakon's— no doubt his hand had touched the detested Angela in ways Gemini didn't even want to begin to imagine!

With an inward shudder she thrust her hand firmly behind her back before taking a determined step away from him. 'There's only one thing you can do for me, Mr Lyonedes,' she assured him flatly. 'And that is to withdraw the offer you've made to purchase Bartholomew House from my father's widow!'

Drakon studied Gemini Bartholomew from beneath narrowed lids, noting the wings of colour that had appeared in those ivory cheeks, and the over-bright glitter of emotion now visible in her beautiful sea-green eyes as she glared at him. 'And why, when the sale is due to be completed in only two weeks' time, would you imagine I might wish to do that, Miss Bartholomew?' he said slowly.

A pained frown appeared between those long-lashed aquamarine eyes. 'Because it isn't hers to sell, of course. To you or anyone else!'

'I believe my legal department have checked all the necessary paperwork and are completely satisfied with their results,' Drakon assured her smoothly, no longer

completely sure what or who he was dealing with. He
certainly had no one else's word but hers that she was
who she claimed to be.

From all accounts her behaviour had been less than
rational ever since she'd entered the building, and the
claim she had just made, along with that slightly wild
glitter in those stunning Aegean-coloured eyes, would
seem to imply a certain wobble in her emotional balance. Perhaps, after all, he should have heeded Markos's
advice and not agreed to meet privately with this unusual young woman?

'I'm sure that they were.' She now gave an impatient shake of that white-gold head. 'When I said
Bartholomew House wasn't Angela's to sell, I meant
morally rather than legally.'

The tension in Drakon's shoulders relaxed slightly.
'I see,' he murmured.

Somehow Gemini doubted that!

And she didn't care for the way in which Drakon
was now regarding her so sceptically with those piercing coal-black eyes of his from between narrowed lids.

No doubt he already thought she was slightly de-
ranged after her behaviour in the reception area, without her now claiming that Bartholomew House wasn't
Angela's to sell, and then admitting that it was! Except
it wasn't. How could it be, when Bartholomew House
in London had been owned by a Bartholomew since—
well, for ever? And Angela wasn't really a Bartholomew.
The other woman had been the second wife of Gemini's
father, and only married to him for three years before
his death six months ago—how could Angela possibly
begin to understand the sense of tradition, of belonging, that a Bartholomew living in Bartholomew House
had given to her family for hundreds of years?

As Gemini knew only too well, it wasn't a question of her stepmother not understanding those things; Angela didn't *want* to understand them, and had made it more than clear these past few months that as she was Miles's widow the house was legally hers. As such, she could do whatever she wanted with it. And if that involved selling Bartholomew House to Lyonedes Enterprises, to the powerful, mega-wealthy man she had implied was her lover, then that was exactly what Angela intended to do!

Gemini scowled her complete frustration with the situation. 'I realise that you and Angela are…involved, but—'

'I beg your pardon?' Drakon raised an arrogant dark brow.

'Oh, don't worry.' She waved a placatory hand at his frowning countenance. 'I don't consider your having a relationship with my stepmother so soon after my father's death as being any of my business.'

'If that's true it's very…magnanimous of you,' Drakon said slowly.

'Oh, it's true,' Gemini assured him—even if, now that she had met him, she couldn't help but wonder how such a powerful and charismatic man could possibly find a woman like Angela attractive.

Her father at least had had the excuse of deep feelings of loneliness after the death of Gemini's mother just a year before he and Angela had been introduced, as well as being deeply flattered by the attentions of a beautiful woman over twenty-five years his junior. But Drakon Lyonedes was as rich as Croesus, for goodness' sake, and as handsome and powerful as any of his Greek gods. As such, he could surely have any woman he wanted. So why would he bother with a mercenary like Angela? There really was no accounting for a man's taste!

'Please continue,' Drakon invited coolly.

'I'm not sure that I should,' she said, suddenly wary.

He shrugged those broad shoulders. 'You obviously disapproved of your father's second marriage…?'

'No, that wasn't it.' Having started this conversation, Gemini now felt uncomfortable revealing too much of her family history to a man she had, after all, only just met. Especially as, if Angela was to be believed, that man was involved with her. 'I just thought perhaps my father should have waited a little longer before remarrying. He was feeling pretty low when he and Angela met—my mother had died the previous year, after thirty years of marriage, and he was desperately lonely.' She shrugged. 'It seemed to me to be a typical on-the-rebound thing.'

'But your father did not agree?'

Gemini winced. 'He had been incredibly unhappy since my mother died, and he seemed so happy with Angela that I just didn't have the heart to voice any of my doubts to him.'

'You loved him very much?'

'Very much,' she confirmed gruffly.

'So he and Angela married despite your misgivings?'

She nodded. 'I just wanted him to be happy again. I'd tried my best to fill the gap that she left, but no matter how close we were it really isn't possible for a daughter to take the place of a life-mate,' she added sadly.

A life-mate…

Having witnessed his own parents' long and happy marriage, Drakon was not unfamiliar with the concept; he had just never heard it described in quite those terms before.

In retrospect, it was a fitting way to describe the closeness that had existed between his own parents—their marriage had been one of friendship and trust as much as love. A love that had encompassed both their 'sons', and which now caused his long-widowed mother to resort to constant lectures on the wonderful state of matrimony whenever he or Markos visited her at her home in Athens and she encouraged at least one of them to marry and give her the grandchildren she so dearly longed for. Unfortunately neither Markos nor Drakon had found a woman they could even contemplate spending the rest of their lives with, let alone be that elusive 'life-mate' Gemini Bartholomew had referred to.

As a child Drakon had just assumed that everyone's parents were as happily married as his own, that their deep love and friendship for each other was the norm. In his teens and twenties, as the Lyonedes heirs, Drakon and Markos had enjoyed dating and bedding a variety of beautiful women, with no thought of falling in love and marrying. It had taken Drakon years to realise that he hadn't felt even the beginnings of love for any of those women—that in fact the type of love his parents had for each other was the exception rather than the norm.

Now, at the age of thirty-six, Drakon believed himself to be too hardened and cynical ever to welcome that emotional vulnerability into his life. Even if he was lucky enough to find it.

'You and your father were close?' he prompted softly.

'Very.' Tears flooded those sea-green eyes.

'I did not mean to upset you—'

'It's okay,' she assured him gruffly. 'I just—I still miss him so much.'

Drakon shifted uncomfortably. 'Are you sure I cannot get you something to drink?'

'No. Really. I'll be fine.' She blinked back those tears as she continued determinedly, 'Things changed between us—became...difficult once Daddy was married to Angela.'

'He was unhappy in the marriage?'

She had already revealed more to this man than she had intended doing; there was absolutely no reason for him to know of the disillusionment that had set in within months of her father's second marriage. 'I'm sure I've already bored you with enough family details for one day, Mr Lyonedes,' she said huskily. 'I've only told you the things I have in an effort to help you to understand the...the awkwardness, of this situation.'

He nodded briskly, obviously accepting her explanation. 'What I fail to understand is what you think I can do about any of it.'

Unfortunately, now that Gemini was confronted with the man himself, she was wondering the same thing! Sitting at home in her apartment, going over the conversation she wanted to have with Drakon Lyonedes, it had all seemed so much simpler than it was in reality. And the fact that the man was so completely and disconcertingly handsome wasn't helping the situation.

Nor was the fact that, in spite of knowing he was intimately involved with the despised Angela, Gemini actually found herself appreciating those tall, dark and dangerous good looks...

How much greater would that appreciation be if she *didn't* know he was involved with Angela? Gemini dreaded to think!

She nervously moistened the dryness of her lips with the tip of her tongue before speaking. 'As I've said, I would like you to withdraw your offer for Bartholomew House.'

'Which, unless I have misunderstood the situation, would not seem to be any of your concern. It was Angela Bartholomew who inherited the house on your father's death and not you,' Drakon pointed out.

'But she shouldn't have done,' Gemini insisted. 'Daddy assured me only weeks before he died that he intended making a new will—one that would clearly state that Bartholomew House was to come to *me* when he died.'

'Something he obviously failed to do before his unexpected death.'

She gave a pained wince. 'Well...yes.'

'He left you nothing?'

Gemini didn't particularly care for the censure she could hear in Drakon's tone. 'I wouldn't call the cherished memories of the love and caring he always had for me nothing!'

That sculptured mouth thinned. 'As I am sure you are well aware, I was talking of what you English refer to as "bricks and mortar".'

'It wasn't necessary. My parents set up a substantial trust fund for me years ago,' she dismissed stiffly. 'But, as I've said, my father assured me that it was his intention to ensure that Bartholomew House came to me after...after his death.'

'Unfortunately we only have your word for that.'

'I am not in the habit of lying, Mr Lyonedes!'

'I was not suggesting that you are.' Drakon sighed his irritation, both with this conversation and his feelings of discomfort at her obvious distress at her father's recent demise and the loss of her family home. 'Only that perhaps you should be discussing all these things with your father's lawyers rather than with me.'

'I already have,' she admitted heavily.

'And...?'

She sighed. 'And they acknowledge that my father informed them only weeks before he died that he was in the process of writing a new will.'

Drakon gaze sharpened. 'But he failed to present this will to them?'

'It would appear so,' she confirmed shakily. 'As such, they agree with you. In the absence of this new will, clearly stating that Bartholomew House was to be separate from all my father's other properties, then Angela is entitled to it as well.'

'It is not a case of my agreeing or disagreeing,' Drakon stated. 'The law is simply the law—no matter what may have been stated verbally. Besides which,' he continued firmly as she would have interrupted, 'if I were to withdraw my own offer for the house and land I have no doubts that your stepmother would simply find another buyer.'

'I realise that—which is why I've come up with another proposal. If you are agreeable, that is?' Those sea-green eyes had brightened excitedly.

Drakon closed his own eyes briefly, before opening them once again to study Gemini from beneath lowered lashes.

From the things she had just revealed to him concerning the Bartholomew family, she was perhaps exactly who she claimed to be. Nevertheless, as she'd come here today with the sole intention of persuading him to stop his company's purchase of Bartholomew House, Drakon somehow doubted this 'proposal' would be any less irregular!

'Of course you would have to agree not to tell Angela anything about it for now,' she added worriedly. 'Otherwise I know she would do everything in her power to prevent it—to the point of withdrawing from the sale of Bartholomew House to Lyonedes Enterprises.'

Drakon's mouth thinned. 'Not without incurring a severe financial penalty for reneging on our present arrangement.'

'That's something, at least,' she breathed shakily.

'Miss Bartholomew—'

'Please call me Gemini,' she invited softly.

'Gemini,' Drakon agreed abruptly, although just voicing that unusual name seemed to add a level of intimacy to this already unusual situation that he wasn't sure he felt altogether comfortable with. 'You are obviously under a misapprehension concerning my—' He broke off as he saw Markos reappear at the top of the private spiral staircase leading directly from the offices below.

Gemini frowned as she sensed that his attention was no longer on her but directed somewhere behind her. Her breath caught in her throat as she turned and found herself looking at a dark and handsome man so similar in looks to Drakon Lyonedes that he surely had to be related to him. No doubt this was Markos Lyonedes, Drakon's cousin.

Whoever he was, Gemini dearly wished he had waited just a few minutes more before making his appearance!

'Sorry to interrupt, Drakon.' The man's deep green gaze was fixed curiously on Gemini even as he spoke to his cousin. 'I expected you to join me in my office some time ago.'

Drakon looked down frowningly at his slender gold wristwatch, surprised to see that he had been talking with Gemini for almost half an hour rather than the ten minutes he had originally thought necessary before dismissing her. Incredible!

'I believe Miss Bartholomew has said what she wished to say...?' He turned to give her a pointed glance.

Instead of taking that as the invitation to leave Drakon intended it to be, she turned and walked gracefully across the room to where Markos stood at the top of the staircase. 'I'm pleased to meet you, Mr Lyonedes.' She smiled warmly as she thrust out her hand.

Markos briefly raised dark and questioning brows in Drakon's direction before turning to take her slender hand in his own. 'I assure you the pleasure is all mine, Miss Bartholomew.' Markos's voice had become dark and smoky.

'Gemini,' she invited lightly.

'Markos,' he returned warmly.

Her smile widened. 'I apologise if I've made your cousin late for an important business meeting.'

'Not at all.' Markos's gaze darkened appreciatively as he continued to hold onto that slender hand and looked down into the pale beauty of her face. 'In Drakon's place I wouldn't have been in any hurry to leave you in order to attend a boring business meeting either.'

Drakon found himself suddenly deeply irritated by the obvious flirtation taking place in front of him, and became even more annoyed as Gemini gave a husky and appreciative laugh before deftly extricating her hand from Markos's. 'I will join you downstairs in a moment, Markos,' he bit out harshly.

His cousin gave him an amused glance. 'I would be more than happy to stay here and keep Gemini company until you return from talking with Bob Thompson.'

Drakon's mouth thinned. 'That will not be necessary.

Miss Bartholomew and I will be meeting for dinner this evening in order to conclude our conversation.'

Wide and startled sea-green eyes turned sharply in his direction. 'We will?'

Drakon bit back his inner frustration, having no idea why he had even made such a statement. Except he had not liked the idea of Markos remaining alone here with Gemini any more than he had appreciated the way in which his cousin had held on to her hand for far longer than was necessary or polite...

Implying what, exactly?

This woman had forced her way into his presence today by making a damned nuisance of herself, before making several surprising statements—including one concerning Drakon's relationship with her stepmother. And as a reward for that unacceptable behaviour he was now inviting her out to *dinner*?

No, he had not invited her out to dinner. He had *told* her the two of them would be having dinner together this evening in order to finish this conversation. Not the same thing at all...

'We will,' Drakon stated flatly. 'I will send a car to Bartholomew House to collect you at seven-thirty this evening.'

'I haven't lived at Bartholomew House for years.' Her nose wrinkled ruefully. 'I'm afraid Angela cornered me several months after she and Daddy were married and asked me to leave,' she explained with a grimace.

Drakon scowled darkly, liking the situation between the two Bartholomew women less and less the more he learnt of it.

Admittedly, as the second wife of Miles Bartholomew, Angela had been perfectly within her rights to ask her stepdaughter to find somewhere else to live—especially

as Gemini must have been twenty-four or five at the
time—but morally…

But as he had already assured Gemini once today,
unfortunately morality often had very little to do with
anything!

'Then you will give your current address to the receptionist downstairs when you leave so that the car
can be directed there,' he ordered.

'I'll go down to Reception with Gemini,' Markos offered.

Drakon shot his cousin a narrow-eyed glance as he
once again sensed Markos's interest in this ethereally
beautiful young woman. 'I am sure Miss Bartholomew,
having already managed to force herself into my presence today, is more than capable of taking herself down
in the lift,' he drawled dismissively, feeling an inner
satisfaction as he saw the guilty flush that instantly
warmed Gemini's cheeks.

Markos gave an amused smile. 'I'm sure she is too.
But wouldn't it be better if one of us were to ensure she
has actually left the building?'

The blush deepened in Gemini's cheeks. 'I resent the
implication that I'm some sort of criminal who needs
escorting from the premises!' she defended irritably.

'Forgive me if I inadvertently gave that impression,'
Markos apologised.

She nodded. 'I only behaved in the way that I did earlier because I needed to speak to your cousin on a—a
personal matter, and it seemed to be the only way to
achieve that.'

Drakon now sensed Markos's speculative green gaze
on him, aware that after their earlier conversation his
cousin no doubt now believed that 'personal matter'
was something totally other than what it actually was.

'Escort the lady downstairs by all means, Markos,' he said as he strolled across the room to join them. 'Until later this evening, Gemini,' he added huskily, before turning to descend the spiral staircase without so much as a backward glance.

'Do I have a smudge of dirt on my nose or something?' Gemini shot a puzzled frown at the man standing beside her in the lift as she sensed his silent appraisal.

'Not at all.' Markos shook his head. 'It's just— Drakon has never mentioned knowing you before today.'

Her brows rose. 'That's probably because he *didn't* know me before today!'

'No?'

'Mr Lyonedes—'

'Markos,' he reminded her smoothly.

Oh, he was a charmer, this one, Gemini acknowledged ruefully—but she had no doubt that there was a will of steel every bit as forceful as his cousin's beneath that outer charm. 'Why don't you just say what you have to say, Markos?' she invited.

He shrugged broad shoulders. 'I am merely curious as to your reason for coming here today.'

Gemini smiled. 'There's really nothing for you to be curious about.'

'No?'

'No,' she stated firmly.

'But I *am* correct in assuming you are Miles Bartholomew's daughter?'

Gemini tensed warily. 'Yes...'

Markos pursed his lips. 'As I thought.'

And he was no doubt thinking a lot of other things if he was aware of his cousin's very personal relationship with Gemini's stepmother!

If Angela were to learn that she was having dinner with Drakon this evening, it would no doubt result in her stepmother throwing one of her temper tantrums. But that was Drakon's problem, not Gemini's; there really was nothing more Angela could do to her that she hadn't already done!

'Well, it's been nice meeting you, Markos.' Gemini's smile was now brightly non-committal, and she stepped out of the lift as soon as the doors opened onto the ground floor. 'I'll be sure and leave my address with the receptionist on my way out.'

Thankfully Markos took that for the dismissal it was meant to be and remained standing inside the private lift. 'I hope you enjoy your dinner with Drakon this evening.' He nodded his farewell, amusement still dancing in those deep green eyes as the lift doors slowly closed.

Whether that amusement was directed at Gemini or his cousin, she wasn't sure...

CHAPTER THREE

'I HAD assumed when you suggested we have dinner together this evening that I would be meeting you at a restaurant.'

Drakon's expression remained unreadable as he stood outside the darkened Lyonedes Tower building and watched Gemini climb out of the back of the silver limousine. The black knee-length dress she wore left her arms and shoulders bare, with a tantalising glimpse of the fullness of her breasts above the scooped neckline, and was a perfect foil for that white-gold hair which fell straight and gleaming about her slender shoulders as she straightened. Blusher added colour to her cheeks this evening, and a pale peach glossed the fullness of her lips. She looked breathtakingly beautiful!

He nodded a curt dismissal of the driver, waiting until the other man had climbed back behind the wheel and driven away before turning back to Gemini. 'You have some objection to us dining here at the apartment?'

Gemini didn't have an objection per se. It just didn't seem exactly...*businesslike* for her to dine with Drakon Lyonedes in the intimacy of that amazing apartment with its magnificent—romantic?—views over London. Even if he *was* once again dressed formally in one of those expensively tailored dark suits—charcoal-grey this time—with another white silk shirt, and a pale blue silk tie meticulously knotted at his throat. That square chin was freshly shaven, and the darkness of his hair appeared slightly damp. As if he had just stood naked beneath the shower—

Imagining Drakon naked in the shower was *so* not a good idea when she was already completely aware of him!

He raised dark brows at her lack of reply. 'This is a business discussion, after all, is it not?'

Well, when he put it like that… 'Of course,' Gemini affirmed gratefully, falling into step beside him as they entered the eerily silent and only semi-illuminated building.

They walked over to the lift, the slender three-inch heels on her strappy sandals sounding over-loud in that unnatural silence. She felt their complete aloneness even more once they had stepped inside the private lift to be whisked silently up to the top floor of the building.

'It really is very good of you to agree to talk to me again so soon.' Gemini rushed into awkward speech in an effort to quell her increasing nervousness as she gripped her slender black evening bag tightly in front of her.

Not that she was normally the nervous type. Far from it. She was usually pretty outgoing. But there was just something so broodingly intense about the man standing beside her…

Drakon gave a tight and humourless smile. 'After your less than orthodox behaviour earlier today, you mean?'

A delicate blush warmed her cheeks. 'Yes.'

He nodded. 'There are certain aspects of our conversation earlier that are…incomplete.'

She blinked up at him. 'There are?'

'Oh, yes,' he said grimly.

Gemini brightened. 'Of course—I hadn't finished telling you about my proposal!'

'That too,' he acknowledged.

Too? What other part of their conversation earlier today had been left 'incomplete'?

Gemini had no more time to dwell on that question as the lift doors opened and Drakon stepped back to allow her to precede him into the sitting room of his apartment. The sitting room seemed much more intimate this evening, illuminated only by four lamps placed about the room, and the glittering London skyline stretched enchantingly in the distance through those floor-to-ceiling windows. A small round table was intimately laid for two in front of one of them, tableware and glasses gleaming, three cream candles in the silver candelabra as yet unlit...

'Would you care for a glass of wine?'

Gemini dragged her gaze away from the intimacy of those place-settings to look across at Drakon as he stood by the bar, his face appearing more harshly brooding in the dimmed lighting. 'I—yes, thank you,' she accepted, placing her bag down on the arm of a chair. 'White, if you have it.'

Drakon smiled slightly to himself as he turned away to open and then pour the wine, sensing Gemini's discomfort as she continued to stand in the middle of the room. 'Was the rest of your day pleasant?' he murmured softly as he crossed the room to hand her one of the two glasses of fruity white wine.

She gave him a startled look as she slowly reached out and took the glass he held out to her. 'Er—busy. As usual.'

'Busy in what way?' Those black eyes studied her over the rim of his glass as he sipped the perfectly chilled wine.

Gemini had hardly expected to be discussing what sort of day she'd had when she next saw Drakon! Almost as if they were out on a real date. Which was utterly ridiculous! Not that she was dating anyone at the moment, her last brief romantic interest having ended months ago, but even so... His relationship with Angela apart, Drakon looked as if he ate up willowy blondes for breakfast, chewed them round for the rest of the morning, and then spat out their bones before enjoying a brunette for lunch!

Although perhaps thinking about Drakon eating her up wasn't the best idea when Gemini now found herself unable to look anywhere but at his sculptured mouth as she imagined how those lips would feel against her skin...

'We're always busy the day before a big wedding.' She rushed into speech in an effort to dismiss those erotic and entirely inappropriate thoughts. 'There's the church to decorate, the bride's bouquet and all the corsages and buttonholes to arrange, then in the morning we'll have to do the top table and twenty others in the reception marquee.' She shrugged. 'I have to be up very early tomorrow too in order to make sure it all gets done well before they return from the wedding at four o'clock.'

Exactly why had she felt the need to add that part? she scolded herself. There was absolutely no way she would still be *here* in the morning!

Drakon looked slightly puzzled. 'I'm afraid I have no idea what you're talking about.'

'Oh. Sorry.' She grimaced before taking a quick sip of her wine.

It was excellent. Of course. A perfectly chilled Pinot Grigio, if she wasn't mistaken. Which she probably wasn't; her father had considered learning to recognise a good wine as an important part of her education.

'Delicious wine.' She nodded her approval before placing the glass down on one of the side tables. Delicious, but definitely lethal for her to drink too much of it when she'd barely had time to draw breath all day let alone eat. Especially as her thoughts had already wandered into what it would feel like to have Drakon's mouth on her!

'I am pleased you approve,' Drakon drawled dryly, even as he wondered about the reason for the blush that had now coloured Gemini's cheeks. 'You were about to explain the reason for your involvement in this "big wedding"?' he reminded her.

She nodded, that white-gold hair gleaming pale and silvery in the lamplight. 'I own and run a florist's shop.'

Drakon scowled. 'I didn't know that...'

Gemini shrugged those slender shoulders. 'There's no reason why you should have done.'

Oh, but there was... As soon as his business meeting this morning had been over Drakon had telephoned down to Max Stanford and asked him to check not only whether Gemini was indeed who she claimed to be, but also into the dynamics of the relationship between Gemini and her stepmother. Perhaps he should have asked Max to put together a more detailed personal dossier on Gemini?

To learn that she had a job at all, let alone owned and ran her own florist's shop, came as something of a surprise to him. Miles Bartholomew had come from old money, and had only added to that wealth during his successful business life; as his only child Gemini would surely have no reason to work. Unless…

His jaw tightened. 'I thought you said you were not left without funds when your father died?'

'I wasn't.' She smiled, revealing small and even white teeth. 'As I said, I have a trust fund. I've owned my shop for five years now—I'm afraid I'm just not the type to sit on my backside looking pretty while I wait for some handsome prince to whisk me off my feet and into marriage,' she declared.

This young woman was ethereally beautiful rather than merely pretty, and Drakon had no doubts that there had been plenty of men during her twenty-seven years who would have wished to 'whisk' her off to somewhere probably a lot less permanent than matrimony. Himself included…?

'And do you enjoy owning and running a florist's shop?' he bit out, annoyed with his own thoughts.

'I love it!' She gave him another bright smile, those sea-green eyes glowing.

'And is your shop successful?'

'Very.' Gemini shot Drakon a mischievous sideways glance. 'And that's not me being egotistical—it just is.'

'Please don't put words into my mouth,' he advised dryly. 'And no business "just is" successful. It takes hard work on the part of someone to make it so.'

She eyed him curiously. 'You sound as if you speak from experience?'

He shrugged. 'My father and uncle were the ones to found Lyonedes Enterprises. My cousin and I have merely continued to add to that success.'

Gemini knew these two powerful men had done so much more than that. Lyonedes Enterprises was now one of the most financially strong and successful companies in the world.

'My father also started and ran his own company,' she said. 'He liquidated it all when he retired at sixty.'

'Because you had no interest in running your father's company? Or because he had no son to continue it?' Drakon prompted curiously.

Her smile faltered slightly. 'Both, probably.'

Was that a note of sadness Drakon could hear in Gemini's voice? Perhaps an underlying wistfulness for having grown up an only child? Having spent much of his life growing up with a boisterous younger cousin, Drakon could not even begin to imagine what that must have been like. His parents' house had always seemed filled to overflowing with the two of them, and also many of their friends.

'Unfortunately my talent always lay with flowers and other things that grow.' She brightened. 'Even as a small child I was obsessed with digging in the garden. To the point that my mother finally persuaded my father to give me my own bed in the garden—no doubt in an effort to stop me from digging up his prize roses!' she added affectionately.

Just her talk of her parents was enough to reveal the deep love that had existed between them and Gemini—making Miles Bartholomew's second marriage, to a woman not so much older than Gemini herself, even more difficult for her?

Drakon made a mental note to himself to thank his mother the next time he saw her for never having put Markos and himself through that same unpleasantness. Not that either of them would have been difficult if Karelia *had* decided to marry again after their father's death; they both loved her far too much to wish her anything but happiness.

'I imagine, as you're the owner of a florist's shop, it must be difficult for a man to send you flowers,' he commented.

'Not at all,' Gemini assured him lightly. 'Yellow roses are my favourites, if you ever feel the—' She broke off abruptly, that delicate blush once again warming her cheeks. 'Sorry. Of course you aren't ever going to want to send me flowers.' She grimaced, before turning away to stroll across to the windows that looked out over the illuminated London skyline. 'This really is a magnificent view.'

Yes, it was. Except Drakon wasn't looking at the London skyline but at Gemini herself.

He didn't believe he had ever met another woman quite like her before. Beautiful, obviously accomplished as she ran a successful shop, and from all accounts a loving and loyal daughter to her father despite the less than harmonious relationship that existed between her and her stepmother. And she now felt such a sense of duty towards the home where she had spent her childhood, which had been in her family for over three hundred years, that she had even risked the possibility of Drakon having her arrested earlier this morning.

'Do you play...?'

He smiled slightly as he saw she was looking across at the piano.

'A little.'

'And do you play well?'

'Passably.' He shrugged.

'I'm sure that if you play even a little you do it very well indeed,' she chided teasingly.

Drakon crossed the room to stand beside her. The

softness of her perfume was an enticing mixture of flowers and beautiful woman. 'Why do you say that?' he prompted.

She smiled widely. 'I don't know you very well, but I already know enough about you to realise you're the type of man who, if he chooses to do something, will never do it "passably" well!' Once again that smile faltered and then disappeared as she seemed to realise exactly what she'd just said. And its obvious sexual implications...

Drakon chuckled huskily as that becoming blush once again coloured the ivory smoothness of her cheeks. 'I will take that as a compliment...'

Gemini wasn't at all comfortable with the sudden intimacy between them—an intimacy she knew *she* was completely responsible for creating with her thoughtless comment!

Was it because she hadn't completely dispelled those earlier images of a naked Drakon Lyonedes emerging from the shower from her mind? Probably. She found it a little difficult to think of him in the abstract at all when he was standing beside her. So hot and immediate. As well as dark and dangerously attractive!

She moistened her lips. 'Perhaps we should just concentrate on our business discussion?'

Those dark eyes narrowed, and his mouth was once again a thin and uncompromising line. 'In that case I believe we must first dispense with your mistaken belief that I am currently involved in a personal relationship with your stepmother.'

Gemini turned, her eyes wide. 'Mistaken...?'

'Certainly.' Drakon frowned. 'I have always made a point of never mixing business with pleasure.'

'But—' She gave a slightly dazed shake of her head. 'I don't understand.'

'It is simple enough, surely?' He raised those arrogant dark brows. 'I have no idea why you should have drawn such a conclusion, but I assure you my only connection to your stepmother is one of business. In the form of my purchase of Bartholomew House,' he added, so that there should be absolutely no doubt as to his meaning.

Gemini stared up at him wordlessly. He looked sincere enough. In fact he looked more than sincere—his handsome face was now visibly showing an expression of extreme distaste at the mere suggestion that he might be involved in an affair with Angela...

But her stepmother had told her—

A lie...?

What possible reason could Angela have had to lie about being involved in an intimate relationship with Drakon?

Knowing the other woman as well as Gemini had come to know Angela since her father had died, she found the answer was suddenly all too obvious.

Gemini had tried so hard to like Angela when her father had first introduced her as the woman he intended to marry. Despite the vast age difference between Angela and Miles. Despite the fact that Gemini had believed her father was rushing too hastily into a second marriage. And in spite of the fact that Angela had given every appearance of being nothing more than a voluptuous blonde beauty attracted to Miles's money rather than the man himself.

Yes, despite all those things Gemini had still tried to like and get along with the older woman. For her father's sake, if for no other reason, because she'd known how much he had wanted his second wife and his daughter to be friends.

Whenever the two women had been in Miles's company that had always appeared to be the case. It had only been when Gemini found herself alone with the other woman that Angela's hostility had become so blatantly obvious, in the form of cutting remarks or long, uncomfortable silences.

It had quickly become obvious to Gemini that, other than Miles, the two women had absolutely nothing in common, and that even that common interest differed greatly in its intent. Angela had wanted and demanded all of Miles's attention for herself. The existence of his twenty-something daughter had been more of an embarrassment than anything else. Whereas Gemini had just wanted to see her father happy again.

Angela asking her to move out of the house once she'd married Miles had certainly been no hardship to Gemini. She had only moved back into Bartholomew House after her mother died so that her father wouldn't be left alone there with only his memories. It had been perfectly natural for her to move out again in order to leave the newly married couple to their privacy.

It was the fact that Angela had made the request without Miles's knowledge and knowing full well that Gemini would never tell him what she had done that had been hard to bear. Angela had made it obvious to Gemini that she resented any time father and daughter spent together—to the point that she'd ensured it rarely happened. It had been an attitude that was never visible whenever Miles was present. Angela's behaviour then had been sickeningly kittenish as she'd continued to wrap her much older and totally smitten husband about her manicured, sexy little finger.

In the circumstances, was it any wonder that Angela had enjoyed implying to Gemini that she had managed to capture the interest of someone like Drakon Lyonedes—a man half Miles's age and probably a dozen times richer?

Knowing Angela as well as she did, Gemini thought the other woman believed it was only a matter of time, anyway, until she made the fabricated affair into a reality. So what did it matter if she'd exaggerated the situation to Gemini now? And if it didn't happen who was ever going to contradict Angela's claims when the man himself was so utterly elusive?

Except Gemini had now met Drakon, and she felt extremely foolish for having believed the other woman's boast about his being infatuated with her. Gemini had no doubt Angela was lying to her; Drakon Lyonedes wasn't the type of man to be infatuated with *any* woman. Besides, being so arrogantly self-assured he obviously never felt the need to lie about any of his actions—least of all his involvement with a woman!

'Am I right in assuming this information was given to you by your stepmother?' he prompted harshly.

Gemini flinched at the disgust underlying his tone. 'Perhaps I misunderstood her.' She gave an uncomfortable lift of her shoulders. 'I— She mentioned how…nice you were.' *Sexily gorgeous* had been her exact words, actually, but Gemini really couldn't bring herself to tell him that! 'Maybe I just let my imagination take that a step further than Angela actually intended—'

'I believe you assured me earlier that you do not lie?' Drakon cut in.

She winced. 'I try not to, no…'

'Then do not do so now,' he advised her coldly.

'I believe I said I might have been mistaken,' she said uncomfortably.

'And do you really believe that?'

'What I believe is that Angela was trying to hurt me by boasting of how quickly she had replaced my father in her bed,' Gemini acknowledged shakily. 'You must have thought I was completely off my head this morning when I started rambling on about the affair you were having with Angela.' She offered him an embarrassed smile.

He gave a derisive snort. 'Not completely, no.'

'You've *never* been intimately involved with Angela, have you?'

'No,' he confirmed.

'Oh, God, I'm so sorry!'

'Here—drink some more of your wine.' Drakon moved to pick up Gemini's glass and handed it to her, inwardly seething at Angela Bartholomew and the lies she had told her stepdaughter. In order to hurt her? No doubt. For himself, Drakon took exception to any woman claiming to have a relationship with him that simply did not, never had and never would exist. Especially in the case of the voluptuous Angela Bartholomew.

Would he resent it quite as much if it had not been the intriguing and beautiful Gemini to whom that lie had been told?

Drakon didn't even want to think about the implications of that question, let alone find an answer for it! 'Not everything your stepmother told you about me was a lie. Lyonedes Enterprises *is* in the process of purchasing Bartholomew House and its grounds from her,' he reminded her softly.

Gemini gave a pained frown. 'I don't understand why

you would even want to own a big house and grounds in London when you have this wonderful apartment to stay in whenever you're in England.'

Drakon drew in a sharp breath even as he stepped slightly away from her. 'It is not my intention ever to live in Bartholomew House.'

She looked puzzled. 'It isn't?'

'No.'

'Then who is—? Perhaps I shouldn't ask that.' She shot him an awkward look. 'Obviously you have your reasons for wanting to own a house in London.'

Drakon's eyes narrowed at Gemini's more than obvious assumption that those reasons probably involved a woman. 'I believe I stated that Lyonedes Enterprises is in the process of completing the purchase of Bartholomew House?' he reiterated firmly.

She frowned. 'What does that mean, exactly?'

His jaw tightened. 'Precisely what I said.'

She gave a confused shake of her head. 'Are you going to open up more offices there, or something?'

Drakon's mouth firmed as he sensed impending disaster. 'Or something.'

Gemini looked at him searchingly, but as usual that dark and harshly handsome face revealed none of his inner thoughts or emotions. This man could have posed for the original Egyptian Sphinx, his expression was so damned inscrutable!

She swallowed before speaking. 'Exactly *what* are you, as President of Lyonedes Enterprises, intending to do with Bartholomew House?' She ensured the preciseness of her question didn't allow for further prevarication on his part.

'Perhaps we should have dinner first—'

'Is that because you're hungry? Or because I probably won't want to eat once you've answered my question?' Gemini prompted shrewdly.

'The latter,' he allowed grimly.

Her chin rose determinedly. 'Drakon, will you please tell me what your intentions are with regard to Bartholomew House?'

He breathed deeply. 'For the house itself? Very little.' He gave a shrug of those broad shoulders. 'For the land it stands upon? Extensive.'

Gemini continued to stare at him, her expression remaining blank even as her thoughts inwardly raced. Bartholomew House was a beautiful three-hundred-year-old four-storey mansion house, standing on half an acre of prime land in the very heart of fashionable London. Land that Drakon Lyonedes seemed to be implying was his main reason for the purchase.

If that was so, then what did he intend doing with the house that stood on that piece of land?

'Oh, my God!' Gemini gasped weakly even as she felt the colour draining from her cheeks. 'You intend to have the house knocked down!'

Drakon scowled darkly as he heard the shocked accusation in her tone.

It was not an entirely incorrect accusation...

CHAPTER FOUR

'PERHAPS you should sit down before you fall down!' Drakon rasped harshly as he clasped the white-faced Gemini's arm to steady her before gently guiding her across the room to sit down in one of the armchairs. Putting his hand at the back of her neck, he pushed her head down between her knees.

Just what he needed. An unconscious Gemini Bartholomew in his apartment!

'Breathe deeply,' he instructed gruffly. The hand he held against the slenderness of her nape revealed that she was shaking. Badly!

Breathe deeply? Gemini wasn't sure how she could be expected to breathe at all when he had just revealed that his company intended destroying the house that had been in her family for hundreds of years! The same house where she had been born and had spent such a happy and carefree childhood…

'Drink this.'

Gemini raised her head enough to see the full glass of white wine Drakon now held in front of her, reaching up to take it from him before downing the contents in one go. 'Could I have some more, please?' she breathed shakily.

'I do not think—'

'Drakon, please!' Gemini rallied enough to look up at him pleadingly through the curtain of her hair.

He shrugged those broad shoulders before taking the empty glass from her shaking fingers and once again crossing over to the bar to refill it. 'I merely wished to point out that your drinking too much wine will not change anything.' He walked slowly back across the room.

Gemini's hands shook as she pushed her hair back over her shoulders before taking the refilled glass from him. 'I don't think I particularly care about that at the moment.'

He raised dark brows. 'Which, unfortunately, will not prevent you from suffering a hangover tomorrow morning.'

She laid her head back against the chair, breathing deeply. 'At this moment I'm more than happy to let tomorrow take care of itself!' She frowned suddenly. 'Are you even able to *legally* demolish a house as old Bartholomew?'

That square jaw tightened. 'Not completely, no.'

'What does that mean?'

He seemed to choose his words carefully. 'It means that our plans for the redevelopment of the site have, by necessity, to incorporate the original house.'

Gemini's heart sank. 'Incorporate it how, precisely?'

He shrugged. 'Plans have already been submitted and approved for the building of a hotel and conference centre.'

Gemini's hand tightened about her wine glass as she felt a sudden wave of dizziness. 'And no doubt Angela has known about these plans from the beginning?'

Drakon drew in a deep breath before turning and walking away, his back towards her as he looked out of one of the floor-to-ceiling windows. 'I believe your stepmother was made fully aware of our intentions at the outset, yes…'

Gemini would just bet that she was! She was sure Angela had been aware of it and no doubt inwardly gloated about it! It wasn't enough that she now owned the home that she knew full well Gemini had wanted for herself; the other woman was selling Bartholomew House to Lyonedes Enterprises knowing it was that company's intention to totally change, if not obliterate, the house and grounds as Gemini knew them…

'Intentions that I assure you I would have done everything in my power to block if I had known of them!' she cried.

'No doubt.'

'It would appear that I'm only just in time to present you with my own offer.'

Drakon's eyes narrowed as he turned slowly, allowing none of the regret he felt at seeing Gemini so pale and obviously distressed to show in the deliberate blandness of his expression. Which didn't mean that at that moment he wouldn't have liked to strangle Angela Bartholomew with his bare hands for being the initial cause of that distress!

He'd had no idea of the rift that existed between the two Bartholomew women when he'd entered into negotiations for the family house and grounds. Not that it would ultimately have made the slightest difference to those negotiations—but he usually made a point of being aware of any extraneous circumstances in his company's dealings.

He did not particularly care for the way Gemini now looked at him as if he were about to commit murder! 'What sort of offer?' he asked.

She stood up, only to sway slightly on her feet as the effects of the wine she had just consumed kicked in. 'Do you have a bread roll or something that I could eat?' she asked self-consciously.

Drakon gave an impatient sigh. 'We will sit down and eat dinner. Afterwards you will tell me about this offer you wish to make me.'

Sit down and eat dinner? Gemini felt as if even attempting to eat the bread roll she had requested would probably choke her! 'I think we've gone well past the stage of politely eating dinner together, don't you, Drakon?' she said dully.

'Then I suggest we *impolitely* eat dinner together.' He pulled one of the chairs back from the table and looked at her pointedly.

She gave a humourless smile as she walked slowly across the room and sat down abruptly in that chair. 'It might be as well if you gave lighting the candles a miss,' she advised heavily.

He nodded as he stepped round the table and began to take food from the hostess trolley and place it in front of her. 'We will not talk again until you have eaten something,' he assured her gruffly as he sat down opposite her.

For all the notice Gemini took of the meal—smoked salmon, followed by individual beef Wellingtons and tiny roasted vegetables, with some intricate chocolate confection to finish—Drakon might as well not have bothered putting it in front of her. Gemini was only able to chew disconsolately on a bread roll as she remained lost in the misery of imagining the beauty of Bartholomew House swallowed up by a hotel complex. It was unthinkable—unacceptable that such a thing should be allowed to happen.

True to his word, Drakon remained silent throughout, only speaking again once they had reached the coffee stage of their meal.

'It's decaffeinated,' he assured her as he placed a cup on the table in front of her.

At any other time, under different circumstances, Gemini would have felt warmed that a man like Drakon Lyonedes had bothered to remember her preference in coffee. Under *very* different circumstances! 'Thank you,' she accepted woodenly, before taking a sip of the black unsweetened brew.

'You're welcome,' he muttered as he resumed his seat opposite her.

'I can't exactly claim to have enjoyed my meal,' she said apologetically.

He shrugged. 'Luckily the chef of my favourite London restaurant is not here to be offended by the fact that you did not eat any of the food he so expertly provided.'

Gemini shot him a frowning glance. 'I could kick myself now for not realising Angela was up to something underhand after she refused my own offer to buy Bartholomew House from her.'

Drakon's brows rose. 'You made her an official offer for Bartholomew House?'

'Oh, yes,' she said. 'Angela just laughed in my face.'

The more Drakon heard about Angela Bartholomew the more he disliked her. And he would certainly have preferred to be more prepared for the distress caused to Gemini by her stepmother's mercenary nature.

He chose his words carefully. 'Admirable as your actions were, I doubt the amount you offered even came close to the offer Lyonedes Enterprises made to your stepmother—'

'I made sure the amount I offered slightly topped yours,' Gemini assured him firmly.

Drakon's eyes widened. 'You have *that* sort of money at your disposal?'

'More or less.'

His mouth twisted ruefully at the way that sea-green gaze now avoided meeting his. 'How much more and how much less?'

Gemini stood up restlessly. 'I *do* have the money,' she reiterated distractedly.

Drakon's lids narrowed as he looked across at her searchingly, noting the glitter in those sea-green eyes, the flush to her cheeks. And the determined set to that full and sensuous mouth...

Under different circumstances he could imagine nothing he would have enjoyed more than making love to Gemini until those sea-green eyes became heavy with desire, her cheeks flushed with pleasure, and those pouting lips swollen with arousal.

Under different circumstances...

As it was, even a hint of the sexual interest he felt for her, which had been growing steadily throughout the evening and intensifying to a physical ache when he'd placed his hand against her nape earlier, would be completely rejected.

Drakon couldn't remember the last time—if ever— a woman had piqued his sexual interest as much as Gemini did. If he were completely honest with himself she had begun to do so from the first moment he'd looked at her on the security monitor this morning, as she'd restlessly paced the room she had been confined to. Markos—damn him—had been quite correct in surmising as much when Drakon had announced it was his intention to talk to Gemini himself. His cousin had also known exactly which buttons to push to get a reaction out of Drakon when he had come up to the apartment and interrupted their conversation.

Drakon had been as surprised as Markos had looked when he had announced that Gemini was to be having dinner with him this evening. Surprised by the need he had felt to reassure her that he was not, nor had he ever been, involved in an affair with her stepmother. And not a little alarmed that the circumstances of their meeting meant he was the very last man Gemini would ever consider becoming sexually involved with.

Over the years Drakon had become accustomed to having any woman he bothered to take an interest in. The cynical part of him knew those conquests were due as much to his extreme wealth as to any personal attraction he may or may not possess, but he already knew Gemini well enough to know that neither his wealth nor the way he looked would be enough to tempt her into a purely physical relationship with him. She was a woman who would require…*more*…

Which left him precisely where?

Attracted—deeply attracted—to a woman he knew there was absolutely no possibility would ever return that attraction, let alone act upon it!

'You do have the money, *but*?' he prompted shrewdly.

Gemini shot him a frown. 'What makes you think there's a but?'

He gave a derisive smile. 'Isn't there?'

Yes, there was. And it was a big one. One that Gemini had desperately been trying to overcome this past month without success…

She sighed. 'I told you earlier that my parents set up a considerable trust fund for me. The interest has been paid to me on a yearly basis since I reached the age of eighteen, and the capital amount is to be made over to me on my thirtieth birthday.' She grimaced. 'I've been trying for the past month to see if I can break that trust and have the capital now, so that I can buy Bartholomew House.'

'And?'

She scowled. 'My father's lawyers assure me the trust was set up in such a way as to be unbreakable. Of course if Daddy had made the new will, as he promised he would…!' She gave a frustrated shake of her head. 'But obviously he didn't, so I'm stuck with not being able to get at the bulk of my money until my thirtieth birthday.'

Dark brows rose over those coal black eyes. 'Which means you will not receive the capital for…what…? Another three years or so?'

'Two years and four months, to be exact,' Gemini acknowledged grudgingly.

Drakon gave a humourless smile. 'By all means let us be exact—' He broke off, a perplexed frown appearing between his eyes. 'That would make your birthday some time in October?'

She nodded warily. 'The twenty-second.'

'But that is not the month for Gemini.'

Her wariness proved merited! 'No…'

'I had assumed your unusual name derived from your birth sign?'

Gemini forced a bright and totally insincere smile to her lips. 'Obviously you assumed wrong.'

Drakon studied her through narrowed eyes, noting that smile and the dull flatness of those sea-green eyes… 'You are being evasive, Gemini.'

'Am I?'

'You know that you are.'

Her expression was pained as she began to pace, slender and long-legged and extremely graceful, her hair a silvery curtain about her shoulders in the moonlight reflecting through the windows behind her.

'I don't see what my birthday has do with the offer I've made you—'

'You have not made me any offer yet—nor do I wish to hear it until we have finished our present conversation,' Drakon assured her decisively as she would have gone on. 'Gemini is the sign of the twins...' he murmured slowly.

The frown deepened between those sea-green eyes. 'Most people would have realised by now—and *accepted*—that I would obviously prefer not to talk about this subject any more!' she muttered crossly.

He nodded. 'I have realised.'

'But you continued anyway?'

'Yes.'

'Why?' she demanded.

Because, painful as he could see this subject was to her, Drakon wanted—*needed*—to know!

She had told him so much about herself already—when her birthday was, what she did for a living, her love for her parents, her disharmonious relationship with her stepmother. And it wasn't enough. Drakon found that he desired to know all that there was to know about Gemini Bartholomew. Almost as much as he desired to make love to her...

'I'm a twin,' she revealed suddenly, her eyes glittering brightly with unshed tears as she turned away. 'I had a brother,' she continued quietly. 'He only lived for three hours after he was born, and my mother chose my name deliberately—not out of the sadness of losing him, but out of the joy of knowing him even for that short amount of time. She didn't want any of us to ever forget him—' Gemini broke off abruptly as her voice choked with tears. The silken curtain of her hair fell forward to hide the depth of emotion so clearly revealed in the rawness of her voice.

Drakon gave a self-disgusted snort and moved swiftly across the room. He took Gemini into his arms, resting her head against his shoulder, and moved his arms firmly about the slenderness of her waist, her closeness allowing him to breathe in the soft perfume of her hair. 'I am so sorry, Gemini,' he muttered. 'You were right. I should not have pushed you in the way I did.'

'No, it's okay.' She shook her head. 'I— It's just that since Daddy died there's no one left who knew about Gabriel—that was my brother's name. Gabriel. Gemini and Gabriel.' She drew in a ragged breath. 'It's strange, because I never really knew him, but I've always felt as if…as if I were somehow incomplete…as if a part of me were missing.' She looked up to give a tearful smile. 'Weird, huh?'

Not weird at all when one considered that Gabriel had been her twin—that the two of them had shared their mother's womb for nine months at the very beginning of their lives…

It also explained that sadness Drakon had recognised earlier in the beauty of Gemini's eyes when he had mentioned there being no son to inherit her father's business. Because he now realised there had been no *living* son…

Gemini had no brother living. No parents, either. Leaving her completely alone in the world.

Much as Markos's flirtatious nature often annoyed him, and much as he sometimes grew concerned about his widowed mother spending months living alone in

Athens, Drakon knew he couldn't imagine being without either of them.

His hand seemed to move of its own volition to touch the softness of her hair. 'I think that is a perfectly natural feeling in the circumstances,' he said as he stroked that silkiness.

Those sea-green eyes widened as she breathed, 'You do?'

'Of course.' Drakon nodded, entwining several of those silky strands about his long fingers. 'I have considered Markos as my brother since I was ten years old, and we have always been close. To know that you could have had that same closeness with your own brother must be difficult sometimes. Especially this past six months, with both your parents now gone too.'

Gemini had no idea what she was doing, virtually spilling out her life history to Drakon Lyonedes of all people! Having only met him for the first time this morning, and having found him so remote and arrogantly sure of himself, she would have thought him the last person she would be confiding her inner emotions to only hours later!

Even more worrying was the fact that she was now completely physically aware of him…

Not that she hadn't been aware of his dark and dangerous good looks from the moment she first looked at him—what woman wouldn't be? But being this close to him…held tightly in his arms, with her body moulded against the lean and muscled hardness of his…every part of her, all her senses, seemed to be screaming with that awareness.

He smelled so good—clean and virile male, with a spicy and insidiously delicious cologne. And his body felt so warm and solid against her own. Those shoulders wide and muscled, his chest and stomach powerfully lean, his long legs placed solidly either side of hers, his thighs hard and—

Oh, help…!

Gemini tensed even as she looked up at Drakon through lowered lashes, barely breathing as she felt the press of his arousal against the softness of her stomach. She was only a few inches shorter than him in her heels, and their faces were even closer as the warmth of his breath brushed against her cheek. There was no doubting that Drakon was aware of that sudden sexual tension too. His jaw was clenched, a nerve pulsing in that tightness, his mouth was compressed and his cheekbones high and prominent. And those dark eyes—

Those dark eyes were burning with the same desire Gemini could feel pressing so insistently against her!

What did she do now? To act on the aching desire flooding her limbs and so desperately clamouring for her to close the distance that separated their parted lips would be asking for trouble. To pull away and run wasn't really an option either, when they still had so much to talk about.

Drakon suddenly solved her dilemma by grasping the tops of her arms and putting her firmly away from him before stepping back.

'Better now?' he prompted coolly. The emotion in those coal-black eyes was now shielded behind hooded lids, his expression once again arrogantly remote as he lifted his glass and took a swallow of the white wine.

Well, Gemini could breathe again, at least! It remained to be seen whether or not she would be able to put that physical awareness behind her as thoroughly as he appeared to have done. 'Much,' she confirmed huskily. 'Thank you.'

Drakon had no idea what Gemini was thanking him for. Allowing her to talk of her family, perhaps? Or the fact that he had decided not to act on the sexual tension that minutes ago had thickened the air in the room to an almost unbearable degree?

It was a sexual tension he would normally not have hesitated to act upon, but in Gemini's case, here and now, it could only have seemed like taking advantage of her vulnerability...

Drakon knew himself to be many things—controlled, arrogant, ruthless—but until this moment he would not have thought self-denial to be a part of his nature. It was a self-denial he would no doubt live to regret if the throbbing ache of his erection was any indication!

He arched arrogant dark brows as he turned. 'For what?'

Gemini shrugged. 'Being a shoulder to lean on when I needed one.'

'I did nothing except listen,' he dismissed abruptly as he placed the empty wine glass back down on the table. 'And I believe it is now time for me to listen to you, as you make your offer to me with regard to Bartholomew House. The same as that you made to your stepmother?' he reminded her.

Gemini looked at him searchingly for several long seconds, but could see nothing of the compassionate and caring man of seconds ago in the harsh implacability of Drakon's expression. The obviously aroused man who had held her in his arms only seconds ago had also gone.

She gave a rueful shake of her head. 'My offer is to Lyonedes Enterprises rather than to Drakon Lyonedes...'

His mouth tightened. 'It is one and the same thing.'

'Not really,' Gemini pointed out. 'Lyonedes Enterprises doesn't consist of just you, does it? There's your cousin to consider, too.'

He looked down the length of his arrogant nose at her. 'My cousin, I assure you, will be more than willing to accept my judgement, as I accept his, in all matters relating to Lyonedes Enterprises.'

Gemini would just bet he would! She had no doubt that not too many people ever went up against this man in any of his decisions—not even the cousin he was obviously so close to. Not in the way that *she* had done today.

Now that she had actually met and spoken with Drakon she realised she was lucky his Head of Security hadn't decided to lock her in the basement this morning after all—and thrown away the key!

'Okay.' She drew in a deep breath. 'My offer to Angela in buying Bartholomew House was that I'd pay over the interest from my trust fund for the next two years, and the remaining amount once the capital was released on my thirtieth birthday. I'm willing to make Lyonedes Enterprises the same offer once the property becomes yours.'

It was exactly the offer that Drakon had been expecting Gemini to make, after hearing the details of her trust fund.

And an offer he had no choice but to refuse on behalf of Lyonedes Enterprises.

CHAPTER FIVE

GEMINI knew what Drakon's answer to her offer was going to be even before he spoke—could see that answer as she looked into those remorseless black eyes.

'Yes. Well. Obviously not.' She moved quickly to pick up her clutch bag from the arm of the chair where she had left it earlier, her face pale in the lamplight. 'I think it's past time I was going, anyway. I'm sorry to have wasted your time.' She turned away.

'Gemini!'

She froze before turning slowly back to face Drakon. 'Yes?'

Drakon scowled at the brief flash of hope he saw in those in those sea-green eyes. 'I cannot let you leave when you are so obviously upset.'

'I don't see how you're planning on stopping me.' She looked at him quizzically. 'Look, Drakon.' She sighed wearily as he continued to scowl his displeasure. 'It's obvious that you aren't any more interested in the deal I'm offering than Angela was, so I think it's best if I just be on my way now. It will save us both the embarrassment of your having to say so.'

No. Unfortunately Drakon could not in all conscience even *consider* a deal in which Lyonedes Enterprises effectively paid out millions of pounds for a prime site the company wanted in the heart of London, then shelved their idea to build a hotel complex there in favour of selling it on to Gemini, who would then pay them back in instalments. From a business point of view the whole idea was ludicrous!

And from a personal one...?

Drakon frowned darkly as he saw the look of defeat in the pallor of Gemini's face. Her eyes now appeared like huge sea-green lakes of bleak despair against that paleness. Because she now knew beyond a shadow of a doubt that she had lost the family home she so obviously loved. The last tie with the father she had also loved and so recently lost...

He gave an impatient shake of his head, knowing that he couldn't back down on his decision. Not only was it the right one in regard to Lyonedes Enterprises, it would be totally against his nature to do so. 'I do not believe for one moment that your father intended your trust fund to be used for such a purpose.'

She gave him a bitter smile. 'We'll never know now what he intended, will we?'

Drakon's jaw tightened. 'The fact that he did not, as he intended, make a new will, perhaps implies that he had rethought his decision to leave you Bartholomew House?'

'Oh, please, Drakon!' Gemini threw him a fiery glance. 'As you didn't even know my father you can have absolutely no idea what he did or didn't decide.'

He winced at the emotion in her voice. 'That is not completely true. I met your father several times at social functions in London over the years.'

That was news to Gemini. Although there was absolutely no reason why her father should ever have mentioned meeting the legendary Drakon Lyonedes to her.

He couldn't have known that Gemini and Drakon would meet one day. Especially under these circumstances!

'And?'

He shrugged those wide shoulders. 'And he always seemed a man of decisiveness and purpose.'

Gemini smiled sadly. 'Then I can only assume you must have met him pre-Angela.'

'Perhaps,' Drakon acknowledged. 'But from a practical point of view what would you even *do* with a home and grounds the size of Bartholomew House? Surely it is far too big for you to have considered living there alone?'

Her stubbornly pointed chin rose. 'I have—*had*,' she corrected firmly, 'no intention of living there alone, Drakon.'

Ah. It was a complication Drakon hadn't but definitely should have considered before now… 'You are engaged. Or intend to be married soon?'

'Of course not.' She looked down pointedly at her bare left hand before adding, 'I wouldn't be here having dinner alone with you if I was!' She shook her head. 'But I don't intend always to be alone. I would like to be married at some time in the future, and to have children of my own one day. Whenever I've envisaged that day I've always thought I would be living in Bartholomew House,' she said huskily.

Guilt was not an emotion Drakon was in the least familiar with, and it now sat uncomfortably heavy on his shoulders. Especially when it was in connection with a young woman he found altogether too attractive for his own comfort! Nor was he particularly happy with the brief feeling of satisfaction he had experienced at knowing Gemini was not seriously involved with anyone else at the moment. The chances of her ever becoming involved with *him*, now that he had refused even to consider her proposal for purchasing Bartholomew House, were also extremely remote!

He looked across at her through narrowed lids. 'I don't see how anyone could have reason to object to your having a business dinner with me?'

Gemini accepted that it might have started out as a business dinner—except for the subdued lighting and those candles on the dinner table—but Drakon certainly hadn't been feeling businesslike a few minutes ago, when she had felt the evidence of his arousal pressing against her. When whether or not they kissed each other had hung so delicately in the balance for several tense and breathlessly expectant moments!

'Probably not,' she accepted briskly. 'But I wouldn't have felt right about coming here if I was involved with someone.'

Drakon frowned his irritation. 'I don't see why not. Or is it your intention, when this "one day" arrives with this as yet imaginary husband and children, to close yourself off from all other social contact?'

'Of course not.' Gemini gave him a derisive glance. 'But going out for the evening to have dinner alone with—well, frankly with another man, who happens to be single and very eligible, really isn't acceptable when you're married to someone else.'

He raised dark brows. 'Even if it is a business dinner?'

'Even then.' She shrugged dismissively. 'I wouldn't be at all happy knowing my husband was out to dinner with some glamorous blonde or brunette, business or otherwise, so I wouldn't expect him to like my doing it either. And I really have no idea why we are even talking about someone who doesn't even exist yet,' she added wryly. 'It's bizarre!'

It was an odd conversation, Drakon acknowledged. One that gave him even more of an insight into the type of woman Gemini Bartholomew was.

At the same time it reiterated his earlier impression that she was not the type of woman to enter lightly into what Drakon already knew, from that brief time of holding her in his arms, would be a highly volatile sexual affair between the two of them. Indeed, she was the type of woman who would need to be in love, rather than just in lust, with any man she went to bed with.

Surely that didn't mean she might still be a virgin at twenty-seven?

Of course it didn't; just because Gemini hadn't married yet it didn't mean she hadn't already fallen in—and out—of love, or had sex. Or *made love*, as she no doubt thought of it!

Drakon's hands clenched at his sides just at the thought of other men making love to her. Of those men having seen her naked, with that beautiful white-gold hair falling caressingly over them as they touched and kissed all those delectable and willowy curves—

Those regrets at his earlier self-denial had occurred even more quickly than Drakon had imagined they might!

He nodded abruptly. 'I will ring for the car and have you driven back to your home,' he said.

'There's no need,' Gemini replied. 'I can easily get a taxi once I'm outside.'

'I arranged for your transport here, and as such cannot possibly allow you to go home in a taxi,' he bit out harshly.

'You aren't *allowing* me to do anything, Drakon.'

Gemini couldn't help smiling a little at his arrogance. 'And I want to go now,' she insisted heavily, that humour quickly fading. 'Not in ten minutes or so when the car arrives.'

He straightened. 'Then I will drive you home myself—'

'That really isn't necessary.' She frowned at the mere idea of being confined in a car with him for the fifteen minutes or so it would take to drive her back to her apartment. Drakon had rejected her offer, and now she just wanted to get out of here—not drag this awkwardness out a moment longer. 'Nor is it a good idea, considering you've been drinking wine—the licensing laws over here are pretty strict.' She drew in a deep breath. 'Thank you for dinner—'

'Which you were too upset to eat.' A nerve pulsed in the tightness of his jaw.

'And the lovely wine—which I certainly wasn't too upset to drink,' she added pointedly. 'And for listening to me, at least…'

Drakon scowled his displeasure at the frown that had reappeared between those magnificent eyes. 'There really is no reason for you to leave so soon—'

'I'm afraid there's every reason, Drakon.' Gemini sighed. 'You were my last hope, I'm afraid.'

He knew that, and inwardly railed against the fact that he had ultimately proved to be so unhelpful to her. But, apart from his immediate family, business had always come first and last with him—certainly for the ten years since he had taken over as President of Lyonedes Enterprises. The appeal of a beautiful pair of sea-green eyes and the allure of a desirable body simply were not justifiable reasons for him to give even a moment's consideration to Gemini's impractical offer to purchase Bartholomew House.

'I will need to come down in the lift with you, at least, in order to let you out of the building,' he rasped.

'By all means come downstairs and see me off the premises,' she accepted teasingly. 'Having already been confined by your security man once today, I would hate for it to happen a second time—and maybe this time involve the police because all the alarms go off as I try to leave!'

As the two of them stepped into the lift together Drakon couldn't help but admire Gemini's cool dignity only minutes after he had dealt her what must have been a devastating blow. Many women, as he knew from experience, would have resorted to shrieking or crying—or even seduction—in order to try and get their own way, but not Gemini Bartholomew. There was no doubting she looked slightly more emotionally fragile than when she had arrived, but otherwise her calm dignity was still firmly in place.

Not that any of those things would have worked where Drakon was concerned—although the seduction would no doubt have been enjoyable. But Gemini had not even tried to exert *any* of her feminine wiles on him.

Was that disappointment Drakon felt? Possibly. In the circumstances, he could not in all conscience act upon his own desires, but having Gemini act upon her sexual awareness of *him*, which he had sensed in her such a short time ago, would have been a different matter entirely!

Gemini was very aware of Drakon standing beside her as they went down in the lift together. And of a return of that sexual tension that had occurred earlier when he had taken her in his arms. If it had ever gone away…

If she were honest with herself, she hadn't really held out much hope of Drakon being receptive to her unusual offer to buy Bartholomew House from Lyonedes Enterprises when she'd agreed to have dinner with him this evening. She had already realised that from a business point of view it really wasn't a very practical offer. So having Drakon turn down the offer had come as no real surprise.

The physical awareness that had sprung so readily to life between them earlier and was still so tangibly evident most definitely had…

Oh, Gemini wasn't surprised that she found Drakon physically attractive—she had realised when she met him this morning that he was a dangerously handsome man!—but that Drakon so obviously found *her* physically attractive too had come as a total shock. She wouldn't have thought she was his type at all—too determined and pushy, too impulsive, and definitely far too outspoken.

If she had thought about it at all she would have imagined that the sort of woman he found attractive would be someone undemanding and elegantly beautiful, with a social charm that acted as a foil for his own more taciturn nature. Someone that her stepmother Angela was only too capable of at least pretending to be. As Gemini knew only too well, Angela's true nature was only revealed after a wedding!

Gemini looked at Drakon from beneath lowered lashes, aware that her breathing had become shallow and her body hot. Her breasts felt full and heavy, the nipples hard and sensitive pebbles, and a telling dampness was flooding her thighs as she wondered what it would be like to make love with such a vitally power-ful and ruggedly handsome man. She had absolutely no doubt that Drakon would be a deeply satisfying and ac-complished lover—that he would be as accomplished at lovemaking as she had so naively commented he prob-ably was on the piano!

Come to think of it, there were quite a few similari-ties between making love and playing the piano—surely it was all a question of running your fingers over the right keys in order to achieve the most satisfying result? In fact—

'What are you doing?' Gemini gasped as the lights flickered and the lift came to a sudden halt between floors. Drakon had reached out and pressed one of the buttons on the panel before turning to look at her, his expression as dark and unreadable as his eyes as he looked down at her for several tension-filled seconds. 'Drakon…?' She looked up at him dazedly.

Drakon reached out and took Gemini in his arms. He moulded the softness of her body against his hard-ness, aware that she wanted this as much as he did as he heard the shallowness of her breathing, saw the swell of her breasts above her dress, the nipples hard against the softness of that material, and felt the warmth of the rest of her body instinctively curve intimately into his.

'Drakon…?' She sounded slightly panicked now, as he studied her intently before moving one of his hands to cup the side of her face, to gently part the softness of her lips. The soft pad of his thumb dipped into the heated moisture of her mouth before slowly spreading that moisture across her lips. 'Drakon…!' she gasped weakly, and she allowed her bag to slide to the floor of the lift and her arms to move about his waist beneath his jacket.

Her hands were warm against his back through the silk of his shirt. It was all the encouragement he needed to lower his head and capture the moistness of her lips with his, groaning low in his throat as those lips parted further and the kiss deepened. Their ragged breathing sounded loud in the still silence of the dimly lit lift as the two of them sucked and bit on each other's lips as they kissed hungrily, passionately.

Drakon only lifted his lips from hers in order to taste the creaminess of her throat as he pushed her back against the wall of the lift and ground the hard and aching throb of his arousal against her. She tasted of warmth and honey, of arousal, and her skin was hot against his lips as he kissed his way down to the swell of her breasts, tasting and licking her there, muttering his dissatisfaction as the fitted bodice of her dress prevented him from going lower.

Gemini was so aroused, so lost in the pleasure of Drakon's kisses and caresses, that she wasn't even aware of his having lowered the zip at the back of her dress and tugged aside the material until she felt his lips against the bareness of her breasts. His tongue was a moist rasp across her nipple before he drew that sensitive peak deep into the heat of his mouth. Her hands grasped his shoulders for support as his fingers cupped her other breast and his thumb moved across it in the same rhythmic caress, causing a warm rush of moisture to pool and dampen between her thighs.

Drakon continued to grind the hardness of his arousal against her and her breath caught in her throat, her arousal tightening to fever pitch as she looked down at him, his lashes long and dark against the olive skin of his hollowed cheeks, those firm and ruthless lips parted over her nipple as he drew on her deeply, hungrily, his teeth biting into the softness of her flesh, his tongue a rough and erotic scrape of pleasure.

She gave a whimper of protest as his lips and tongue reluctantly released that turgid nipple, only to moan low in her throat as he turned their attention to her other breast. Her fingers became entangled in the darkness of his hair as the ache between her thighs intensified to a burn of need that caused her to shift restlessly against the long length of his shaft, crying out softly as she felt his hardness rub against her swollen flesh through the fine fabric of their clothes, groaning, gasping, as she continued to move rhythmically against him, feeling herself spiralling out of control as the intensity, the depth of pleasure, hurtled her towards release.

'Hello? Mr Lyonedes? Do you need assistance?'

Gemini stiffened dazedly and Drakon stilled against her breast as that intrusive voice pierced the heat of their arousal.

'Mr Lyonedes? Do you require assistance, sir?'

Gemini recognised the voice as belonging to Max, the Head of Security for Lyonedes Enterprises she had met that morning, even as Drakon released her abruptly before stepping away from her.

His expression was tight and extremely grim as he looked down at her darkly for several seconds, before turning away to lift the receiver beside the lit panel. 'No assistance needed, Max,' he barked into the mouthpiece.

'Are you sure, sir? The lift appears to be stuck between the thirteenth and fourteenth floors…?'

'Not stuck, Max, just not moving,' he assured the other man tautly. 'Miss Bartholomew and I will be descending to the ground floor in a few moments.'

There was a brief, telling silence before the other man spoke again. 'Very good. Thank you, sir.'

'Miss Bartholomew' had quickly pulled up the bodice of her dress while Drakon spoke to his Head of Security, the heat now in her cheeks due to intense embarrassment rather than arousal. Not only had she almost made love with Drakon in a lift—which was surely mortifying enough?—but after that brief conversation with his employer, no doubt Max was also fully aware of exactly why the lift had been stopped between floors!

Good Lord, she had almost made love with *Drakon* in a *lift*!

Drakon Lyonedes…

Even more frustratingly, his hair smoothed back into style and his suit jacket and tie now straightened, he now looked just as smoothly self-contained as usual. Whereas she—goodness knew what she must look like, with her dress still unzipped at the back and her hair in a tangle about her shoulders, her cheeks hot and the peach gloss kissed from her lips!

'Turn around.'

Gemini raised startled lids and looked warily up at Drakon. She moistened her slightly swollen and sensitive lips before speaking. 'Sorry…?'

His own mouth was a thin, uncompromising line in the arrogant planes of his face, his eyes as hard as the onyx they resembled. 'If you turn around I will re-zip your dress.'

Gemini clutched the material to her breasts and quickly turned away from him, trembling when she felt every cold inch of that zip against her heated skin as Drakon deftly refastened it. She wondered what on earth she was supposed to do now… How was she supposed to behave towards the man she had almost made love with in a lift? Was there a precedent for that sort of thing? Some sort of protocol that she—never having made love in a lift before—didn't have a clue about?

Of course there wasn't a protocol for this type of thing! And hysteria really wasn't an option either—which meant Gemini had to get a grip as quickly as possible and stop behaving like an inexperienced idiot. Even if she was one...

Oh, she had dated often at university—had even thought she might have been in love a couple of times and mildly experimented with lovemaking. But once she'd bought and started to run the shop her time had pretty much been taken up with making it into a success, leaving little opportunity for dating, let alone falling in love. In fact, now that she gave it some thought, dinner this evening with Drakon was as close as she had got to having anything that even resembled a date for well over a year.

Which was absolutely no excuse—and definitely not an explanation—for the explosion of arousal and passion that had just happened between the two of them!

She might be inexperienced, but Drakon certainly wasn't. And after her behaviour just now she doubted that he would believe she was either...

'Do you intend to stare at that wall for the rest of our journey down?'

Gemini flinched at the hard amusement she could hear in Drakon's voice as she felt the lift begin its descent. 'Not at all,' she denied briskly, and she turned, bending down to retrieve her clutch bag from the floor of the lift before forcing herself to look up and meet the hardness of his gaze. 'Well, that was certainly...different,' she said lamely.

'Yes.' Drakon's mouth twisted in self-derision. 'Different' was certainly one way of describing the way in which the situation had totally spiralled out of his control once he had taken Gemini into his arms!

He hadn't meant to kiss her at all, let alone touch her in that intimate way, but once he had done so and she had responded…! It hadn't mattered to Drakon at all that at that moment they were in a lift together. Nor had he given any thought to the fact that stopping the lift in between floors in that way would alert whoever was on security duty this evening. He had just wanted to touch her, taste her—damn it, he had wanted to eat her up until he had totally devoured her! He still wanted to do that…

His jaw tightened. 'I do not fly back to New York until next week. Perhaps we could have dinner together again tomorrow evening?'

Those beautiful sea-green eyes widened incredulously. 'I don't think that's a good idea, do you?'

Drakon raised dark brows. 'Why not?'

Gemini shook her head. 'I'm sure I don't really have to explain that to you!' She glanced gratefully out into the hallway as the lift doors opened out onto the ground floor.

'Nevertheless…' Drakon stood back to allow her to precede him out into the dimmed hallway, his expression grim. 'We have already established that neither of us is involved with anyone else.'

That might or might not be true—the fact that Gemini had believed Drakon when he'd claimed not to be involved with Angela didn't mean that he didn't have someone else waiting for him in New York! And it certainly didn't mean that they should see each other again before he left England.

Not when agreeing to see him again would no doubt be seen by him as a tacit agreement from her for a repeat—no, a *conclusion* of that explosion of passion that had just occurred between them in the lift...

CHAPTER SIX

GEMINI gave a definite shake of her head. 'I'm sure to be exhausted after working on the wedding flowers all day tomorrow, but thank you for asking.'

Drakon had regretted making the invitation virtually as soon as he'd made it! Regretted it and inwardly berated himself for even *thinking* of seeing her again.

This woman had a way of slipping beneath his guard. Of totally demolishing the tight rein he always kept over his self-control. Of tempting him to behave in ways he never had before. If Max hadn't interrupted them when he had then Drakon had no doubt he would actually have made love to Gemini—in a lift, of all places!

It was unacceptable to a man who totally rejected any and all hint of emotional vulnerability, and instead preferred to remain detached and in control at all times. Wanting to push a woman up against a wall and make unbridled love to her couldn't be called either of those things!

No, it was better by far if Drakon never saw or spoke to her again. And after this evening there was absolutely no reason why he should ever need to do so...

'Very well.' He nodded stiffly. 'But I will come outside with you and see you safely into a taxi.'

Gemini could have argued that she had lived in

London all her life and as such was perfectly capable of seeing herself into a taxi, thank you very much! But no doubt Drakon would then argue the point, and delay her departure by doing so. Which she certainly didn't want when she so desperately needed to get away from him.

It wasn't in the least apparent from Drakon's cool and controlled expression as he looked down the length of his arrogant nose at her that only minutes ago he had almost made love to her with a fire and intimacy no other man ever had. But she was only too well aware of it. Her breasts still ached with sensitivity, and she could feel that telltale dampness between her thighs...

As was to be expected, there was no scarcity of available taxis when Drakon Lyonedes needed one, and he had no trouble flagging down one of London's black cabs almost immediately they stepped to the edge of the pavement; he was the type of man for whom life always ran the way in which he wanted it to.

Unlike Gemini, who had no choice but to accept that Bartholomew House was now totally beyond her reach.

She felt numbed and slightly hollow as she climbed into the back of the taxi, only half listening as Drakon leant in to give the driver the address of her apartment.

'I can be contacted through my cousin Markos if you ever have need of me.'

Gemini blinked up at Drakon from the back seat of the taxi. Why would he suppose she might ever have need of him? 'Managing to speak to one of the Lyonedes family didn't work out too well for me last time,' she reminded him pointedly, just wanting to be on her way so that she could lick her wounds in private.

All her wounds. Losing Bartholomew House *and* responding so uninhibitedly to this grim-faced man's earlier passion. At the moment she wasn't sure which of those things was going to be the more difficult to understand, let alone accept.

Drakon's mouth was set firmly. 'I will leave instructions that you are to be allowed to make an appointment to see either Markos or myself at any time.'

Gemini's eyes widened. 'Why on earth would you want to do that?'

A good question. And one that he wasn't sure he had a logical answer to. Except to say that his Greek upbringing did not find it acceptable that Gemini had effectively been left completely alone in the world since her father died.

'The instruction will be given,' he reiterated firmly. 'You may please yourself as to whether or not you ever choose to use the privilege.'

She sat back against the seat. 'I'm pretty sure that I won't.'

He had asked for that response, Drakon acknowledged ruefully, knowing that his present attitude was less than gracious. But this young woman had become like a burr under his skin—a discomfort he couldn't seem to ignore.

'I hope you do not have to work too hard tomorrow.' He stepped back and closed the door, leaving a pale-faced Gemini bathed only in moonlight as the taxi drew away from the kerb.

Drakon stood on the pavement and watched the taxi until its tail lights disappeared amongst the other London evening traffic, then turned sharply on his heel and went back into Lyonedes Tower, knowing—well, hoping—he had seen the last of Gemini Bartholomew...

* * *

'We may have a problem.'

Drakon looked up from where he had been packing the last of his papers into his briefcase in preparation for his flight back to New York early this evening, frowning as he saw the unhappy expression on Markos's face as his cousin came into the study of the penthouse apartment at the top of Lyonedes Tower.

'What sort of a problem?' Having spent a quiet weekend in the apartment in preparation for two days of lengthy negotiation with Thompson Oil—which had, of course, been concluded to Lyonedes Enterprises' advantage—Drakon wasn't in the mood to deal with any hiccups that might now have occurred in the finalising of that contract. Nothing which could threaten his return to New York today. He had been away from his own office for long enough.

Markos grimaced. 'Mrs Bartholomew came to see me this afternoon—'

'*Miss* Bartholomew,' Drakon corrected, wondering why, when he hadn't yet left the country, Gemini had chosen to make an appointment with Markos rather than himself. And for what reason... 'Gemini is not married.'

'If I'd meant Gemini then I would have said Gemini,' Markos reasoned impatiently.

Drakon eyed his cousin guardedly as he slowly stepped away from the desk. 'So it was her stepmother who came to see you today?'

His cousin nodded. 'Well, I had the distinct impression she would have preferred it to have been you, but as you weren't available this afternoon she settled for seeing me instead.'

Drakon had spent the past four days trying not to think about Gemini. Not too successfully, admittedly.

Several times he had found himself lost in thoughts of making love with her, and usually at the most inappropriate of times. The last thing he had been expecting was a visit to Lyonedes Tower by her stepmother.

'What did she want?'

'You. Or, alternatively, me.' Markos gave a disgusted snort.

He shook his head. 'Is there some problem with our purchase of the Bartholomew property?' Such as a more recent Miles Bartholomew will making a sudden and unexpected appearance? That would certainly solve all Gemini's problems—whilst at the same time opening up a legal nightmare for Lyonedes Enterprises!

'Not that I'm aware.' Markos immediately dismissed that possibility. 'Angela Bartholomew's interest in the Lyonedes family appeared to be completely personal,' he added, with a contemptuous curl of his top lip. 'She invited me out to dinner this evening,' he expanded when Drakon still looked nonplussed. 'And she left me in no doubt that dinner would very swiftly be followed by bed.'

It was so much in keeping with the things Gemini had implied if not said about her stepmother that Drakon found it difficult to hold his smile in check. 'And did you accept the invitation?'

'Don't be so damned stupid! Have you ever *met* the woman?' His cousin glared at Drakon's obvious amusement. 'She's a barracuda wrapped in designer-label silk!'

Drakon bit his top lip to stop his smile from deepening. 'I have had the...pleasure of meeting her once, yes. When the contracts were signed.'

'And?'

'She's a barracuda wrapped in designer-label silk,' he agreed.

'This isn't funny, Drakon.' Markos scowled. 'I thought it was a business meeting, and I was so surprised by the obvious sexual intent in her invitation that I'm afraid I was less than my usual discreet self.'

Drakon's humour instantly faded. 'What did you do?'

His cousin looked annoyed. 'I merely commented what a charming stepdaughter she has—at which she asked very sweetly when and how I had met her stepdaughter.'

'Did you tell her?' Drakon rasped sharply.

'At the time I didn't think there was any reason not to.'

'Exactly what did you tell her, Markos?' Drakon demanded.

'I said we had both met her when she came here last week to talk to you. That was when that sweetness completely disappeared and I saw the true nature of the woman.' Markos winced at the memory. 'I've never seen such a change in anyone. She was muttering something about killing her as she left.'

'How long ago was that?'

'Only ten minutes or so—where are you going?' Markos asked in surprise as Drakon strode forcefully towards the door.

He turned in the doorway. 'To ensure she does not succeed in harming Gemini, of course.'

His cousin raised dark brows. 'What about your flight?'

Drakon shrugged dismissively. 'If necessary I'll reschedule the jet for tomorrow. Right now I believe I need to go and ensure Gemini's safety.'

Markos looked shocked. 'You really think Angela Bartholomew would physically harm her?'

Drakon gave a humourless smile. 'From what I have learnt, I don't believe that woman needs to lay a finger on Gemini in order to hurt her. Or to enjoy every moment of doing so,' he added grimly.

'Do you want me to come with you? Probably not.' Markos raised placatory hands as Drakon turned to glare at him.

'I think you've already done enough for one day, don't you?' he asked accusingly.

'I really had no idea how she felt about Gemini until she changed from sex-kitten into tigress just at the mention of her name!' his cousin defended.

No, in all fairness, Markos *hadn't* known of the depth of animosity that existed between Gemini and her stepmother. Drakon had chosen to tell his cousin only the rudimentary details of the reason for her visit to him the previous week. And he had only told Markos that much out of self-defence—to illustrate that it had been a business meeting and nothing more—after his cousin had teased him over the weekend about whether or not he would be seeing Gemini again before he returned to New York.

Much as it irked Drakon to admit it even to himself, these past four days he had wanted to see her again. He had wanted it very much. Those occasions when he had been unable to succeed in putting her from his mind had usually resulted in him having to take a cold shower. Yes, Drakon had *really* wanted to see Gemini again.

He had just never imagined it would be under circumstances such as these...

* * *

'Exactly what did you think you were doing?'

Gemini had taken advantage of a brief lull in the day's business and left her assistant in charge of the shop while she retired to her office, intending to go through the accounts and check on the rest of the month's bookings. The last thing she had been expecting late on a Tuesday afternoon—or at any time, in fact—was a visit from Angela!

She drew in a deep breath before glancing up at her father's widow, not in the least reassured by the angry glitter she could see in Angela's eyes and the bright spots of colour in her cheeks. The rest of her appearance was as elegantly beautiful as usual; her hair was perfectly styled, the blue silk knee-length suit a perfect match in colour for her eyes, the three-inch heels on the matching shoes making her legs appear both slender and shapely. An elegantly beautiful viper!

'What did I think I was doing in regard to what?' Gemini enquired calmly as she placed her pen carefully down on the desktop in front of her.

'Don't try and play the innocent with me!' Angela snapped as she stepped fully into the office and slammed the door behind her before striding over to stand in front of the desk and look down at Gemini contemptuously. 'You've always acted so primly self-righteous. I never would have guessed that you would attempt something so underhand!'

Gemini looked at her blankly. 'Flattered as I am to have so obviously succeeded in surprising you, I still have absolutely no idea what you're talking about.'

Angela's pale blue gaze swept over her scornfully. 'You know exactly what I'm talking about.'

Her patience with this woman had worn thin long ago, and now that her father was dead, and Angela was selling everything he had ever worked for and owned, Gemini saw absolutely no reason why she should even attempt to hide her dislike any longer.

She stood up impatiently. 'If you don't tell me what you're doing here in the next few minutes then I'm afraid you'll leave me with no choice but to demand that you leave.'

Those blue eyes flashed angrily. 'Perhaps the name Drakon Lyonedes might help to jog your memory?'

Gemini felt the colour drain from her cheeks. Drakon? Angela was here because she *knew* Gemini had been to Lyonedes Tower to talk to him concerning Bartholomew House? Did Angela also know she'd had dinner with him there on Friday evening? That they'd kissed? And, if so, *how* did she know? Surely Angela could only have learnt those things from Drakon himself?

Did that mean he had been lying to her, after all, when he'd denied any personal involvement with Angela?

Gemini eyed the other woman guardedly. 'What about him?'

Angela gave an inelegant snort. 'I told you not to try and play the little innocent with me.' She looked daggers at Gemini. 'And to think Miles always believed you were such a sweet little thing too.'

'Whatever problem you think you have with me, you will leave my father out of this,' Gemini said, her hands clenched so tightly at her sides that her nails were digging painfully into her palms.

'Will I?' the older woman challenged derisively as she perched one slender hip against the side of the desk. 'I wonder what Miles would have thought about your having thrown yourself at a man like Drakon Lyonedes.'

'I did not throw myself at him!' Gemini protested.

'Liar!' Angela straightened abruptly, her eyes once again glittering. 'I always knew you didn't like me, Gemini—and, believe me, the feeling is completely reciprocated. As far as I'm concerned you've always been far too much of a reminder of the perfect first wife that Miles so obviously adored.'

'How could you possibly have been jealous of a dead woman?' Gemini gasped.

'I was never jealous of Rosemary!' Angela glared furiously.

'It sounds distinctly like jealousy to me,' she retorted.

'And what would you know about it, little rich girl?' the other woman demanded. 'You lived in a mansion all your life, doted on by rich and indulgent parents, you owned your own pony, attended private schools, and holidayed in exotic places all over the world several times a year. What would you know about growing up on the twelfth floor of a tenement building in a family of six who had nothing to look forward to but the next dole cheque?'

'I— That was you?'

'Oh, yes,' Angela sneered. 'Until I reached sixteen and was old enough to break my ties with my family in order to reinvent myself and use the one asset I have— my body and the way that I look. Of course I had to put up with the pawing of a succession of wealthy old men, but it was all worth it when I finally persuaded the wealthiest one into marrying me.'

Gemini went deathly white at these revelations. 'You told my father that your father had gambled away your family fortune before committing suicide—'

'And he did gamble—probably still does. What little money the government gave us always went to the bookies or on another bottle of whisky to throw down his throat,' Angela said harshly. 'He rarely, if ever, gave my mother enough money to actually *feed* any of us.'

'You told my father that both your parents were dead.'

'I lied,' Angela admitted. 'I've never been back, but as far as I'm aware both my parents are still alive—and no doubt living in exactly the same squalor as always.'

Gemini could perhaps understand what had driven Angela into seducing Miles into marriage now that she knew the truth of the other woman's background—obviously any wealthy man would have done. Could understand and even sympathise with her. What she couldn't accept was the unhappiness that selfishness had caused her disillusioned father before he died...

She took a deep breath. 'I'm sorry if that truly is how you were forced to live as a child—'

'Oh, it's all true,' Angela assured her. 'And you can keep your sympathy for someone who might actually appreciate it. After all, I came out the winner in the end, didn't I?'

Oh, yes, Angela had certainly triumphed. Spectacularly, in fact, with regard to Gemini's father.

'I suppose Drakon Lyonedes was to be your second, even wealthier husband?'

'Why not?' Angela demanded aggressively.

Gemini gave a pained frown. 'Don't you have enough money now, having sold off everything my father left you?'

'I'll *never* have enough money,' the older woman said with hard determination.

'And never care who you have to trample over in order to get it, apparently,' Gemini said dully.

'That's rich, coming from you!' Angela jeered.

'You're still so desperate to own Bartholomew House that you would even stoop to trying to seduce Drakon yourself to get it!'

Gemini felt ill. In fact she thought she might actually be sick if she had to stand and listen to this woman for too much longer. 'Considering your claim that *you're* involved with Drakon, I'm surprised you believe he could be seduced—by me or any other woman.'

'I believe I said you had *tried* to seduce him,' Angela scoffed. 'I'm sure you very quickly learnt that a man like Drakon requires a woman who's a little more adventurous and experienced than a mere baby like you!'

Just thinking of Drakon and Angela together intimately, after the passionate way he had kissed her in the lift four days ago, brought on another wave of nausea. She swallowed hard. 'I'm afraid I'm going to have to ask you to leave after all.'

'I'm not going anywhere until I've made it perfectly clear to you that Bartholomew House—and Drakon—will never be yours!' Angela announced.

Gemini gave a slow and disbelieving shake of her head. 'What on earth could a man like Drakon possibly see in someone like *you*?'

Those blue eyes flashed angrily. 'Oh, climb down off your alabaster pedestal, Gemini. If you haven't realised it yet, your own pathetic attempt to seduce Drakon makes you exactly like me!'

Gemini closed her eyes and gave a shudder of distaste. 'God, I hope not.'

'Offends your naive little sensibilities, does it?' Angela taunted.

'Everything about you offends my sensibilities,' Gemini shot back.

'Why, you little—'

'I think not,' interrupted a dangerously soft voice that Gemini instantly recognised.

She opened wide, startled eyes in time to see Drakon take hold of the arm that Angela had raised with the intention of slapping Gemini on the face.

The older woman's face twisted into an ugly mask of hatred as she turned to see who her assailant was. The change that came over Angela's expression then was even more sickening than all that had gone before it. Her eyes softened to a sultry blue as she looked up at Drakon. Her painted red lips curved into an inviting smile, the anger leaving her body as she leant into him.

'Oh, dear, Drakon, I'm afraid you've been caught in the middle of a rather silly argument between two even sillier women,' she murmured throatily.

Gemini felt nausea rise up inside her, and knew she was actually going to be ill after witnessing this sickeningly kittenish display. She only had time to gasp 'Excuse me!' before she brushed past Drakon, heading for the stairs and the privacy of the bathroom in her apartment above the shop.

CHAPTER SEVEN

DRAKON took one look at Gemini collapsed on the floor beside the toilet in the bathroom of her apartment, her face a deathly clammy white after obviously having been violently ill, before striding over to the sink and dampening a flannel with cold water. He went down on his knees beside her to begin bathing her face.

Gemini pushed the flannel away, her eyes a deep and pained sea-green. 'What are you doing?'

He raised dark brows as he sat back on his heels. 'I believe I am endeavouring to make you feel better.'

She gave a humourless smile. 'I'm afraid it's going to take a lot more than the application of a cold flannel to my forehead to succeed in doing that!'

'Gemini—'

'Would you please just go away, Drakon?' She avoided looking at him directly as she reached up and self-consciously flushed the toilet for a second time before lowering the lid and using it as leverage to rise shakily to her feet. 'It's bad enough that I allowed that woman to upset me enough to actually make me physically sick, without the added humiliation of having you witness it,' she muttered, and she picked up her toothbrush and toothpaste and left the bathroom without so much as a second glance in his direction.

Drakon rose slowly to his feet and threw the damp flannel back into the sink. He concentrated on drawing in deep, controlling breaths in an attempt to dampen down the worst of his own anger at the scene he had walked in on a few minutes ago. His hands clenched into fists at his sides as he fought the need to slam one of them into the mirror inset into the wall over the sink.

Following the veiled insights Gemini had given him into Angela Bartholomew's true nature, he had expected the older woman to come straight to the florist's shop and confront Gemini. But, even knowing that, Drakon hadn't been prepared for the scene of violence he had walked in on earlier.

Or his own reaction to it…

A haze of red had literally passed in front of his eyes on seeing Angela's hand raised with the obvious intention of striking Gemini, and for the first time in his life Drakon had actually felt himself tempted into using violence against a woman.

He hadn't done so, of course. That would have been totally against his nature, as well as his parents' teachings. But it had taken every ounce of his self-control not to shake Angela until her perfectly straight white teeth rattled in her vicious head!

Instead he had taken a tight hold of the woman's arm and escorted her from the shop, closing the door firmly behind her before informing Gemini's wide-eyed assistant that her employer was indisposed and probably wouldn't be downstairs again for the rest of the day.

Coming up the stairs to Gemini's apartment and finding her collapsed on the floor of the bathroom, and then having his offer of assistance totally rejected by her, had brought a return of that furious red haze.

So much so that Drakon knew he still didn't have his emotions completely back under iron control when he went in search of her.

Gemini looked up warily as Drakon joined her in the sitting room. She had already hurried into the kitchen and washed her face and cleaned her teeth, but still felt mortified by the scene he had witnessed downstairs, as well as her own physical and embarrassing reaction to it.

But she was even angrier with Drakon for having been the real cause of Angela's vehemence. 'What are you doing here, Drakon?' she demanded dully. 'Isn't it enough that I've had to listen to your mistress insult both my father and myself this afternoon, without having to now suffer your company, too?'

A nerve pulsed in his tightly clenched jaw. Those black eyes glittered darkly. 'I believe I assured you last week that that woman is not, and never will be, my mistress,' he bit out harshly.

Gemini gave a disbelieving snort as she stood beside the unlit fireplace. 'Have you told *her* that?'

'I have no need to tell a woman such as her something she is already only too well aware of,' he said arrogantly.

'Could we please stop the lies?' Gemini pushed the length of her hair back from the paleness of her face. 'We both know that Angela only came here at all today because *you* told her I'd seen you last week.'

That nerve in his jaw pulsed even harder. 'Markos was the one to tell her about that.'

She looked stunned. 'What?'

Drakon sighed at her look of hurt disbelief. 'In self-defence. He had no idea of the trouble it would cause when he did so.'

Gemini stared across at him incredulously. 'You really expect me to believe that?'

He rose up to his full height, appearing every inch the arrogant billionaire industrialist he was in one of his expensively tailored dark suits, pale grey silk shirt, and a darker grey silk tie. The darkness of his hair looked as if it had received a trim since the last time she had seen him.

'I am no more in the habit of lying than you have assured me you are,' he told her coldly.

'I just find it a little hard to believe that Markos needed to tell Angela anything out of self-defence,' she said sceptically.

Drakon looked slightly uncomfortable. 'Apparently she had just propositioned him. Markos was so taken aback by the suggestion that he fell back on his brief acquaintance with you in order to change the subject.'

The first part of that statement sounded a lot like the Angela Gemini now knew far better than she'd ever wished to. It was the second part of the statement that sounded so improbable. 'Your cousin implied that he and I are involved in an attempt to deflect Angela's interest in him?'

Drakon's jaw tightened. 'I believe Markos might have implied that it is you and I who are involved, and that he is also acquainted with you.'

That would certainly explain the arrival of the wrathful Angela. 'And exactly how did he think telling her something like that was going to succeed in saving him from what I'm sure was Angela's less than subtle proposition?'

'Markos obviously had no idea of the animosity with which Angela regards you.' Drakon's nostrils flared. 'Apparently I was her real target, and Markos only second choice. I believe he merely hoped to distract even those second-hand attentions by drawing attention to our own acquaintance.'

Gemini stared at Drakon wordlessly for several seconds. The directness of that unwavering dark gaze challenged her to continue disbelieving him. Which she found she couldn't do. The explanation was so ridiculous—and sounded so exactly like something Angela would do—that Gemini couldn't help but believe it.

She felt some of the tension leave her body as she gave a rueful sigh. 'Poor Markos.'

'Poor Markos?' Drakon repeated incredulously, knowing that at this moment in time he could cheerfully have pummelled his cousin to a pulp—something he hadn't done since they had been children together—for being the cause of Angela's verbal and physical assault on Gemini.

Gemini nodded. 'I like Markos.'

Drakon noted grimly that she did not say she felt that same liking for him. Not that he could exactly blame her. So far in their acquaintance Gemini had believed him to be involved in an affair with her father's widow, to be responsible for denying her the right to purchase her family home, and to add insult to injury he had then proceeded to make love to her against the wall of a lift in Lyonedes Tower!

No, unfortunately he had no one but himself to blame if Gemini's feelings towards him were more than a little ambivalent.

Drakon looked up as she gave a sudden splutter of laughter. 'Sorry—I was just imagining Markos's panic when Angela propositioned him!' she explained at his questioning look.

'Certainly not his finest hour,' Drakon acknowledged

dryly. 'Although he did at least have the good sense to come to me immediately after she had departed and inform me of what he had done,' he added with a frown. 'I am only sorry I did not arrive soon enough to prevent the unpleasantness of your stepmother's verbal attack.'

'You at least stopped the physical one.' Gemini gave a shrug of her slender shoulders. 'And the verbal stuff was no worse than some of her other outbursts, actually. Better in some ways, because for the first time I actually learnt a little of what motivates her.' She grimaced. 'Not a pretty story, I'm afraid.'

And not one she intended sharing with him either, Drakon guessed. Not that he had any wish to know anything more of Angela, or the reasons she behaved in the way she did. His only concern was Gemini—not the unpleasant woman whom her father had married.

'What did she say to make you physically ill?'

She was very pale still, but even so Drakon couldn't help but appreciate the way the colour of Gemini's short-sleeved blouse perfectly matched the colour of her eyes, making her hair appear even more white-gold. Black jeans fitted smoothly over her bottom and thighs; her bare feet were thrust into flat, open-toed sandals.

Gemini sobered. She was very aware that it was the shock of thinking Drakon was involved with Angela after all, and then his unexpected arrival so quickly after Angela—which at the time had only seemed to confirm his involvement—that had caused her to be so violently ill.

The question was, *why* had it?

She had thought about Drakon a lot these past four days—of their time together in the lift, of her own loss of control—so maybe it had been the thought of his having discussed any of that with Angela which had made

her feel so ill? Although if that had really been the case
she had no doubt that Angela would have taken great
pleasure in telling her so!

'I told you—nothing worse than usual.' Gemini gave
a dismissive shake of her head. 'Shouldn't you have
flown back to New York by now?'

He glanced down at the plain gold watch on his
tanned wrist. 'I was scheduled to leave for the airport
an hour ago, yes,' he admitted, before shrugging broad
shoulders as he saw her surprised expression. 'I thought
it more important that I come here instead, to help you
deal with your stepmother,' he explained.

Gemini felt a warm glow inside at the thought of
Drakon having changed his arrangements out of concern for her. 'That really was very kind of you,' she
murmured huskily. 'Perhaps you'll be able to book another flight later today?'

He smiled tightly. 'It is of no matter; the Lyonedes
jet will fly whenever I instruct it to do so.'

'Of course it will.' She nodded ruefully. Silly her—
of *course* there was a Lyonedes jet! Her father had been
extremely wealthy, but she knew the Lyonedes family
were rich beyond her imagining. Hence Angela's obvious interest in ensnaring one of them for herself...
'What on earth did you say to Angela to finally get her
to go?' she prompted curiously.

Drakon's top lip curled with distaste as he recalled
the unpleasantness of that conversation—the details
of which he had no intention of sharing with Gemini.
But it had left Drakon feeling it might be of benefit to
all concerned if he were to have further investigations
made in regard to Angela Bartholomew. If for no other
reason than that Lyonedes Enterprises was about to

complete an important and costly business transaction with a woman who could not be trusted.

Except Drakon knew there was another, equally important reason for his concern about Angela. And that reason was standing across the room from him.

He'd had every intention of returning to New York this evening—of putting Gemini Bartholomew and the desire that had blazed so hotly between them the previous week firmly from his mind. But now that he had seen her again he knew he no longer felt any inclination to leave England—either today or tomorrow. In fact, he had no desire to leave England until he was reassured that this matter between Gemini and her stepmother had been settled.

And it *would* be settled, Drakon inwardly decreed grimly. One way or another. In such a way that would ensure Gemini was no longer in danger from Angela's viciousness.

'I merely told her that it was time for her to leave,' he answered economically, having no intention of boring Gemini with the truth of her stepmother's flirtatious manner—almost as if he had not witnessed the viciousness of her attack on Gemini!—or the fact that she had dared to invite him out to dinner this evening. It was an invitation Drakon had left the other woman in absolutely no doubt he would refuse—along with any others she might care to make in the future.

The sneering remarks she had made about Gemini following that refusal had been enough to alert Drakon anew concerning Gemini's safety...

'Are you free for dinner this evening?'

Gemini had been lost in thought during Drakon's lengthy silence, but now she looked across at him sharply. 'You're inviting me to have dinner with you again?'

He nodded briskly. 'It is obvious that we need to discuss the continuing problem of your stepmother further, and as I will no longer be flying back to New York today—'

'You won't?' Gemini blinked owlishly, not sure whether that lurch in her stomach was due to a residual nausea from earlier or if it was solely to do with the fact that Drakon apparently wasn't returning to New York today as planned, and had actually invited her out to dinner with him this evening!

It was an invitation she knew she shouldn't accept…

Couldn't accept.

Not when she had spent the past four days telling herself that her heated response to this man had been just a figment of her imagination. An overreaction to everything else that was going on in her life at the moment.

She'd only had to look at Drakon again to know she had been fooling herself…

This man—the way he looked, the aura of power he wore like a mantle about those broad and muscular shoulders—appealed to Gemini on a level she had never experienced before. He somehow made her feel safe, protected, while at the same time being aware that Drakon himself was the biggest danger of all to her. Physically and possibly emotionally as well…

'No. I—' Drakon broke off as a knock sounded on the internal door of the apartment. 'That's probably your assistant. I instructed her to let you know when she was ready to lock up for the day.' He shrugged as Gemini raised her brows.

Yes, Drakon Lyonedes was a man she knew she

should beware of—for more reasons than the obvious one of finding him so mouthwateringly attractive. Left unchecked, he was more than capable of taking over her life if he chose to do so—and was certainly arrogant enough.

'You—' It was Gemini's turn to break off as a mobile phone began to ring. It had to be Drakon's, because the ringtone of hers was one of her favourite songs rather than a normal ringtone like this. 'That's probably Markos, checking to see if you arrived here in time to save me from the clutches of my evil stepmother!' she guessed dryly.

'This situation is not in the least amusing, Gemini.' Dark brows lowered over those coal-black eyes as he removed a mobile phone from the breast pocket of his tailored jacket. 'And I believe my cousin knows me well enough to know I will most certainly have saved you— if indeed you needed saving,' he declared, before taking the call. 'Yes, Markos,' he said, at the same time giving Gemini a small inclination of his head in acknowledgement of her correct guess as to the identity of the caller.

Gemini decided to leave him to the privacy of his call and left the room to answer the door to Jo, reassuring her assistant that she was fine before accompanying her down the stairs to close the blinds and lock the door behind her as she left for the day.

Leaving Gemini completely alone with Drakon...

She lingered downstairs in the shop for several minutes after Jo had gone on her way, restlessly tidying where no tidying was necessary as she thought over Drakon's invitation to dinner this evening. So that they might discuss the problem of Angela further, he had said. Although quite what that meant she had no idea. It was now more than obvious to her that Angela's dislike of her wasn't necessarily personal but was directed towards what Gemini represented. An inborn resentment that she doubted any amount of talking between herself and Drakon would succeed in changing.

Which was reason enough for her to turn down his dinner invitation, surely?

If she wanted to turn it down...

She had total recall of her visit to Lyonedes Tower. Of Drakon's cool arrogance. His remorseless power. Most telling of all, she clearly remembered what it had felt like to have those chiselled lips and those long elegant hands on her body as he made love to her in the lift.

Which was precisely why she shouldn't even *think* about agreeing to have dinner with him again this evening.

'What are you doing alone down here in the darkness?'

Gemini turned sharply to face Drakon, instantly noting how the width of his shoulders almost filled the doorway leading out to the stairs of her apartment. Immediately she was reminded of just how tautly muscled his chest and shoulders had felt beneath her hands...

Not a good memory to have when she was still debating whether or not it would be sensible, even sane on her part, to spend another evening with him!

'Just tidying up,' she said lightly. 'Are you ready to leave now?' she added hopefully.

Drakon looked across at her speculatively. The blinds that had been pulled down over the windows shrouded the shop in half-light, making it impossible for him to see her clearly—although he thought he could make out two bright wings of heated colour in those ivory cheeks.

She also seemed slightly nervous and she avoided meeting his gaze.

'You are not recovered enough to go out to dinner this evening,' he said slowly.

'I—'

'Perhaps you would prefer it if we were to remain here and I prepared something for us to eat?' Drakon suggested swiftly when he sensed she was about to use her earlier indisposition as a way of refusing to have dinner with him. A refusal he had no intention of accepting...

Her eyes widened as she gave a disbelieving huff of laughter. 'You can cook, too?'

'Of course.'

Of course he could cook, Gemini chided herself derisively; he was a man who gave the impression that he could do absolutely anything he chose to. 'Well?' she asked in a reminder of the conversation they'd had the previous week when she'd asked if he played the piano in his apartment.

'Passably.' His mouth curved into a wry smile in acknowledgement of that conversation.

Gemini laughed. 'In that case you can certainly cook for me some time.'

He quirked dark brows. 'But not this evening?'

She shrugged. 'I really don't see that there would be any point. Angela is—well, Angela.' She grimaced. 'And whatever bee she currently has in her bonnet over me will no doubt pass when she gets some other multi-billionaire in her matrimonial sights.'

Drakon frowned. 'Did you really believe earlier that I was involved with her in a personal way?'

Yes, briefly, she *had* once again believed that. How could she have thought anything else when the other woman had appeared here like an avenging angel and accused Gemini of trying to seduce Drakon?

Gemini shrugged again. 'It really doesn't matter what I do or don't believe on that subject, does it?'

'Oh, but it does,' Drakon murmured as he stepped further into the shadows. 'To me it matters very much.'

Gemini swallowed hard as she watched him approach with lithe, purposeful strides, only coming to a halt when he stood mere inches away from her. 'I—it's all been sorted out now, so no real harm done,' she dismissed nervously.

He raised an eyebrow. 'Surely that is for me to say, and not you?'

She drew in a deep breath and let it out slowly. 'Stop making such a big thing out of it, Drakon.'

'But it *is* a big thing to have one's word doubted, is it not?' he pressed softly.

Gemini gave him an irritated frown. 'You want me to apologise for ever having doubted you? Is that it?'

Those sculptured lips curved in a smile. 'That would certainly be a start, yes.'

'A start?' she repeated warily, not sure she was comfortable with the way Drakon stood so overpoweringly close to her. Or with the direction this conversation appeared to be going in.

'A start,' he echoed huskily as he closed the small distance between them, his hands moving up to lightly grasp the tops of her arms as his head began to lower towards hers.

Yes, their conversation was going in exactly the direction Gemini had thought it might!

CHAPTER EIGHT

SHE swallowed hard. 'Drakon—'

'Gemini…' he murmured throatily, his breath a warm caress across her lips.

She felt trapped, very like a rabbit caught in the glare of the headlights of a car, as she continued to stare up at him in the semi-darkness and felt the unmistakable pull of physical attraction. 'This isn't a good idea at all.'

Those dark eyes glittered. 'I disagree.'

Gemini blinked. 'You do?'

'Oh, yes,' Drakon muttered, and her nearness, the heady seduction of her perfume, took over all of his senses as he finally claimed her lips with his own.

He had thought often of doing this again, he realised as her lips parted, yielded to his, and he drew her fully into his arms to deepen the kiss. Taking. Possessing. His hands moved restlessly, searchingly over the sweet curves of her back and the smooth roundness of her bottom, pulling her into him and making her fully aware of the hard pulse of his arousal.

Yes, he had thought of this many times these past four days. Yearned for this. Ached for it.

There was no room for other thoughts now except to indulge those senses. No time for gentleness as his tongue plundered the sweetness of her mouth until he knew every warm and delicious inch. The warm swell of her breasts was crushed against the hardness of his chest, her thighs were hot against him, and the air filled with the raggedness of their breathing and their low moans of pleasure.

To Gemini it was as if no time at all had passed since Drakon had last made love to her. The passion was instant—the need, the aching pleasure even more so. She gasped as his fingers touched her skin beneath her blouse seconds before his hand cupped the lace of her bra, groaning in her throat as her nipple rubbed against the heat of his palm.

He moved back slightly to unbutton her blouse and reveal those lace-cupped breasts to his glittering black gaze before he expertly removed the skimpy item of lingerie and let it fall on the floor, along with her blouse.

Gemini slid the jacket from his shoulders and down his arms before dropping it onto the floor to join her discarded clothing, allowing the briefest moment of humour as she imagined the horror of Drakon's tailor at her cavalier treatment of a jacket that she was sure had cost thousands of dollars.

But it was only the briefest of thoughts before Gemini released the knot of his tie and tossed it aside, unfastening the buttons of the white silk shirt and revealing the muscled perfection of his olive-skinned chest. The shirt met the same fate as his jacket, and her breath caught in her throat as she was finally able to touch the glorious contours of his bared flesh.

Steel encased in velvet…

Gemini could feel the play of muscles beneath that velvet warmth as Drakon's mouth once again claimed hers, and she moved her arms about his waist to caress the long length of his naked back, down over the tautness of his fabric-covered buttocks and then up along the length of his spine.

He dragged his lips from hers to taste the delicate skin of her throat, the top swell of her breasts, before moving lower, capturing the hard nub of her nipple and drawing it into the heat of his mouth.

She gasped, her bare back against the brick wall as Drakon curled his fingers about her thighs and lifted her up and into him until her legs were about his waist. Her fingers became entangled in the darkness of his hair and pleasure coursed through her as she felt the hard throb of his arousal against her core.

That pleasure pooled between her thighs in a warm rush of moisture as he began to move slowly against her. At the same time his hand moved to cup her other breast, sliding a rhythmic thumb again and again over that second throbbing peak until she wanted to die from the arousing onslaught of his clever lips and hands and fingers.

Gemini could only cling to the dampness of Drakon's bare shoulders as she felt herself spiralling high, ever higher. He continued pleasuring her breasts at the same time as his throbbing shaft rubbed against that sensitised nub between her thighs. Her breath was coming in short and painful gasps as she hurtled closer and closer towards a release that filled her with a longing to pull Drakon closer at the same time as a fear of completely losing control of her senses urged her to push him away.

Drakon seemed to sense that confusion in her. His eyes were dark and glittering as he slowly released his mouth from her breast and looked up at her. 'I'm not hurting you, am I?'

'God, no!' she choked out, trembling, shaking from the force of her own arousal.

An arousal that he seemed to incite in her at will...

An arousal that was rapidly fading, to be replaced by embarrassment as she realised exactly what they were doing—and where!

'I just—I'm finding all of this a bit overwhelming, Drakon. Making love for the first time was somehow always more...romantic in my imaginings.' She made an attempt at humour as she forced her knees to relax their death grip about his waist, her legs feeling slightly shaky as she allowed her feet to slide down to the concrete floor.

He blinked. 'Sorry?'

'It's silly, I know,' she gabbled. 'But I'd always thought that the first time I made love it would at least be in a huge feather bed—maybe even a four-poster.'

'A four-poster bed?'

'Mmm. With curtains blowing in a gentle breeze,' Gemini mused as the idea of making love with Drakon in such a romantic setting began to take flight.

'I beg your pardon?'

'And maybe rose petals scattered about the room,' she continued dreamily. 'Don't you think that would be romantic, Drakon?'

'Undoubtedly,' he rasped.

Gemini snapped out of her romantic musings as she became aware of the wariness in his tone. And not just wariness, but utter disbelief.

And a healthy dose of shock!

No doubt it *was* a shock for him to realise that the spoilt and pampered daughter of Miles Bartholomew was a twenty-seven-year-old virgin...

What on earth had she been thinking, drivelling on like that in front of a man like him?

Her cheeks burned hotly. 'What did you imagine,

Drakon?' Her embarrassment deepened as she picked
up her blouse and quickly put it on over her bare breasts.
'Did you think that I make a habit of behaving in this
uninhibited way with every man I meet?'

His jaw tightened. 'Not every man, no.'

'Just the rich and powerful ones?'

A scowl darkened his brow. 'Gemini—'

'If you really thought that, then I'm afraid you have
me confused with my stepmother,' she cut in before he
could answer her.

'I know exactly who and what you are, Gemini,' he
grated.

The rustle of clothing behind her told her that Drakon
had probably pulled his shirt back on at least. The shirt
she had only minutes ago unbuttoned before throwing
on the floor!

What was it about this man in particular that made
her behave so completely out of character? Gemini
barely recognised the wanton she became every time
Drakon took her in his arms.

And a drivelling, romantic idiot too, apparently!

Something a man like him would certainly be re-
pelled by.

Gemini kept her back towards him and moved to the
safety of the other side of the shop before turning. Only
the whiteness of Drakon's shirt was visible where he
still stood in the shadows. She licked her lips. 'Don't
misunderstand me, Drakon. I'm really very grateful for
the help you gave me earlier in getting rid of Angela,
but not grateful enough to—'

'I strongly advise that you don't insult me by finishing that sentence,' he warned, the tone of his voice
dangerously soft.

Gemini shivered as she felt the chill of his warning

down the length of her spine. A warning she would be insane not to heed! 'I don't mean to insult you—'

'No?' he rasped as he bent down to pick his jacket and tie up from the floor.

'No,' she reiterated wearily. 'That's the last thing I want to do when you've been so...kind.' She shrugged. 'It's just been one hell of a day. Emotions are running high, and I really think it would be best if you just left now.'

Drakon agreed with the logic of her reasoning. At least he would have agreed with it if he could have thought logically at all. As it was, he was still reeling from the knowledge that, although Gemini was a sophisticated young woman in her late twenties, she was a physically inexperienced one.

How was such a thing possible in this day and age? Especially for a beautiful young woman whose father's wealth would have ensured she had lived her life in privilege and self-indulgence? When her late teens and early twenties would have been spent socialising with men of wealth and experience? When Gemini's own stepmother was an acknowledged seductress?

But perhaps Gemini's contempt for the latter was the very reason she had chosen a completely different path for herself?

Whatever the explanation for her physical innocence, Drakon was stunned by it. Stunned and at the same time wary. He had been sexually active for more than twenty years now, and never in all his thirty-six years had he made love to an innocent. As much as he still wanted and desired Gemini—and it seemed he had only to look at her to want her—he had no intention of complicating his own life or hers by becoming her very first lover.

His movements were measured, deliberate, as he

shrugged back into his jacket and then neatly folded his tie and placed it in one of his pockets before looking across at Gemini once more. 'After witnessing her behaviour earlier, I don't believe for a moment that you have seen the last of your stepmother,' he remarked with obvious distaste.

Gemini didn't think so either; she knew her stepmother far too well to ever believe that. Angela seemed to have set her sights on ensnaring one of the Lyonedes men as her next husband—preferably Drakon—and, as Gemini knew only too well, the older woman wasn't easily deterred once she had set her mind on making a conquest.

Knowing of Gemini's acquaintance with both men— these encounters with Drakon were far too physically volatile for her ever to think of them as friends—was surely only guaranteed to make Angela even more determined to capture one of the Lyonedes cousins. If only out of spite towards Gemini.

She shrugged ruefully. 'As long as you and Markos stay well away from her in future there shouldn't be a problem.'

Drakon gave a humourless smile. 'That may be a little difficult when we are in the middle of a business transaction with her.'

Gemini stiffened at this reminder that Lyonedes Enterprises was in the process of purchasing her family home from Angela. 'I believe you walked yourself into that particular situation,' she said unsympathetically.

'Indeed,' he accepted dryly. 'And it is a situation I am more than capable of dealing with. But I would advise that you do everything in your power to avoid any further confrontation with her.'

Gemini looked him directly in the eyes. 'Maybe you should just give her what she wants and take her to bed?'

Drakon drew in a harsh breath at the very thought of having a sexual relationship with the avaricious widow. Not that she was unattractive—if a man did not mind knowing her interest was mainly in his bank balance!

Which, he acknowledged, was something that had never particularly bothered him before. Indeed, it was the reason he had become so cynical and jaded about ever finding a woman who might love him for himself, and whom he could love in return. Years of having women attracted to the Lyonedes name and his excessive wealth had resulted in unemotional and consequently fleeting relationships with women.

His continued attraction to Gemini—a young woman whom he now knew was neither avaricious nor experienced—was unsettling to say the least.

He eyed her dispassionately and nodded abruptly. 'I will give your suggestion all the consideration it deserves.' Which, as far as he was concerned, was none whatsoever.

Gemini recoiled as if Drakon had physically struck her. Which, in a way, he had.

For the past four years she had stood back and watched as dozens of men had fallen prey to the allure of Angela's voluptuous beauty—her own father included—and to think of Drakon, a man whose attraction she seemed unable to resist herself, becoming another one of Angela's conquests brought a return of Gemini's earlier nausea.

She frowned. 'Obviously you must do what you think best...'

Those almost black eyes glittered coldly. 'I invariably do,' he rasped harshly.

Yes, she had no doubt that he was a man who answered to no one for any of his actions. And really she had brought this current situation on herself. Out of self-defence and confusion over her attraction towards Drakon, maybe, but nevertheless she had instigated this particular conversation.

'Thank you once again for your help earlier.'

'You're welcome.' He gave a brief inclination of his head.

'No doubt you'll be returning to New York now?'

Drakon had decided earlier that to leave England before the issue of Angela Bartholomew was settled to his satisfaction would be an error of judgement on his part. But this time spent with Gemini, when he had once again found himself unable to resist making love to her, only to learn that she was an innocent, told him that it would perhaps be an even bigger error of judgement on his part if he were to remain. Only perhaps? It could become a catastrophic error of judgement for both of them if he were to remain in England at this present time!

'No doubt,' he replied noncommittally as he strolled over and opened the shop door. 'Lock the door behind me.'

Gemini glared at his autocratic back as she followed him. 'I have every intention of doing so.'

Drakon looked down at her wordlessly for several long seconds before sighing. 'Don't hesitate to call on Markos if it should become necessary.'

Call on Markos, not him, she noted heavily as she shut and secured the door after Drakon left. He couldn't have told her any more plainly that their own brief association, whatever it might have been, was very definitely over as far as he was concerned.

Drakon waited only long enough to hear Gemini lock the door behind him before taking his mobile out of his pocket and pressing a quick-dial button as he walked the short distance to where he had parked his car earlier.

'Have Max arrange for a twenty-four-hour watch to be kept on Gemini,' he instructed economically when his cousin answered the call on only the second ring. 'And first thing in the morning have him do a thorough check on Angela Bartholomew,' he added grimly before Markos had time to respond to that first instruction. 'I also want him to look into the possibility of Miles Bartholomew having drawn up a will dated later than the one that was presented for probate.' He unlocked and opened the door of the Mercedes and slid into the leather seat behind the wheel. 'A will that may have left Bartholomew House to his daughter rather than his wife.'

'Do you think that's a possibility?'

'After today, I think Angela is a woman capable of doing anything that is in her own best interests.'

'Including illegally suppressing her husband's will?'

'Including that, yes,' Drakon confirmed grimly.

'Hell!' Markos groaned heavily. 'That could leave Lyonedes Enterprises in one almighty legal tangle.'

It would also, if it existed, leave Gemini in a position of great vulnerability… 'Yes,' he agreed tersely.

'And where will you will be while I'm instructing Max to do these things?' Markos prompted curiously.

Drakon glanced across at the closed and shuttered flower shop that Gemini owned and ran. His gaze was drawn upwards to where a light had come on in what he now knew to be the sitting room of her apartment. 'I have decided to leave for New York this evening after all.'

'Really?' Markos sounded surprised.

'Really,' Drakon echoed dryly. There was no reason for him to return to Lyonedes Tower; he rarely carried luggage with him anyway, as he kept a full wardrobe of clothes in both his New York apartment and the one here in London.

'But Gemini is okay?'

He frowned his irritation at his cousin's obvious concern. 'She appeared to be perfectly well when I left her two minutes ago,' he snapped.

'And her stepmother?'

'Is a bitch from hell, and we should never have entered into a business transaction with her,' Drakon felt no hesitation in announcing harshly.

There was a brief pause before Markos spoke again. 'I'll talk to Max straight away.'

'Do that.'

Drakon ended the call as abruptly as he had started it. His second call to the pilot of the Lyonedes jet was even briefer as he sat and watched Gemini's shadowy outline inside her apartment as she moved to pull the curtains across the two windows that faced down onto the street.

He was still sitting there in the silence of the Mercedes fifteen minutes later when a black Range Rover, with Max himself seated behind the wheel, pulled into the parking space behind. He turned in his seat, and the two men nodded brief acknowledgement of each other before Drakon started his engine and drove away.

* * *

'Well!' Gemini huffed indignantly as she slowly replaced the telephone receiver on its cradle.

'Problems?' Jo looked across at her curiously as she came to collect her jacket from the office of the shop in preparation for leaving for her lunch break on what was turning out to be a very busy Friday.

Drakon Lyonedes had been a problem before Gemini had even met him! And he had become even more of one—for totally different reasons—since she had first forced herself into his presence. Had that really only been a week ago? It somehow seemed so much longer.

Gemini still inwardly cringed every time she thought about the last time she had seen him three days ago.

Considering how the time usually flew by when she was at work, it had been a surprisingly long three days. Three days during which Drakon had completely disappeared from her life.

No, not completely…

She had slept badly the night after he'd left her so abruptly. Not because she had wasted any more of her time thinking about that awful scene with Angela, but because she hadn't been able to stop thinking about Drakon and her response to him. Consequently it had taken her until late the following morning to notice the black Range Rover parked just down the street from the flower shop, and several more hours to realise that Max Stanford was seated behind the wheel, his steely gaze fixed unwaveringly on the flower shop. On her?

Gemini had decided she was being paranoid, and the Range Rover had disappeared when she'd gone out later that morning to buy her lunch from the deli two doors down the street. And then she had realised that another black car had taken the place of the Range Rover, and the man sitting inside seemed to be watching her from behind concealing sunglasses. By the time she'd shut up shop for the night the black Range Rover and Max were back, and the other car and its driver had disappeared.

Still feeling ever so slightly paranoid, Gemini had nevertheless felt no hesitation in walking over to the Range Rover and tapping on the window to ask an obviously less than pleased Max exactly what he was doing, parked outside her shop. His curt explanation had been enough to send Gemini hurrying back inside to put a call straight through to Markos.

Charming and roguish as ever, Markos had assured her that he was simply carrying out his cousin's instructions, and that Max, or one of his security team, was to remain as her protection until Drakon told him otherwise.

Gemini had been stunned. And not a little annoyed. She accepted that Angela had been verbally abusive the last time the two women had spoken, and that Drakon had walked in on that heated scene just in time to prevent her stepmother from actually hitting her, but surely he didn't imagine Angela would actually try to harm her?

That question had unfortunately remained unanswered, because Gemini's efforts to contact Drakon in New York had proved as difficult as contacting him at Lyonedes Tower had been the previous week. She had managed to get as far as talking to his personal assistant this time, only to be informed that Mr Lyonedes was unavailable. Nor had Drakon bothered to return her call.

She had now received a telephone call from that same personal assistant, telling her that, 'Mr Lyonedes has instructed me to inform you that he will be arriving in

England later today and will be calling on you at your apartment at eight o'clock this evening.' It just added insult to injury. Gemini had a good mind to make sure she was nowhere near her apartment at eight o'clock tonight!

Although she accepted that wasn't likely to achieve very much when the current watchdog parked outside would no doubt tell Drakon exactly where she had gone. Still, it was the principle of the thing that mattered; damn it, Drakon couldn't just walk in and out of her life and take charge whenever he felt like it! Well…apparently he could. But that didn't mean that she had to make it at all easy for him.

She looked up now and smiled reassuringly at Jo. 'It's nothing I can't handle,' she assured her assistant firmly.

At least Gemini sincerely hoped she *could* handle seeing Drakon again…

CHAPTER NINE

'ARE you expecting someone to join you?'

Gemini had been aware of Drakon the moment he entered her favourite Italian restaurant. Just as she had been aware of the female interest directed towards him as he inexorably made his way across that restaurant to where she sat at a table in one of the more private booths at the back of the happily noisy and crowded room. A table set for two.

Her own heart had skipped a beat at how dark and dangerously attractive Drakon looked this evening, in a casual black silk shirt, unbuttoned at the throat, and black trousers tailored to the long length of his legs. The darkness of his hair was slightly tousled and damp, as if he had recently taken a shower. Which he probably had, she accepted, if he had only flown in from New York a few hours ago.

She put down her glass of Chianti to lean back against the leather bench seat. She looked up and smiled at him. 'Yes, I'm expecting someone to join me,' she confirmed lightly.

Drakon looked more than a little irritated. 'Did my assistant not telephone you earlier to tell you I would be calling at your apartment this evening?'

'Oh, yes, he telephoned me,' Gemini said blandly.

'Then—'

'Obviously I had plans for this evening other than sitting at home waiting for the great Drakon Lyonedes to grace me with his magnificent presence,' she continued as though he hadn't spoken.

He would have to be blind not to notice the way those sea-green eyes flashed with temper. And unfortunately he wasn't in the least visually impaired where Gemini Bartholomew was concerned! 'You are annoyed that I asked my assistant to telephone you.' It was a statement not a question.

'How astute of you, Drakon!' she came back with saccharine sweetness.

If anything Gemini looked more beautiful this evening than when Drakon had last seen her: those sparkling eyes were surrounded by long dark lashes, colour highlighted her cheeks, the fullness of her lips was glossed peach, and her hair was a silky white-blonde curtain about her slender shoulders. The fitted cotton sweater she wore was the same sea-green colour as her eyes, and a short black skirt revealed the length of her legs.

Drakon's mouth thinned as he realised he was not at all pleased to know she had dressed like that for the pleasure of another man. 'Are you saying you would rather I had telephoned and spoken to you personally before I left New York?' he queried.

Her eyes once more glowed with temper. 'I'm saying I would rather you had bothered to return my call two days ago, or at the very least telephoned me yesterday and *asked* if it was convenient for us to meet this evening, rather than just having your assistant call and *tell* me that we were!'

Yes, that would have been the more acceptable, the

more polite way of doing things, Drakon acknowledged impatiently. Except he had not been feeling in the least polite—either yesterday or any of the other days he had been back in New York. Because of this woman. Because he had not been able to stop thinking about Gemini and the last time the two of them had been together. Or how much he wished to see her and be with her again...

That knowledge alone had been enough to make his temper and mood unpredictable at best these past three days, and volatile at worst. Nor, he acknowledged irritably, had he been in the least sure of how much she would have welcomed the call if he had been the one to telephone today...

Drakon had accepted long ago that he was a man of strong sexual appetites, but also a man who rarely if ever thought of any of the women he made love to when he was not sharing her body and her bed. Gemini Bartholomew, he had learnt these past few days, was the exception to that rule—and he didn't like it one little bit.

He had found himself thinking of her far too often for comfort since flying back to New York, both at work and during the long evenings spent at his penthouse apartment in Manhattan. Neither did he have to look far to find the reason for his feelings of frustration where she was concerned.

Gemini's admission of physical innocence...

Drakon had been stunned. It was incredible, unbelievable, that a woman of her beauty and years should still be a virgin. It also put her beyond the reach of his normal casual affairs. Unfortunately that in no way lessened the desire Drakon felt for her...

Just seeing her again, being with her again, was enough to make his body harden with a ferocious desire!

'Oh, for goodness' sake sit down and stop making the place look untidy, Drakon,' she snapped as the waiter arrived at the table and handed her two menus before departing again.

He frowned. 'I thought you said you were waiting for someone.'

'I was,' Gemini said. 'And now he's arrived. I was waiting for you, Drakon,' she admitted as he continued to stare down at her.

His eyes widened. 'Me?'

'I was pretty sure one of your watchdogs would be only too happy to tell you exactly where to find me at eight o'clock this evening,' she told him. 'And, as you very kindly gave me dinner at your apartment last time, I thought the least I could do was buy you dinner at my favourite Italian restaurant this evening. Would you care for a glass of red wine?' She lifted up the bottle of Chianti she had ordered when she arrived and held it poised over the empty wine glass at the place setting opposite her own.

'Thank you,' Drakon accepted quietly as he slid onto the bench seat opposite, more relieved than he cared to consider at the knowledge that Gemini was not spending the evening with another man after all. That she had, in fact, dressed this way for his pleasure. 'I apologise if you found my assistant's telephone call impolite.'

Gemini looked across the table at Drakon from beneath lowered lashes, knowing she was once again slightly overwhelmed by the sheer presence of this man. Even dressed in casual clothes he exuded that aura of power and authority. 'Your assistant was perfectly polite, Drakon—you're the one I consider rude and high-handed in asking him to make the call in the first place.'

Drakon returned her gaze quizzically. 'You don't intend to let me off the hook lightly, do you?'

'Should I?' Gemini deliberately showed none of the inner turmoil she felt at seeing Drakon again as she casually picked up her wine glass and took a sip of the deliciously fruity red wine.

'Probably not.' He shrugged those broad shoulders.

'Definitely not,' she corrected pointedly.

Drakon sighed. 'Very well. I apologise unreservedly, Gemini, for not telephoning you myself and requesting a meeting with you.'

'You're forgiven.' She gave a graciously acknowledging inclination of her head.

'So this is your favourite restaurant...' Drakon looked about them appreciatively, finding the warm and cosy atmosphere of the restaurant also to *his* liking.

There were red-and-white-checked cloths on the twenty or so occupied tables, with candles alight in empty wine bottles on each one, lots of greenery trailing down from above, brightly coloured pictures of Italy adorning the terracotta-coloured walls, and the delicious smells of garlic and Italian sauces coming from the kitchen were enough to make his mouth water.

'Not what you were expecting?'

Drakon's gaze returned across the table to Gemini as he heard the amusement in her voice. Inwardly he acknowledged that nothing about this young woman was what he would have expected from the only daughter of the wealthy and influential Miles Bartholomew. Which, he knew, was becoming a serious problem for him; Gemini was rapidly throwing all his previous experience with women off-balance. Throwing *him* off-balance…

He shrugged as he picked up the menu. 'I'm sure the food here is adequate.'

She gave an indelicate snort. 'The food here is fantastic!'

Drakon perused the extensive menu. 'What would you recommend?'

Gemini studied his bent head, noting the way his hair had started to curl slightly as it dried in the warmth of the restaurant. The sharp angles of his face were softened by the warm glow of candlelight, and the silky dark hair visible at the base of his throat where his shirt was unbuttoned instantly made her remember how that soft pelt went all the way down to his—

'Gemini?'

A blush warmed her cheeks as she raised her startled gaze to meet Drakon's glittering black one. 'Anything,' she answered abruptly. 'All the food here is good.'

Those dark eyes continued to study her for long, timeless seconds. Tense, still seconds, when even the chatter of the other diners faded into the background and there seemed to be only Gemini and Drakon in the room, and she found herself totally unable to look away from that compelling gaze.

Gemini had hoped that if she ever saw Drakon again she would find she had got over whatever madness had possessed her the last time she had seen him—well, the last two times she had seen him! That she would be able to look at him, speak to him, spend time with him and see him for the arrogant, powerful man that he was. And it was impossible *not* to see those things in him. Unfortunately she knew he was also dangerously seductive; he only had to touch her, kiss her, to send her over the edge of self-control. Something that had never, ever happened to her before, but seemed to happen constantly with him. As she'd said, he was extremely dangerous...

She straightened, determined to break the sensual spell that once again threatened to engulf and claim her. 'So, how has your week been?' she asked with brittle brightness.

'Busy.' Drakon put down his menu. 'Yours?'

She shrugged. 'The same.'

'There have been no more visits from your stepmother?'

Gemini gave him a cool look. 'I'm sure Max has duly reported that there haven't.'

Drakon's mouth thinned. 'Markos informed me that you were less than pleased at Max's watchfulness.'

'Did he?' she mused. 'Didn't seem to make much difference to the outcome, did it?'

Drakon sighed heavily. 'Would you rather I had left you completely at the mercy of that woman's vindictiveness?'

'Once again, I would rather you had asked first,' she said pointedly.

He raised dark brows. 'And if I had done so?'

'I would have assured you that it wasn't necessary.' She waved an elegant hand. 'You were the reason Angela went off the deep end in the first place, and with you out of the picture...'

Drakon gave a humourless smile. 'Unless it has escaped your notice, I have returned.'

As if any woman could be unaware of the presence of Drakon Lyonedes! The man only had to enter a room in order to dominate it. A point that was ably demonstrated only seconds later, when Benito came to take their order and completely deferred to Drakon throughout the entire conversation.

'What?' he prompted when he saw Gemini frowning across the width of the table at him once they were alone again.

She shook her head. 'You totally ruined my usual couple of minutes of flirting outrageously with Benito when he comes to take my order.'

Drakon's brows rose. 'You flirt with the waiter?'

'I flirt outrageously,' she corrected. 'And Benito is the owner of the restaurant, not the waiter.'

He glanced across to where the dark-haired, handsome young man was passing their order to a shorter, portly man to take to the kitchen, before resuming his place behind the desk at the entrance to the restaurant. 'You come to this restaurant because you like to flirt with the owner?' His gaze was hard and glittering when he turned it back to Gemini.

'No, I come here because the food is excellent—*and* I like to flirt with the owner,' Gemini added with a teasing smile.

Drakon failed to see anything in the least amusing about her obvious attraction to Benito. 'Your usual male companions must find that very...unflattering.'

'What do you mean by that?' she asked.

Drakon scowled. 'The men you usually bring here on a date.'

She sat back on the seat, her brows mockingly high. 'I wasn't aware *this* was a date.'

It wasn't. At least it hadn't been Drakon's intention that it should become one when he had decided he and Gemini must meet again this evening. And yet the two of them were sitting together in a cosy Italian restaurant. At a secluded table for two. With a lit candle in its centre. And an evening of possibilities stretching before them. Yes, it certainly had all of the ingredients of a date, he recognised heavily.

He shrugged. 'For the sake of appearances let us say that it is.'

For the sake of Gemini's sense of self-preservation she would rather say that it wasn't! Admittedly she had been the one to instigate this evening's meeting taking place at a restaurant rather than her apartment, as he had stipulated through his assistant.

But that was the whole point, wasn't it? She had made her own arrangements for the evening because she had resented Drakon's arrogance in issuing that instruction through a third party!

Except she didn't seem to have thought it through as thoroughly as she ought to have done. Hadn't even considered that the two of them sitting here, talking and eating a meal together, would take on all the appearance of a date. Which was a bit late in the day when you considered she'd already allowed him to make love to her. *Twice!*

'I do hope you intend to give poor Max a couple of hours off, at least, while we eat dinner?' she said sweetly.

Drakon instantly recognised her deliberate attempt to remind him exactly why she would never consider their having dinner together as being a date—his arrogant high-handedness in having her watched over by his security team.

'Poor Max?' he queried.

She nodded once their first course had been delivered to the table and the waiter had departed. 'I'm sure you pay him and the rest of your security team well, but even so it must still have been very boring for them to just sit outside my apartment for the past three days and nights.'

Yes, Drakon had read Max's daily reports with interest, noting that Gemini spent her days in her shop and her evenings and nights alone in her apartment. 'You are correct. I do pay them very well,' he said. 'And I believe you very kindly offered Max some variation in your routine when you closed the shop yesterday afternoon.'

She gave a mischievous grin. 'He told you about that?'

Even in reading Max's e-mailed report Drakon had been able to pick up on the older man's discomfort at having to follow Gemini into a large beauty salon, where she had proceeded to have her hair styled, then a manicure and a pedicure, before disappearing into a private room in order to have various parts of her delectable body waxed.

'He may never recover from the experience,' Drakon commented.

Gemini had actually come to like and respect Max Stanford during the past few days—had even invited him into the shop a couple of times for coffee when she'd thought he might be in need of a drink. She just hadn't been able to resist teasing him a little when it came to the usual relaxing way she spent her Thursday afternoons off. Besides which, she had been fully aware of the fact that, as with everything else she had done the past three days, he would report her movements to his employer.

She eyed Drakon quizzically. 'And not you?'

He shrugged those broad shoulders. 'My mother usually spends her Saturday afternoons in the same way, I believe.'

His widowed mother, Gemini knew, had lived alone in Athens since the death of her husband ten years ago. In fact, she knew quite a lot more about Drakon now than she had three days ago; the internet was a marvelous although potentially dangerous thing, offering any amount of information on someone as famous as him.

Such as the extent of his business interests around the world, as well as his extreme wealth. He owned homes in New York, London, Hong Kong, Toronto and Paris, as well as a private island in the Greek Aegean—although how he ever found the time to live in most of those homes was a mystery to her when he obviously worked so hard adding to the Lyonedes millions.

She also knew that he was thirty-six years old. And single. With not so much as a hint of an engagement in his past...

She eyed him curiously now. 'Are you and your mother close?'

'Very,' he said economically.

'And you and Markos are close too?'

'Like brothers,' he confirmed.

'I noticed that.'

Drakon raised dark brows. 'You find it strange that I not only feel affection for my family but also engender a return of that affection?'

'Not in the least,' she dismissed lightly. 'Why would I? I'm sure you're a very attentive son, and the closeness between you and Markos was all too obvious when I saw you together last week.'

The slightly wistful note in Gemini's voice reminded Drakon that her twin brother had died before she'd even had a chance to know him, and that with the death of both of her parents she now had no family of her own that she might call on for affection. Or protection.

'Try your ravioli before it goes cold,' she encouraged, as if she were aware of his thoughts and felt uncomfortable with them. 'Benito's father is the chef, and his spinach ravioli is to die for.'

Drakon, guessing that she was deliberately changing the subject, forked up some of the ravioli and found it to be every bit as excellent as she said it was. 'This *is* good.' He nodded his approval, not having realised how hungry he was until he bit into the succulent food.

'Would I lie to you?' Gemini grinned her satisfaction at his obvious enjoyment.

Drakon stilled, not quite sure how to answer that comment. Or if he should answer it at all. It had been his experience over the years that most women did indeed lie, and usually for the same reason.

Initially to pique his interest, and afterwards to hold that interest.

Gemini had been honest—brutally so on occasion—from the very beginning of their acquaintance. Something else that made her so different from any other woman he had ever known.

In fact, the whole evening turned out to be something of a surprise to Drakon as they ate more delicious food prepared and cooked by Benito's father. They discussed such far-ranging subjects as films they had both seen—in his own case privately, because he hated to go to noisy and overcrowded public cinemas—agreed the merits or otherwise of books they had both read, and discovered that they both had a love of opera.

'When Daddy was alive he and I would attend the

opera together once a month,' Gemini told him wistfully.

'But not your stepmother?'

'The only thing Angela liked about the opera was being able to dress up and show off the latest piece of jewellery my father had bought her,' Gemini said. 'Luckily even that wore off after the first couple of times, so my father and I were able to go alone together after that. Our monthly visit to the opera was the one thing he flatly refused to give up, even though Angela was so demanding of his attention.'

A stubbornness her father had no doubt paid a high price for, Drakon recognised with a frown, once again wondering what sort of woman Angela was that she had wanted to possess and own Miles to the exclusion of his only child. Certainly she was a woman he knew he wanted nothing more to do with than was absolutely necessary.

'What is your favourite opera?' he asked.

'Any and all of them,' Gemini answered without hesitation.

Drakon nodded. 'It's something that you either love or hate, is it not? Markos and I were lucky enough to be introduced to that love at an early age by our parents. We were both a little wild during our teenage years, and my mother was determined to instil at least some measure of refinement into us before it was too late,' he told her with a smile.

Gemini somehow couldn't imagine the controlled and haughty Drakon Lyonedes as ever being wild. She was surprised at how quickly and enjoyably the evening had passed, with Drakon proving to be an interesting as well as an entertaining dinner companion. To the extent, she now realised, that she had become so charmed by his company she had completely forgotten the reason they were having dinner together at all this evening!

'So.' She sat back with a smile as they lingered over their coffee. 'Will you be letting Max off the hook now so that he can go back to his usual duties?'

His long eyelashes lowered over suddenly guarded dark eyes. 'We won't complete on the purchase of Bartholomew House for another ten days.'

Gemini gave a sudden pained frown at the reminder that his company was buying her family home with the intention of turning it into a hotel. Something she had certainly forgotten in the last enjoyable three hours or so.

'So Max stays?' she said stiffly.

'For the time being, yes,' Drakon confirmed.

'It's time I asked Benito for the bill.' She smiled across at the owner of the restaurant. 'And please don't even suggest paying,' she added warningly as she sensed he was about to do exactly that. 'I prefer to pay my own way, thank you very much.'

Drakon was annoyed at the realisation that by introducing the subject of his purchase of Bartholomew House he had succeeded in bringing about a return of her feelings of resentment towards him.

Had that perhaps been his intention all along in order to keep her at a distance?

Pleasant and enjoyable as this evening had undoubtedly been, it had also confirmed that Gemini was unlike any other woman Drakon had ever met. To the extent he had found himself completely relaxing in her company. He had even talked of his family and his work with her—something he had never done before with any woman. Admittedly she had been just as open with him, but nevertheless he still found the experience slightly disturbing in a way he could not entirely explain.

The sooner this situation between Gemini and her stepmother was resolved, the sooner he could return to his own previously uncomplicated life!

CHAPTER TEN

'I ENJOYED this evening,' Drakon admitted once he had parked his car beside the pavement outside Gemini's shop and apartment, their journey from the restaurant having been made in complete, brooding silence.

He sensed that she had once again deliberately erected barriers between them—which was what he had intended, was it not? But having achieved his objective, he now found himself wishing for a return of that previously animated Gemini...

'Will you allow me to take you out to dinner tomorrow evening as my way of saying thank you for tonight?' he asked gruffly.

The streetlamp outside allowed him to see the frown between her brows as she turned to look at him.

'Wouldn't that rather defeat the whole object, when I took *you* out to dinner this evening as my way of saying thank you for dinner at your apartment last week?' she said slowly. 'We could go on saying thank you like this for ever!'

For ever was not something Drakon had ever considered with any woman...

Nevertheless, it was very necessary that Gemini spent tomorrow evening with him, at least. 'I thought we could have an early dinner and then perhaps we might attend the opera together?'

Pleasure instantly glowed in those beautiful sea-green eyes before the emotion was very firmly brought under her control and she gave him a chiding look. 'That isn't playing fair, Drakon!'

After their conversation earlier it had never been his intention to play fair! It was important to his plans for this weekend that Gemini spend tomorrow evening in his company. If he had to use what she considered unfair means in order to achieve that end, then so be it.

'So, what is your answer?' he prompted tensely.

'Isn't it a little late to get tickets for tomorrow—? No, of course it isn't,' Gemini answered her own question as Drakon merely raised those mocking dark brows at her; of *course* he could obtain tickets for the opera—for tomorrow or any other evening!

She knew it would be madness on her part to agree to spend another evening with Drakon—she enjoyed his company too much, found him far too dangerously attractive to be able to continue resisting the impulse she felt to simply lose herself in him.

And yet...

She hadn't attended the opera since her father had died—had wondered if she would ever be able to do so again when it would hold such painful emotional memories for her. And yet the thought of going to the opera with Drakon, of sharing that enjoyment with him when their earlier conversation had revealed how much he also loved it, was simply too much of a temptation for Gemini to be able to resist.

'I would love to go to the opera with you,' she accepted huskily.

'Good.' Drakon nodded his satisfaction with her answer. 'Is six o'clock too early for me to call and collect you so that we might enjoy an early supper together first?'

Saturdays were always Gemini's busiest day of the week, but she didn't have a wedding or a party to provide floral arrangements for tomorrow, and no doubt Jo would be happy to shut up shop just this once, while her employer went upstairs to get ready for her evening out.

'Six o'clock sounds perfect,' Gemini said, happiness bubbling up inside her at how much she was already looking forward to seeing him again tomorrow.

Only because he was taking her to the opera, she told herself firmly. It had absolutely nothing at all to do with the fact that she had enjoyed his company so much this evening she felt a slightly hollow feeling inside at the thought of parting from him.

And if she really thought she could fool herself, then she was being totally delusional!

Not only had she been completely physically aware of Drakon all evening, but she had enjoyed his company and conversation in a way she never had with any other man. He was intelligent and well read, as well as lazily charming when he wished to be, and she had found it heart-warming when he'd talked so affectionately of his family.

All of which meant Gemini was now seriously in danger of falling even deeper under his spell.

Who was she kidding? If she became any more deeply attracted to him she was likely to go up in flames at his slightest touch!

Which was reason enough not to give him the opportunity to touch her again this evening, at least.

'Six o'clock tomorrow,' she confirmed abruptly as

she pushed open the car door and quickly stepped out onto the pavement. 'No need to get out, Drakon; the cavalry has arrived!' she said dryly as she turned and saw Max's familiar black Range Rover pulling into the kerb a short distance behind Drakon's Mercedes.

'Nevertheless, I have every intention of seeing you safely to your door.' Drakon frowned his irritation at Max's sudden arrival as he got out of the car, his hand moving up to lightly cup her elbow as he nodded a brief acknowledgement to Max. 'My mother would be horrified if she were ever to hear of such a shocking lack of manners on my part after she took such care to instil gentlemanly behaviour in both Markos and I,' he teased gently when Gemini looked up at him questioningly.

She chuckled softly as they walked to the outer door leading up to her apartment. 'Your mother sounds utterly charming.'

A remark that instantly caused him to wonder what his mother would make of Gemini...

He had no doubt that Karelia would approve of Gemini's independence and determination. Of the way she had survived the loss of first her mother and then her father in but a few years. Of the way she remained calm in the face of her stepmother's relentless vindictiveness. And no doubt his mother would be amused by the way Gemini had quietly shown herself to be more than a match for his own indomitable will and arrogance.

Yes, he knew his mother would approve of and like Gemini as much as Markos did.

Drakon's mouth compressed, and his hand dropped away from Gemini's elbow at the thought of his cousin's open admiration for her. 'I will call for you at six

o'clock tomorrow.' He turned sharply on his heel and
left her.

Gemini watched the stiffness of Drakon's back as he
returned to his car, got behind the wheel and drove off
without so much as a backward glance in her direction.

Surely that couldn't be disappointment she was feeling—especially after her earlier decision not to allow
him to touch her again—just because he hadn't so much
as attempted to kiss her goodnight?

If it was then she was already far too deeply emotionally involved with him than she'd feared...

'I don't understand...' Gemini turned to look dazedly at
Drakon the following evening as they sat in the back of
the chauffeur-driven limousine he had collected her in.

The chauffeur had just driven into what looked to
be a private airport, before stopping the car beside a
small, sleek jet and getting out from behind the wheel
to come round and open Gemini's door for her.

'I thought you said we were going to have an early
supper before going to the opera?'

'We are,' Drakon said.

He'd already taken her breath away once tonight,
when she'd opened the door to him and seen how dev-
astatingly handsome he looked in an obviously expensively tailored black evening suit, with a snowy white
shirt and white bow tie. Now he'd stunned her once
again.

Gemini stepped slowly out onto the tarmac, too surprised to do anything other than allow him to clasp her
elbow as he led her up the steps into the sleek plane.
'Where are we going?' she asked breathlessly as she
took in the opulent comfort of what she now realised
must be the Lyonedes jet Drakon had mentioned.

Four soft white leather armchairs were placed about a table where Drakon now saw Gemini seated before sitting down opposite her. There were another six armchairs for more casual seating, a thick black carpet on the floor, and an extensive bar towards the back of the cabin where a male steward stood pouring two glasses of champagne. A huge screen—no doubt where Drakon viewed some of the films they'd discussed over dinner the previous evening—took up most of the wall next to the cockpit.

'You may close the door now, Malcolm, and inform Drew that Miss Bartholomew and I are ready to leave.' Drakon smiled up at the steward as the other man placed the glasses of champagne on the table in front of them.

Gemini decided to take a sip of the bubbly wine before she attempted to speak; her throat was feeling unnaturally dry. 'Leave for where?' she queried, relieved when her voice came out sounding almost normal—she felt anything but.

How could she feel in the least normal when, instead of sitting in one of the small and expensive restaurants in London that catered to the opera crowd, she was on a private jet, the engines now roaring as the plane began to taxi down the runway in preparation for flying them off to goodness knew where?

'Verona,' Drakon told her with satisfaction as he relaxed back in his own comfortable chair.

Gemini gave a gasp, knowing there was only one place in Verona they could possibly attend the opera—and that was the open-air amphitheatre!

'I didn't think to ask—are you nervous about flying?' Drakon sat forward in concern as he saw the way the colour had suddenly drained from her cheeks.

He'd had no hesitation in complimenting her earlier

on how elegantly beautiful she looked this evening. She wore a simple black knee-length sheath of a dress, with a black silk shawl thrown casually about the bareness of her arms and shoulders. Her jewellery was matching teardrop emerald and diamond earrings and a slender bracelet, and the removal of the black silk shawl revealed she had on a matching necklace—an emerald the size of an English penny suspended from the clasp of a one-carat diamond nestling between the firm swell of her breasts.

None of which detracted from the fact that the colour had now bleached alarmingly from the creaminess of her cheeks...

'Gemini?' Drakon reached across the table to grasp both her trembling hands in his.

Her throat moved convulsively as she swallowed before speaking. 'I—ignore me. It's just...I've only ever attended the opera in Verona once before, and it was with my parents, as a treat for my twenty-first birthday,' she revealed huskily.

Drakon winced. He had thought Gemini would enjoy attending the opera in the Italian city—there truly was nowhere else in the world quite as magnificent as the amphitheatre in Verona for the opera. Instead he had only succeeded in bringing back memories of a happier time, when both her parents had still been alive and they had been a family.

'Would you rather I instructed Drew to turn the jet around and we returned to—?'

'Heavens, no!' Gemini exclaimed as she blinked back the tears that shimmered in her eyes. But they were tears of joy rather than unhappiness. 'For one thing, I wouldn't dream of denying Max his night off—'

'Your continued concern for my Head of Security is touching!'

'And for another, I can't imagine anything more wonderful than the opportunity to attend the opera in Verona again,' she continued emotionally. 'Thank you so much for arranging this, Drakon. I can't tell you how much I'm looking forward to this evening.' She turned to clasp and squeeze his hands reassuringly.

'You're welcome,' he murmured gruffly.

'What are we going to see?'

'*Aida*—don't tell me it's the same opera you attended with your parents,' Drakon said heavily when she drew her breath in sharply.

'Yes, it is.' Gemini gave a shaky smile, slightly stunned by the coincidence.

Her parents had arranged their trip to Italy six years ago, as a surprise for her, and the three of them had flown out to Venice and spent three days there before taking the train to Verona. Even then Gemini hadn't realised what her real twenty-first birthday treat was to be, as they had enjoyed a leisurely lunch and then strolled about Verona for the afternoon, viewing the remains of the Roman amphitheatre from the outside, enjoying the romanticism of the 'Romeo and Juliet' balcony, and then lingering at an outside café to enjoy a delicious Italian coffee before returning to their hotel to change for the evening.

It had been only as they'd left their hotel after an early supper, joining the hundreds of other people dressed in evening clothes and strolling towards the now brightly lit amphitheatre, that Gemini had realised they were going to attend *Aida* at the world-famous open-air amphitheatre.

It had been an enchanted evening—beyond spectacular—with Gemini sitting with her parents in starry-eyed wonder as the evening slowly darkened and amber lights reflected the ancient theatre in all its pageantry, a perfect and magical backdrop for the magnificent voices performing on the stage.

And tonight she was once again going to attend that magical place—with Drakon Lyonedes, of all people...

'This is perfect, Drakon,' she assured him as she smiled across at him tremulously. 'Absolutely perfect!'

Drakon was unable to make any response because he found himself held captive by the genuine happiness of Gemini's smile. Those sea-green eyes appeared as warm and glowing as the emeralds that adorned her earlobes, throat and wrist, her lips were full and sensual, her hair a beautiful white-gold halo about the delicacy of her face and the slenderness of her shoulders.

At that moment hers was a beauty that glowed brightly from within, and her pleasure and happiness were such that Drakon almost felt as if he could reach out and touch it. As he longed to reach out and touch *her*.

'Are you ready for me to begin serving dinner now, Mr Lyonedes?'

It was an effort for Drakon to drag his gaze away from Gemini in order to look up at the steward who stood beside the table, looking down at him enquiringly, his expression deliberately impersonal.

Instantly Drakon was made aware of the fact that not only had he been totally captivated by Gemini seconds ago, but they were still holding hands across the table! Which was totally out of character for a man who *never* showed public affection—even for his family.

'Are you ready to eat now, Gemini?' He smiled tightly as he extracted his hands from within her grasp and saw the confused blush that coloured her cheeks, the way she suddenly avoided his gaze.

She appeared self-conscious, and continued to avoid his gaze by smiling up at the steward. 'I would just like to visit the bathroom first, if that's okay?'

'Certainly, Miss Bartholomew.' Malcolm visibly responded to the friendly warmth of her smile. 'If you would just like to follow me I'll show you where it is.'

Drakon found he was unable to stop himself from watching the soft sway of her hips as she followed Malcolm down the cabin to the bathroom, admiring the simple elegance of her appearance. The black sheath dress was a perfect foil for that elegant diamond and emerald jewellery and the pale gold colour of her hair.

Once again he was assailed with the knowledge that Gemini Bartholomew was both a beautiful and unusual woman. Unusual in that if she was aware of that beauty—and how could she not be?—then it was not something she attempted to use to her advantage in the way most beautiful women did, as they wheedled and charmed whatever they could out of the men in their lives.

At least, that was how the women Drakon had so far met in his own life usually behaved. And there had been many. Far too many, he acknowledged ruefully. Which probably accounted for his cynicism where all women were concerned. A cynicism he would do well to remember, he warned himself, especially when in the company of this particular woman.

'That's better.' Gemini resumed her seat opposite Drakon, her hair newly brushed, the peach gloss on her lips refreshed. 'It must be all the excitement,' she added with a smile.

Drakon raised an eyebrow. 'I was not aware you found my company so stimulating.'

Gemini felt a prick of disappointment that her brief absence seemed to have brought about a return of his mocking humour. Although this timely reminder of exactly who and what he was like was a good thing, when minutes ago she had felt herself enchanted by both Drakon and the evening ahead.

'It was probably the champagne,' she excused lightly.

Those dark eyes narrowed. 'No doubt.'

'This is delicious!' Gemini enthused once Malcolm had served their first course of asparagus tips and prawns enhanced with a delicate minted sauce.

'The food is from the same restaurant that provided the meal you did not eat last week,' Drakon revealed.

'You must be one of their best customers.'

'Perhaps.'

Gemini absolutely refused to have her spirits dampened by that terse response. 'I was far too busy to find the time to eat today, so I intend to enjoy every mouthful.'

That dark gaze raked over her mercilessly, lingering on the emerald nestled against her breasts. She obviously had a taste for expensive jewellery—so perhaps she wasn't so different from every other beautiful woman he knew…

'No matter how busy you are, today or any other day, I very much doubt running a florist's shop allows you to purchase such expensive jewellery.'

Gemini stiffened at the insult she heard underlying Drakon's tone, slowly placing her knife and fork down onto the side of her plate. 'Exactly what are you implying?'

Broad muscled shoulders moved in a shrug beneath his black evening jacket. 'It was merely an observation.'

Gemini moistened her lips and took her time before answering him. 'I take it you're referring to the necklace and earrings I'm wearing this evening?'

'And the matching bracelet,' he drawled.

'Oh, we mustn't forget the matching bracelet.' Her eyes flashed the same colour as the emeralds that sparkled so brightly at her ears, neck and wrist.

Drakon raised mocking hands. 'There's no reason for you to become so defensive.'

'Isn't there?' Gemini asked. 'What's wrong, Drakon?' She leant back in her chair to study him speculatively. 'Is it that you're regretting your decision to take me to the opera in Verona, even though you know how much I'm looking forward to it? Perhaps you would rather we didn't go? That we asked the pilot to turn the plane around, after all, and returned to England?'

'Don't be ridiculous!' He looked deeply irritated, his eyes very dark, his mouth a thin, angry line. 'I was merely commenting on—'

'I know exactly what you were doing, Drakon—and it wasn't "*merely*" anything.' She gave him a direct look. 'The earrings, necklace and bracelet were my mother's. My father gave the earrings to my mother on their wedding day, the bracelet on their tenth wedding anniversary, and the necklace on their twenty-fifth.' Gemini frowned as she heard her own voice break emotionally. 'My father decided to give them all to me after she died. There would have been her emerald engagement ring too, but—' She broke off abruptly, irritated with Drakon for having succeeded in baiting her into revealing this much, and even more annoyed with herself for feeling defensive enough to speak of things that would be better left unsaid.

'But what?' Drakon prompted astutely.

Gemini avoided that piercing dark gaze as she picked up her knife and fork again. 'Could we just eat our dinner before it goes cold?'

'The first course is meant to be served cold.'

She shot him a fiery glance. 'I'm trying to change the subject here.'

'I am aware of that. But what?' he repeated insistently.

She had never before met a man who could take her through such a gamut of emotions in so short a space of time: puzzlement, excitement, pleasure, irritation, and now sheer frustration at his obvious determination that she would give him an answer to his question

She pressed her lips together stubbornly. 'Will there be anyone famous singing in the opera this evening?'

'You *will* answer my question, Gemini.'

Gemini gave a huff of incredulous laughter. 'I really can't believe that there are any women left who would still fall for that "me man, you woman" routine!'

'Oh, but there are.' His jaw set. 'Some men too.'

'Then more fool them,' she came back pertly. 'I assure you it isn't going to work on me!'

Drakon was certain that Gemini was using this conversation to hold something back from him. As certain as he was that minutes ago he had tried deliberately to insult her in an effort to put some distance between them. In retrospect, the insult had backfired on him when she had revealed that all the diamond and emerald jewellery she was wearing this evening had once belonged to her mother, and as such obviously had a sentimental value rather than a monetary one.

Yes, he had made a mistake by attempting to insult her, and it was a mistake he regretted—but that did not detract from the fact that he had every intention of knowing exactly what it was she wasn't telling him.

'Perhaps if I were to apologise for my earlier insensitivity?' he said awkwardly, not used to finding himself in a position where he needed to apologise to anybody.

'Perhaps.'

He nodded in satisfaction. 'Now you will tell me why you do not have your mother's engagement ring.'

Gemini looked across at him incredulously. '*That* was your apology?'

'Yes.'

'That's really the best you can do?'

His jaw tensed at her obvious teasing. 'For the moment I believe so, yes.'

She laughed softly. 'Gosh, it's so hard to resist when you've apologised so...*prettily.*'

'Gemini!' Drakon ground his teeth together at her obvious prevarication.

She gave a weary sigh. 'If you really must know...'

'I believe I must, yes.' A nerve pulsed in his tightly clenched jaw.

Gemini's face was once again pale. 'I accepted the earrings, necklace and bracelet after Mummy died because my father so obviously wanted me to have things that meant so much to both of them. But I could see how painful it was for him to even think of giving me Mummy's engagement and wedding rings.'

Drakon nodded. 'I can understand that.'

He knew that his own mother kept his father's wedding ring safely locked away in her jewellery box. Occasionally she took it out just to sit and hold it in her hands and think of the man she had loved and still did

love—so deeply she had never even contemplated remarrying.

Drakon's gaze sharpened as he thought of Miles
Bartholomew's remarriage, and the vindictive woman
who had become his second wife. 'Where are those
rings now?'

Gemini smiled sadly. 'I think we both know you've
already guessed exactly where my mother's rings are,
Drakon.'

He could certainly take a good and accurate guess as
to what had become of the rings. It was unbelievable.
Unacceptable!

'Tell me anyway,' he ground out harshly.

Gemini sighed. 'The will my father left was made
shortly after he and Angela were married. At a time
when he still believed her to be an honourable woman,
as well as a warm and loving one,' she added dully.

Drakon looked aghast. 'Your father expected that
Angela would be honourable enough to give your mother's rings to you after he had died?'

'I believe he did, yes.'

'Which she has not done?'

Oh, it was much worse than that—not only had
Angela not given those rings to Gemini, but she had
taken great delight in wearing the emerald and diamond
engagement ring herself...several times.

'Which she hasn't done,' Gemini confirmed flatly.
'Now, could we finish eating our dinner?' Although,
in truth, she wasn't sure she had an appetite for it any
more.

Any more than she had for the long evening in
Drakon's company that now stretched ahead of her...

CHAPTER ELEVEN

A SECOND chauffeur-driven limousine was waiting for them at a private airport near Verona, but Gemini sat alone in the back of the luxurious car for several minutes after Drakon excused himself to make a brief telephone call.

'Everything okay?' she asked when he finally joined her.

'Perfect.' He turned to give her a brief, hard smile as the car moved smoothly forward.

The unpleasant memories resurrected by their earlier conversation about her parents and Angela had thankfully dissipated as they'd continued to chat casually during the delicious dinner Malcolm had served to them so efficiently during the flight, and now Gemini was once again anticipating the evening ahead, and the opera she had no doubts would be a feast for the senses.

It wouldn't dare be anything else when she had Drakon Lyonedes as her escort for the evening!

Which, when she thought about it, was pretty incredible, considering she had been feeling so angry and upset with him just over a week ago.

The reason for her initial animosity still existed, of course—especially as Drakon's company was about to take possession of Bartholomew House. But his personality was such, and this unexpected time in Verona so magical, that it was difficult if not impossible for Gemini even to think of reverting back to resenting him.

But that didn't mean she wasn't fully capable of resenting the dozens of glamorous women who looked at Drakon so covetously once they had reached the amphitheatre and joined the other patrons of the opera in the exclusive bar for a glass of champagne before the performance began.

Not that she could exactly blame any of those women. Tall, broad-shouldered, and dressed in that designer-label black evening suit and white silk shirt and bowtie, his dark hair slightly tousled from the warm and sultry breeze, Drakon was by far and away the most handsome and distinguished man present.

'Please don't let my being here stop you from being with any of your friends,' she said, after watching Drakon nod aloof acknowledgement as he was greeted by various people.

'They are mainly business acquaintances, not friends.' Drakon looked down the length of his arrogant nose at her and them. 'And I have no wish to be with any of them.'

It was a sentiment so obviously not shared by several of the more beautiful women present. 'I don't think the sexy redhead near the bar regards you as a business acquaintance!' Gemini teased, noting the other woman's sultry glance in his direction.

'I am not responsible for what other people think of me.' Drakon didn't so much as spare a glance in the redhead's direction. 'The champagne is to your liking?'

It was slightly exhilarating, Gemini realised, to know that a man whose attentions were as welcome as

Drakon's so obviously were was concerned only with *her* welfare. 'The champagne is perfect, thank you.' She smiled up at him warmly.

Drakon felt himself bathed in the warmth of that smile—a feeling he found surprisingly pleasurable after observing that several of the men present had been eyeing Gemini with acute interest since their arrival a few minutes ago. An interest she seemed totally unaware of. Or was perhaps just uninterested in? Whatever the reason—

'Gem? My God, Gem, is that really you?'

Drakon stiffened as this excited greeting interrupted his train of thought. A greeting directed at Gemini.

She confirmed that it was as she turned, her expression slightly puzzled, only to have her face light up with pleasure as she obviously recognised the blond-haired man now making his way determinedly towards her through the crowd of people.

'Good grief! What on earth are you doing here, Sam?' Gemini asked excitedly.

'The same as you. I'm here to watch the opera, of course!' The younger man seemed elusively familiar to Drakon as he reached out to grasp both of Gemini's hands in his and beamed down at her. 'My God, Gem, you can't believe how good it is to see you again—and in Verona of all places!' He laughed exuberantly.

'Unbelievable, isn't it?' Gemini acknowledged the beauty of their surroundings.

At the same time she became aware of the dark and brooding man standing stiffly disapproving beside her.

She glanced up at Drakon from beneath lowered lashes, able to feel the leashed displeasure just below the surface of his urbanity and knowing by the coldness of his expression and the chill in those glittering black eyes as he regarded the other man haughtily that he resented Sam's intrusion.

She left her hands clasped within Sam's as she made the introductions. 'Drakon—Sam Middleton. Sam, this is Drakon Lyonedes.'

'As in Lyonedes Enterprises?' Sam gave him a startled glance even as he released her to hold out a perfunctory hand in greeting.

'Middleton,' Drakon returned tersely, neither confirming nor denying his identity as he briefly returned the handshake.

'Pleased to meet you.' Sam continued to look into that harshly chiselled face for several seconds before giving a perceptible shake of his head as he turned to look back at Gemini, a dozen unasked questions in his widened bright blue eyes. 'Maybe we can get together for a longer chat during the interval?' he urged, obviously eager to pump her for answers.

'I—'

'That will not be possible, I'm afraid.' Drakon was the one to answer dismissively. 'Gemini and I will be meeting other friends then.'

She gave him a surprised look; that was the first she'd heard of it. Although, as Drakon had been the one to fly her here to Verona in his private jet, she could hardly complain if he had now decided he wanted to talk to some of his business acquaintances later on, after all.

'Sorry about that.' She gave Sam a regretful smile.

'I'll be back in London next week, so maybe we can meet up again then?' Sam suggested.

'Perhaps. *If* Gemini is back in London by next week,' Drakon said frostily at the same time as his arm moved about the slenderness of her waist.

Gemini gave him another startled glance, surprised at the possessiveness of that gesture as much as by what he had said. 'But—'

'If you will excuse us?' Drakon murmured as the bell sounded to announce the start of the performance, not even waiting for Sam's reply before moving away to join the people now making their way to their seats.

Gemini had time to turn to shoot Sam an apologetic glance over her shoulder before glaring up at Drakon. 'What on earth was all that about?' she demanded, bewildered by his behaviour.

He spared her only the briefest of glances as he concentrated on guiding her safely through the milling crowd. 'What was what about?' he said evasively.

'Well, for one thing, of course I'll be back in London next week. In fact I'll be back in London later this evening—'

'No, you won't.'

Gemini came to an abrupt halt, and then was forced to mutter a distracted apology to the couple whose way she was blocking.

'What do you mean I won't?' She frowned at him as he took a firm grasp of her arm and moved them to a less crowded and thankfully more private area.

He shrugged as he released her arm. 'The opera won't finish until very late, so naturally I have arranged for us to stay at a hotel here in Verona tonight.'

'What? Without so much as asking me if that was okay?' Gemini gasped incredulously.

He raised arrogant brows. 'I brought you to Verona without asking your permission, too.'

'Well…yes. But—' She flung up her hands in dismay. 'Not only have I not brought any other clothes or toiletries with me, but you *can't* just make decisions like that without even consulting me!'

'I believe I already have.'

Gemini's cheeks burned at what she considered his bloody-minded arrogance. 'You—'

'And the second thing?' he interrupted calmly.

'What?' she said, confused.

'You said "for one thing", so I assumed there must necessarily be a second thing?' he replied.

Gemini ground her teeth in frustration at his obvious lack of interest in discussing their overnight stay any further. 'The second thing is what was all that about with Sam just now? You deliberately gave him the impression that we're—well, that we're—'

'Involved?' he supplied dryly.

'Yes!' she hissed, uncomfortable with Drakon's continued calm when she was feeling anything but.

He looked down at her wordlessly for several long seconds. 'We had dinner together last week. And again yesterday evening. We have had dinner together again this evening. We are now in Verona, attending the opera together. And somewhere in amongst those evenings together we have twice been intimate with each other, for want of a better expression. Do all of those things not indicate that we might possibly be involved?' He arched those arrogant dark brows.

Gemini looked annoyed. They had done all those things together, yes, but as far as she was aware not one of those earlier evenings had been arranged and agreed between them. Dinner last week had been to discuss Lyonedes Enterprises buying Bartholomew House. She had organised their dinner together yesterday evening at the Italian restaurant because she had been angry with

Drakon for setting his watchdogs onto her. Which only left this evening...

Admittedly Drakon had actually invited her out this evening. And she had accepted. She just hadn't expected it would involve being whisked off to a private airport and wined and dined on the Lyonedes jet before arriving in Verona to attend the opera.

But that didn't mean she and Drakon were involved. Did it?

She shook her head firmly. 'That's still no reason for you to have behaved like—like a Neanderthal in front of Sam!'

Drakon drew in a sharp breath. 'A Neanderthal?'

Gemini's anger left her as quickly as it had flared into being when she saw his stunned disbelief at her accusation. 'A Neanderthal.' She nodded confirmation as she deliberately repeated the word. 'That "me man, you woman" thing again. Or, in this case, "you *my* woman"! Which, besides being patently untrue, was especially inappropriate seeing as Sam happens to be my cousin,' she added.

Drakon's expression of haughty disdain turned to one of puzzlement. 'I didn't realise—your surnames are not the same.'

'Could that be because Sam's mother is my mother's sister?' she asked sarcastically.

'I thought he looked vaguely familiar...' Drakon looked down at her blankly for several seconds. 'Yes, I see now that was due to the family resemblance.'

'The family that by this time tomorrow will all have been informed that I'm staying in Verona with Drakon Lyonedes! And don't you dare laugh,' Gemini warned as she saw those chiselled lips begin to twitch. 'The only family I have left are my Aunt Beatrice, Uncle Joseph

and Sam—and now they're all going to think that for
some reason I've allowed myself to become Drakon
Lyonedes's latest bimbo!'

Drakon's humour faded as quickly as it had appeared,
his eyes turning to ebony chips of ice as he looked down
at her. 'As far as I am aware I have never associated with
bimbos,' he informed her frostily.

'Kept woman. Mistress. Whatever,' Gemini said
crossly. 'I don't enjoy having the only family I have
left in the world believing I'm no better than Angela!'

Drakon looked down at her searchingly, noting the
over-bright sheen to those glorious sea-green eyes, the
slight pallor to her cheeks, and realized—no matter
how much he might resent her accusations—that her
distress concerning what her small immediate family
might think of her was very real.

He drew in a deep breath. 'We will seek out your
cousin at the interval and I will endeavour to put the
record straight with regard to our relationship.'

She raised surprised brows. 'And exactly how do you
intend doing that?'

'By informing him that our association is primar-
ily a business one. Also that we have separate rooms
booked at the hotel tonight. No…?' he said with a frown
as Gemini gave a firm shake of her head.

'No,' she said. 'I'm afraid that all sounds a little like
protesting too much.'

'I could always apologise for my earlier manner—
explain that I had no idea he was your cousin—'

'Which would only give the impression that we *are*
involved, after all!' She sighed. 'Never mind, Drakon.
I'll sort it out with Sam when he gets back to London
next week.' She ran an agitated hand through her hair.
'Let's just go and listen to the opera, hmm?'

The last thing Drakon had intended this evening was to create a reason for any more unpleasantness in Gemini's life—in truth, bringing her to Verona, well away from England, had been deliberately designed to do the very opposite. But that unexpected meeting with her cousin certainly seemed to have cast a shadow over her enjoyment.

Because, as she had so succinctly pointed out, Drakon had behaved like a Neanderthal when confronted with a younger man who seemed to be on far too intimate an acquaintance with her!

He had assumed, from the warmth of their greeting to each other, that Gemini and Sam must have been romantically involved in the past. And he had not liked it. Not one little bit. Which was really no excuse for his proprietorial behaviour towards her.

'You're right. We should take our seats now,' he said.

Drakon's inner feelings of disquiet resulted in him spending the first hour of the opera looking at Gemini more than he did the spectacle taking place on the stage: the smooth sheen of her white-gold hair, the creaminess of her brow and cheek, the clear brightness of those sea-green eyes as she gazed at the performers with rapt attention, the sensual fullness of her lips, the slender arch of her throat, and the tempting swell of her breasts.

The knowledge of her innocence told Drakon she was a young woman of principle. Her love and respect for her father, despite his disastrous second marriage, indicated that she was a woman of loyalty. She was a young woman who, because she had grown up protected and cosseted by her father's wealth, could so easily have chosen to become one of the idle and bored debutantes Drakon had met so many times in the past at social events all over the world. But she had instead chosen to forge her own life and career by opening her own shop and working—working hard—with the flowers she so obviously loved.

All of which made her the most beautiful and unaffected young woman Drakon had ever met.

And he wanted her badly.

He ached to hold her softness in his arms as he moulded her body against his. To kiss every inch of her face and throat before claiming her lips with his. To cup her bared breasts in his hands as he slowly pleasured their stiff peaks. To caress the slenderness of her waist and hips before gently stroking the heat between her thighs—

'Isn't this wonderful!' Gemini breathed, having placed her hand excitedly on Drakon's arm as she turned to look at him with eyes that seemed to glow the same intense green as her emeralds. The earlier tension between them, and the reason for it, had obviously been forgotten. And forgiven, he sincerely hoped.

'Wonderful,' he echoed gruffly as his hand moved to capture and keep the warmth of her fingers pressed against his arm, but he was looking at Gemini and not at the stage above.

She gave him another one of her warm smiles before turning back eagerly to the opera, seemingly unaware that her hand still lay clasped within Drakon's.

Exactly when, he wondered, had this woman slipped beneath his guard of cynicism? When, exactly, had he ceased to regard Gemini as nothing but an intrusive nuisance, one he wished out of his life as quickly as she had thrust herself into it? When had that protectiveness he had felt after learning of Angela Bartholomew's viciousness towards her become so all-consuming?

He had no need to wonder *why* it had happened.

He had realised only too well during this past hour of watching her, of looking at her, exactly the reasons she was now such an important part of his life.

If not the *most* important...

'Wasn't that absolutely amazing?' Gemini exclaimed several hours later as she and Drakon emerged onto the lamplit cobbled street outside the amphitheatre, her hand resting on the crook of his arm so that they wouldn't be separated amongst the crowds of happy people milling around them.

Drakon had seemed distant towards her during the interval, although true to his word they had sought out Sam. Drakon had insisted on the younger man joining them for a glass of champagne. As she had requested, Drakon had offered no apology for his earlier behaviour, but instead had warmly encouraged her cousin to talk of the places he had already visited during what was apparently a touring holiday of Italy—something the enthusiastic Sam had been only too happy to do.

Gemini shot Drakon a concerned glance now. 'You know, I was only being half serious earlier when I called you a Neanderthal.'

To her relief he gave her a wry smile. 'It was a perfectly justified accusation on your part.' He grimaced. 'I behaved badly.'

'You made up for it by being charming to Sam during the interval,' she said.

Drakon came to a halt as he looked down at her quizzically. 'Are you always so ready to forgive?'

She shrugged. 'Life's really too short to do anything else, don't you think?'

His mouth thinned. 'Some people are beyond forgiveness.'

'Well…yes.' Gemini didn't need to ask which person he was referring to! 'But in those circumstances surely the best thing to do is simply cut them out of your life rather than reduce yourself to their level?'

Drakon looked down at her in open admiration. 'Enjoyable as the opera undoubtedly was, *you* are what I have found amazing this evening, Gemini.'

She gave him a startled look. 'I am?'

'Oh, yes.'

'Despite the Neanderthal remark?' she teased.

He laughed softly. 'In spite of it.'

'Oh…'

Drakon tilted his head as he looked down at her quizzically for several long seconds. 'You really have no idea how unusual a woman you are, do you?' he finally said warmly.

Gemini wasn't quite sure what to make of Drakon in his current mood. His cynicism she had learnt to cope with. His arrogance, too. Even his mockery was easily deflected if she didn't allow it to get to her. What Gemini had no idea how to deal with was this admiring, almost gentle Drakon…

'I'm just me, Drakon,' she protested.

'Exactly.'

Gemini frowned up at him in the lamplight, her heart starting to beat loudly in her chest. She saw the warmth in his obsidian eyes as he gazed steadily back at her, a nerve pulsing in his jaw, those chiselled lips softened and slightly parted.

Oh, good Lord!

Physically innocent she might be, but she would have to be a moron not to recognise the look in his eyes for the desire that it was. Ditto the parted invitation of his lips. It was a desire the nerve pulsing in his jaw would seem to indicate he was holding firmly under his control. Unless Gemini were to indicate she wished it otherwise.

The question was, did she want to do that?

When she had come to Verona six years ago it had been as a beloved daughter being given a special birthday treat by her parents. Being here now with Drakon was absolutely nothing like that.

Their slight disagreement apart, she had been absolutely, totally aware of him all evening—despite the magical opera. That awareness had been humming beneath the surface of her skin all evening, with a tingling that made her sensitive nipples ache and heat pool between her thighs. It was an ache that she knew Drakon was more than capable of satisfying.

She looked up at him in the golden glow of the lamplight. The strong angles of his face were thrown into shadows, his dark eyes were looking down at her, and she knew that she wanted him to make love with her more than she had ever wanted anything in her life before.

She moistened her lips before speaking, her cheeks feeling warm as she saw the hungry way his gaze followed the tip of her tongue as it swept over that pouting softness. 'So you booked separate rooms for us at the hotel, did you?' she asked.

It was only as Drakon breathed in deeply that he realised he had not been breathing at all for the last minute or so. 'I requested a suite with two bedrooms.'

Gemini chuckled. 'Hedging your bets, Drakon?'

Had he been? Had he hoped that the evening would be so successful, so enjoyable, that he and Gemini would spend the night together?

Certainly not consciously. 'I doubt that there will be

a four-poster bed in either of them,' he told her apologetically.

'Probably not, no,' she agreed quietly.

'Or rose petals to perfume the room,' he added gruffly.

'I'm sure I won't notice with the light off,' Gemini murmured.

The fact that Drakon had bothered to remember her romantic fantasies was enough for now. More than enough to sustain her tingling awareness as they walked the short distance to an exclusive hotel.

That awareness had been elevated to an almost overwhelming swell of anticipation by the time they had booked in and Drakon had used a keycard to allow them to enter the sitting room of a suite on the top floor.

'No.' Gemini moved to stop his hand as he would have reached out and turned on the light. The moonlight streaming into the room through the two floor-to-ceiling windows provided the necessary illumination as she stepped into his arms. 'Make love to me, Drakon,' she whispered, her face lifting invitingly to his as her arms moved about his waist.

Drakon's hands moved up to cradle each side of her face as he gazed down at her hungrily. The softness of her creamy cheeks felt like velvet against his palms as he committed the perfection of her face to memory, to be taken out at some later date to please or torment him.

'You are so overwhelmingly beautiful, Gemini, inside as well as out,' he muttered, and the rasp of their breath was the only sound in the room as his head lowered and his lips at last laid claim to hers.

Their passion, their need for each other, was like a dam bursting, and the kiss that had started so gently quickly became something else as they took eagerly, hungrily, from each other, and gave back just as much in return. Lips devoured, teeth gently bit, and tongues duelled in devouring demand.

Drakon groaned as he felt himself spiralling quickly out of control. Gemini's fingers became entangled in the hair at his nape as they continued to kiss hungrily. His skin felt hot and feverish, his shaft a hard and pulsing ache as he pressed into the heated softness between her thighs, wanting—oh, God, how he wanted her. It was suddenly all too much…

'Drakon?' Gemini's eyes were huge bewildered pools of dark green as he suddenly wrenched his mouth away from hers and put her firmly away from him.

He breathed in raggedly before looking down at her from between lowered lids. 'As I pointed out earlier, we do not have the four-poster bed or the perfume of rose petals that you said were required for your seduction,' he reminded her distantly.

'My seduction?' she repeated painfully.

Drakon's mouth compressed but he didn't reply.

She clasped shaking hands in an attempt to steady them. 'I don't understand…' Minutes ago, seconds ago, he had seemed on the point of devouring her—and goodness knew she had been more than willing. The passion between them had been so intense they had seemed in danger of going up in flames.

He dropped his gaze. 'For us to go to bed together now would be wrong on levels I cannot begin to explain.'

'For whom?' Gemini prompted shrewdly. 'Is it that you don't want the so-called responsibility of taking my innocence? That you maybe even think, in my naivety, I might imagine myself to be in love with you?' she pressed.

Drakon stood unmoving as her words rained down like daggers entering his flesh. 'It is a possibility, is it not?'

'No!' she gave a shocked gasp. 'No, Drakon, it isn't a possibility!' She stepped back, her gaze anguished as the heat of tears drenched those sea-green depths. 'You—' She broke off as the sound of his mobile phone intruded into the tension. 'You should answer that. It might be one of the women from the opera earlier, wanting to meet up with you. An *experienced* woman!' she spat.

'Possibly,' he said coolly.

Gemini gave him one last fulminating glare before turning on her heel and hurrying across the room to enter one of the two bedrooms and slam the door behind her.

Leaving Drakon alone in the moonlight as each and every one of those daggers pierced deeply into a part of him he had believed until tonight to be invincible...

CHAPTER TWELVE

GEMINI felt emotionally exhausted by the time the chauffeur-driven limousine drew to a halt beside the pavement outside her shop at twelve o'clock the following day. She hadn't slept at all the previous night, listening as Drakon talked briefly on the telephone before she heard the sound of the other bedroom door softly closing—evidence that he obviously wasn't taking her up on her suggestion that he go out again.

Neither of them had had any appetite for the breakfast Drakon had ordered to be delivered to their suite at eight o'clock this morning, and the drive to the airport and their flight back to England had been made in tense silence.

She could have sat down and cried for the awful way their evening together in Verona had ended. Apart from that brief awkwardness with Sam it had been such a magical time: the delicious dinner on the plane, the beautiful sights and smells of Verona, the pageantry of the opera, the romantic walk along the cobbled streets to their hotel with the warmth of Drakon's arm draped possessively about her waist, the wild heat of passion once they were finally alone together in their suite.

And then the icy coldness of Drakon's rejection.

Even now, after hours of thinking of virtually nothing else, Gemini didn't understand it, let alone accept it. He had known from the outset that she'd had no other lovers, and it certainly hadn't seemed to bother him during the walk back to the hotel, or when they had kissed so passionately.

She turned to look at him now as he sat so distant and unmoving beside her in the back of the limousine. 'Drakon—'

'We should go up to your apartment now,' he cut in as the chauffeur got out of the car and opened Gemini's door for her.

'We?' Gemini had assumed from his aloofness the past twelve hours that once they were back in England Drakon would be anxious to get rid of the responsibility of her before returning to New York.

'Max has arrived.' He nodded to where the black Range Rover had just parked in front of the limousine. His grim-faced Head of Security was getting out from behind the wheel. 'The two of us need to talk to you privately,' Drakon added before opening the door beside him and striding over to greet the older man.

Gemini got slowly out of the car, vaguely smiling her thanks at the chauffeur at the same time trying, and failing, to hear what Drakon and Max were saying to each other. Their voices too soft for her to make out any of their conversation, although their expressions didn't look reassuring.

She frowned as the men walked briskly back to join her. 'Drakon, what—?'

'We will go inside, where we cannot be overheard.' He took a firm grasp of her arm.

Considering it was lunchtime on a Sunday—a time when most people were either at home or in the local pub eating lunch—the area was virtually deserted, with only two uninterested joggers passing by on the other side of the road—which was probably as well, when Gemini and Drakon were both so obviously wearing the clothes they had worn the evening before.

'Aren't you being a bit cloak-and-dagger?' she protested.

'Privacy would be best.' Max was the one to answer her gruffly.

'I don't think so.' Gemini stubbornly dug her heels in as she glared at first one man and then the other. 'In fact I'm not going anywhere until one of you tells me what's going on.'

A grudging amusement entered Max's steely blue eyes before he turned to raise questioning brows at his employer.

Drakon's jaw clenched. 'You are the most stubborn woman!' He sighed impatiently. 'Bartholomew House was broken into last night,' he revealed economically.

Gemini recoiled slightly in shock. 'I—is Angela all right?' she gasped breathlessly.

Drakon's impatience turned to incredulity at her concern for a woman who had been nothing but vicious and cruel towards her. A woman who had tried to do everything in her power, since Miles's death, to make Gemini miserable in every way possible. A woman, in fact, who deserved no one's sympathy—least of all Gemini's.

'Your stepmother was not at home at the time,' Drakon assured her coolly.

'Thank goodness!' She looked relieved. 'Was anything taken?'

'That is what we need to talk to you about,' he answered pointedly.

Gemini continued to look at him dazedly for several long seconds, a frown between her eyes. 'I don't understand…' She shook her head. 'How do you even know about the break-in if it only happened last night?' she finally said slowly. 'Let alone that Angela wasn't at home at the time?'

He raised dark brows. 'That is the reason that Max and I would prefer this conversation took place in private.'

Sea-green eyes widened as Gemini obviously took in the full import of what he had said. She glanced at the stoic Max and then back at Drakon. 'Perhaps it might be better if we did go up to my apartment, after all.'

'A canny lass; I knew there was a reason I liked you!' Max nodded approval.

'That's a pity—because I'm still reserving judgement on *you*!' Gemini threw back as she unlocked the door leading up to her apartment.

Max gave a throaty chuckle—the first that Drakon could remember hearing from him in the five years Max had worked for him. 'Give it time, lass, maybe I'll grow on you.'

'I wouldn't count on it,' Gemini muttered as she led the way upstairs, still feeling slightly stunned about the break-in at Bartholomew House and the unspoken implications of Drakon's knowledge of it. Let alone what Max's presence here might indicate.

'Okay!' She threw her wrap and bag down on the coffee table in her sitting room before turning to face the two men. 'One of you tell me exactly what's going on. And I sincerely hope your explanation doesn't include telling me that Max, for reasons as yet unknown, was the one who broke into Bartholomew House last night! Drakon?' she prompted.

Max was now avoiding her gaze as he took a thick envelope from the breast pocket of his leather jacket and handed it to Drakon, before turning his back on the room to stare out of the window onto the street down below.

Drakon smiled ruefully as he recognised the light of challenge in Gemini's eyes. 'I have no intention of telling you that Max was anywhere near Bartholomew House last night.'

She eyed him reprovingly. 'The wording of that statement isn't exactly reassuring.'

'It wasn't intended to be,' Drakon said dryly. 'I believe you should look at this before you say anything else,' he continued firmly as Gemini would have spoken, and reached into the envelope. He took out what looked to be a legal document of some kind before holding it out to her.

Gemini made no effort to take the document but eyed it as if it were a snake about to uncoil and sink its fangs into her. Her mouth had gone dry. 'Tell me what it is first...'

Drakon drew in a sharp breath before answering her. 'It was locked away in the safe at Bartholomew House, and it is the last will and testament of Miles Gifford Bartholomew, signed and witnessed by two members of his household staff two weeks before his death. In it he bequeaths an apartment in Paris and a villa in Spain, plus a yearly sum for the rest of her life, to his wife, Angela Gail Bartholomew, and Bartholomew House, plus the remainder of his estate, to his only daughter—namely Gemini Bartholomew.'

All the colour bleached from her cheeks, and a loud buzzing noise sounded in her head. The room began to dip and sway, before—thankfully—complete darkness descended.

* * *

Gemini didn't believe she had ever fainted in her life before, but as she roused herself groggily, and found herself lying on the sofa in her sitting room, Drakon crouched beside her, a concerned expression on his face, she knew that was exactly what had happened.

Because Drakon had told her of the existence of a more recent will than the one which had previously been presented by her father's lawyers...

Gemini blinked up at him. 'Is it really true? There was a newer will all the time?' She pushed the hair back from her face as he helped her to sit up.

'There was a newer will,' Drakon confirmed as he straightened, his hands clasped tightly behind his back in an effort to contain the rage he felt towards Angela Bartholomew. A rage which had been steadily growing since learning the truth from Max during the other man's telephone call to him late the previous evening. 'A legal will which, for obvious reasons, your stepmother decided it was in her best interests to repress,' he added harshly.

Gemini looked up at him with tear-wet eyes. 'Daddy kept his promise after all...'

Drakon's hands tightened painfully. 'Yes, he did.'

Those tears overflowed to fall softly down the paleness of her cheeks. 'Bartholomew House is really mine?'

'Yes.'

'That's— I can't tell you how— Oh!' She raised startled sea-green eyes. 'But that must also mean, if Angela is no longer the legal owner of Bartholomew House, that the contract Lyonedes Enterprises has with her to buy the house and land is no longer valid?'

Drakon's smile was humourless. 'No, it is not.'

Gemini caught her bottom lip between her teeth. 'I'm so sorry, Drakon.'

'You're *sorry*?' he exploded incredulously. 'That woman attempted to deny you your true heritage, that which is legally and morally yours, taking great delight in doing so, and you are *apologising* to me? Unbelievable!'

'Not just a canny lass but a generous-hearted one too,' Max murmured admiringly from where he still stood beside the window.

'A woman like no other,' Drakon acknowledged huskily as he turned to look at the other man. A wealth of understanding passed between them in that single brief glance. 'This is a time for rejoicing in your good fortune, Gemini.' Drakon turned back to her. 'Not a time for you to concern yourself with any legal ramifications for Lyonedes Enterprises.'

A frown appeared on the creaminess of her brow. 'But how could you possibly have known where the will was?'

'You can thank Max for that,' Drakon said. 'I merely voiced my suspicions. He was the one who made discreet enquiries of some of your father's present and ex-employees.'

'I struck gold with a young woman—Jackie—who was your father's personal assistant and stayed on for several months to assist your stepmother after he died,' Max said dourly. 'She doesn't work for Mrs Bartholomew any longer, but once I explained who I was, and the reason for my interest in the possibility of a newer will, she was only too happy to supply the combination number to the safe in your father's study. I gather she has her own reasons for disliking your stepmother.'

Gemini grimaced. 'I believe Angela's way of thanking Jackie for her assistance was to have an affair with her fiancé only weeks after my father died.'

'That would do it,' Max agreed.

'But is this will still legal if it was…obtained in the way it was?' she asked.

'It is most certainly legal.' Drakon nodded firmly. 'And I don't think Angela Bartholomew would care to go to the authorities with accusations of theft when to do so would mean she would have to explain why she did not admit to knowing of the existence of this will months ago.'

'I wonder why she didn't simply burn it?' Gemini mused.

'I don't know, and I don't particularly care,' he rasped. 'Admittedly it would have been better for all concerned if your father had gone to his lawyers and left the signed will with them, but perhaps he believed a private will, with the signature of two members of his household as witnesses, would be a safer way of dealing with the matter.'

'Less obvious to the eagle-eyed Angela, you mean?' Gemini guessed. 'Yes, I'm sure you're right. Although she obviously found the new will anyway, after Daddy died so suddenly.'

'Unfortunately, yes,' he agreed. 'Max has also ascertained this morning that she dismissed the two witnesses to the will from their employment at Bartholomew House shortly after your father's death. In an effort, no doubt, to prevent them from stepping forward with knowledge of the existence of a new will.'

'Knowing Daddy, they wouldn't have been aware of the exact contents of the will anyway,' she said. 'It was really in the safe at Bartholomew House all this time, then?'

'Yes.'

She glanced across at the stony-faced Max where he still stood in front of the window. 'And you were the one who...*found* it there?'

He grimaced. 'I think I'll take the fifth on that one, if you don't mind.'

Gemini knew that was the only admission she was likely to get that he had indeed been the one to enter Bartholomew House the previous evening.

She stood up to cross the room and throw her arms around his waist. 'Thank you, Max!' She hugged him tight. 'Thank you so much!'

He stood uncomfortably in her arms for several seconds. 'I think your hug is misdirected, lass,' he finally murmured gruffly, and patted her back awkwardly.

Gemini knew exactly who she had to thank for her sudden change of fortune—knew perfectly well that Max had been acting directly under Drakon's orders.

She gave Max another brief hug before turning to face Drakon, knowing that what he had done, what he had asked Max to do, was going to cause him and Lyonedes Enterprises serious problems.

The new will proved Angela a liar and a cheat. And because of that Lyonedes Enterprises would no longer acquire the much-coveted site in London on which it had intended building a hotel complex. Drakon himself could come in for serious legal ramifications if Angela decided to go to the authorities after all. In fact, the only one to benefit from the actions of the past twelve hours would appear to be Gemini herself...

'I don't know how to thank you—'

'No thanks are necessary,' he assured her stiffly.

She threw Max an amused glance. 'Now you know why I thanked you first,' she murmured exasperatedly.

'Don't bring me into this.' The older man held up his hands in mock protest before turning back towards the window. 'Uh-oh—I believe trouble has arrived,' he announced.

'Angela?' Gemini said knowingly.

'Oh, yes,' Max confirmed as he turned back to look at Drakon. 'Do you want me to go down and—'

'Let her come up.' Gemini was the one to answer him. 'Drakon, if Angela has somehow worked out who was responsible for the break-in at Bartholomew House last night then we'd only be delaying this confrontation by ignoring her now,' she reasoned, just as he was about to issue instructions to Max.

Drakon's admiration for Gemini grew by the minute, it seemed. Admittedly she had fainted once she knew of her father's more recent will, and realised she was the owner of Bartholomew House after all, but that had been understandable. Her stoicism since then had been indomitable.

As he had told Max earlier, Gemini truly was a woman like no other...

The intercom buzzed in announcement of Angela's presence downstairs.

Drakon sighed. 'Gemini is right, Max. We might as well get this over with now.'

'I think that's best.' Gemini walked over to the speaker on the intercom. 'Come up, Angela,' she instructed the other woman coldly, and pressed the button to open the external door.

Drakon frowned. 'Gemini—'

'Don't worry, Drakon,' she said as her stepmother

could be heard coming up the stairs. 'Now that I know the truth I'm more than capable of handling her.'

Drakon was sure that she was; he only feared what further emotional damage Angela might do to her in the meantime...

The older woman's expression was contemptuous as she entered the room. 'I should have known that *you* would be here too.' She gave Drakon a scathing glance. 'And no doubt this is one of your henchman!' she said, glaring at Max.

'Mrs Bartholomew.' Max gave a terse nod, his steely gaze narrowed in warning.

Blue eyes glittered angrily as Angela turned to Gemini. 'You do realise that I could have you arrested for theft, as well as for breaking and entering at Bartholomew House?'

'There has been a break-in at Bartholomew House?' Drakon was the one to address her smoothly.

'You know damn well there has!'

He raised dark brows. 'And why on earth should I know that?'

'Oh, please!' Angela snapped. 'You even arranged for your cousin to take me to dinner last night in order to make sure I was out of the house.'

Drakon turned as he sensed Gemini looking at him incredulously, nodding slightly in confirmation when she mouthed, *Markos took her out to dinner?*

'What does your date with Markos last night have to do with me?' he asked.

'It worked very effectively as a means of ensuring you could sneak in and do your little Houdini act with certain contents of my safe!'

Drakon shrugged. 'I assure you I have absolutely no

control over my cousin's actions. Nor do I understand
what you mean by my "Houdini act".'

Angela gave a disbelieving snort. 'I didn't even discover there was anything missing until I went to the
safe this morning to return the jewellery I wore to go
out last night.'

'And you believe *I* am the one responsible for those
items being missing?' He raised haughty brows.

'I know you are!'

'I am afraid you are under a misapprehension, Mrs
Bartholomew,' Drakon bit out coldly. 'Neither I, nor indeed Gemini, were even in England last night. We flew
to Verona for the evening. For the opera, you know. We
returned only a short time ago.'

Gemini looked at Drakon sharply as it became glar-
ingly obvious to her exactly why they had flown to
Verona and stayed the night there; by doing so Drakon
had ensured that they both had an alibi for the break-in.

Angela seemed to notice their evening clothes for
the first time, and her cheeks became flushed. 'Then
you had your henchman do it for you—'

'I believe this conversation is over, Mrs
Bartholomew,' Drakon cut in repressively.

'A word of advice, Drakon,' Angela jeered. 'Never
try to deceive a deceiver.'

'At last we seem to be agreed on something,' he replied.

Angela's face darkened angrily. 'Why, you—'

'That's quite enough!' Gemini stepped forward to
grip Angela's arm as she swung it with the obvious intention of slapping Drakon's face. 'You may have done
your best to make me miserable, Angela, but you will
never—*ever*—attack any of my friends.' She thrust

her face in front of the shorter woman's. 'Is that understood?'

'Is that what you call him? 'Your "friend"?' Angela
sneered.

Gemini drew in a sharp breath at the deliberate insult, but at the same time she knew the accusation was
far from the truth; Drakon wasn't, never had been, and
now probably never would be her lover, as Angela was
implying he was. Unfortunately...

"Not having any of your own, you probably wouldn't
recognise friendship if it bit you on the nose,' she said
coldly. 'But, yes, Drakon is my friend. And this is my
home. As such, you will not insult one of my friends
in my home. Is that understood? *Is it?*' she pressed.

A grudging respect entered the glittering blue eyes
that stared up into Gemini's. 'Yes,' Angela finally
grated tightly.

'Good.' Gemini released her arm and stepped back.
'Now, for my father's sake, not yours, I'm willing to let
you walk out of here and take up permanent residence
in either the Paris apartment or the Spanish villa you
apparently own. If,' she continued firmly as Angela
would have spoken, 'you don't do either of those things,
then you will leave me with no choice but to go to the
police and tell them of your duplicity.'

'If you did that you would only implicate yourself
and your "friends" in the robbery at my home.'

'Actually, that would be *my* home,' Gemini corrected.
'And, as such, the contents of the safe there would also
be *my* property,' she added challengingly.

Angela's face paled. 'But you didn't know any of that
when the will was taken.'

'I know it now,' Gemini pointed out. 'Which I believe will be all that matters in the eyes of the law,' she

added, with much more confidence that she actually felt. 'But feel free to challenge my claim if that's what you want to do.'

Angela scowled. 'Exactly when did you develop claws?'

'Oh, they were always there,' Gemini assured the other woman. 'Merely sheathed for my father's sake. So which is it to be, Angela? Paris or the villa in Spain? Whichever one you choose, I will give you two days to vacate Bartholomew House and leave England for good,' she added. 'Oh, and I also expect you to return the rather large deposit you received from Lyonedes Enterprises when you agreed to sell them a property you knew you didn't actually own.'

The older woman seemed to fight an inner battle with herself for several long seconds, as if she were exploring each avenue of escape open to her, and her shoulders finally dropped in defeat as she obviously found they all ended in a cul-de-sac.

'You should have just burnt the new will,' Gemini said.

'Yes, I should.' Angela sighed. 'I just couldn't quite bring myself to do it. For what it's worth, I *did* love Miles,' she finally admitted tightly. 'In my own way.'

Gemini gave a weary shake of her head. 'I'm not sure whether that makes your behaviour better or worse.'

'No,' Angela acknowledged heavily before glancing at Drakon and Max. 'Touché, gentlemen. Now, if you will all excuse me,' she drawled, 'it appears I have a lot of packing to do. And a visit to make to my bank to return funds to Lyonedes Enterprises. I take it you will deal with the legal side of things?' She looked enquiringly at Drakon.

'Already being dealt with,' he confirmed.

Angela nodded again before turning on one three-inch heel and leaving. The door downstairs closed quietly behind her seconds later.

Gemini sank down weakly into one of her armchairs, more relieved than she could say that the situation had finally been resolved in such a way that it took Angela out of her life for good and at the same time gave her back Bartholomew House.

And it was all thanks to Drakon…

CHAPTER THIRTEEN

DRAKON had watched and listened proudly as Gemini completely dominated the woman who had taken advantage of the deep love Gemini felt for her father in order to manipulate and steal from her.

But at the same time he'd felt a heavy weight in his chest at Gemini's insistence that she considered him only as a friend.

'I'll go too now, if that's okay?' Max murmured.

'Gemini?' Drakon prompted gruffly.

She roused herself enough to look up and smile at Max. 'Thank you once again. For everything.'

'No problem.' He nodded to them both before leaving.

Drakon was unsure what to say in order to breach the tense silence left behind by the other man's departure. Uncertainty, in any given situation, was not an emotion that sat well on his shoulders.

Gemini looked across at him. 'Do you think we'll—I'll—ever hear from Angela again?'

He smiled confidently. 'Somehow I think not. You were like a tigress just now in defence of your...friends.'

She nodded. 'And I meant every word. You and Max, and poor Markos, have all been wonderful.'

'I believe I may speak for the others when I say it

was our pleasure,' Drakon said. 'I should leave now as well,' he added. 'You will no doubt need time and space in which to properly absorb your change of circumstances.'

Gemini gave herself a mental shake, knowing that this was Drakon's way of saying goodbye. 'Did Markos really take Angela out to dinner last night in order to make sure she was out of the house for several hours?'

'Yes.' Drakon's mouth twisted. 'He felt it was the least he could do after his error earlier this week.' He shrugged those broad shoulders. 'I believe he also likes you.'

And Gemini liked Markos too.

But she *loved* Drakon...

Completely.

It was a discovery, an admission she had made to herself, as she'd lain awake and alone in her bed in the hotel in Verona the previous night...

She loved everything about Drakon. The way he looked obviously made her feel weak at the knees, and when he kissed her, made love to her, she simply melted. But it was so much more than that. She loved his obvious love and loyalty towards his family, his integrity in business, his self-confidence in any situation, his ability to make Gemini feel protected while at the same time respecting her freedom of choice.

Alone in her bed last night she had realised that Drakon was everything, and more, she could ever have wished for in the man she loved.

That love had only deepened today in the knowledge that he had believed in her, cared enough—even if it was only as a friend—to ensure that Bartholomew House was returned to her.

She moistened her lips before speaking. 'Will you be returning to New York now?'

Drakon was silent for several seconds. Several long seconds. 'That depends on you,' he finally answered.

Gemini gave him a startled glance. 'Me?'

'Yes,' he confirmed wryly. 'Shall I go back to New York today, Gemini, or shall I remain here in London, so that we might perhaps start again?' His expression was strained.

'Start what again?' Gemini was aware that she sounded idiotic, virtually repeating every word Drakon said, but she was afraid of misunderstanding him, and by doing so causing embarrassment to them both.

Drakon breathed heavily. 'Everything,' he bit out forcefully. 'We met in unusual circumstances, and our relationship has continued in that unusual way ever since.' He moved forward until he was close enough to crouch down beside the chair in which she sat. 'I am asking, Gemini, if we could not begin again?' He reached out to take one of her hands in his, and became aware of the envelope he still held. 'I totally forgot...' He frowned down at the bulky envelope. 'I should have given you this earlier.'

'Haven't you given me enough already?' Gemini looked totally bewildered.

Drakon reached into the envelope and drew out a small green box before resting it in his palm and holding it out to her. 'I believe this also belongs to you,' he said.

Gemini could only stare down blankly at the ring box in Drakon's hand, still befuddled by the possibilities of what Drakon had just said to her. It had seemed as if he wanted another chance with her.

'What is it?' she prompted breathlessly.

He smiled gently. 'I am sure that you already know.'

Yes, she did know. Was positive that inside the ring box would be her mother's emerald and diamond engagement ring and her plain gold wedding band!

She blinked in an effort to clear the tears that suddenly stung her eyes. 'Was this the private telephone call you made yesterday evening when we arrived in Verona?'

'Yes,' he acknowledged simply.

Gemini reached out and took the box tentatively before slowly raising the lid. The familiarity of the rings inside caused her to close her eyes, sending those scalding tears cascading down her cheeks.

'Oh, Drakon…' She began to sob in earnest.

'Don't cry, Gemini!' He reached out and gathered her into his arms, pressed her face into the warmth of his chest. 'I thought only to make you happy,' he murmured huskily as he crushed her to him. 'Please don't cry, *agapi mou*,' he entreated. 'I cannot bear it!'

Gemini couldn't seem to stop crying. She couldn't remember anyone—not even her father, whom she had adored and who had adored her—doing anything so absolutely, unselfishly wonderful for her. Put that together with Drakon's earlier conversation, and his endearment just now, and her earlier hopes began to take flight…

She raised her head and looked at Drakon, seeing his concern for her in those dark, dark eyes. And something else…

She moistened her lips before speaking, and saw emotion darken those now jet-black eyes. 'Drakon, why, when it must have been obvious how willing I was, did you change your mind about making love to me last night?'

His expression became strained. 'In the circumstances, it would have been wrong of me to take advantage of you…'

'And?' Gemini pressed, her heart pounding loudly in her chest.

He gave a tight smile. 'I told you—there was no four-poster bed and no rose petals.'

'But I told you those things didn't matter to me any more…'

His mouth firmed. 'They matter to *me*!' he told her fiercely. 'Damn it, I love you, Gemini—and, difficult as it was to walk away from you last night, I could not in all conscience make love to you until everything else in your life had been settled.'

'You *love* me?' she repeated breathlessly, her heart seeming to falter and then stop, before starting up again, stronger, quicker.

Drakon gave a pained wince. 'I had not meant to say that to you just yet.'

She looked at him quizzically. 'Why not?'

'Because you deserve more. You deserve to be wooed and courted, to be spoilt and cosseted, before I so much as broach the subject of the depth of my feelings for you.'

The beating of Gemini's heart soared out of control. 'And what of the depth of my feelings for you?'

He blinked. 'You have feelings for me? Of course you do.' A muscle twitched in his jaw. 'They are feelings of friendship. And gratitude.'

The tears once again began to fall down her cheeks. 'Yes, of course I'm grateful to you—how could I not be when you've done something so wonderfully unselfish for me? And I do believe you're the best friend I've ever had! But haven't you realised yet that I love you, too?'

His throat moved convulsively. 'You love me?'

'So very much, my darling, so very much!' Her eyes glowed with emotion as she gazed up at him adoringly. 'Admittedly you can be arrogant and bossy, and you're incredibly single-minded...'

'But...?' He laughed shakily as she listed his faults.

'But I love you anyway,' she assured him with an incandescent smile. 'Drakon, do you remember I once told you that I've felt incomplete all my life?' she said. 'As if a part of me were missing?'

'Because you lost your twin.'

'You complete me, Drakon. Totally and utterly,' Gemini told him fervently.

Drakon took a deep breath. 'And I am so consumed with love for you I don't know how I ever existed without you.'

'I feel exactly the same way,' Gemini vowed, before Drakon's lips claimed hers and there was no more talk from either of them for a considerable amount of time.

'We must stop now, my darling.' Drakon drew back reluctantly in one of the armchairs, Gemini nestled comfortably in his arms. 'I have waited this long to make love with you. I can wait a little longer,' he insisted as she looked up at him in silent reproach. 'But first—will you marry me, Gemini?'

Her eyes widened. 'Marriage, Drakon? Are you sure?'

'Totally and utterly.' He firmly repeated her words of earlier. 'I love you to distraction. I had no idea what loneliness was until I was faced with the thought of never seeing you again, never being with you again.' His arms tightened about her. 'Will you marry me and complete me also, Gemini?'

'Oh, yes, Drakon, I'll marry you,' she accepted, before throwing her arms about his neck and kissing him enthusiastically. 'But where will we live?' She sobered. 'At the moment your business and home is in New York, and I live and work here in London.'

Drakon smiled. 'I am sure that Markos will not mind moving to New York in my place. I will transfer to the offices here, to London.'

Gemini's eyes were wide. 'You would do that for me?'

'My love, have you not realised yet that I would do and be anything for you?' He gazed down at her with those intense dark eyes.

Oh, yes, Gemini knew exactly what lengths Drakon was willing to go to in order to ensure her happiness. 'Then perhaps it's time I made some sort of sacrifice for you?' she said.

'In this instance it is not necessary that you do so,' he replied. 'Besides, would you not prefer that our children grow up in Bartholomew House?'

Drakon's children. And hers... Gemini had thought she couldn't possibly be any happier than she was, but the thought of having Drakon's children made her feel full to bursting.

'Do you regret having to give up Bartholomew House?'

He shrugged. 'To Lyonedes Enterprises it was only ever a piece of real estate, but to you it was always so much more. We will find somewhere else in London to build our hotel. Besides,' Drakon added teasingly, 'I haven't given up anything; Bartholomew House now belongs to my future wife and the mother of my children.'

It was truly unbelievable that she could be this happy.

'In that case, I would like it very much if you moved to London,' she breathed softly.

His arms tightened about her. 'Then it shall be so. And tomorrow we will go out and buy an indecently expensive engagement ring— No?' he said, when he saw the uncertainty in her face.

'I—would you mind very much if we used my mother's engagement ring instead?' Gemini looked up at him anxiously.

Drakon smiled down at her indulgently. 'You do not wish for a new and indecently expensive ring?'

She smiled ruefully as she shook her head. 'We can have new matching wedding bands. But if you don't mind I would really like to wear my mother's engagement ring.'

Drakon reached down and picked up the box from where it had fallen when they'd begun to kiss each other, flicking open the lid and taking out the emerald and diamond ring.

'I will love you for eternity, Gemini,' he pledged as he slipped the ring onto her finger.

'As I will love you, Drakon,' she vowed in return.

Two weeks later, on their wedding night, Drakon carried Gemini into the master bedroom of his house on the island in the Aegean Sea, pushing aside the gauzy curtains around a four-poster bed surrounded by the perfume of dozens upon dozens of rose petals. They lay down upon the covers and made long and beautiful love with each other...

* * * * *

THE ENIGMATIC
GREEK

CATHERINE GEORGE

Catherine George was born in Wales, and early on developed a passion for reading which eventually fuelled her compulsion to write. Marriage to an engineer led to nine years in Brazil, but on his later travels the education of her son and daughter kept her in the UK. And, instead of constant reading to pass her lonely evenings, she began to write the first of her romantic novels. When not writing and reading she loves to cook, listen to opera, and browse in antiques shops.

CHAPTER ONE

His island had lain in the sun in this remote part of the Aegean Sea long before Bronze Age Minoans had sought refuge here from cataclysmic disaster on Crete. Normally Alexei Drakos relished its peace. Today, not so much. From his office in the *Kastro* he gazed down, frowning, and then abandoned the view of brilliant blue sea lapping at the golden beach far below to make a comprehensive check of the banks of technology across the room. But for once they failed to hold his attention. Feeling restless, and plagued by something unfamiliar he refused to identify as loneliness, he turned back to the windows to watch a ferry in the distance discharging its cargo of holiday-makers into the *tavernas* lining the harbour of the neighbouring island.

Tomorrow tourists like these would flock here to his island for *Agios Ioannis*. Bonfires would blaze on the beaches to celebrate the feast of St John and visitors would come in droves for the festival and for the highlight of its entertainment, the bull dance famed for origins which reached far back into antiquity. Those Minoans again. But it was worth the sacrifice of privacy for a single day. The islanders who made a living from fishing here on Kyrkiros had reaped big benefits from his decision to revive the festival. It brought tourists who paid them an entrance fee, ate their food and bought their crafts, sampled their olives and honey, drank the wine from the island vineyards and ordered more from the websites he'd set up. But otherwise left the island in peace.

Suddenly tired of his own company, he made the descent by the ancient, winding stairs for once to burn off some of the energy buzzing through his system and entered the big, modernised kitchen on the ground floor of the *Kastro* to exclamations of pleasure from the women working there.

'You should have rung, *kyrie*,' scolded his housekeeper, pouring coffee. 'I would have come up to you.'

He shook his head as he took one of the pastries she offered. 'I knew you would be busy, Sofia.'

The woman smiled fondly. 'Never too busy to serve you, *kyrie*. And nearly all is ready now for tomorrow. A good meal is prepared for the dancers, and Angela and her daughters have done marvels.'

'They always do.' He smiled at the women who every year fashioned traditional costumes based on designs discovered on ancient, barely discernible frescoes during the *Kastro's* restoration.

Sofia smiled lovingly as her son came hurrying in. 'Is all in place, Yannis?'

The youth nodded eagerly. 'You wish to check, *kyrie*?'

Alex downed his coffee and stood up. 'Lead on.'

In contrast to the normal peace of the island, colourful stalls had been set up on the sweep of beach below. Higher up, on the natural shelf overlooking the terrace where the dancers would perform, a vine-wreathed pergola sheltered tables reserved in advance by the forward-thinking of the influx of visitors expected the next day. He nodded in approval to the men finishing up there. 'Well done, everyone.' With a reminder to check that all the necessary signs were in place, he returned to his office, but this time via the lift he'd installed years before as one of the first steps towards making the *Kastro* penthouse habitable. His phone rang as the doors opened and he smiled as he saw the caller ID.

'Darling,' said a lilting, unmistakeable voice. 'I'm tired and thirsty and I've just landed at your jetty.'

His eyebrows shot to his hair. '*What?* Stay right there. I'm on my way.'

The moment the lift hit ground level again, he raced out of the *Kastro* and down the beach to the main jetty where a woman stood waiting, her face alight with laughter as she held out her arms.

'Surprise!'

'You certainly are!' He hugged her tightly for a long moment, then held her away from him and raised a mocking eyebrow. 'You were just passing?'

Talia Kazan's eyes sparkled as she smiled up into the hard, handsome face. 'Passing! I've been travelling for so long I hardly know what day it is!'

He motioned to the beaming Yannis to help bring the bags. 'Give it up, Mother, the ditzy-blonde act doesn't work with me. You know exactly what day it is.'

She shrugged, unrepentant. 'Who better? I had a sudden desire to see my son so I packed my bags and came to do that—you are pleased, I trust?'

He kissed the hand he was holding. 'Of course; I'm delighted! But you took a risk. I might not have been here.'

Her eyes gleamed in triumph. 'Since I am *not* ditzy, I contacted your admirable Stefan to make sure you would be here for the festival and swore him to silence. He said you were coming alone, as usual.' She shook her head in reproof. 'You should have brought some pleasant company with you.'

'If by pleasant you mean female, the women I know demand the sophisticated pleasures of the city, Mother. Arcane festivals on a remote island just don't do it for them.'

'Then invite someone with a higher cultural threshold.'
The luminous violet eyes were suddenly serious. 'It is time
you put that nonsense from Christina Mavros behind you
and found a real woman.'

He shrugged that off with an impatient smile. 'Did Takis
bring you over?'

'No; he was so busy over there with guests checking in
at the *taverna*. A very kind young man assured me it was
a pleasure to bring me to Kyrkiros and so save Takis the
trouble.'

'Who was this man?' demanded her son sharply.

'I did not catch his name over the noise of the boat engine. Now, lead me to Sofia so I can beg her for coffee.'

Sofia and her crew were clustered at the kitchen door,
faces wreathed in smiles as they greeted '*kyria* Talia' in
rapture and pressed her to have coffee, wine, pastries or
anything her heart desired that they could provide.

One of the new arrivals on the neighbouring island of Karpyros felt a rush of excitement as she focused her discreet
little binoculars on the action across the water. At this distance it was hard to be sure, but the man hugging a blonde
over there surely had to be the rare sight of Alexei Drakos,
the boy-wonder entrepreneur famed for his hostility towards the media.

Eleanor tucked the binoculars away when her lunch arrived and with a smile thanked the young waiter in the basic
Greek she'd crammed for her current assignment: a series
of travel articles on lesser-known Greek islands well off
the tourist trail. It was more ambitious than anything she'd
worked on to date, and before grudgingly signing off on expenses her editor had dropped a bombshell by stipulating a
shot at an interview with Alexei Drakos as part of the deal.

'Since the Mavros woman did the dirty on him a few

months ago, he's kept a very low profile, but apparently he always visits his island in June. Make damn sure you get there in good time because tourists swarm there for some festival he's put on every year since he bought the island. There's no accommodation, so book a room somewhere else, plus a boat to get you there on the day.' Ross McLean had flashed his bleached veneers at her. 'And wear something sexy to beard the lion in his den.'

'Drakos translates as dragon, not lion,' she'd retorted. 'And I don't do sexy!'

On her way out Eleanor had heard him muttering about college girls who thought they knew it all and rolled her eyes. There was fat chance of getting a reporter's job these days without a college degree, and to augment hers she'd worked her socks off to add photography to her journalism qualifications; something greatly to her advantage with Ross McLean because it saved him the expense of a photographer.

Now she was almost literally in sight of her quarry, Eleanor refused to spoil her appetite by worrying about how to achieve the scoop her boss was so hot for. But succeed she would, somehow, if only to show him just what a 'college girl' could do. Maybe the reclusive Mr Drakos would be in a sociable mood now the blonde had arrived to keep him company. Though Ross, drat the man, knew very well he was asking the impossible. Alexei Drakos had been famous for stonewalling journalists even before the lurid exposé by a furious ex-lover. But who had he been hugging today? No matter how hard she'd dug, Eleanor had learned frustratingly little about the man's private life other than the woman-scorned outpourings of Christina Mavros. Her research into his professional persona had built up a picture of a *wunderkind* who achieved success while still at school with some kind of genius software technology, and as an adult entrepreneur went on to put his money to good use with investments in pharmaceuticals, property and more technology. But, other than his reputation for philanthropy she had no clue to the man behind the public persona.

The taverna owner's son rushed over as Eleanor got up to leave and carried her luggage the short distance to one of the small apartments. He set her bags down on the small veranda fronting the last of the square white cubes overlooking the harbour and unlocked the blue door. Eleanor smiled in approval at the scrupulously clean, white-walled room as Petros carried her bags inside and told him she intended dining at the taverna that night.

'Then I will reserve a table for you, *kyria*. Many people will be here tonight before the festival tomorrow,' he told her, and flushed with pleasure when she thanked him and gave him a hefty tip.

Petros was right, of course. The place would be heaving with visitors ready to swarm across to Kyrkiros tomorrow. But if Alexei Drakos was such a private man why did he open his island to all and sundry, even if it was for just one day? While she dined later she could gaze across the sea and speculate to her heart's content about the king of the Kastro on the island over there. In the meantime, she'd haul her bags up the ladder to the open mezzanine bedroom, do her usual minimum unpacking and take a short nap.

Eleanor showered later in the tiny, spotless bathroom and dressed in her usual trademark jeans and T-shirt. As a gesture to the island night-life the jeans were white and the clinging top black and scooped low enough to show a hint of suntanned cleavage; and in a practice run for dragon-slaying the next day, she brushed on mascara and lip gloss. Eleanor eyed her reflection critically. Two weeks of island-hopping in the sun had added a satisfactory bronze glow to her skin, but the effect was more healthy than sexy. She shrugged. If Ross was rat enough to fire her for failing to get the exclusive he was panting for, she would go freelance.

The taverna was buzzing with holidaymakers and locals when Petros darted out to conduct her to a tiny table which gave her a good view across the boats bobbing in the harbour to the lights just visible on the dark outline of Kyrkiros on the horizon. She was served with bread and olives to nibble on while she waited for the red mullet, which arrived sizzling, dressed with lemon juice and olive oil, and accompanied by a salad and half a carafe of local wine.

Eleanor thanked Petros warmly and asked about the festival next day. 'Is the bull dance for men only?'

He shook his head. 'The *taurokathapsia* is for both men and women. Enjoy your meal, *kyria*.'

Eleanor peered at the distant lights across the water, wondering about Alexei Drakos. From what little she'd learned about his personal life, it seemed unlikely he was looking forward to the invasion on his territory next day, but at least he now had the blonde to cheer him up when the hoi polloi descended on him. Her research might have turned up nothing about any current love life, but she'd made the deeply intriguing discovery that his mother had been one of the most famous photographic models of her day. Talia Kazan's heyday had been short. Her exquisite face had never graced magazine covers again after she married Milo Drakos and produced the son who, allegedly, was estranged from his father. Eleanor's journalistic antennae buzzed like bees with the urge to find out why.

As she left the taverna Eleanor complimented the owner about her dinner, and when she ordered lunch for next day remembered to confirm that a boat had been booked for her trip over to Kyrkiros afterwards. Once there her plan was to soak up the festival atmosphere, take lots of photographs and then sit back people-watching at her reserved table while she waited for the lord and master of the island to show. Or not.

Back in her room, Eleanor soon regretted her nap. After a while she gave up trying to sleep and switched on her laptop to do more digging. She went back to the piece about Christina Mavros, the socialite from Crete who had failed in her aim to marry Alexei Drakos and subsequently sold her vindictive, highly coloured story to the press. Stupid woman, thought Eleanor as she went on with her search, but by the time her eyes began to droop at last her only new find had been a photograph of Alexei's father. From the cut of his hard, handsome face it seemed that Milo Drakos would make a bad enemy.

Eleanor woke late next morning and hurriedly climbed down the ladder to make coffee to kick-start the day. After her shower she followed Ross McLean's instructions and pulled on a dress for once, instead of jeans. Not that it was remotely the kind of thing her boss had in mind. The navy-striped white Breton number was as simple and comfortable as a T-shirt, but at least it showed off legs the Greek sun had toasted to an even darker shade of bronze than her face.

Later on at the taverna, Eleanor enjoyed an entertaining lunch hour as she watched seagoing craft of all descriptions making for the other island. When Petros finally came to say her boat was waiting for her, the sun was so fierce she was glad of dark glasses and sun hat for the trip across the sea, her excitement mounting at the approach to the steep, rocky island dominated by an ancient kastro. She breathed in the familiar sage and lavender scent of the Greek *maquis* lining the paths winding up through sun-baked hillside; the sound of music and chattering crowds in festive mood added to her anticipation as her genial ferryman docked at a jetty.

Eleanor thanked him and settled a time for the trip back later that evening, then got straight to work to take shots of the houses which clustered around the Kastro and climbed the slopes above it to a summit crowned by the blue dome of an icing-white church. Groundwork done, she threaded her way through the chattering, animated crowds to claim the place she'd reserved at one of the tables under the pergola. Musicians were playing at the far end of the terrace, but she'd learned from Petros that the main event would be after dark when bonfires were lit for the performance of the famous bull dance. She eyed the stage with misgiving. She'd seen pictures of the frescoes on Crete, depicting dancers somersaulting over a bull, but there was no visible way to restrain an animal here if it got out of hand, which was worrying.

She promptly forgot about bulls when the doors to the Kastro opened and three people emerged to descend the steps to the terrace. Of the two men in the group, it was obvious who was king of this particular castle. Alexei Drakos was smiling down at his blonde companion, and Eleanor realised in sudden excitement that she was Talia Kazan in the flesh, from this distance as beautiful in maturity as she had been in her heyday. The blonde was no pillow-friend after all, but Alexei's mother, in a hyacinth-blue dress of exquisite cut, a large straw hat on her gleaming hair.

The son was equally striking. His curling hair was only a few shades darker gold than his mother's, instead of black as Eleanor had expected before she'd researched him, but his face was carved from different, utterly masculine clay, with heavy-lidded dark eyes and handsome, forceful features which bore an unmistakeable resemblance to his father. He was slim-hipped and broad shouldered, and even in conventional linen trousers and white shirt, which merely hinted at the muscles beneath, there was a powerful masculine grace about him. Alexei Drakos was a magnificent specimen of manhood by any standards.

Eleanor watched, riveted, as Alexei linked his arm
through his mother's to inspect the goods on display at
each stall for a brief moment and exchange a few words
with the vendors before leaving the field clear to the purchasing public. From under cover of her table's parasol,
Eleanor took a few shots of mother and son with the
Kastro as backdrop then turned her lens on the festive
crowd milling about in the hot sunshine.

Eventually she put her camera away and went off to
browse among the stalls for presents to take home. The
crafts on display were of good quality. She soon found
carved worry-beads that would amuse her father and a
small, exquisitely embroidered picture perfect for her
mother. With regret she passed by the displays of pottery
and copper pots as too difficult to transport home, but then
reached a stall with goods that made her mouth water. She'd
read that it was hard to find really good jewellery outside
the larger towns in Greece, but the wares on sale here were
the real deal and obviously came from the mainland. When
enough space cleared to let her get a look, she passed over
the striking pendants and earrings way out of her price
range and concentrated on trays of small trinkets, one of
which caught her eye and said 'buy me'.

'Copy of Minoan ornament,' the man on the stall stated,
but in such strongly accented Greek Eleanor barely understood. 'You like it?'

The tiny crystal bull had a gold loop on its back; perfect
to attach to her charm bracelet. She liked it a lot.

'How much?' she asked, but when he mentioned the sum
she shook her head regretfully, which prompted an unintelligible spiel from him on the virtues of the charm. The man
only broke off when space was made for someone who addressed Eleanor in Greek to ask if she needed help with the
problem. Her most immediate problem, due to the sudden

sight and scent of Alexei Drakos at such close quarters, was trying to muster enough breath and vocabulary to answer.

'I don't speak enough Greek to bargain,' she said at last in English.

'Ah, I see. Allow me.' He began a rapid exchange with the stall holder and turned to Eleanor with a smile that rocked her on her heels as he named a price just within her budget.

'Thank you so much!' She hastily counted out money to hand over before the stall holder could change his mind, and tried to concentrate as the man said a lot more she couldn't understand. Standing so close to Alexei Drakos was scrambling her brain!

'He will attach it to your bracelet if you leave it with him for a while,' he translated for her, the hint of attractive accent adding to her problem.

'Thank you.' Eleanor unfastened the heavy gold chain from her wrist and handed it to the vendor, pointing to a link near the lock.

'I told him to bring it to you later,' said Alexei. 'Do you have a table?'

Eleanor nodded dumbly, certain by now he thought she was a total idiot.

'Alexei *mou*, I heard you speaking English,' said his mother, hurrying to join them. 'Won't you introduce me?'

He smiled. 'I've only just met the lady myself.'

'Then I will make the introductions. I am Talia Kazan, and this is my son, Alexei Drakos.' Her accent was equally fascinating, but more pronounced than her son's, the words spoken with friendly warmth that unlocked Eleanor's tongue.

'Eleanor Markham,' she said, smiling. 'How do you do?'

'Delighted to meet you. Are you here with friends?'

'No, I'm travelling alone.'

'Then would you care to join me for a drink?' said Talia.

Would she! Eleanor beamed. 'I'd love to. Perhaps you'd come over to my table.'

'I'll send someone,' said Alexei, and went off to speak to a waiter.

Talia gave Eleanor the smile that had made her famous. 'I am so glad of some company. Alex is very busy today.' When they reached the table, to the intense interest of people sitting nearby, she sat down with a sigh of pleasure. 'Are you just here for the day at the festival, or are you staying on Karpyros?'

Eleanor explained about her assignment.

Talia's violet eyes were instantly guarded. 'You are a journalist.'

Eleanor met the look steadily. 'Yes. But I'm not a gossip columnist. I work in features, mainly on travel, so I won't capitalise on meeting the famous Talia Kazan.'

The slender shoulders shrugged. 'It is a very long time since I was famous.'

'Yet you've hardly changed at all.' Eleanor spoke with such obvious sincerity the beautiful eyes warmed.

'How kind of you to say so. You are here to write about the festival?'

Eleanor nodded, hoping she didn't look guilty. Bad move to reveal that an interview with Alexei Drakos was her main objective.

'I have not been here for the festival for a while,' Talia told her. 'But Alex always leaves his calendar clear for it, so I came on impulse to surprise him.'

'He must have been delighted!'

'Fortunately, he seemed to be. Not every man welcomes a surprise visit from his mother.' Talia smiled up at the youth setting down glasses, bottles of mineral water and fruit juice. '*Efcharisto,* Yannis.' She eyed Eleanor with gratifying interest. 'So, tell me about your assignment.'

Eleanor described the lesser-known islands she'd visited for her series. 'I take my own photographs, so I nearly always travel solo.'

'But you must have someone in the UK waiting impatiently for your return?' The blue eyes sparkled, unashamedly curious.

Eleanor shook her head, smiling. 'The only one waiting impatiently right now is my editor. But I'm lucky enough to have good friends, and I'm close to my parents.'

'I am most fortunate myself that way. My son may be a busy man, but he makes time for regular—if brief—visits to his mother. Do you live at home with your parents?'

Before Eleanor could reply, Alexei Drakos joined them. Talia smiled at him warmly. 'Sit with us for a while.'

He shook his head. 'Stefan tells me I have calls to return. Miss Markham, has your bracelet been returned to you?'

'No, not yet.'

'I'll hurry the man along.' With an abstracted smile, he strode off again.

His mother looked after him anxiously. 'The world does not leave him alone, even here at his retreat—though Stefan, his assistant, does his best to keep it at bay over this particular holiday.'

'This festival is obviously important to—to your son,' said Eleanor.

'To me, also,' said Talia, and looked up with an enquiring smile as a boy approached the table, holding out a package.

'Ah, that must be for me,' said Eleanor, and took out her bracelet, now adorned with the crystal bull. '*Efcharisto*!' she said, pleased, and handed over a tip. She smiled guiltily as she displayed the charm. 'Very expensive, but I couldn't resist it after your son was kind enough to bargain the price down.'

Talia leaned closer to examine it. 'Exquisite—and a most perfect souvenir of Kyrkiros.'

Eleanor fastened the bracelet on her wrist. 'There. No more extravagance for me this trip.'

Alexei Drakos' assistant came towards them, smiling respectfully. 'Forgive me for interrupting, but Sofia says a light supper is ready, *kyria* Talia. She apologises it is early tonight because of the *taurokathapsia*.'

'Of course,' she said, getting up. 'Miss Eleanor Markham, meet Stefan Petrides, Alexei's man in Athens.'

Stefan bowed formally to Eleanor. '*Chairo poly, kyria* Markham.'

'*Pos eiste*,' she returned.

'I am not happy leaving you alone here, my dear,' said Talia, frowning. 'Please join us for dinner.'

Eleanor smiled gratefully, but shook her head. 'That's so kind of you, but I purposely ate enough lunch to see me through the evening. Goodbye—it's been such a pleasure to meet you.'

'Likewise, Eleanor Markham, though the day is not over yet,' said Talia, and with a smile went off with her escort.

Eleanor gazed after them a little wistfully, then sat down and began writing up the events of the afternoon. She was soon so deeply absorbed she jumped when someone rapped on the metal table. She looked up with a smile to find Alexei Drakos eyeing her notebook with hostility.

'My mother is concerned about leaving you alone here,' he said coldly. 'But you're obviously busy. She tells me you're a journalist.'

Her smile died. 'Yes, I am.'

'And my island is providing an even richer source of material than you expected?'

Eleanor's defences sprang to attention. 'It is indeed.'

'Write one word about my mother, and I will sue,' he said with menace.

Eleanor's chin went up. 'I'm here solely to report on this famous festival of yours, Mr Drakos. But, since you ask so *nicely,* I'll leave out my chance meeting with Talia Kazan. Though, since I would be reporting fact, suing would not be possible.'

'Maybe not.' His cold eyes locked on hers. 'But believe me, Miss Markham—whatever rag you work for I can get you fired as easily as I helped you out earlier.'

He strode off, cursing at the chance that had involved his mother with Eleanor Markham. Since the notoriety Christina Mavros had brought on him, he had avoided contact with any woman other than his mother. Until today, that was, when an attractive tourist's rueful little smile had seduced him into offering help to someone who was not only a woman but a reporter, for God's sake!

Eleanor stared after him balefully. No chance of an interview with Talia Kazan's baby boy, then. And no prize for guessing how Alexei Drakos had made his fortune, either. He'd probably just stepped on the necks of everyone who got in his way. Her mouth tightened. Romantic fool that she was, the chance meeting with him had been one of the major experiences of her life, whereas to him she was just a petty little problem to solve by threats.

Her eyes sparking like an angry cat's behind her glasses, she noted that all the reserved tables were now full, other than the one adjoining hers. Everyone was eating and drinking and having a wonderful time in laughing, animated groups, which emphasized her solitary state—a common enough situation on her travels, and not one that had bothered her in the slightest up to now. Eleanor shrugged impatiently. Her blood sugars obviously needed a boost after

the clash with the dragon of Kyrkiros. She walked over to
the stalls, bought a couple of nut-filled honey pastries from
one of them, and returned to her table to find a teenaged
lad waiting there.

'*Kyria* Talia sent for you,' he informed her, indicating
the tray on the table.

Eleanor smiled warmly and asked him to convey her
thanks to the lady. She sat down to pour tea into a delicate
china cup and smiled when she tasted an unmistakeably
British blend. The pastries were doubly delicious with the
tea as accompaniment. By the time Eleanor had finished
her surprise treat, lamps were glowing along the terrace,
the sudden darkness of the Aegean night had fallen, a singer
had joined the musicians and she had almost recovered from
the blow of her encounter with Alexei Drakos. She stiffened when an audible ripple of interest through the crowd
heralded the arrival of the man himself as he ushered his
mother to the adjoining table. One look at him revived her
anger so fiercely it took an effort to smile when Talia beckoned to her.

'Do come and join us, Eleanor. The dancing will start
soon.'

Eleanor shook her head firmly; grateful it was too dark
for her feelings to show. 'It's very kind of you but I wouldn't
dream of intruding.'

'Nonsense! Why sit there alone? Stefan will bring your
things.'

And, short of causing a scene, Eleanor was obliged to
accept the chair Alexei Drakos held out for her next to his
mother. She thanked him politely and smiled at Talia. 'And
thank *you* so much for the tea. It was just what I needed.'

'I hoped it might be. I made it with my own fair hands.'
The radiance of Talia's smile contrasted sharply with the

expression on her son's face. 'Do stop looming over us and sit down, Alexei *mou*—you too, Stefan.'

Eleanor tensed, her stomach muscles contracting as a bull bellowed somewhere deep inside the *Kastro*, loud enough to be heard above the music and the noise of the chattering crowd.

'Ah, we begin,' said Talia with satisfaction.

Alexei eyed Eleanor sardonically. 'Is something wrong, Miss Markham?'

'Nothing at all,' she lied, but sucked in a startled breath as the lights died. They were left in darkness for several tense seconds before the torches encircling the raised wooden platform burst into flame, and bonfires ignited one after the other along the outer edges of the beach.

'How is that for Greek drama?' crowed Talia, touching Eleanor's hand. 'My dear, you are so cold. What is wrong?'

'Anticipation,' Eleanor said brightly. With a defiant look at Alexei Drakos, she took out her camera. 'For my article,' she informed him.

'You may take as many photographs of the dancers as you wish,' he assured her, his message loud and clear. One shot of his beautiful mother and Eleanor Markham would be thrown off his island.

'Thank you.' She turned her attention to the stage, intrigued to see that the musicians had exchanged their modern instruments for harps and flutes which looked like museum exhibits. Along with some kind of snare drums, they began to make music so eerily unlike anything she'd ever heard before the hairs rose on the back of her neck and her blood began to pulse in time with the hypnotic beat.

With sudden drama, the great *Kastro* doors were flung open and a roar of applause greeted the dancers who came out two by two, moving in a slow rhythm dictated by the drum beat as they descended to the terrace. At first sight

Eleanor thought they were all men after all, but when they moved into the dramatic ring of torchlight the girls among them were obvious by the bandeaux covering their breasts. Otherwise all the dancers wore loin guards under brief, gauzy kilts, glinting gold jewellery, black wigs with ringlets and soft leather sandals laced high up the leg.

Eleanor forgot Alexei Drakos' hostility and sat entranced. The entire scene was straight off a painting on some ancient vase, except that these figures were alive and moving. The procession circled the torch-lit stage twice in hypnotic, slow-stepping rhythm before the dancers lined up in a double row to look up at the table where Alexei Drakos sat with his guests. The leader, a muscular figure with eyes painted as heavily as the girls, stepped forward to salute Alexei and Eleanor shook herself out of her trance to capture the scene on film in the instant before the lithe figures began to dance. They swayed in perfect unison, dipping and weaving in sinuous, labyrinthine patterns which gradually grew more and more complex as the beat of the music quickened. It rose faster and faster to a final crescendo as a bull bellowed off-stage, the doors burst open again and a figure out of myth and nightmare gave a great leap down into the torchlight. The crowd went wild at the sight of a black bull's head with crystal eyes and vicious horns topping a muscular, human male body.

CHAPTER TWO

ELEANOR'S relief was so intense she had to wait until her hands were steady enough to do the job she'd come for as she focused her lens on the fantastic figure. She smiled in recognition as a new player leapt into the torchlight to face the beast, the testosterone in every line of the bronzed muscular body in sharp contrast to his painted face and golden love-locks; Theseus, the blond Hellene, come to slay the Minotaur.

Eleanor took several shots then sat, mesmerised, as Theseus and the dancers swooped around the central half-man half-beast figure, taunting him like a flock of mockingbirds as they somersaulted away from his lunging horns. She gasped with the audience as Theseus vaulted from the bent back of one of the male dancers to somersault through the air over the Minotaur's horns. He landed on his feet with the grace and skill of an Olympic gymnast, an imperious hand raised to hush the applause as the troupe launched into a series of athletic, balance-defying somersaults, spinning around the central figure while the Minotaur lunged at them in graphically conveyed fury. In perfect rhythm the dancers taunted him with their dizzying kaleidoscope of movement as again and again Theseus danced away from the menacing horns. The music grew more and more frenzied until the dance culminated in another breath-taking somersault by Theseus over the great bull's head, but this time he snatched up a golden double-headed axe of the type Eleanor had seen in photographs of Cretan artefacts.

The Minotaur lunged with such ferocity the audience gave a great, concerted gasp again as Theseus leapt aside to avoid the horns and held the axe aloft for an instant of pure drama, before bringing it down on the Minotaur's neck. There was an anguished bellow as the man-beast sank slowly to his knees and then fell, sprawled, the great horned head at Theseus's feet.

To say the crowd went wild again was an understatement. But, even as Eleanor applauded with the rest, her inner cynic warned that the sheer drama of the moment would end when the beast was obliged to get to his all-too-human feet as the performers took their bow. But, though the applause was prolonged, there was no bow. Still blank-faced as figures on a fresco, the dancers formed a line on either side of the fallen figure. With Theseus and the lead dancer at the impressive shoulders, the male members of the troupe bent as one man to pick up the Minotaur and heaved him up in a practised movement to shoulder height. The women went ahead, hands clasped and heads bowed as, still in rhythm with the wailing flutes and now slow, solemn, hypnotic drumbeat, the vanquished man-beast was slowly borne around the torch-lit arena, horned head hanging, then up the steep steps and through the double doors into the Kastro, to tumultuous applause and cheers from the crowd.

'So what did you think of our famous *taurokathapsia*, Ms Markham?' asked Alexei Drakos as the musicians took up their modern instruments again. 'You seemed nervous before it started. Were you expecting something different?'

'Yes.' She exchanged a rueful smile with Talia. 'I was afraid a real live bull was involved.'

'I rather fancied you were, but I couldn't spoil the drama

by reassuring you!' Talia smiled indulgently and exchanged a glance with her son. 'Was the dance originally done with an actual animal?'

'According to myth and legend, yes, and the wall paintings on Knossos in Crete seem to bear that out. But not here.' He looked very deliberately at Eleanor. 'I assure you that no bulls have danced on Kyrkiros since I acquired the island. Though I can't answer for what happened back in prehistory, Ms Markham.' He beckoned to Yannis, who came hurrying to ask what the 'kyrie' desired, and Alexei turned to Stefan.

'Join your friends now, if you like. I shan't need you anymore tonight,' he said in English.

'Thank you, kyrie,' the young man replied. 'Kalinychta, ladies. This has been a great pleasure.'

'Thank you for your company, Stefan.' Talia gave him her hand. He kissed it formally, bowed to Eleanor and hurried off to the far end of the terrace, where he was absorbed into an exuberant crowd at one of the tables.

'So, what would you like?' asked Alexei.

Talia asked for coffee. 'After all the emotion expended on that performance, I am not hungry. How about you, Eleanor?'

'Coffee would be wonderful, thank you.' Eleanor glanced at her watch as Yannis hurried off with the order. 'I'll be leaving soon.'

'How are you getting back?' asked Talia.

'The boatman who brought me is coming to pick me up.' Eleanor smiled at her gratefully. 'Thank you so much for inviting me to join you.'

'We were very pleased to have your company.' Talia fixed her son with an imperious blue gaze. 'Were we not, Alex?'

'Delighted.' He looked directly at Eleanor. 'Do you have all you require for your article?'

She nodded. 'Your festival will make a wonderful finale to my series. Of course, I'll make it clear that this is an annual event, and stress that Kyrkiros is a private island, not a holiday destination. Was the original bull dance performed as a mid-summer celebration?'

'According to historians it was probably a regular attraction on Crete.'

'It is performed here at this time to commemorate the feast of St John, which also happens to be Alex's birthday,' said Talia, with a smile for her son.

'Then I wish you many happy returns, Mr Drakos,' Eleanor said with formality. 'As I said earlier, nothing will appear in my article that you could object to.'

'Earlier?' said Talia sharply.

Her son shrugged. 'I had a conversation with Ms Markham on the subject of reprisals. I told her what would happen if she mentioned your name.'

His mother stared at him, appalled. 'You *threatened* her?'

'Yes,' he said, unmoved. 'She may write all she wants about the festival and the island. But if there's a single reference to you personally, I'll sue the paper she works for.'

Crimson to the roots of her hair, Eleanor stared at her watch, willing the hands to move faster as Talia shook her head in disbelief.

'Forgive my son, Eleanor. He is absurdly protective about me.' She frowned at him. 'After all, even if I was mentioned, who would remember me after all these years?'

'Don't be naive, Mother.' His mouth tightened when Talia very deliberately poured only two cups of coffee.

'We shall excuse you now, Alexei,' she informed him sweetly. 'You must have people to see.'

Eleanor thoroughly enjoyed the sight of Alexei Drakos dismissed with such relentless grace.

He got to his feet, and gave Eleanor a cool nod. 'I'll say goodbye then, Miss Markham.'

She inclined her head in cool response. 'Goodbye.'

'I'll come back for you after your guest leaves,' he informed his mother.

She smiled indulgently. 'I am perfectly capable of walking indoors on my own, Alexei.'

'I will come back for you,' he said with finality.

Talia sighed as she watched him go. 'My dear, I promise you that Alex will not carry out his threat.'

'It won't be necessary. I won't say a word about you in my article—hugely tempting though it would be,' admitted Eleanor. 'But I confess that I've taken a couple of photographs of you, Ms Kazan—purely personal shots to show my mother. She was a huge fan of yours.'

Talia smiled radiantly. 'Really? I fear she will be disappointed to see me as I am now. I would not have been brave enough for cosmetic surgery—not that I had the slightest need to bother, once I left the cameras behind. These days I use so-called miracle creams and try not to eat too many wicked things—like Sofia's savoury pastries, which are my guilty pleasure. I should have ordered some for you to try, Eleanor.'

'I'm sure they're delicious, but I'm not hungry.'

Talia frowned. 'My son upset you so much?'

Eleanor shrugged, smiling. 'A thick skin is a basic requirement in my profession.'

Talia Kazan was so easy to talk to, Eleanor had soon described previous assignments and felt guilty when Yannis came to inform them a man was asking for the *kyria* at the ferry. 'I've been talking so much I forgot the time!'

'And I have enjoyed listening!' Talia told Yannis he could go, that she would accompany her guest to the boat herself.

'Your son won't like that,' said Eleanor quickly, and cast a glance along the terrace, where Alexei Drakos was talking to the troupe of dancers, who looked very different out of costume.

'My dear, Alex can play the autocrat as much as he likes with the rest of the world, but not with me.' Talia's smile cleared a way for them through the crowd. 'Yannis said the south jetty, which is odd, because it's so much farther away. No matter; a little exercise is good, yes?'

Eleanor disagreed, growing more and more uneasy when she found that the jetty in question was on one of the beaches out of bounds to the public, with no bonfires to guide them. Her misgiving intensified once they'd moved out of range of the Kastro lights. It was hard to make out the path to the jetty and progress was slow.

'Follow me,' said Talia. 'I know the way. Keep close behind—' She gave a sudden shriek as a dark figure shot out of the shadows and snatched her up in his arms to make a run for the jetty. In knee-jerk reaction, Eleanor tore after him as Talia screamed for her son and struggled so fiercely the man stumbled, cursing, and dropped his flailing burden. Eleanor swung her tote bag at his head while he was still staggering and sent him down hard on the jetty, then jumped on him and got in a few punches before he reared up with a furious roar and kicked her into the sea. She sank like a stone and panicked for endless moments until self-preservation instincts finally kicked in. Lungs bursting, she managed to swim up to the surface, coughing and spluttering, and struggling wildly against powerful arms that restrained her.

'Stop!' panted Alexei Drakos. 'I'm trying to rescue you, woman.'

Limp with relief, Eleanor let him tow her through the water to thrust her up into Stefan's grasp before heaving himself out of the water onto the jetty.

'Is your mother safe?' Eleanor demanded hoarsely, and then wrenched herself away from Stefan to cough up more of the Aegean as Talia pushed him aside to get to her.

'Tell me exactly what happened, Mother!' ordered Alexei, thrusting wet hair back from his face.

While Eleanor coughed up more water, Talia explained breathlessly up to the point where the attacker dropped her. 'Then this brave, brave girl knocked him down with her bag and beat him up.'

'But not hard enough. The swine kicked me into the water,' croaked Eleanor hoarsely through chattering teeth. 'Did he get away?'

Alexei's smile turned her blood even colder. 'No, he did not.'

'Where is he?'

'On his way to the Kastro, in company with a pair of angry jailers.'

'Excellent! We should go inside, too,' said Talia firmly. 'You two need to get dry.'

Alexei turned as Yannis came hurrying to say that someone else was asking for the *kyria*. 'What the devil now?' he demanded irritably, turning on Eleanor.

'It must be the real boatman—the one who brought me here earlier,' she said through chattering teeth.

'So, how did the other man contact you?'

'Yannis told us a man was waiting at the jetty,' explained Talia.

Alexei spoke to the boy sharply and, after listening to his explanation, gave him instructions which sent him running off into the Kastro to fetch his mother. 'Apparently our prisoner said he was here for the lady. Yannis knew you were about to leave, Miss Markham, so assumed it was you.'

'Then I'm to blame. I'm so *sorry*,' croaked Eleanor in remorse, but Talia shook her head fiercely.

'Nonsense, it was not your fault!'

By this time Eleanor was so desperate to get back to the taverna and a hot shower she was past caring whose fault it was. 'Now my real ferryman has arrived, I'll take myself off—'

'Absolutely not, Eleanor,' Talia said flatly, and beckoned to the woman hurrying towards them with towels. 'This is Sofia, the housekeeper here. I'll explain to her and then we'll soon have you in a hot bath and into bed.'

'But I can't do that! I need to pay the boatman and get back to the taverna,' protested Eleanor hoarsely, turning away to cough.

'Stefan will see to that—also, send a message to Takis,' said Alexei. 'You must stay here until I interrogate the kidnapper. In the meantime, go indoors with my mother—please,' he added.

'My bag!' said Eleanor in sudden alarm.

'The assault weapon?' His lips twitched as he handed it over. 'Stefan rescued it, but I can't answer for the contents.'

'I hope your camera is undamaged!' exclaimed Talia.

'If not, I shall replace it,' said Alexei, shrugging.

'That won't be necessary, thank you.' Eleanor breathed more easily as she investigated. 'My phone took a direct hit, and the glass on a picture I bought for my mother is cracked. But the camera seems all right.' She was horribly conscious of her bedraggled appearance as Talia bundled her up in a towel. So much for looking sexy! 'The memory card will have survived, anyway. I won't lose any of the pictures.'

'Excellent. Now we must go inside and get something

hot into both of you.' Talia spoke to Sofia, who nodded vigorously and hurried off.

To Eleanor's surprise the musicians were still playing and singing on the terrace, people were talking at the tops of their voices at the tables and a large crowd was still milling around on the beach, where youngsters were shouting as they took turns in leaping over the traditional St John's bonfires. 'Didn't they hear all the commotion?'

'Too much noise, and I got there so quickly I doubt that anyone noticed,' said Alexei, rubbing his hair. 'I followed when I saw you leave the table with my mother and hurried after you in time to hear her scream for me. But I regret that I arrived too late to stop the intruder kicking you into the water. Stefan and a couple of my security men were behind me as I caught him, and they took charge of him while I went in after you.'

'I wish I'd known all that when I was trying not to drown,' said Eleanor wryly.

'Alex dived in after you almost at once,' Talia assured her.

My hero, thought Eleanor, and won herself a sharp look from her dripping rescuer as he escorted them into the cavernous hall of the Kastro and into the anachronism of a modern lift. After a swift, quiet ascent it opened onto the hall of an apartment that could have been part of a modern building. Impressed by the contrast to the ancient Kastro which housed it, Eleanor wrapped her towels around her more tightly to avoid wetting the beautiful floor as Talia led her to a surprisingly feminine bedroom.

'You must get into my shower, as hot as you can bear it. You've lost your lovely glow.'

'You look pale yourself,' said Eleanor anxiously. 'You had a horrible shock, too.'

'But I wasn't kicked into the sea, my dear! Use any of my bath stuff you want.'

'Thank you.' Eleanor's teeth began chattering again.

Talia wagged a finger. 'Be quick; you need something hot to drink. Wrap yourself in the bathrobe behind the door.'

Eleanor bundled her sodden clothes up in the damp towel and put them in the slipper-shaped bath. To her relief her waterproof watch had survived undamaged and, even more miraculously, the crystal bull-charm was still intact on her chain bracelet. Feeling limp as a rag doll as her adrenaline drained away, she turned on hot water in the shower and used some of Talia's shampoo. After a few warming minutes under the spray to rinse her hair she dried off, wincing as she encountered various aches and pains, the most painful a large welt on her ribcage, courtesy of a male shoe. Swathed in towels, she slumped down suddenly on the edge of the elegant bath. What a day! She brightened suddenly as she rubbed at her hair. Now she'd helped save his mother from kidnap, maybe Alexei Drakos would give her an interview by way of thanks. And maybe the moon would turn blue tonight!

Eleanor ran one of his combs through her hair, eyed her reflection without pleasure and reached for the hooded white bathrobe on the door. She replaced her watch and bracelet and opened the door in answer to a quiet knock.

Talia came in, wrapped in a long navy bathrobe, her wet hair tied back from her beautiful face. 'You feel better now, Eleanor?' she asked anxiously as she applied moisturiser.

'Lots better, thank you. How about you?'

Talia grimaced. 'I stripped off every stitch after contact with that man. I had a quick shower in Alex's bathroom and borrowed his bathrobe so, now I have washed away *eau de kidnapper,* I am fine.'

'Thank God for that,' said Eleanor fervently. 'What shall I do with my wet clothes?'

'Sofia will deal with them. She has brought food to the tower room, so come and eat something.'

Suddenly so tired she wanted nothing more than to crawl into the nearest bed and sleep, Eleanor followed Talia to a room with a panoramic sweep of windows and a tray with savoury steam rising from it on a low table in front of a huge leather sofa.

'Sofia's special lentil soup will get you warm,' said Talia. 'After all this drama, you need something nourishing.' She shuddered. 'I thought I was done for when that monster grabbed me, but you attacked him like an avenging fury.'

'He made me so angry,' agreed Eleanor, and took the bowl Talia handed to her. 'Something exploded inside me when the brute snatched you.' She managed a smile. 'But you were pretty ferocious yourself. Between the two of us, the man must have wondered what hit him.'

'I wrenched my shoe off in the struggle and stabbed at his face with the stiletto heel.' Talia laughed unsteadily. 'What an adventure!' She turned as Alexei, now in dry clothes, came into the room with Stefan. 'Did he tell you anything?'

'Nothing useful,' Alex thrust his fingers through damp curls. 'He was insane with fear, certain I intended to kill him for hurting my mother. But eventually he confessed that he was paid to seize the *kyria* and take her to the man waiting at the jetty in a boat. The "dog" who left him to my mercy without paying him.'

'And just who *was* the man in the boat?'

'A stranger he met on Karpyros today who offered him money to do a job for him, if he can be believed. He swears he doesn't know any names, but after some persuasion he gave me his.' Alexei's look chilled Eleanor to the bone.

'He calls himself Spiro Baris, and he's now locked away for the night, moaning about injuries suffered during the struggle.' He shook his head in contempt. 'A struggle with two unarmed women!'

'Not unarmed, exactly. I had my shoe and Eleanor her useful bag,' his mother reminded him, eyes sparkling.

Stefan gave a smothered laugh, and Alexei thawed enough to grin.

'Which of you amazons gave him the black eye?'

'That would probably be me,' said Eleanor, contemplating grazed knuckles. 'I might have got him in the mouth too.'

'You did, *kyria*. He has a split lip,' Stefan said with relish.

'Do you have any other injuries, Eleanor?' asked Alexei.

He'd finally brought himself to use her name! She shook her head. 'A few bruises—the worst one in the ribs from where he kicked me off the jetty.'

'Oh my dear,' said Talia, appalled. 'You must be so sorry you ever set foot on Kyrkiros.'

Alex shot a hard look at Eleanor. 'Will you mention the incident in your article?'

Oh, for heaven's sake! She sucked in a calming breath and winced as her ribs protested. 'And broadcast your breach of security? Of course I won't.'

'Thank you.' He exchanged a glance with Stefan. 'Go down and have a word with Theo. His crew must make very sure no one's stayed behind after the last boat leaves the island.'

'Two of them are guarding the intruder, so I will help him with that,' Stefan said quickly. He wished them goodnight and hurried from the room.

'I'd better get down there too,' said Alexei. He eyed Eleanor with the air of a man with an irritating problem to solve. 'Tomorrow I'm taking my mother to Crete for her return flight to London. You must go with us—Eleanor. I'll try to get you on the same flight.'

'That's very kind of you, but I'm not due back to work for another week.' She smiled politely. 'I've paid out of my own pocket for a week's stay on Karpyros just to lie in the sun and do nothing now I've completed my assignment...' She trailed away at the frowns on both faces.

'It is not wise to do that, dear,' said Talia hastily, before her son could start laying down the law. 'You might get snatched off the beach there.'

Eleanor stared. 'Why? It wasn't me the kidnapper wanted.'

'We can't force you to leave, of course,' said Alexei curtly. 'Think about it while I go down to check with Theo.' He gave his mother a significant look. 'Persuade her, please.'

He strode off to the lift, leaving a tense silence behind him.

'Alex is just trying to do what's best for you,' said Talia soothingly. 'He feels responsible for what happened tonight and wants to keep you safe until you go home. If you go back to Karpyros, he can't do that.'

Eleanor frowned. 'But I'm not his responsibility. It's only natural he's anxious about you, but I'm a complete stranger.'

'Who was injured and half-drowned trying to save his mother from heaven knows what fate. Now show me this bruise.'

Eleanor drew the robe aside from her ribs.

Talia breathed in sharply. 'My dear girl—are you sure nothing is broken in there?'

'Quite sure. I cracked a rib playing hockey in school once, so I know what that feels like. This hurts a bit, but I'll mend.' Eleanor yawned suddenly. 'My wrestling match has left me a bit tired, though. You must be, too. And you must surely have a few bruises yourself!'

Talia nodded ruefully. 'But none as spectacular as yours; the only medication I need is hot tea. I keep a tray in my bedroom, so drink some with me after I see to your hand. I need a talk with Alex before I can think of sleeping.'

'What will he do with the intruder?'

'Call the police here tomorrow to deal with him, I imagine.'

There was something infinitely soothing after all the drama to sit in a comfortable blue velvet chair in Talia's white-painted bedroom, drinking tea from a fine china cup.

'You are quite a girl, Eleanor Markham.' Talia laughed at Eleanor's startled look. 'I mean it. You were very brave tonight.'

'It was pure gut instinct rather than bravery.' Eleanor's eyes flashed angrily. 'I was so furious with the man I wanted to kill him, but in the end the wretch tried to drown me instead.'

'I was in despair until Alex brought you to the surface,' said Talia with a shudder. 'My son was most impressed with you.'

'Only because I attacked the man who tried to kidnap his mother,' Eleanor said flatly. 'This afternoon he was rather less pleasant when he threatened to sue the paper I work for.'

Talia sighed. 'Try to forgive him for that. He is over-protective where I'm concerned. His hostility to the press began when he looked me up online on the computer his father gave him. My ex-husband is a powerful man, but even he failed to stop the speculation about our divorce. Unfortunately, that is the part Alex remembers.' Talia sighed and fixed Eleanor with her famous violet eyes. 'Since then he has further cause to hate the press. You must have researched us before you came. What did you discover?'

'Not that much, except that an ex-girlfriend of your son's sold a colourful story about him to a gossip-column reporter.'

Talia's eyes lit with a tigerish gleam. 'Christina Mavros is a liar, also a fool. She swore she would blacken Alexei's name if he didn't marry her, so he followed your famous Wellington's example and told her to publish and be damned.' She hesitated. 'Did you learn anything about me?'

Eleanor nodded. 'I read that you divorced Milo Drakos—"before the ink was dry on your marriage license", to quote a popular tabloid of the time.'

Talia wrinkled her nose. 'A little exaggerated, but not far out. You must surely want to know why?'

'Of course I do. I'm only human, Ms Kazan.'

'Please—I am Talia!'

Eleanor smiled ruefully. 'I'm wary of appearing familiar. But, just so there's no misunderstanding, none of this will appear in my article. You have my word on it.'

Talia smiled. 'I know that. And I must talk to you about this tonight because Alex is going to rush me away tomorrow and I will not have another chance.'

'For what, exactly?'

'To make a suggestion. If you do not wish to go home yet, why not stay on Kyrkiros until your flight? You will be safe here.'

Eleanor went cold at the mere thought. 'I couldn't possibly.'

'Why not? Once Alex has seen me off at the airport, he can get the ferry back here. I shall insist that he takes a holiday.'

'Even if he agrees, he won't want me around.'

'My son needs to relax, Eleanor, and also needs some intelligent feminine company to relax with. He would never admit it, but his constant aim in life is to achieve bigger and better things than his father.' Talia smiled sadly. 'If you did some research on Milo Drakos, you know that is not easy. It worries me that my son leaves no room in his life for normal relationships. With his looks and money, there have always been women available to him as playmates, but since the affair with Christina Mavros he is wary.' She sighed. 'I so much want him to enjoy the companionship of an intelligent woman. What can I do to persuade you to stay here for a few days and provide him with that?'

Eleanor's first instinct was to assure Talia nothing would persuade her, short of locking her in the Kastro dungeons. But then she had a better idea. 'If you get me an exclusive interview with your son, I will stay for a day or so. My boss is so desperate for his scoop he even ordered me to wear something sexy to persuade your son to talk to me.'

'So you were not really here for the festival at all!'

'Oh yes, *I* was, to round off my series. But Ross McLean is panting for an in-depth interview with the entrepreneur who never talks to reporters. Your son's warning killed all hope of that.' Eleanor looked Talia in the eye. 'But I swear that securing a scoop wasn't my motive for beating off the kidnapper. I just couldn't bear the thought of the man laying hands on someone like you.'

'Someone like me?'

Someone so charming and delicate that the thought of some bruiser manhandling her had sent Eleanor into battle without a second thought. 'Someone I liked so much,' she said, flushing again.

'The feeling is mutual, Eleanor, as I have already made clear.' Talia winced at the sound of raised voices outside. 'What now?'

Alex appeared in the doorway, his face like thunder. 'I apologise for disturbing you, Mother, but we have another intruder. He insists on speaking with you before he leaves.' He turned to the man behind him. 'In deference to our guest, please speak English.'

Talia's eyes widened as Milo Drakos, a commanding figure in a pale linen suit, strode into the room. He bowed to both women and lifted Talia's hand and kissed it, his eyes locked with hers. 'Forgive my intrusion. I was watching when you left the terrace and saw Alexei race after you with some of his men. I could not leave until I knew all was well with you,' he told her, in a voice exactly like his son's.

A delicate flush rose in Talia's face as she freed her hand. 'This is a surprise, Milo. What are you doing here?'

'It is our son's birthday, is it not?'

Alex made a hostile move, but at a look from his mother he backed off.

'A card would have done, Milo,' she observed, in a tone so sweet and cold it sent shivers down Eleanor's spine.

He surveyed her bleakly. 'Instead I came to mingle with the crowds, hoping to give my wishes myself. To my surprise, I was granted the unexpected privilege of seeing you here, Talia, and so I stayed, even knowing I risked instant ejection from my son's island if he saw me.'

'Of course I saw you,' grated Alex. 'But throwing you off Kyrkiros would have attracted unwelcome attention to my mother.'

Eleanor got to her feet hastily. 'If you'll excuse me, I'll say goodnight.'

'Goodnight, my dear.' Talia smiled at her son. 'Escort Eleanor to your room, please, Alexei *mou*.'

In silence so thick it seemed to drain the oxygen from the air, Alex led Eleanor along the hall to his own bedroom, his reluctance to leave his parents alone together coming off him like gamma rays.

'I hope you'll be comfortable in here,' he said stiffly as

he ushered her into a starkly masculine bedroom so unlike Talia's it could have been in a different building.

'I'm sorry to turn you out of your room,' she said, equally stiff.

He shrugged. 'In the circumstances, the least I can do. But I must collect some belongings before I leave you to the rest you must be desperate for by now.' He looked back along the hall, his jaw clenched. 'I apologise. I should have introduced you back there.'

'I recognised your father from his photograph.'

'Of course you did. You're a reporter.'

'Yes. I am.' Eleanor sighed wearily. 'And, before you ask, I won't mention Milo Drakis in my article either.'

'Thank you.' To her surprise, Alex actually smiled. 'Keeping the lid on all this drama must be hellish frustrating for you.'

'True. But to avoid any hurt to your mother I'll make do with a colourful account of the festival and say nothing about the rest.'

'Even though someone tried to drown you?' For the first time his eyes held a touch of warmth. 'I hope this paper you work for pays you well. You earned danger money today.'

Her lips twitched. 'According to my editor, I get money for old rope. He calls this kind of assignment a paid holiday.'

'Not quite the way it went down today!' He crossed to a wardrobe and looked over his shoulder. 'Help yourself to a T-shirt, or whatever, to sleep in.'

The intimacy of the situation put Eleanor on edge as Alex went into the bathroom.

'Tomorrow night,' he said when he emerged, 'You can sleep in my mother's room.'

She stared at him in surprise. 'I thought you were hustling me back to the UK tomorrow.'

He shrugged irritably. 'I was, but while you were getting

cleaned up earlier my mother pointed out that you should be allowed to enjoy the rest of your holiday as planned. I can't guarantee your safety on Karpyros, but I can if you stay on here. You'd have Sofia to look after you and give you meals, and Theo Lazarides for security. You can have the run of the place, other than my office, and if you find the Kastro too intimidating to sleep in alone I can ask Sofia to move up here until you leave.'

'Why are you doing this?' she asked, astonished.

A flash of respect lit the dark eyes. 'I owe you, Ms Markham. You risked your own safety, even your life, to help my mother today. I pride myself on paying my debts. Or do you have a different reward in mind?'

She nodded. 'Actually, I do, but I'll let your mother fill you in on that. Right now, I'm so tired I can hardly keep my eyes open.'

He hesitated, and then surprised her by shaking her hand briefly. 'Thank you again, Eleanor Markham. Goodnight.'

'Goodnight.' She watched the door close behind him, wishing she could be a fly on the wall when he re-joined his parents.

Instead of doing so immediately, Alexei Drakos went into the tower room to stare out at the night sky, his mind more occupied with Eleanor than his parents who, much as he hated to admit it, were probably both pleased to be left alone together for a while. Besides, they were not his immediate problem—unlike the woman occupying his bedroom tonight.

He shook his head impatiently. He'd obviously gone too long without the pleasure of a woman to warm his bed. Since the degrading business with Christina, he'd avoided all women, which meant that part of Eleanor Markham's appeal was her appearance in his life at a time of sexual drought. But the bright eyes in that narrow face had caught his eye this afternoon, otherwise he wouldn't have offered his help. The discovery that she was a journalist had been like a punch to the ribs.

He winced. It was she who had taken that kind of blow tonight, in her fight to save his mother. No getting away from it, damn it. He owed her. He turned away abruptly, squaring his shoulders. Time to knock on his mother's bedroom door and politely request that his father leave. God, what a night!

CHAPTER THREE

ELEANOR woke next morning to a knock on the door, and for a moment stared blankly at her surroundings. She heaved herself up in Alexei Drakos' vast bed, wincing as her various bruises came to life.

Sofia backed in with a tray, smiling. '*Kalimera, kyria.*'

Eleanor returned the greeting, and asked after Talia.

'*Kyria* Talia has gone, but she left you this.' Sofia took a letter from her apron pocket. 'She told me to see you rest. Eat well,' she added as she went out.

Eleanor tore open the envelope quickly.

My Dear Eleanor,

I looked in on you earlier but you were so deeply asleep I did not disturb you. Our intruder is now on his way to police custody but my son insists on escorting me on the ferry to Crete to catch my plane. On the voyage I shall ask him to give you your interview. Enjoy your stay on Kyrkiros. Alex is returning there later, so make sure he gives you your reward for your bravery last night.

Please contact me at the address and telephone numbers above when you get back. In all the excitement, I forgot to ask for yours, and I would so much like to see you again, Eleanor.

With my grateful thanks,
Talia.

Eleanor folded the letter very thoughtfully and turned her attention to the tray. She was hungry, and not even the thought of Alexei Drakos returning to play hell about an interview spoiled her enjoyment of orange juice, rolls warm from the oven and all the coffee in the pot. When Sofia returned she escorted Eleanor to the immaculate guest bedroom, where Eleanor's clothes, including canvas deck shoes, were now dry and ready to wear.

Eleanor thanked the woman warmly, and asked when *kyrie* Alexei was returning.

Sofia looked puzzled. 'He is not returning here from Crete, *kyria.* But you are to stay as long as you wish.'

Eleanor washed her bitter disappointment away in the shower. So there would be no interview with Alexei Drakos after all. Get over it, she told herself irritably. Comfortable again in her own clothes—other than the canvas flats, which seemed to have shrunk a size after their dunking—she made for the lift and took it down to ground level. Voices led her along the hall to a vast kitchen where Sofia was drinking coffee with two other women.

'*Kalimera,*' Eleanor said in general greeting, and received warm smiles in response. She was introduced to buxom Irene and thin Chloe, both of whom, as far as she could make out, praised her for her bravery of the night before.

'You saved *kyria* Talia,' stated Sofia, and scowled venomously. 'The dog has gone with the police. Did he hurt you?'

Eleanor patted her ribs. 'His foot,' she explained, illustrating with a kick. 'When he pushed me in the water.'

'You could have died!' exclaimed Irene with drama.

Eleanor shook her head. '*Kyrie* Drakos saved me.' Not that it had been necessary. She could swim well enough. She smiled hopefully. 'Could someone take me over to Karpyros now, please?' If Alexei Drakos wasn't coming back here was no point in hanging around. Besides, her belongings were back in the *taverna,* and she needed her laptop to get some work done.

'Yannis will take you after you eat,' Sofia said firmly. 'I will bring lunch to the tower room.'

Taking this as her cue, Eleanor left the kitchen and went up in the lift to spend a long time gazing at the spectacularly beautiful view of vine-clad slopes rising from cobalt-blue sea before she settled down to make notes about the day before. She sighed in frustration as she wrote, wishing she could spice the account up with details of the bungled kidnap. But even without it the article on Kyrkiros would be the most interesting one of the series, partly because of the photographs she'd taken of the bull dance and partly because the island was owned by Alexei Drakos. He could hardly object if *his* name was mentioned. It would have been common knowledge to everyone at the festival. She was hard at work when Sofia arrived with a tempting asparagus salad.

'Eat well, *kyria,*' said Sofia. 'When you have finished, Yannis will take you over to Karpyros and wait as long as you wish until you are ready to return.'

Eleanor explained, as well as she could with her limited vocabulary, that she was not returning, that she would stay at the *taverna* there until she flew home to England.

This news brought heated protests but in the end the woman left her to her meal and departed, making it plain she disapproved of the change of plan. The *kyrie* would not be pleased.

Pleasing Alexei Drakos was pretty low on Eleanor's list

of priorities now there was no chance of an interview. She finished her lunch, collected her bag and went down in the lift to the kitchen, where she delighted the women by asking to take photographs of them, both in the kitchen and outside in the sun with the Kastro as a backdrop. And, when Yannis came to transport the *kyria*, Eleanor took shots of the youth with his beaming mother.

'I shall send the photographs to you when I get home,' she promised, and followed Yannis down to the main jetty, feeling regret at leaving Kyrkiros, if only for failing to get her interview.

Eleanor was touched by her reception back at the *taverna*, where Takis and Petros informed her that until receiving her message they had been very anxious about her the night before. She explained as well as she could about her lack of mobile phone, and when she reached her small, blessedly private apartment she sat in the sun for a while on the veranda and looked out over the harbour towards Kyrkiros. So much had happened since leaving the room to go over to the island, it was amazing to realise that only a day had elapsed. Suddenly Eleanor thought of her camera. She went inside to check it, and heaved a sigh of relief to find it was still in full working order as she transferred the photographs of the festival to her laptop.

Her first shots of the Kastro and the village houses were good, but the true colour and animation of the day came through with her capture of the festival mood as laughing, chattering tourists toured the stalls for souvenirs. She lingered when she came to the shots she'd taken of Alexei and his mother. In one he was looking down at Talia with a tenderness which gave Eleanor a pang of emotion hard to identify as she went on with the rest of her slideshow. She crowed in jubilation over shots of the torch-lit stage and the bull dancers, who looked even more unreal on the screen, as though she'd flung open a window on the prehistoric past and captured the moment on film.

The money shots were those of the Minotaur when he first burst onto the stage, and Theseus with golden double-axe held aloft. There was also something very special about the sight of the Minotaur borne off the stage on the shoulders of his conquerors. Perhaps her efforts would console Ross McLean for her failure to get an interview with Alexei Drakos. And pigs might fly! Eleanor shrugged philosophically and settled down to write the article that would round off her series.

Due to his mother's inevitable refusal to make the journey in his helicopter, Alexei had been obliged to take the ferry to Crete to see her onto the plane, and spent most of the trip promising her he would take more time in future to relax and enjoy life. It was a wrench, as always, to part with her; and on the way back he occupied himself with calls to Athens and London. For the remainder of the trip he leaned against the rail, calling himself all kinds of fool for letting his mother cajole him into returning to Kyrkiros to babysit a journalist. And, not only a journalist, but one he had fleetingly suspected of involvement in his mother's kidnap. And because Talia rarely asked anything of him—not even more of his company, which he well knew she wanted most of all—he would do as she wanted. It would do him good, he was assured, to get away from it all for a while, in the company of an intelligent, attractive woman who, she pointedly reminded him, he was indebted to for his mother's safety. All Eleanor wanted by way of appreciation was an in-depth interview, Talia had informed him, which had to be a refreshing change from the usual women in his life, who probably demanded very different rewards for their company at his dinner table and or bed...

Alex frowned, wondering exactly what Ms Markham meant by 'in-depth' for the interview. If she imagined he would lay his soul bare, she was mistaken. Only a fool would do that with anyone, least of all a journalist—even one as appealing as Eleanor. He might be many things, and not all of them admirable, but a fool wasn't one of them. Christina Mavros' malicious spin on their brief affair had been merely a fleeting embarrassment. His hostility towards reporters had begun long before then. From the day he'd found the online accounts of his parents' divorce, the press had been irrevocably linked in his mind with the shattering discovery that his father, his hero, had hurt his mother badly enough to make her divorce him. The hero had crashed from his pedestal and from that day on Milo Drakos' efforts to maintain a normal relationship with his son had met with little success.

When Alex had questioned his mother about the reasons for the divorce, he was told it was something private between her and his father. Talia had refused to say another word, but his grandfather, Cyrus Kazan, had been more forthcoming. If Alex was old enough to ask the question, he was old enough to cope with the answer, had been his grandfather's justification for telling the boy that Milo, though madly in love with his wife, was so insanely jealous he had refused to believe that the child was actually his.

'The problem,' Talia had explained years later when Alex demanded the truth, 'Was the inconvenient fact that I grew large very early on in the pregnancy, which aroused Milo's suspicions. When you were born exactly ten months from our wedding day, Milo was desperately repentant and begged my forgiveness. I'll spare you the details, but it was a long, difficult labour and, because I was exhausted and at the mercy of my hormones, and so furious and heartbroken at his lack of trust, I refused to listen to him. My father, of course, had been ready to kill Milo, but my mother persuaded him to calm down. She pointed out that the best revenge would be to collect Milo's wife and son from the hospital to drive them to the Kazan family home, which would then be barred against him.'

Alex's face was grim as he watched the water streaming past. In the clash between his father and mother it had been a classic case of Greek meeting Greek, which probably explained Talia's vengeance. But, although she was a fiercely protective mother, she was also a practical one determined for the best for her son. Because Milo could provide the best, she had given him the right to have the child baptised Alexei Drakos, rather than Kazan, her original intention.

Milo had also demanded the right to provide for his son's expensive education, with the stipulation that Alex made regular visits to him in Athens and his holiday home on Corfu. When the boy was young these were experiences eagerly anticipated by both father and son. After the shock of his grandfather's revelations, teenage Alex still kept to the agreed visits to his father because his mother was adamant that he should, but he spent most of his time there either swimming in the pool in Corfu, or in Athens glued to the latest thing in computers Milo had bought his son in an effort to win the hostile boy's approval.

Thus began Alex's early passion for technology, which in time led to his development of innovative software which made him a fortune. He had still been at the famous British school his father had insisted on mainly, Alex knew, to prevent him from becoming a 'mother's boy' as Milo feared would happen if his son was left to grow up with only female supervision once old Cyrus died. But Alexei had a parting gift ready for his father during their final holiday together. Due to a stomach bug he left Corfu after only a few days, and at the airport handed Milo a cheque which covered the full amount expended on his education over the years. 'Now I owe you nothing,' he told his father, and left Milo standing stricken as his son boarded the plane. These days Alex felt more regret than satisfaction at the memory, and quickly shut it out by contacting Theo Lazarides to say he was about to dock.

Eleanor was so deeply immersed in her article she almost jumped out of her skin when someone hammered on her door. She flung it open and stared in shock into the dark and angry eyes of Alexei Drakos.

'What the hell are you doing here?' he demanded, his accent more pronounced than usual.

'I might ask the same of you,' she retorted. 'You frightened the life out of me.'

'I damn well hope I did. You threw open the door without even checking to see who it was. After what happened last night are you mad, woman?' He glared at her. 'I rang Theo Lazarides when I was on the ferry and he said you'd gone. Why the devil didn't you stay on Kyrkiros as arranged?'

'Once the intruder was in custody it was unnecessary.' Eleanor's chin lifted. 'In any case, why are *you* here? Sofia told me you weren't coming back to Kyrkiros.'

He shrugged impatiently. 'That was the original plan before all the melodrama yesterday. But after sorting everything with the police, and the rush to get my mother over to the ferry on time this morning, I forgot to tell Sofia I was returning to the island for a while after all. Look,' he added more reasonably, 'Must we discuss this outside? Let me in.'

Eleanor shook her head. 'I think not.'

He made a visible effort to control his temper. '*Why* not?'

Her chin lifted. 'Because you're angry with me.'

Alexei closed his eyes for a moment, as though praying for patience. When he opened them again he stepped back a fraction and raised his hands. 'Ms Markham—Eleanor—I come in peace. I have no intention of harming you in any way. I'm here to take you back to Kyrkiros to make sure you come to no further harm than you've already suffered. There I can keep you safe. Here it is impossible. My mother would never forgive me if anything happened to you that I could have prevented.'

Eleanor frowned, perplexed. 'But I don't need to be kept safe now the kidnapper's locked up.'

'The man who hired him is still out there.' His mouth tightened.

'Look, Mr Drakos...'

He raised a mocking eyebrow. 'It's a bit late for formality!'

She shrugged. 'Alexei, then.'

'Alex.'

'I have a much simpler solution to the problem—Alex.'

'Which is?'

'I forget the holiday and catch the first possible flight home.'

Alex gave her an unsettling smile. 'But if you do that you'll go without your reward. My mother told me—in great detail—what you want, and persuaded me to agree. So to achieve your ambition, Eleanor Markham, you must stay on for a while.'

Her heart leapt. He really meant to give her an interview? She moved back at the sound of people approaching the other apartments. 'You'd better come in.'

'Thank you.' Alex stepped inside, an eyebrow raised as she closed the door. 'Why the change of heart?'

'The possibility of an interview was worth the risk,' she said bluntly.

'You're not at risk from me, Eleanor.'

'Good to know.' She waved him to the couch. 'Do sit down.'

'No time for that. I want you to come with me right now. I'll sort Takis out.'

'Certainly not. *If* I decide to come, I'll do that myself.' Eleanor gave him an assessing look as she considered the pros and cons of a stay on Kyrkiros. 'You would really give me an interview?'

'With certain subjects off-limits, yes.' He smiled cynically. 'Your editor would be pleased.'

'Ecstatic,' she agreed, resigned. 'But I still can't see why I have to stay on Kyrkiros to do it. Why would anyone bother about me now your mother's gone home?'

'You were seen on the island, sharing my table in company with her. You are therefore perceived as important to me.' Alex's eyes hardened. 'From a ransom angle the attempt on my mother failed, so you're the next best thing.' He thrust a hand through his hair. 'Besides, I have a gut feeling that you're in danger. Laugh if you want, but I've been subject to feelings like this at times all my life. I've learned the hard way not to ignore them.'

'Premonitions, you mean?'

'Not exactly. The nearest explanation I can give is the electricity in the air before a storm breaks. And, though the weather's set fair, I'm feeling it on the back of my neck right now. So for God's sake pack your bags and let's get out of here.'

The promise of an interview decided Eleanor. She saved her work on the laptop, stuffed her notebook and camera into her tote bag and went up the ladder at top speed to pack the rest of her belongings.

'I must take the key to Takis,' she told Alex as she handed the bags down to him.

'The ferry to Crete is about to leave. Tell him you've

changed your mind and you're catching it. I moored my boat well out of sight of the *taverna* this morning when I brought my mother over, so with luck we can get away unseen.'

The enormity of what she was doing suddenly struck Eleanor full force. 'I must be mad! My phone is broken, and I'm taking off with a virtual stranger without telling anyone where I'm going. I could disappear off the face of the earth with no one the wiser.'

Alex gritted his teeth. 'I can tell you write for a living! Plan B, then. I'll get Takis over here so that you can tell him where you're going and I'll swear him to silence to keep you safe. I'll speak slowly so you understand me. Deal?'

She nodded reluctantly. 'Deal.'

'Good. Lock the door behind me and stay inside until I come back.'

Eleanor waited, her belongings at her feet, not sure whether she was setting out on an adventure or making the worst mistake of her life. But it was worth the risk to get the interview. And hopefully Alex would see that she got to Crete to catch her plane home afterwards. Any other journalist would be jumping for joy, and professionally she was. But on a personal level she had serious reservations about spending time with a hostile man who was only suffering her company to ensure her safety—and even then only because his mother had used emotional blackmail to get him to agree.

Alex returned quickly with Takis and ushered the *taverna* owner into the room. 'Right then, Eleanor. Muster your best Greek and explain to him yourself.'

Eleanor felt awkward as she told Takis she was leaving with *kyrie* Drakos to stay on his island. But when Alex explained the kidnap threat to him, slowly and clearly so she could understand, the man's kindly face darkened and he swore that they could trust him to say nothing. He advised them to go down to the boat via the little-used path beyond Eleanor's apartment, and thus avoid passing any curious eyes at the *taverna*s along the harbour.

There was no lighting on the path. It was both narrow and steep, but Alex kept up a punishing pace in silence on the way down to the harbour. When Eleanor, gasping for breath, was finally sitting amongst her belongings in the stern of a sleek boat, the engine noise was too loud to ask questions. She felt a surge of alarm when she found Alex was taking a much longer route than her trip the day before but eventually calmed down, embarrassed, when she realised he'd merely made a wide detour around the island to a mooring behind the Kastro. When a man appeared from the quayside buildings to secure the boat, Alex jumped up onto the dimly lit jetty and leaned down to take Eleanor's luggage, before helping her out.

'This is my private dock, and this is Theo Lazarides, who takes care of security here. Ms Markham will be staying here for a few days, Theo.'

'Welcome back, Ms Markham,' he said politely.

She smiled. '*Efcharisto, kyrie* Lazarides.'

Alex picked up the luggage and Eleanor took charge of her tote bag and laptop. 'Let's get inside.' He looked at Theo. 'Has everyone been warned?'

'Yes, *kyrie*.'

With a brisk nod Alex shifted both bags to one hand, and took hold of Eleanor's arm with the other. 'Careful, it's a rough surface along here and there are no lights. I keep it that way on purpose.'

'To repel intruders?'

'More or less, though until now we've never had any. The man you had the bad luck to run into last night is the first since I took the place over. But he was just someone's tool, so vigilance is now doubly necessary. Careful,' he added as she stumbled.

Infected with Alex's urgency, Eleanor felt safe only when they came in range of the lights from the Kastro and entered the old citadel from the back via a passageway with several more doors opening off it. Alex dumped the bags and locked the outer door behind them, then took her to Sofia in the kitchen.

The woman smiled warmly as she welcomed Eleanor back. 'I will take you to your room.'

'I'll do that, Sofia,' said Alex quickly, and added a lot more that Eleanor couldn't understand.

'What were you telling her?' she demanded as they went up in the lift.

'Merely that we would both need time for baths before we eat.' Alex gave her a sardonic smile as the doors opened. 'Was that imagination of yours at work again, cooking up something sinister?'

'No.' Eleanor shrugged. 'I just get frustrated when I don't understand what's going on, so make allowances, please.'

'I could give you lessons,' he offered, surprising her.

'I won't be here long enough for that. But thank you,' she added, and smiled politely as she went into the bedroom ahead of him. 'In fact, thank you for a lot more than that. I'm very conscious that I'm keeping you from returning to Athens.'

Alex put her bags down on the chaise at the foot of the bed and turned to look at her very directly. 'I can spare a few days. Stefan is already back there, and I can keep in contact with him and everyone else in the world I need to from my office right here in the *Kastro*.'

'You like to be in control,' said Eleanor, making mental notes. 'I did some research on you before I came.'

'Of course you did,' he said, lips tightening. 'And what

did you learn, Eleanor? Colourful details about my private life?'

She looked at him very directly. 'You know perfectly well there aren't many.'

He looked sceptical. 'You must have found the account of my private life by one Christina Mavros!'

'Yes, but I dismissed that as sheer "woman scorned" invective. I also read about your parents' divorce and that your mother was one of the most beautiful photographic models of her generation. But other than Miss Mavros's nasty little piece I found very little, except that you were a boy genius who achieved success very young.'

'Oh, I was clever enough,' he said harshly. 'But my first taste of British public school was hell—' He broke off with a curse. 'That's strictly off the record. I'll give you a formal interview tomorrow. In the meantime, have a rest or bath or whatever before dinner, which will be in an hour or so. I'll knock when it arrives.'

'Thank you.' Eleanor's eyes were thoughtful as she closed the door behind him. He need have no worries about her discretion. Having achieved the impossible dream of an interview with Alexei Drakos, there was no way she would risk having him set lawyers on her by writing anything he would object to seeing in print.

After a shower, Eleanor rolled her dress in a ball and stuffed it in one of her bags. Sophia's careful laundering had done wonders but she would never wear it again. She shrugged. Alex might be accustomed to women in designer finery at his dinner table, but tonight he would have to put up with a guest in jeans and one of a dwindling supply of clean T-shirts. On the bright side, a touch of make-up and a spritz of perfume was a definite improvement on the drowned-rat look of the night before, especially if she left her hair down. No curls, but there was a lot of it—shiny as chocolate sauce, according to one old flame—and her shoulder-skimming bob was still in good shape, courtesy of the haircut she had splashed out on before leaving home.

She sent a message to her parents via her laptop, but took a paperback out of her holdall instead of getting down to work. She climbed up on the pretty white bed to settle against the pillows, and sighed with pleasure at the thought of reading something that wasn't research. And, after days of hopping on and off ferries to go in search of various accommodations she'd organised herself, it was rather good to feel all responsibility had now been taken out of her hands until she flew home.

When she heard the expected knock, Eleanor put a bookmark in her novel and got off the bed to thrust her feet into yellow canvas espadrilles in place of the shrunken navy flats. 'Come in.'

Alex put his head round the door. 'I thought we'd have a drink before the meal.'

'Thank you.'

He smiled briefly as she joined him in the hall. 'I see we both had the same idea about dressing down tonight.'

'Not much choice for me. I packed only two dresses.'

'You look just as good in jeans,' he said casually, with a look which sent a jolt of unwelcome heat through her. 'We have no one here to impress, so after all the drama yesterday the priority tonight is comfort. I hope you *are* comfortable with me, Eleanor?'

She sat down in a corner of the sofa, thinking it over. 'I will be eventually.'

'But not yet?'

'I hardly know you,' she pointed out. 'We're strangers, after all.'

'Yet you were at ease with my mother right from the first.'

Eleanor smiled. 'She's a very special lady.'

'True.' His eyes softened. 'I was the envy of my friends when she came to prize days and cricket matches. She bought a house in Berkshire within easy travelling distance of the school when I first started there, and my grandfather flew over to accompany her as often as he could so I wouldn't feel out of it when other boys had fathers to cheer them on.' He eyed her quizzically. 'Your research didn't turn up mention of Cyrus Kazan?'

'No.' Eleanor held her breath, astonished that she was hearing personal details of Alexei Drakos' life.

'What would you like to drink?' he asked. 'A cocktail or some of this wine?'

'Wine, please,' she said, willing him to go on about his family.

'It comes from vineyards here on the island. Under my friend Dion Aristides' expert guiding hand, most of it is exported these days—part of my ongoing development programme for Kyrkiros.' Alex filled two glasses and sat down beside her.

'After the festival yesterday orders will be flooding in,' said Eleanor, tasting with pleasure. 'It's really excellent. But surely you would do even better if you opened the island to visitors more often?'

'It depends on what you mean by better. At present supply keeps pace with demand. Expansion would mean a bigger workforce we've no room to house. As things stand, the export of wine, olives and various crafts made by the islanders keeps the population in steady income throughout the year to augment the living from fishing. The quality of life is good here.'

'I'd love to explore your island,' she said hopefully.

He shook his head. 'In normal circumstances I would be

glad to show you, but after the drama of getting you here that would be counterproductive.'

'But surely the islanders will know I'm here?'

'Of course. But Theo has made sure no one talks to outsiders.' Alex eyed her narrowly. 'You don't look happy.'

Eleanor smiled ruefully. 'I hate to sound ungrateful, but after my travels I'd really looked forward to lazing around on a beach for a while before flying home.'

'Tomorrow I'll show you a place where you can sunbathe to your heart's content in complete privacy.' He got up as Sofia and Yannis arrived with a serving trolley, the former voluble with apologies she addressed to Alex at such speed Eleanor soon gave up trying to understand.

Alex held up a hand, laughing, and translated for Eleanor. 'Sofia thought I was leaving today and apologises for serving such simple food tonight. Tomorrow she will do better.'

Eleanor sniffed at the appetising aromas coming from the trolley and assured Sofia that it all smelled delicious.

'Eat well to recover strength,' said the woman, slowly and deliberately this time so Eleanor could understand.

'*Efcharisto.*' Eleanor included Yannis in her smile as the pair left.

'As you can probably tell,' said Alex, 'Sofia, like everyone else on the island, was impressed by your bravery last night. We are instructed to eat the cold dish first,' he added, and seated her at the table under the window before sitting opposite her.

Eleanor mentally raised an eyebrow as she transferred stuffed aubergines to their plates. Alexei obviously took it for granted she would serve him.

'I would have asked Sofia to stay to serve the meal,' he said, apparently reading her mind, 'But I thought you might prefer less formality.'

'You were right.' She tasted the aubergine's spicy tomato filling. 'This is very good. On my travels I've kept to fish and salad mostly.'

'You don't eat meat?'

'I do, but in some places goat was on the menu, and my courage failed!'

He laughed. 'You're safe tonight. I'm told the *entrée* features pork.'

Eleanor felt like pinching herself from time to time as she ate, to be sure she really was dining with Alexei Drakos. She'd been bowled over by his charisma from the first, so deeply attracted to him on sight his threats had been a bitter blow. But right now, instead of enduring her company politely as she'd expected, he was pulling out all the stops to put her at ease. And to be fair he was really something to look at now his hair, damp from a shower earlier on, had dried to a sun-streaked gold halo. Well, maybe not a halo. This man was no saint.

'Is a penny enough for your thoughts?' he said abruptly, and smiled slowly as a wave of scarlet flooded her face. 'Obviously not!'

'This is all so unreal,' she said, going for part of the truth. 'When I came to the island to report on the festival I never thought for a minute that you would speak to me at all, let alone agree to an interview.'

'You can thank my mother for that. She asked me to give you the reward you asked for, and because we are both indebted to you I will do so. But,' he stated with emphasis, 'I will personally check every word of the article when it's finished. And if and when I'm satisfied it must go off before you leave.'

'By all means. You can stand over me while I press Send!'

Alex raised a cynical eyebrow. 'And how do I know your

editor will print it exactly as it stands? He could apply his own spin and make something completely different out of it.'

'I'll give you his email address so you can hit him with the threats you made to me. Believe me; Ross McLean will do whatever you want to get his exclusive.' Eleanor took their plates to the trolley and returned with the hot *entrée* dishes. She set them on the table and handed Alex a pair of large serving spoons. 'There you go.'

'Ah! I obviously took your help for granted earlier.'

'Not a problem.' Eleanor smiled demurely. 'I'm grateful to you for the food I'm eating, whoever serves it.'

Alex shook his head in sorrow as he filled their plates. 'A beautiful woman is sharing a meal with me and feels only gratitude?'

'Not at all.' And wasn't that the truth. 'As I said before, I feel the unlikeliness of it too.'

He laughed. 'Nevertheless here we are, sharing a meal as men and women do everywhere. But in return for this supper you're so grateful for, *kyria* journalist, you must sing for it. Tell me more about Eleanor Markham.'

She eyed him challengingly. 'I will if you return the compliment.'

'I have promised to do so!'

'But that will be an interview with Aléxei Drakos, the public figure, with every word I write subject to your approval.' She smiled persuasively. 'I'd like to know more about the private man. Strictly off the record, of course.'

He gave her a hard look. 'No notebook or camera?'

She shook her head. 'Just my sworn oath to tell no one. Ever.'

Alex concentrated on slow-cooked pork of melting tenderness for a moment or two. 'I'm not in the habit of discussing my personal life with anyone, least of all a journalist.'

'Forget I'm a journalist. Just think of me as a woman,' Eleanor said promptly.

His eyes moved over her in deliberation which sent her pulse up a gear. 'Impossible to do otherwise,' he assured her. 'Very well, Eleanor Markham. You give me your life story and I'll respond with some of mine.'

'Some?'

'That's the deal.'

'Done.' She got up, serving spoons in hand. 'In that case, I'll help you to more of this delicious meal.'

When he threw back his head and laughed Eleanor's heart did a quick forward roll against her sore ribs. 'You're happy to wait on me now.'

'Absolutely.'

'Then I accept. And now you talk.' He filled their glasses and looked at her expectantly.

Eleanor topped up his plate and resumed her chair. 'There's not much to tell,' she began, wishing there were. 'My career began with a Saturday job on a local newspaper when I was a schoolgirl. I was offered a full-time job there later, but went to university instead. I graduated with a respectable English degree, worked hard to add qualifications in journalism and photography to go with it and gained experience with various newspapers before my present job.' She looked up to meet the intent dark eyes. 'That's it, really.'

'For a writer, there's very little human interest in your story, Eleanor. Where are the tales of wild student parties and the men in your life?' he demanded.

She sighed. 'In my past, regretfully.'

Alex eyed her thoughtfully as he drained his glass. 'All of them?'

'The ones from the wild student days, yes.'

'How about in the present?'

'As I told your mother, my job is hard on personal relationships. But I have good friends so the drawback doesn't bother me too much.' She pulled a face. 'Compared with your life mine sounds numbingly dull.'

'Not recently,' he reminded her, and picked up her hand to examine her bruised knuckles. 'It was anything but when that reprobate kicked you into the sea last night.'

Eleanor agreed with a shiver which had more to do with his touch than the incident. 'I haven't thanked you properly for rescuing me—though when you first grabbed me I thought it was the man, trying to drown me for real.'

'It was like trying to rescue an eel!' he agreed and eyed her quizzically. 'But did you really need rescuing?'

'No. I'm a fairly strong swimmer. Once I made it to the surface, I could have swum back to the jetty easily enough. Well, maybe not easily. The wretch hurt me quite a bit.'

'Which is why I dived in after you. When you'd just laid into my mother's kidnapper it was the least I could do.'

'And much appreciated,' said Eleanor and sat back. 'Your turn now.'

He leaned over to refill her glass. 'What do you want to know?'

'Anything you care to tell me. Perhaps I could just ask some questions? It's entirely up to you whether you answer them.'

'If you wish,' said Alex, resigned.

'Can we go back to the time when you started in prep school? Why was it such hell?'

He was silent for some time, wondering why it felt so easy to confide in her, when normally he refused to talk about himself to anyone at all other than his mother, and even then only rarely. 'To admit this is very bad for my image, but at first I missed my mother so much I buried my face in the pillow every night so no one heard me cry. I was a pretty average size at that age, and cursed with this hair. I could speak English fluently enough, due to tutors my father employed to prepare me for the new school, but I spoke it with an accent—as I still do. When the rugby season started, things looked up. In the front row of the pack in a scrum I learned a few tricks—not all of them in the rule book—which were a great help. I put on a burst of growth, grew taller very quickly, did well at other sports and life became bearable.'

'How old were you when you went away to school?'

'Too young,' Alex said without inflection.

Eleanor eyed him with compassion, picturing a little boy with golden curls crying at night for his mother. 'I didn't go away to school, at least not until I went to university, so by the time I flew the nest I was raring to go.'

'A much better arrangement.' He shrugged. 'But, hard though school was in the beginning, I made good friends there in time, including the master who opened up the world of technology to me.'

'I read that you made a fortune from it while you were still in school.'

Alex shrugged. 'I have two people to thank for that: my grandfather, who put up the money to back me on my venture, and my father.'

Eleanor stared at him in surprise.

'Milo Drakos bought me the latest and most expensive computer to play with every time I went to stay with him.' He smiled grimly. 'This only stopped when I refused to go there any more.'

'He gave up buying expensive bribes?'

'No. He became involved with a woman who hated me.' He shot her a look. 'Surely your research turned up that bit of information?'

'No, it didn't. Is your father still involved with her?'

Alex shook his head. 'The relationship was short-lived,

because the lady not only objected to my visits but demanded that he marry her and adopt her son from a former marriage; a huge mistake on her part.' The dark eyes hardened. 'She had no hope of it anyway. It annoys the hell out of me to admit it, but I'm sure Milo's still in love with my mother.'

Eleanor could well believe it. The electricity in the air had fairly crackled when Milo Drakos had walked into his ex-wife's bedroom the night before. 'May I ask how she feels about him?' she said carefully.

'I can't tell you. If I bring the subject up she refuses to discuss it. My beautiful mother may look sweet and malleable, but she has a will of iron, and pride to match.' He broke off at a knock on the door and smiled at Sofia as she came in to put a coffee tray on a table in front of the sofa.

'The meal was delicious,' Eleanor told her.

'*Efcharisto*,' said the woman, pleased, and began clearing the dinner table. 'Do you need anything else, *kyrie?*' she asked Alex.

He shook his head. 'Nothing more tonight.'

She wished them both good night and went out with the trolley.

'Yannis didn't come back with her,' said Eleanor. 'Does she live nearby?'

'Right here in the *Kastro*, in a ground floor apartment adjoining the kitchen.'

'She's a widow?'

Alex nodded soberly. 'When her husband died a year or so after I took over the island I offered her the job of housekeeper, with rooms in the *Kastro* for her and the boy.' He gestured towards the sofa. 'Let's move over there.' He smiled blandly. 'Perhaps you'd even pour my coffee.'

Eleanor grinned at him. 'My pleasure!'

Alex shot her a probing glance as they sat down. 'Do

you feel happier now you know that Sofia and Yannis sleep in the building?'

She stared at him in surprise. 'No. I wasn't unhappy before.'

'So you really do believe I mean you no harm.'

'It never occurred to me to think otherwise.' She paused. 'I assume Sofia is accustomed to catering for guests?'

Alex gave her a smile which transformed his face from merely handsome to off-the-charts breath-taking. 'If that's a way of asking whether I bring a lot of women here, the ladies I know are city dwellers who demand venues more sophisticated than a remote island lacking even a *taverna*. Besides, this place is my retreat. And, if you're worried about the proprieties, your deeds yesterday ensure that your reputation can survive a couple of nights alone here with me.' He reached for the coffee pot and refilled their cups. 'Tell me more about yourself and the life you lead.'

CHAPTER FOUR

ELEANOR shook her head. 'I'd much rather talk about Alexei Drakos.'

He raised a dark eyebrow. 'You had no trouble in talking about yourself to my mother.'

'That's different.'

'Because you liked her from the moment you met, whereas you're still not comfortable with me.'

Her eyes flashed. 'Do you blame me? It's not every day I meet a man who threatens me with a lawsuit!'

He shrugged impenitently. 'I will always do everything within my power to protect my mother. And at the time of my threat I'd only just met you. But since then I have compelling reasons to be grateful to you.'

'I see. So when will you give me the interview?'

'In the morning—early, if you wish.'

'I do.' And once she'd written the piece and Alexei had vetted it she would send it off to Ross McLean and then catch the first possible flight back home. Alex might be the most powerfully attractive man she was ever likely to meet, but she disliked the idea of being marooned here with no way of getting off his island until he agreed to take her to Karpyros to catch the ferry. As soon as he did she would leave whether she could get an earlier flight or not. She could spend the waiting time exploring Crete.

'What are you thinking about now?' he demanded. 'Nothing pleasant, by the look on that expressive face of yours.'

'On the contrary, I'm glad that you're willing to get on with the interview right away.' She smiled politely. 'The moment you approve it I'll send it off and get the ferry to Crete out of your way.'

He raised a dark eyebrow. 'This is rather different from the woman who insisted on a week's holiday. What's changed your mind?'

Her chin lifted. 'On Karpyros I could have left any time I wished. Here I can't.'

Alex frowned. 'You're not a prisoner, Eleanor. The precautions are purely for your own safety. I will take you over to Karpyros early in the morning if you want.' He paused. 'Of course, if you do that you won't get your interview.'

She nodded, resigned. 'Which leaves me with no choice.'

'Exactly.' He got to his feet and held out his hand. 'You're obviously tired. I'll see you to your room.'

She ignored the hand as she got up. 'Thank you. But I don't need an escort.'

'My intention,' he assured her, 'Was to leave you at your door, I swear.'

A wave of heat flooded her face. 'I didn't think otherwise,' she said stiffly, and to her embarrassment gave a sudden yawn.

The eyes that looked so dark under the crown of dark-gold hair glittered with mockery. 'I've offended you and embarrassed the hell out of you, and now I've bored you to death.'

'Absolutely not.' Eleanor smiled sweetly. 'I've been hanging on your every word—as I will tomorrow during the interview.'

'Is that all you can think about—?' He stopped short,

eyes narrowed in hostile speculation. 'Is *that* why you tried to rescue my mother? Was the blasted interview so vital you actually risked your life to make me agree to it?'

Eleanor glared at him, incensed. Fists clenched, she turned on her heel and made for the door but he was there before her to open it. She brushed past and hurried ahead of him along the hall to reach his mother's room in time to shut the door in his face.

'Open this door!' Alex called, equally furious, by the sound of him as he hammered on it.

She gave the paintwork a look vitriolic enough to strip it to the bare wood and went into the bathroom to shut out the pounding. It was a good thing Sofia lived out of earshot. She bit her lip, not sure that it was such a good thing after all. She hadn't thought of it before he brought the subject up, but the fact remained that she was alone up here with Alexei Drakos, who was now in a towering rage. She gritted her teeth. He wasn't the only one. She needed another shower to cool off before she could think of bed. She turned on the water and opened the bathroom door a crack. All was quiet. Alex had obviously stormed off to his room, or his office, or wherever.

Eleanor swathed a towel round her head to protect her hair, then stood under a lukewarm shower until she felt calmer. Later, in the camisole and boxers she wore to bed, she leaned back on the bed to read for a while, but soon gave up trying to concentrate. Strange. Alone in the little apartment over on Karpyros, she had felt perfectly safe, but here, locked away at the top of what was virtually a citadel, she felt anything but. Alexei Drakos' fault, damn him.

A quiet knock on the door brought her bolt upright. 'Who is it?'

'Who do you think? Open up, please.'

'Why?'

'I want to speak to you.'

With reluctance Eleanor slid off the bed and pulled on her dressing gown. She opened the door a crack and peered through it.

Alexei Drakos made no attempt to move nearer, but she tensed at the look in his eyes.

'You said you meant me no harm,' she said sharply.

'I don't. But I object to having doors shut in my face in my own home.'

'It was either that or get physically violent. As I did yesterday with the intruder,' she reminded him.

'Quite a temper you lost back there.'

'Do you blame me? You actually accused me of helping your mother just to get an interview!' Her eyes speared his. 'For the record, *kyrie* Drakos, my sole thought was getting her away from the man who snatched her. I was so furious I could have killed him with my bare hands.'

'You had a damned good try,' he agreed, his tone lighter. 'I suppose I must be grateful you slammed the door instead of attempting to murder *me*!' He moved nearer. 'I came to apologise. May I come in?'

With reluctance Eleanor opened the door wider and retreated to sit bolt upright on one of the blue velvet chairs where she'd felt so at ease with Talia Kazan.

Alex eyed her speculatively as he took the other chair. 'Do you feel better now?'

'I'm working on it.'

'I apologise for the crack about the interview.' He laid his hand on his heart. 'I'm sure your motives were of the purest when you went into battle for my mother.'

'Are you?'

'Am I what?'

'Sure.'

He crossed his long legs and sat back, eyeing her objectively. 'Now I've had time to think I am sure, yes. But consider it from my angle—you had only met my mother that day. It was hard to believe you'd put yourself at such risk for a stranger without *some* kind of ulterior motive.'

'I acted on basic gut instinct. Motives didn't come into it. Your mother needed help; I did my best to give it.'

Alex smiled wryly. 'Yet you're no amazon. Our man Spiro refused to believe a woman was responsible for his injuries.'

'He would have had a few more if he hadn't kicked me into the sea!'

'I think the worst part for him was the scorn from Theo Lazarides.' His lips twitched. 'He is deeply impressed by you, Eleanor.'

She shrugged. 'It's nice to know somebody respects me.'

'I do.' Alex leaned forward, hands clasped loosely between his knees. 'Even if the interview *was* part of your motive, I respect a woman willing to go to such lengths to gain her heart's desire.'

'I suppose I take that as an apology.' She smiled sweetly. 'I trust the door incident didn't dent your male hubris too much?'

'It was a new experience. Not one I cared for.' His eyes held hers as he got up. 'I apologise for hammering on the door.'

'For the second time today, if we're counting.'

'I must cure myself of the habit. Tomorrow I promise to be sweetness and light all day.' He smiled sardonically. 'At least I promise to try. Goodnight.'

'Goodnight.'

Alex went out and closed the door behind him. 'Now lock it,' he called as he left, and strode along the hall to his own room when what he really wanted was to go back to Eleanor and take her to bed. Having a door slammed on his face had fired up his libido to the point where he needed a cold shower. He shook his head, baffled. Eleanor appealed to him more than any woman he'd met in a long time, though for the life of him he couldn't say why. Her figure was boyish, and her temperament abrasive, but he wanted her. And since they were alone here, shut away from the world for a day or two, it would be only natural for a man and woman to take the best possible advantage of the situation.

Even with the door securely locked it was a long time before Eleanor went to sleep, and when she did she dreamed about monsters that chased her into the sea. It was a relief to wake to sunlight and the knowledge that today she could get the interview done and be free to go. Powerfully attractive though Alexei Drakos might be, the constant hint of danger about him kept her on edge all the time. Eleanor shrugged irritably and slipped out of bed to unlock the door, ready to admit Sofia with her breakfast, then washed, dressed in denim shorts and one of her dwindling supply of fresh T-shirts and secured her hair back in its pony-tail, ready to get to work.

When the expected knock sounded on her door, Eleanor opened it to find Alex outside, damp of hair and radiating vitality, as though he'd been up for hours.

'*Kalimera*, Eleanor Markham.'

'Good morning,' she said, surprised. 'I was expecting Sofia.'

'I asked her to serve breakfast in the tower room. Will you join me?'

'Thank you, but I don't eat much breakfast,' she warned as she followed him.

'A pity you couldn't have joined me for a swim first to give you an appetite, but in the circumstances it's not advisable. I can provide a pleasant place for the sunbathing you yearned for, but you must keep to a bath for your water fix.' He held out a chair at the table which was laid with hot rolls, fresh fruit and two steaming pots, one of which was tea, he informed her. 'My mother left some of her favourite brand for you.'

'How kind!' Eleanor was struck again by the fantasy aspect of the situation as she faced Alexei Drakos across a breakfast table with a backdrop of sunlit blue Aegean below. After their little altercation of the night before, she had expected him to be hostile; instead he was slaying her with that smile of his. 'It must be wonderful to live in a place like this.'

'I don't live here. Kyrkiros merely serves as an occasional escape-hatch from life in the real world.'

She smiled. 'Like a kind of holiday home, complete with castle and state-of-the-art office where you can keep tabs on your empire.'

'I do that wherever I am.'

'And Stefan keeps you in touch from Athens?'

'Stefan heads a team there, yes.' He watched her buttering a roll, his eyes amused. 'Shouldn't you be noting this down?'

Eleanor shook her head. 'I'll put my journalist's hat on later when we get down to business.' She picked up the coffee pot and filled his cup.

'Thank you,' he said in mock surprise. 'Are you softening me up to get at all my secrets?'

'Whatever works,' she said cheerfully.

'How long an interview do you want?'

'I'll take all the information you'll give me.'

'It won't be that much,' he warned. 'After you've finished, I'd like to show you something before you get down to work.'

Eleanor smiled hopefully. 'You're going to show me over the *Kastro*?'

He shook his head. 'It's still a work in progress down in the basement area. It was made safe when I first took over here, of course, before the living quarters were done. But I keep to local labour for the renovation work, with fishermen who transform into builders and stone masons in winter when wild winds and rough seas put a stop to fishing, so the progress is slow. Right now I'll show you my garden instead.'

After breakfast Alex led the way along the hall past the bedrooms and the lift, and on round a bend which brought them to the head of the spiral stone staircase ascending from below, with a further short flight leading up to what she thought must be an attic of some kind.

'I'll go first,' he said. 'But be careful, the steps are uneven in places.'

Intrigued, Eleanor kept close behind him. At the top Alex opened a door to let in a glare of sunlight and turned to help her up the last couple of steps.

'Welcome to my secret lair.'

Eleanor gazed in delight at a rooftop garden. Huge terracotta pots overflowing with greenery and flowering plants surrounded a central paved space furnished with chairs and tables shaded by parasols.

'How absolutely lovely.' She smiled as she noticed a screen suspended between two pillars. 'Surely you're not worried about privacy up here?'

Alex shook his head. 'When the *meltemi* blows at the end of summer the screen is very necessary.'

She laughed. 'I can relate. Cowering behind a windbreak on a windy beach was part of the deal on childhood holidays. How about you?'

'I spent my summer holidays at my father's house on Corfu.'

'I remember. You were too busy swimming and sailing and playing with your computer to need windbreaks as we ordinary mortals do.'

'Most ordinary mortals fly off to the sun for their holidays.'

'*Touché*,' she conceded and sat down on one of the reclining chairs. 'My parents were never keen on air travel, so my first holidays abroad were spent with college friends. The travelling was the big attraction in my present job.'

Alex drew up a chair beside her. 'Will your editor give you a promotion when you send him the article?'

She laughed. 'Highly unlikely.'

'I could make it a condition.'

'Absolutely not—thank you.'

'I can at least insist that your name is on the article.'

She thought about it. Her name would be above the travel series as usual, but the Alexei Drakos exclusive was so important to Ross he would want it under his own by-line.

Alex frowned. 'You don't want that either?'

'No, thank you. I don't.' She could just imagine Ross's reaction.

'As you wish. When do you want to start?'

'In half an hour? I'll get my things together.'

'No tape recorder!'

'No problem. Where shall we do this?'

'In my office. I'll show you.'

They went back down the steep stairs to the hall and on to the lift, which took them down a floor to his office. When he made no move to invite her inside, Eleanor smiled politely, told him she'd return in half an hour and went back up to the guest room.

Alex watched her go, already regretting he'd agreed to

this. He shrugged impatiently and reminded himself that Eleanor deserved her reward. But in return for the interview he had given no other journalist he deserved a reward too, of the kind that Ms Markham was supremely equipped to give him. He smiled as he checked the array of technology lining the room, had a brief conversation with Stefan and then placed a chair in front of the desk he'd had shipped from London. He transferred all paperwork to the drawers and sat back behind the desk to wait.

CHAPTER FIVE

ELEANOR took a minute or two to tidy up then packed her bag, which looked very much the worse for wear after its use as a weapon. She went down in the lift to tap on the office door, and when bidden to enter halted on the threshold, deeply impressed.

'What an amazing workplace,' she commented, and smiled at Alex as he stood up. 'I'm a bit early.'

'Can't wait to get to work?' He waved a hand at the chair in front of the desk and seated himself behind it. 'Let's make a start.'

Eleanor pulled the chair close, took the tools of her trade from her bag and looked across at the man enthroned in his massive leather chair. 'May I take a photograph?'

Alex nodded reluctantly. 'But just of me, please, not the room.'

She focused on his face and took two shots, then opened her notebook and sat with pencil poised.

Eleanor had not expected the interview to be easy, but getting Alexei to talk about his achievements was uphill work. There was to be no mention of anything personal, including his family. He was willing to discuss the company he'd founded in his teens because it had given him the means for expansion into the other ventures which had brought him global success. He gave her concise information about most of his interests, but on the subject of his philanthropy he was more guarded. His financial support was given to certain deserving causes only after careful research to make sure the funds went straight to those most in need, rather than into the pockets of administrators.

'May I mention the work here on Kyrkiros?' asked Eleanor.

'Certainly—good PR for the project.'

'What made you take on this particular island?'

'I had good reason to be grateful to the inhabitants.'

'May I ask why?'

Alex was silent for a moment then shrugged as though coming to a decision. 'You can stop there for a minute.'

Eleanor frowned. 'Can't you explain why you're grateful to them?'

He fixed her with a dark, warning eye. 'I can, but only in confidence. Since I brought the subject up, I suppose it's only fair to explain, but solely on the strict understanding that you write about the work being done here and not my personal reasons for developing Kyrkiros.'

She put her pencil down and closed the notebook, then sat back. 'Off the record then.'

Alex was silent for a while as though picking and choosing how much information to give her, then began describing a holiday taken after graduation—a stay in the home of a university friend on Crete.

'Sailing in the Aegean was a great way to de-stress after the hard graft of finals. I spent most of that last fortnight with Ari in the family dinghy,' Alex told her. 'But one day we went farther than usual and when a storm blew up it swept us God knows how far off-course. We both fought hard to keep her afloat but when the dinghy finally capsized the boom caught Ari's head as we went overboard. I managed to hook an arm in Ari's lifejacket and held on for what felt like eternity until we were rescued.' He smiled grimly. 'Poseidon must have been watching over us.'

Eleanor gazed at him in sudden comprehension. 'You were rescued by people here on Kyrkiros?'

'*I* was, yes. I passed out at some point, so I was pretty much out of it for a while. When I finally woke up my broken arm was in a cast, I had the mother of all headaches, every bone in my body was throbbing in sympathy and I was lying on a bed here in the *Kastro*, in what is now the kitchen. I woke with total recall, wild with anxiety about Ari.' Alex smiled grimly. 'Sofia's husband had hauled me into his boat, but Ari had been detached from me by Dion Aristides and taken to his place on nearby Naros.'

'Wouldn't it have been easier to take care of you both in the same place?'

'Dion ordered the others to wait to find out exactly who we were and whether we were married.'

'*Married*?'

Alex smiled. 'My fellow castaway was Arianna Marinos. She was cared for by Dion's female servants, while Sophia and Georg looked after me. Anxious parents soon arrived on the scene, but it was some time before Ari was well enough to travel. Her mother stayed with her at Dion's place and after a visit to check on her I left with my parents. Ari and I both recovered, I got on with my life and eventually attended her wedding on Crete,' he said wryly. 'One look at Dion's handsome face when she finally woke up, and Ari had no eyes for anyone else, including me.'

Wow, thought Eleanor. 'Does she live there with him now?'

'When they're there on the island, yes. Dion does great things with the vineyards there, and after I took over here he agreed to extend his expertise to our Kyrkiros vines. He also oversees those on part of the estate on Crete that

Arianna inherited from her father, the place where I'd holidayed with her before she deserted me for another man.' He smiled crookedly. 'It was bad news for this famous hubris of mine. I broke my arm in the process of saving her life, while she broke my heart.'

'It obviously mended,' said Eleanor briskly, secretly sympathetic. 'Was she here for the festival?'

He shook his head. 'Not this year. She's expecting their second child soon, and Dion persuaded her to stay home on Naros.'

Alex's face betrayed no hint of emotion at the mention of children, but something in his tone touched a chord in Eleanor. Or maybe she was attributing sensitivity where he merely felt indifference. 'So what happened next?'

He told her he'd eventually liaised with the newly-wed couple as to the best way to show appreciation for the kindness shown to him by the people of Kyrkiros. At first Dion had been hostile, not only jealous of Alexei Drakos' past relationship with his wife, but suspicious of the young entrepreneur's motives where Kyrkiros was concerned. Alex had made it very clear that his sole aim was to provide steady income for the islanders, show them how to market their produce and thus free them from the financial vagaries that threaten a lifestyle based on fishing. Dion was quick to grasp the advantages of a wider market for the Kyrkiros olives and wine. The grapes grown on the island produced wine with a unique bouquet and flavour, and once marketed with the products of the Aristides and Marinos vineyards the new venture took off at speed after the festival was established as a PR exercise.

Alex had resolved to restore the *Kastro* the first time he returned to Kyrkiros with his mother to express his thanks to the inhabitants. When he eventually took over the island, Talia expressed her personal gratitude by contributing part of the cost of creating an apartment in the *Kastro* for her son's special retreat, with as much work as possible given to the islanders on restoration of the main building.

'God knows when it will ever be finished,' said Alex. 'But the end result is less important than the security the work gives to the people here. Besides,' he added, 'I quite like the old place the way it is.'

'Whose idea was the bull dance?' asked Eleanor.

'Arianna's. The three of us talked over the best way to attract attention and, Cretan that she is, she suggested putting on some viable version of the bull dance depicted at Knossos. She did the research, devised the dance with a professional choreographer and with his help eventually found a team of dancers acrobatic enough to perform it. Stefan helped with the PR and advertising, and the very first performance was such a success we've never looked back. Though this year's dancers surpassed all the others,' he added. 'You were impressed?'

'An experience I'll never forget,' she assured him. She opened her laptop, pressed a few keys and turned the screen towards him. 'See for yourself.'

Alex studied them then looked up at her with respect. 'These are good—very good. You've captured the antiquity of the scene.' His eyes gleamed as he scrolled to the Minotaur's entrance. 'Zeus! If I didn't know he was flesh and blood I could swear he was the monster he's portraying.' He frowned. 'Theseus is far too pretty, but you were clever to catch him with his axe poised for the kill.' He pushed the laptop back to her. 'So, Eleanor Markham, do you have enough information for this article you've worked so hard to achieve?'

'I think so.' She gathered her belongings together. 'I'll go back to my room now and work on it. I'll give you the draft as soon as it's ready.'

'I thought you wanted to laze in the sun for a while.'

'Work before pleasure,' she said absently, her mind already busy. 'Where will you be when I finish?'

'Here probably, or I might go down and lift some weights for a while.' He took a mobile phone from a drawer and handed it over as he saw her to the door. 'I should have given you this before.'

'I sent emails to my parents instead, but I'm glad of the phone.' She smiled politely. 'Thank you.'

'My number's keyed in on it. If I'm not here, just ring me when you want me. Or I'll ring when I want *you*.'

Something in his tone sent the now-familiar streak of heat through Eleanor as she hurried back to her room, deeply conscious that he was watching her all the way. Shorts had been a risky choice. On the other hand her legs were good. Her *derrière* wasn't bad, either and she was female—and human—enough to be glad of it in the circumstances. She closed the bedroom door behind her and settled down to concentrate on the task in hand as she plugged in her laptop to type up her notes. With only the official facts Alexei Drakos had given her, it would be no easy task to deliver the earth-shaking interview Ross McLean was salivating for, but at least she could describe this beautiful island and give a plug to the work going on here. To add colour she could weave in a little about the owner's aspirations. She sighed. If she could write about the sailing accident and Alex's personal reasons for taking over Kyrkiros, she'd have Ross dancing on his desk.

When she'd finished Eleanor worked up her notes into a first draft. She broke off for a tidying up session in the bathroom and then went back to the laptop. It was just a draft, she reminded herself irritably as she edited it. At last she saved her work, unplugged the laptop and took it down to the office. She knocked and put her head round the door, but the room was empty. She ground her teeth. Now she'd stiffened her resolve enough to let him read the damned article, the man was missing. She left the laptop on the desk and turned to run smack into a hard male body.

Alex seized her by the waist to steady her. 'Careful! Where are you going?'

'To look for you.' The contact sent Eleanor's pulse so high into overdrive she said the first thing that came into her head as she saw his hair. 'You've been swimming again?'

He shook his head as he let her go. 'I've been working out and had a shower afterwards. I made one of the ground floor rooms into a gym. You're welcome to use it.'

She shook her head, smiling ruefully as she backed away. 'Not really my thing, thank you. I just do a bit of Pilates now and then to keep in shape.'

The dark eyes moved over her in a slow head-to-toe scrutiny as she sat down at the desk. 'It works!'

Eleanor firmly ignored the sizzle of heat his comment sent streaking through her and booted up the laptop. She scrolled to the draft of the article and pushed the machine across the desk to him. 'I kept to the letter of the law with your restrictions so it won't take long to read.'

He raised an eyebrow. 'Do I detect a note of censure, Eleanor? What additions would you make to it if I gave you free rein?'

'Personally, I would put in the human interest of how you were rescued by the people of Kyrkiros and that your investment in their welfare is your way of thanking them.'

Alex shook his head with finality. 'That would mean involving others who value their privacy.' He drew the laptop nearer. 'While I read it, go up and sit in the sun in the roof garden.'

'I'd rather read in my room for a while. I'll take to the roof as a reward after the article's gone.' She gave him Ross

McLean's email address. 'If you approve, contact my editor and read the riot act to him before I send it off.'

But back in her room there was no way she could concentrate on someone else's written word. She sat at the window to look down on a view of boats, and a hot sun-baked beach edging ultramarine sea, feeling like a character in some novel herself, maybe in a fairy tale, looking down from her tower on the world below. Except that she was no princess, and the handsome prince was right here in the tower, probably cutting her article to ribbons as he read it.

When the expected knock came Eleanor braced herself as she opened the door.

Alex smiled. 'It's good. I've made a few minor adjustments, so come back to the office and sort out the final draft. Then send it off and you can relax in the sun at last.'

'Thank you,' she said, relieved. 'Did you contact Ross?'

'I did, and laid down the law about my requirements. His immediate reply gave assurances that no syllable would be changed.'

'I wish I'd been there to see his face when he got the email!'

'You could have waited to give him the piece until you got back.'

She shook her head. 'Better this way.'

'But you won't be there to see the article in print.'

Eleanor grinned. 'Knowing Ross, he'll have it framed on his office wall of fame by the time I get back.'

Alex held out the chair in front of his desk for her, and pushed the laptop over, along with a page of notes. 'These are my revisions. Shall I leave you to it?'

She cast her eyes over the list. 'It won't take long.'

He leaned back in his chair. 'Then I'll stay.'

She nodded absently and set to work.

Alexei watched the intent, sun-bronzed face with pleasure which reinforced his plan of the night before. Strands of glossy dark hair had escaped their moorings to lie against Eleanor's cheeks, but she seemed unaware of them, or of him or anything else, as she incorporated his alterations into her text. She finished very quickly, but then sat, teeth caught in her bottom lip as she read through the article twice before she was satisfied.

He felt a surprising pang of something very like tenderness at her total absorption. Eleanor Markham was no beauty, but there was something about her narrow, intelligent face that appealed to him as much as—even far more than—the glossy, highly finished ones he mixed with socially here in Athens and London, also in New York from time to time. He was certain that nature alone was responsible for the curves outlined by her shirt and, though she had worn make-up the night before, there was none in evidence today. He might dislike her profession, but he liked Eleanor.

He must like her a lot, he thought sardonically. It was not a habit of his to discuss his personal life with anyone, not even his mother, yet he'd found himself actually describing his schooldays to Eleanor. Even more unusually, he had complete confidence in her assurance that what he required kept off the record would stay that way. His mother had been right—as always. The company of an intelligent woman was a refreshing change, and he was by no means ready to part with this one just yet.

'There,' she said at last and slid the laptop over to him. 'If you're satisfied I'll get it off to Ross.'

After which, of course, she would want to take off immediately for Crete to catch a plane home. As Alex read the revised draft his brain, long accustomed to dealing with several things at once, began devising ways to keep her here longer—not only to take her to bed but because he enjoyed her company. Persuading a woman to stay with him was new. From the time he'd reached his present stature in his early teens, women had been there for the taking, from the neighbours' daughters he met in Corfu to the women encountered in college and in the business world afterwards. But, with his parents' union as example, marriage held no appeal. His normal male appetites were catered for by sophisticated beauties who appealed to his senses only, never to his heart. Loving someone madly, as both his parents had done, was a fate he had taken pains to avoid. Not, he realised, frowning, that he had any knowledge of pain in a romantic relationship. Arianna might have dented his pride a little, but his heart had survived undamaged.

'Is it that bad?' demanded Eleanor. 'Shall I do more work on it?'

Alex shook his head. 'No. It's fine as it is. I always frown when I concentrate.'

'You don't object to the touches I put in?'

'No. They make me sound human, so leave them. You write well.' He pushed the laptop back to her. 'All yours; make your editor happy.'

Eleanor was only too glad to speed the article on its way, along with the photograph which really pleased her. It portrayed Alexei Drakos in exactly the right light, his air of power unmistakeable.

'Just wait for McLean to acknowledge it,' said Alex. 'Then afterwards you can relax and enjoy some lunch before you go up to the roof to sunbathe.'

'An attractive programme,' she agreed, and smiled wryly as the expected email popped into her inbox. 'Here it is.'

Alex came round the desk to look over her shoulder.

'"Good girl! Many thanks, RMcL."'

'Good girl!' said Eleanor in disgust, and shut the laptop.

'You prefer "woman"?' said Alex, amused.

'Would you like it if someone said "good boy"?'

'Point taken. Let me soothe your indignation with a glass of vintage Kyrkiros wine.'

Eleanor agreed gratefully. She felt utterly wrung out, which was ridiculous. Spending the morning on one solitary article wouldn't normally be exhausting, but getting one so important so absolutely right, and with Alexei looking on as she worked, had been a draining experience. To sink into a comfortable sofa and look out at the view as she drank her celebratory wine was a treat she deserved after the effort taken to get the interview. Though she had Talia to thank for that, she knew only too well.

'I need a wash before lunch,' she told Alex. 'I won't be long.'

'Take your time.' He smiled. Something he was doing a lot more lately since he'd met Eleanor Markham. 'But not too much. You need sustenance after all your hard work.'

'Fifteen minutes,' Eleanor promised, and hurried off to her room. Since she was finally going to enjoy her time in the sun later, she put on the relatively conservative swimwear she wore when travelling alone, covered it with a loose pink shirt and white jeans and thrust her feet into pink flip-flops. She slapped on some moisturiser and lip gloss, brushed out her hair and put sun block, book and dark glasses in the tote bag.

'You're on time,' said Alex as she joined him in the tower room. 'A pearl among women. You notice I said *women*?'

She laughed, feeling suddenly euphoric now she'd achieved the impossible and not only written, but actually sent off, her exclusive about Alexei Drakos. 'Duly noted,' she assured him and accepted the brimming glass he handed her. 'Thank you. I really need this.'

'I asked for a salad with some of Sofia's bread for ballast,' said Alex, indicating the meal set out on the table. 'We can eat something more substantial for dinner.'

Eleanor felt a little bubble of excitement rise somewhere inside at the prospect, and sternly reminded herself that their evening together was a matter of obligation for Alexei Drakos, not a dinner date. 'Right now a cold meal is exactly what I need.' She raised her glass in toast. 'Plus this, of course. You make seriously good wine here on Kirkyros.'

'Dion is a notable winemaker and a hard task-master on the subject of quality. I just make sure the wine sells. And drink it,' he added as he touched his glass to hers.

Eleanor took another sip and rolled it round her tongue. 'It has a flavour all its own—something like a rosé, but with more body. And,' she added, smiling at him, 'Delicious though it is, I'll stick to one glass. It's heady stuff.'

Between them they polished off most of the savoury bread with the entire platter of crayfish salad, talking so easily together, for a change, during the meal that Eleanor almost accepted when Alex offered more wine, but then shook her head and filled a glass from a jug of ice water instead.

'Prudent lady,' he observed lazily.

'I've been looking forward to my session in the sun too much to risk a headache!' She got up. 'Talking of which, if you'll excuse me I'll now make my way to your roof garden at last.'

Alex offered to accompany her, but Eleanor smiled at him politely and shook her head.

'I'm sure you have things to do, so I'll leave you in peace. Tell Sofia the lunch was fabulous.'

'It was.' Alex opened the door for her. 'But for me that had more to do with the charming company than the food.' He touched her hair fleetingly and smiled into her eyes. 'It would be wise to wear a hat.'

She nodded jerkily. 'I'll pop into my room and collect one on the way.'

Alex leaned in the doorway, watching her as she rushed along the hall at such speed she lost one of her flip-flops and had to bend to snatch it up. He smiled. Eleanor was very wary of him, which was all to the good. Her lack of coquetry was so appealing, he would take great pleasure in coaxing her into his bed. But instead of following her, as instinct urged, he turned away to his office to ring Stefan. He would give Eleanor her half hour in the sun before he joined her to make sure all was well with his guest, as any host worth his salt would do. After a report from Stefan, he gave his assistant a few comprehensive instructions then went back to the window to look down at the beach below, feeling restless again after the business discussion. The part of him that detested idleness was urging him to get back to take the reins in Athens, or to London to do the same there. But the part of him he usually kept in firm control was happy to stay here lotus-eating for a while.

A pity he couldn't take Eleanor on a tour of the island rather than keeping her locked up with him in the *Kastro*, but it was better to take no chances until he saw her off on her flight from Crete. His hands clenched. He would never forget the horror of hearing his mother scream his name as she was snatched almost from under his nose, nor the harsh censure he'd received from his father for not taking more care of her—which had stung all the more for being deserved. He would make damned sure nothing happened to Eleanor Markham.

At the thought of his mother Alex felt a sudden urge to make sure all was well with her, and rang to tell her he'd done her bidding like a good son and Eleanor's article had been sent off to her editor. Talia was delighted. She praised him lavishly and advised him to make the most of the time he was spending with his guest.

'You are right to keep her safe there with you, Alexei *mou*,' she said lovingly. 'Give Eleanor my good wishes and make her promise to visit me when she gets home.'

CHAPTER SIX

ELEANOR lay perfectly still on one of the long chairs in the roof garden, her face in the shade under the parasol, and the rest of her—liberally coated with sun block—stretched out in the sun to top up her tan. For once she had no desire to read. Her mind was occupied with Alexei, and the abundance of physical attributes bestowed on him by nature. The few natural blondes of her acquaintance would kill to possess curling lashes like his; she shook her head in sudden impatience. It was time to leave this magical place. If she stayed any longer she'd risk falling for the man, which would be the height of stupidity from so many points of view she should put it out of her mind—and less cerebral parts—right now. After their hostile start he'd now warmed towards her to a very gratifying degree, it was true; enough to talk on subjects she was pretty sure he never discussed with anyone other than his mother. And on the subject of Arianna, maybe not even to Talia. But anything hotter than that was out of the question, as she well knew.

She smiled bleakly. The only man in her past she had ever felt actual lust for had made it clear he looked on her as the perfect friend. Sexy bed-mates were two a penny, he'd told her, but an intelligent female friend like Eleanor Markham was a pearl beyond price. Alex had brought up the pearl thing, too. She was tired of it.

Alex opened the door onto the roof garden quietly, and stood very still at the sight of Eleanor lying in the sun in a relatively modest bikini. Strangely, it made her far more desirable than the flaunted assets of most holiday makers, even with a dark bruise visible on her ribcage. Hands clenched at the thought of the man who had caused it, and he stood looking at her so long she stirred.

'I disturbed you,' he said quietly, joining her.

Eleanor sat up and pulled her shirt on. 'I've had enough sun for now anyway.' She smiled at him brightly. 'This is a perfect place to sunbathe. Do you spend a lot of time up here?'

'Very little.' He sat down beside her, close enough to breathe in the scent of warm, sun-kissed female, and had to clench his hands to keep from touching the glowing skin. 'It was the general idea when I had the work done up here but I rarely have the time.'

She shook her head in mock-disapproval. 'Your empire would hardly disintegrate if you took half an hour off now and then, surely?'

He smiled wryly. 'You sound just like my mother—who, by the way, asked me to pass on her good wishes when I spoke to her earlier.'

Eleanor's eyes softened behind her dark lenses. 'How sweet of her. Does she come up here to sunbathe?'

Alex gave a snort of laughter. 'Never! She keeps that complexion of hers well protected from the sun. Christo, the photographer who made her famous, laid the law down from the start.'

Eleanor nodded. 'I bought my mother the book of portraits he published, solely because the majority of them were of Talia Kazan. He described her in his foreword as his Greek goddess muse.'

'He was furious when she gave up her career to marry

my father.' Alex smiled sardonically. 'Christo is a Londoner from the East End, real name Chris Higgins, who discovered her when she was a schoolgirl on holiday in London. The camera loved her and because she was in love with London, and excited by the idea of independence, she persuaded her father to let her work with the celebrated Christo. My grandfather could never deny her anything, so Talia Kazan stayed in London and became famous almost overnight. Her face was on the cover of every glossy magazine at one time or another.'

Eleanor nodded. 'My mother still has some of them. She always wondered why Talia Kazan's career ended so abruptly.'

'Christo blamed my father for his muse's desertion, but in actual fact the novelty of a modelling career wore off for her very quickly. The ex-policewoman my grandfather hired as Talia's companion and minder was leaving her to get married, and if it hadn't been for Christo and his pleas my mother would have given it up long before she met Milo Drakos. She was involved in a fashion shoot in winter near the Greek embassy in London. It was a bitterly cold day and my father came out of the building to see her shivering in a flimsy summer dress. He stripped off his coat, wrapped her in it and, ignoring Christo's violent objections, swept her into a taxi with her minder and took her home.'

'How romantic!' Eleanor smiled at him. 'It was love at first sight?'

His mouth twisted. 'If it was, it didn't last long.' He turned away as Yannis appeared, carefully carrying a tray. 'I thought you might be thirsty.'

'How kind of you.' Eleanor smiled at the boy. '*Efcharisto,* Yannis.'

Alex filled two glasses with fruit juice and ice and handed one to Eleanor. 'I trust you're taking note.'

'That you're waiting on me? I'm honoured.'

'As you should be.' He touched his glass to hers, giving her that calculated look again.

'You mean the women you know are perfectly happy to wait on you all the time?'

'If they're not, they've never said so.'

Of course they hadn't!

He chuckled. 'You have a very expressive face, *kyria* journalist. Those cat's eyes of yours shoot off sparks of disapproval.'

'*Cat's* eyes!' she retorted. 'Thanks a lot.'

'I mean that they are gold in some light, like a lioness,' Alex said, surprising her.

'Hazel,' said Eleanor, and downed some of her drink. 'That's what it says on my passport,' she added as he looked blank.

'Hazel,' he repeated. 'I'll remember that.'

Eleanor gave him a sidelong, suspicious look. If he never came up here normally, why was he here now?

'What is it?' he asked.

She put her sunglasses back on. 'Would you be kind enough to take me over to Karpyros tomorrow to get the ferry to Crete, please?'

Alex frowned. 'You're so desperate to get away?'

Not nearly as much as she should be. 'I'm very conscious that I'm keeping you here when you should be wherever you're due next, so—'

'So now the article has gone off, you're unwilling to stay a second longer than necessary.'

'That's not what I meant. I'm just trying to be as little trouble to you as possible.'

He reached out and whipped the sunglasses from her face. 'I dislike staring into blank lenses. The earliest flight

I could arrange is in two days' time. So you must endure your captivity until then.'

'I'm sorry to be such a nuisance for you.' Eleanor found it hard not to fidget under the black, relentless gaze. 'But you don't have to stay with me. I'm safe enough here with Sofia and Yannis and your security people. Just organise someone to get me over to Karpyros to catch the ferry on the day and you can be on your way first thing tomorrow. Or even tonight.'

His smile set her alarm bells ringing. 'You are unflatteringly anxious to get rid of me, while I am only too delighted to spend extra time in *your* company.' His eyes hardened. 'I will not let you out of my sight until I see you safely on that plane, Eleanor Markham.'

She stared at him in surprise. 'Why? It's not so long since you threatened to have me fired from my job.'

'I admit that in my concern for my mother—and my aversion to the media—I was too quick to accuse. But I have atoned for that. If nothing else, you can add a unique qualification to your CV should you seek another job—the only journalist to achieve an interview with Alexei Drakos.'

Eleanor grinned. 'There goes that hubris again.'

He shrugged his formidable shoulders. 'If you mean I am proud of what I have achieved in my life, I admit that. But is it so strange that I prefer to keep my personal life private?'

'Not in the least. Yet you talked to me about some of it. Why?'

'I wish I knew. And wish now I had not.' The compelling eyes locked on hers again. 'Do not betray my confidence, Eleanor Markham.'

'I won't, ever,' she assured him.

'Even though you could be paid big money for some of the information I gave you?'

'Only if I sold it to another paper. And, since I like the

job I have now, I won't do that. Besides,' she added. 'I gave you my word.'

'So you did.' Alex handed the sunglasses over. 'Tell me about your life in England. You have a house there?'

'I share one with a college friend. Originally there were four of us, but due to career changes the other two left, so now I live upstairs and the ground floor is Pat's territory.' She smiled. 'It works well because I'm away so much.'

'Who owns the house?'

'The landlord. We rent.'

Alex looked at her curiously. 'Wouldn't it be better to buy a house?'

'Of course. But only when I can afford to live alone in one.'

'You have no wish to marry?'

She smiled wryly. 'I'm all too familiar with the stress of sharing a house. I'd have to think long and hard before sharing my entire life with a man.'

He nodded. 'I understand that. When I see the life Arianna has made with Dion, I have no envy, even though I once cared for her.'

'You said she broke your heart!'

'I was dramatic to win your sympathy,' he said shamelessly and grinned. 'Did I succeed?'

'Fleetingly.' She hesitated. 'Don't you want children?'

He shrugged. 'I would like a son one day, but marriage is unnecessary for that.'

Her eyes flashed. 'You mean you would just select an appropriate mother for your son? What then? Would he just spend his summer holidays with you?'

'*Ochi*! He would live with me permanently.'

'How about the mother?'

'She could stay also, if she wished.'

'Big of you! But if she's the normal breed of mother you

won't separate her from her son with a crowbar.' She smiled. 'Not that I need tell you that.'

'True,' he conceded. 'My mother found it hard to part with me for just the brief times I spent time with my father. Even so, she kept rigidly to the terms of their agreement until I was eighteen, at which point the delightful Melania came into his life. I spent only one holiday in Corfu with them and never went back.' He smiled sardonically. 'No one enjoyed that holiday—my father, his mistress and I least of all. I became ill soon after I arrived, and left after only a few days. That was my last holiday with my father.'

'It must have been hard for your mother to bring you up alone.' Eleanor's sympathy for Talia was growing by the minute.

'Until I went to England to school my grandfather was always there to help her when I got out of hand, as boys do. My grandmother died when I was young, and I hardly remember her, but Cyrus was a big part of my life. He adored my mother. It must have been hard for him to let her work with Christo.' He shook his head suddenly. 'Amazing! I find myself telling you things I never speak of to anyone else, Eleanor Markham.'

She smiled. 'Probably because I have infinite experience in providing a listening ear—right through school, college and afterwards when I shared a house with friends. When they had man trouble—a pretty regular occurrence—I provided tea and sympathy and even mopping up.'

'Did they return the favour?' he said, amused.

She shook her head. 'I kept my woes to myself.'

'As I said before, a pearl among women!'

The pearl thing again! 'You've forgotten my temper.'

Alex laughed. 'I assure you I have not. Those eyes of yours flash like warning lights when you are angry. I admire such passion in a woman.'

She tried to keep her expression neutral. No one had ever said anything like that to her before. 'Contrary to your belief, *kyrie* Drakos, I hardly ever lose my temper.'

'Beating men up is not a habit for you?'

'No.' She chuckled. 'So rest easy, you're in no danger from me.'

'A great relief,' he said with sarcasm, then frowned as a sudden gust of wind rattled the screen. He got up to look out from the balustrade. 'Eleanor, we must go down. A storm is coming. You can read in the tower room instead.'

She pulled on her jeans hurriedly. 'I can read in my room.'

'Then I will feel like your jailer. I shall work in my office. You can have the tower room to yourself and watch the storm coming.'

Not a prospect Eleanor fancied at all. But she fancied solitude in her room even less. 'Thank you. I'll run my laptop on the battery and do some work.'

A gust of wind caught her as she made for the door. Alex shot out an arm to steady her, took charge of her bag and thrust her through the doorway as the wind began to rise in earnest. He slammed the door closed behind them and followed her down to her room.

'You are quite safe here, Eleanor. If the electricity fails we have an emergency generator.'

'Good to know.' She smiled brightly.

'I will see you later.' He handed her bag over and strode rapidly along the hall rather than surrender to the urge to stay with her and forget about work for once.

Eleanor closed the door as the wind rose to new heights. She crossed to the windows to see people rushing to haul boats up the beach out of danger and shivered enough to decide on a hot shower. She had just finished dressing when Sofia came to tell her tea was waiting in the tower room.

'*Efcharisto,* Sofia.'

The woman nodded in approval at Eleanor's heavy cotton sweater. 'Good. It will be colder soon.'

Eleanor grabbed her laptop and hurried along to the brightly lit tower room to check the storm's progress from the windows but found the view obscured by spray. She ate one of Sofia's pastries and settled back with her tea as the wind mounted in increasing fury. Thankful she'd been spared weather like this during her island-hopping, she got down to some serious editing on the first of her travel articles. She worked steadily in an effort to ignore the escalating storm until lightning sizzled through the room accompanied by a deafening crack of thunder, and the lights went out.

Alex raced in, training one of the torches he held on her face. 'Eleanor—are you all right?'

'Just startled,' she assured him breathlessly, hoping he hadn't heard her screech of fright.

He laughed. 'I almost said good girl, but remembered you don't like that.'

Eleanor grinned. 'Anyway—' She was just about to assure him she was perfectly fine when more flashes and bangs cut her off. 'Wow,' she said shakily when she could be heard. 'The storms are mega-noisy in these parts.'

'But you are safe here, Eleanor. I regret that I must leave you to go down to check on Sofia and give Theo a hand with the generator. I can't use the lift, obviously, but I'll be as quick as I can. Will you be all right alone?'

'Of course.' What else could she say?

'I'll leave you a torch.'

'Thank you.' Eleanor winced as the room was lit up by lightning, but this time the thunder was less immediate. 'There,' she said brightly. 'Farther away already.'

Alex laughed and startled her by bending to plant a kiss on her mouth. 'I'll be back as soon as I can.'

Eleanor listened to his footsteps as he raced along the hall to the stairs, then took in a deep breath and returned to her work. But the storm made concentration impossible. Alex's kiss hadn't helped, either. Those lips of his tasted as good as they looked. She closed the laptop and went back to the sofa with the torch alight on the table beside her, passing the time by counting the seconds between each flash and crack of thunder. She surprised herself by actually chuckling when some of the cracks and flashes still came together. Her childhood method didn't apply to Greek storms; Poseidon ruled in these parts.

The lights finally came on after a wait so long the storm had retreated to other parts of the Aegean and stars were blazing in a clear sky. Eleanor turned from the windows in relief when she heard someone in the hall and ran to the door with a smile, which faded abruptly when she saw no sign of Alex. Nor of anyone else. She spun round to collect her laptop and flew along the hall, the creaks and groans of the ancient building rocketing her in a headlong rush to her room. She locked the door behind her and switched on the light, laughing at herself when she had her breath back. Who was she keeping out, for heaven's sake? It took a few deep, even breaths before she calmed down, only to jump yards as the phone Alex had given her rang in her bag.

'Hello?' she said breathlessly.

'Sorry to be so long, Eleanor, are you all right?'

'Now the storm's moved away, yes.'

'Good. I'm just finishing up here. Sofia says dinner will be ready in half an hour or so, which gives me time to clean up.'

The news that Alex was on his way was hugely welcome. Eleanor frowned. But if he was still down below, whose footsteps had she heard? This might be a very modern apartment, but alone up here she was very conscious of the antiquity of the rest of the building. It would hardly be surprising if there were ghosts. Hoping any in residence were the benevolent kind, she tidied up, collected her book and left her room as Alex emerged from the lift.

'I'm filthy,' he told her, grinning like a schoolboy. 'Sofia wanted me to wash in her kitchen, but I need to stand under a very hot shower. Will you wait for me in the tower room?'

'Of course, take your time. Something wrong with the generator?'

He nodded. 'But we put it right—eventually.'

Eleanor went back to the tower room, feeling a lot happier, even able to laugh at herself for scurrying along the hall earlier like a scared rabbit. Not something she would share with Alex. She doubted he was scared of anything. She crossed the beautiful, uncluttered room to look out at the view of moonlight reflected on the now flat calm of the sea. It was easy to picture Jason, back in the mists of time, passing by out there in the *Argo* on his quest for the golden fleece. She stiffened at the sound of footsteps, but this time it was the solidly real Sofia arriving with a tray of olives and nuts.

'Are you well, *kyria*?' she asked anxiously. 'I was worried for you alone up here in the storm, but I cannot manage the old steps in the dark. I thank the good God—and *kyrie* Alexei—for the blessing of the lift.'

Having understood about half of that, Eleanor nodded, smiling. 'I'm fine.' It was true enough now that the lights were on and Alex was close at hand.

'Dinner very soon,' Sofia promised, and went hurrying off to exchange a word with Alex in the hall.

Eleanor made no attempt to hide how glad she was to see him. His thin shirt clung to him as if he'd put it on while his skin was damp, revealing musculature so impressive she was seized with an overwhelming desire to run her hands over his chest and whipped them behind her back to avoid temptation.

'Sorry to be so long,' Alex smiled with sympathy. 'It must have been quite an ordeal up here on your own in the storm. Did you work to pass the time?'

'I tried but I couldn't concentrate so I reverted to counting the seconds between the lightning strikes instead.'

'Then you must need a drink as much as I do.' He filled two glasses and handed one to her.

Eleanor settled down in a corner of the sofa with a sigh of pleasure. 'Is power failure a regular occurrence here?'

'Yes.' He joined her and touched his glass to hers. 'But tonight there was a problem with the generator.' He grinned. 'I rather enjoy the challenge of mastering the thing.'

She laughed. 'You mean you were having fun down there?'

'Not this time. I was concerned about you up here on your own.'

'It's a bit daunting in the dark,' Eleanor admitted, and smiled as Sofia came in with a dish of savouries. 'No Yannis tonight?'

'His friend Markos is spending the night with him,' said his mother, looking anxious. 'They were out in the rain to secure boats and needed a hot bath.' She put a platter of small savoury pies on the table in front of them. 'Eat now while they are warm; I will be back soon with your dinner.'

Alex smiled at her affectionately. '*Efcharisto,* Sofia. Did the power cut affect the meal?'

'No, *kyrie*, it is slow-cooked lamb and kept its heat,' she assured him as she hurried out.

'Thank God for that,' said Alex devoutly and pushed the platter of pastries towards Eleanor. 'These are my mother's favourites, so you're honoured. Sofia rarely makes them for anyone else, except for the festival, where they sell like—'

'Hot cakes?' Eleanor grinned and sampled one, enjoying the taste of cheese and herbs so much she finished it before saying a word. 'Wow. You'd better make a start or I might eat the lot.'

He looked amused. 'Instead you shall share the rest with me before any more accidents prevent us.'

'If the lights go again, I'll come with you to help.' Eleanor's eyes sparkled as they sat down together. 'I'm pretty handy with a screw driver.'

'Then I should have taken you with me tonight.' He toasted her with his glass. 'To a lady of many talents.'

She shook her head. 'Not really. I pride myself on being good at my job, and I can cook a bit, but I can't sing or play a musical instrument.'

'But you have a talent for friendship.'

Eleanor sighed. 'I shouldn't have boasted to you about that.'

'You had no need. I know just how good a friend you can be.'

She turned on him. 'How, exactly?'

'Because you flew to my mother's aid without a thought for your own safety.' He frowned. 'Your eyes are giving off angry sparks again. You dislike the label of good friend?'

'By some people, no.'

'But others you object to?'

'Just one, really—a man who once told me beddable women were two a penny, but I was that rarity, a woman he valued as the perfect friend.' Eleanor turned away. 'Not what I wanted to hear. I'd fondly imagined he wanted me as a lover.'

'He was the stupid one if he did not.' Alex turned her face to his. 'You are a very desirable woman, Eleanor Markham.'

'Thank you.'

'It's the simple truth,' he assured her.

Face hot, Eleanor changed the subject. 'I hope Yannis won't have caught cold.'

'He won't care as long as he secured his boat—which is the love of his life. He takes it over to Karpyros with Markos at weekends to hang out with friends there.'

'You bought it for him?'

'I bought it for his use, yes. My own is powered by a bigger engine. Yannis is forbidden to go near it.'

'By you?'

'By his mother. His father drowned in a storm while fishing, so it took much persuasion for her to let Yannis out in a boat at all at first. But, because life without one is difficult here, she eventually gave in.' Alex eyed the empty plate in rueful surprise. 'I've devoured the lot. My apologies, Eleanor.'

'None needed. Dinner's on its way.'

'So it is. You have very sharp ears!'

'Not always a blessing. I sometimes hear things I'd rather not.' Or weren't even real, like phantom footsteps in the hall. She got up as Sofia trundled the trolley into the room, and with a smile began transferring dishes of vegetables to the table while Sofia removed parchment from a joint of meat to release a mouth-watering aroma into the room.

'Lamb,' Sofia informed her. 'You like it?'

Thankful it wasn't goat, Eleanor nodded fervently. 'I love it.'

'I will be back later to clear. Eat well.'

Alex got to work with a carving knife while Eleanor served the vegetables, and silence reigned for a while as they fell on the food with hunger fuelled by hard labour on Alex's part and post-storm euphoria on his guest's.

'This is just wonderful,' she told him after a while.

He nodded. 'Sofia is a skilled cook. We were lucky she prepared a dish which survived the power cut.'

'Very lucky!' She hesitated. 'Is there any news about who hired Spiro Baris?'

'No, but my people are working on it,' Alex said grimly. 'When I find out I will report to my father, as he demanded. And then the man responsible will curse the day he thought of kidnapping my mother.' His laugh was short and mirthless. 'Because my parents are divorced, the idiot was unaware he risked Milo Drakos' revenge as well as mine.'

'Would an enormous ransom have been demanded?'

'Probably. I would have given all I possess to get my mother back. And, to be fair, so would my father.' Alex smiled. 'But due to your bravery, Eleanor, my mother and my bank balance survived unharmed—and so, thank God, did you. I owe you more than I can ever repay.'

She shook her head. 'The interview was reward enough.'

'Yet it benefited your editor more than you.'

'But it gave me enormous satisfaction. I don't believe Ross McLean thought for a moment that I would actually persuade you to talk to me.' Eleanor's eyes sparkled. 'It's a personal triumph to prove him wrong.'

'You don't like him?'

'Actually, I do. He's very good at his job, and I've learned a lot from him. Ross just has this thing about college graduates because he's had to rely on experience and hard graft to achieve his success in the profession, and never tires of saying so.' She got to her feet. 'Sofia's on her way so I'll just stack these things in the trolley, ready for her.'

'You really do have extraordinary hearing,' said Alex, amused when Sofia arrived as Eleanor put the last of the plates away.

'How is Yannis, Sofia?' she asked.

The woman looked anxious. 'Very hot, and he is coughing, but he won't let me send Markos home.' She shrugged. 'It is company for him.'

Alex smiled in reassurance. 'In the morning, if he's not better I'll get him to a doctor.'

Eleanor searched through her bag for some painkillers and handed them to Sofia. 'Would this help?'

Alex eyed her with respect as he translated the instructions on the medication for Sofia, who responded with a flood of gratitude for the *kyria* and went hurrying off with the trolley.

'It was just four pills, enough for tonight and in the morning,' said Eleanor. 'So he won't come to any harm.'

'How did we all survive on Kyrkiros before you arrived?' said Alex, and took her by the shoulders, shaking her slightly when her eyes flashed fire at him. 'I was joking. I'm sincerely grateful to you, Eleanor.'

'I don't need your gratitude,' she retorted, trying to get free, but he held her fast, his eyes filled with sudden heat.

'So what *do* you need?' His hands tightened. 'You've had the interview as your reward. Now, *kyria* journalist, I'll take mine.' He bent his head and kissed her, then kissed her again with heat that made her head reel, the meeting of tongue with tongue a match applied to kindling. He pulled her up on her toes, shaping every inch of her against his aroused body as his mouth seduced hers into such helpless response they were both breathing like long-distance runners when he raised his head at last. Very slowly he slackened his hold until she was standing square on her feet again, but he held her fast when she tried to move away. 'Are you so desperate to get away from me?' he demanded hoarsely.

Since it was obvious that her body was deliriously happy where it was, she didn't bother to lie. 'No,' she blurted. 'But I should be.'

'Why? Because my body is telling you I want to be your lover?'

Eleanor heaved in as deep a breath as she could; held so close to his chest. 'You mean you want to sleep with me tonight?' she demanded.

'Not sleep.' The note in his voice made her knees tremble. 'I want to make love to you—and not just tonight but every moment possible before you leave.'

And there it was. She sighed as the adrenaline drained away. 'This may sound coy and unbelievable to you,' she said into his chest, 'But the word "leave" is the clincher. I don't do holiday romances.'

He tipped her face up, his dark eyes locked on hers for an instant; then the heavy lids came down like shutters as he let her go to put space between them. 'But you do much damage to this famous hubris of mine, Eleanor Markham.' He shrugged, suddenly nonchalant. 'Ah well, if you won't sleep with me let us have coffee and go off to our separate beds.'

His about-turn was so deflating Eleanor had to force a smile. 'I'll pass on the coffee, thanks. Sofia's brought some mineral water. I'll take that with me instead.' She paused on her way to the door to look up into the sculpted, handsome face, now blank as a mask bar the nerve throbbing at the corner of the mouth that had just kissed her into a response new in her life. 'Goodnight. And, by the way, thank you.'

'For wanting you for a lover, not a friend?' he said, so quick on the uptake she smiled ruefully.

'Exactly.'

'Honest lady.' His eyes darkened. 'Now go. Take your scruples off to bed.'

Eleanor smiled sweetly and marched off down the hall at speed, fuelled by disappointment when he made no move to follow her.

CHAPTER SEVEN

Due to a new fondness for the miracle of electricity, Eleanor left the bedside lamp on for company when she was ready for bed, but sleep was hard to come by. She tossed and turned for what seemed like hours, prey to unfamiliar sexual frustration. She finally drifted into an uneasy, restless doze, but woke suddenly, heart pounding. She sat bolt-upright, cold sweat breaking out over her forehead as she stared in horror at the nightmare apparition in the open doorway. She uttered a hoarse scream and scrambled out of bed, so awkward in her terror she tripped and fell and for the first time in her life fainted dead away.

Eleanor came round pressed against Alex's bare chest, his heart thumping like a drum against her cheek.

'You're safe, *agapi mou*,' he assured her, breathing hard. 'You had a bad dream.'

She opened her eyes a crack, afraid of what she might see, but there was no monstrous, terrifying figure in the open doorway. She heaved in a deep, unsteady breath. 'It was just a nightmare?'

'A very bad one, by your scream.' He rubbed his cheek against her hair, his arms tightening protectively. 'It took years off my life.'

'Off mine too. It was so real. He was standing in the

doorway with those great crystal eyes staring at me.' She swallowed convulsively.

Alex tipped her face up to his. 'Crystal eyes?'

Eleanor nodded. 'Like the dancer. A bull's head on a human male body.'

He smiled indulgently. 'A nightmare indeed!'

'Sorry to involve you in it—why are we sitting on the floor?'

'I found you there. I broke the Olympic sprint record to get here when you screamed, and found you unconscious on the floor.' He got to his feet, picked her up and put her back against the pillows. 'You gave me such a scare. Are you better now?'

She shook her head. 'Not really.'

'I'll go down to the kitchen and look for my mother's tea.'

'*No*! Please. Don't leave me alone up here.' She tried to smile. 'Sorry to be such a coward, but the monster in the doorway seemed horribly real.'

Alex sat on the edge of the bed, eyes narrowed. 'You left your door open?'

Eleanor frowned as she raked her hair back from her perspiring forehead. 'Of course not. I was hardly likely to get ready for bed with it wide open.'

'Not after the conversation we'd just had,' he agreed dryly. 'This apparition you saw. It was in the open door-way—not outside in the hall?'

'It—he—was there in the doorway, Alex. I froze in hor-ror, and for an instant I couldn't tear my eyes away. Then I screamed my head off and jumped out of bed in such a panic I actually passed out. A first for me, by the way,' she informed him, and shivered. 'I need a shower.' She licked her dry lips, eyeing him in appeal. 'Would you stay here while I'm in the bathroom?'

'Of course.' He frowned. 'But be quick, because I must

search the *Kastro*. If what, or who, you saw here was real and not a dream, he must be found. I'll ring Theo.'

'*No*! Please don't,' she said, appalled. 'It was just a dream.' Vivid and horrible, but what else could it have been?

Alex nodded reluctantly. 'As you wish.'

'Thank you, Alex.' She smiled brightly. 'Sorry for the fuss. One way or another, you'll be glad to see the back of me.'

He shook his head. 'On the contrary. My mother—as always—is right. The company of an intelligent woman is a very desirable thing.'

Her smile was ironic. 'But you must know lots of women. With your reputation and wealth and—and the rest of it— you must be beating them off with a stick!'

Alex threw back his head and laughed. 'What a picture you paint of me.' He raised an eyebrow. 'What do you mean by "the rest of it"?'

'You know very well.'

'Tell me.'

'The physique and the looks, of course,' she said irritably.

'You find me good to look at?'

She rolled her eyes. 'You know perfectly well I do.'

'You are good to look at too, Eleanor,' he said, in a tone which made her quiver. 'I stood looking at you in the sun this afternoon before you knew I was there.'

He was wrong about that. She'd known the moment he stepped onto the roof, and not just because her hearing was acute. Alexei Drakos had a way of making his presence felt.

'You made a very charming picture lying there.' His eyes lit with sudden fury. 'Then I saw the bruise at your waist and I could have strangled Spiro with my bare hands.'

Eleanor smiled shakily. 'Thank you. I think. I'll have that shower now.'

Alex got up and stood over her. 'Can you stand?'

'Yes,' she said firmly, embarrassed to find her camisole and shorts soaked with sweat. 'I'm fine now,' she said, face hot, and made for the bathroom as fast as her shaky knees would allow.

'Be quick, in case you feel faint again,' Alex ordered.

Eleanor groaned in despair at her reflection. She would have to wash her hair. She got on with it as fast as she could but, with shaking hands and legs threatening to fold under her, it took time before she was dry and wrapped in Talia's robe. She combed her hair through and swathed it in a towel then slapped moisturiser into her cheeks to bring some colour back to them. When she opened the door, Alex was eyeing the stripped bed, perplexed.

'The sheets were so damp I took them off, but where does Sofia keep the replacements?'

Eleanor crossed to the dresser and began opening drawers until she found a stack of perfectly laundered bed linen. '*Voila!*'

'Excellent! But there is still a problem. The mattress is also damp. You can't sleep here tonight.'

She cringed at the thought of drenching his mother's bed with sweat. How gross was that? 'Of course I can. Those chairs are really comfortable.'

'For sitting only. You shall sleep in my bed again.' His lips twitched at the look on her face. 'I'll take the couch in my office.'

Eleanor shook her head vehemently. 'Thank you, but that's unnecessary. I can sleep on the settee in the tower room.' Even though she quailed at the prospect. The thought of spending the night alone in any room in the apartment scared the living daylights out of her.

'No, Eleanor. You take my bed; I'll take the office couch.' He raised an eyebrow as she chuckled. 'It's good to hear you laugh, but what is funny?'

'I once worked on a paper where the boss's office couch was a way of getting a promotion for some women on the staff,' she told him.

He grinned. 'Not for you, of course.'

Eleanor batted her eyelashes. 'When it was suggested to me, I cried prettily, insisting it was against my religion to have sex before marriage. The M word frightened him so much he avoided me like the plague after that—though he gave me a glowing reference when I left. Another man glad to see the back of me!' She removed the towel and ran her fingers through her hair. 'I'll just get something else to wear.'

'Be quick, then,' he ordered. 'You need sleep. Bring your phone.'

In the bathroom Eleanor pulled on her one and only nightgown, replaced the robe and slipped the phone into her pocket. Alex held out his hand as she emerged, and she clung to it as they went along the hall, half-expecting the apparition to leap out at them until Alex closed his bedroom door behind them.

Eleanor eyed his bed with respect. 'You must be a very tidy sleeper.'

He shook his head. 'I was not in bed. I did some work in the office after you left me. I was undressing when I heard you scream.' He turned the covers back on one side of the bed. 'No more nightmares tonight, *parakolo*,' he commanded.

She hugged her arms across her chest. 'If it was a nightmare. He looked very real to me.'

'In which case, I should have searched for him.' Alex smiled at the look of dismay on her face. 'But I will leave it until the morning. Now get into bed.' He frowned as Eleanor hesitated. 'You're still not happy?'

'Not really, no.' She braced herself. 'Could you possibly sleep in here tonight, Alex? Please?'

His dark eyes flared for an instant before narrowing to the familiar, assessing look. 'Your dream frightened you that much?'

Oh yes. It had felt too real for a dream. The more she thought about it now she was calmer, the more she was convinced that the apparition had been a flesh-and-blood man—from the neck down, at least. In that second of sheer, blazing terror his image had imprinted itself on her mind so indelibly she had only to shut her eyes to see him again in every detail. Every detail... Her eyes flew open again as she turned to Alex in sudden dread. 'He had a tattoo on his arm.'

He frowned as he sat on the edge of the bed. 'Are you sure you're not remembering the dancer who played the Minotaur at the festival?'

'Absolutely sure. In my photographs he definitely has no tattoo.'

'Can you describe this?'

'No. I stared for only an instant before I screamed and passed out,' Eleanor said bitterly.

'If he's that real to you, I have no choice. I must search the *Kastro* immediately.' Alex looked suddenly older, his mouth and eyes grim as he pulled on his clothes.

She cursed herself for convincing Alex that her intruder wasn't a figment of her imagination. 'If you must, please take someone with you!'

'I am more concerned with your safety than mine, Eleanor.' His eyes softened as he sat down beside her. 'Now listen to me, *agape mou*. When I leave, lock the door and do not open it until I get back. I shall turn every light on up here on this floor. You are completely safe locked here in my room, but ring me if you need me.'

She nodded forlornly, filled with a sudden overpowering desire to go home, back where she belonged.

Alex looked down at her for a moment, then pulled her up into his arms and kissed her very thoroughly. 'Get into bed and try to sleep,' he said huskily and strode to the door with her. 'Lock the door,' he repeated his order, and closed it behind him.

Alex flicked on lights as he went along and rang Theo as he went up the stairs to the roof door to confirm it was locked. When he took the lift down to the ground floor he opened the outer door a crack at the back entrance to the *Kastro* and Theo Lazarides left his house and hurried to meet him. Alex spoke in a rapid undertone as he described his guest's nightmare and stated his intention to search the warren of ancient rooms in the Kastro basement. Theo promptly offered to accompany him, but Alex shook his head. 'Just get ready to catch him when I flush him out.'

'You think the lady really saw someone then, *kyrie*?'

'At first I was sure it was just a bad dream, but later she remembered a tattoo, so it might be possible it was not. Sorry to involve you, Theo. You must be tired.'

'Not so tired I could sleep, knowing you were searching down there alone with no one to watch your back. You think someone is lying low somewhere in the old part?'

'No, I do not. But I'm going to make sure.' Alex smiled grimly. 'I was lucky enough to achieve a meteoric success rate early on in life to get where I am now, but I'm not fool enough to believe I did it without making enemies. Someone's out to cause me pain of some kind, financial or personal, but the fool made the biggest mistake of his life when he paid someone to kidnap my mother. I'm indebted to Ms Markham for her share in preventing that, so the least I can do is make the search to ease her mind. And mine.'

Theo looked worried. 'You think this is all connected to *kyria* Talia?'

'Because it would hurt me most, yes.' Alex tested a couple of torches. 'My method of dealing with opponents has been pre-emptive all my life—to get in with my strike before they get in with theirs. I learned that very early on with all the opponents lurking along my road to success. So now I'm going to flush out this man and get rid of him before he does any more harm.'

'You think he is real, then.'

'In my head, no, but I can't take any chances, Theo.' His eyes glittered coldly. 'If he is real, I could kill the swine just for frightening my guest. And I've left Ms Markham alone up there, so I'd better get on with it.'

Theo caught his arm. 'Let me go in there with you, *kyrie*!'

'No. I appreciate the offer, but I've got more chance of catching him unawares if I go in alone.'

In time, when the reconstruction was completed, Alexei intended this oldest part of the *Kastro* to function as more storerooms for the island's produce, but in the beginning his priority had merely been making the basement structure of the place sound. Once that was done, he organised transformation of the ground floor into kitchen and living quarters, plus a personal exercise room, and went on to convert the top floor into his private apartment with offices on the floor immediately below it. Come the autumn, the majority of the male population would get to work on the network of rooms and passages in the cellars and basement.

Armed with a torch, Alex left Theo standing guard by the door which opened from the hall on to the ancient steps and descended cautiously, his deck shoes noiseless on the ancient stones picked out by the solitary beam of light.

It was eerie work, hunting a phantom quarry. But

Eleanor's terror had been so genuine her scream had given him the same dread he'd felt when his mother shrieked his name as Spiro snatched her at the festival. His eyes glittered coldly. If whoever was lurking in his *Kastro* was involved in either incident, he would pay for it, and pay dearly. Alex moved silently through the familiar stone maze, feeling his way along walls which gave way to doorways and narrow passageways, until he was satisfied that even the last possible hiding place was empty. It was slow, nerve-straining work, his entire system on full alert, prepared for attack which never happened. No one was there. Cursing silently, he mounted the ancient steps, shaking his head in response to Theo's raised eyebrows as he emerged.

'It must have been a dream after all.' He shrugged. 'Ms Markham was fascinated by the bull dance, and took some extraordinary photographs. The dancer who played the Minotaur made such an impression he surfaced in her dreams.'

Theo nodded gravely. 'But you had to make sure.'

'No choice, really,' said Alex grimly. 'I object to intruders on our island.'

'Your island now, *kyrie.*'

Alex shook his head. 'Ours, Theo.'

The man smiled. '*Efcharisto*! If I can be of no more help I will go home.'

'Right.' Alex looked down at his clothes in distaste. 'I must clean up. I'll be glad when we've got the place in shape down there; it's a damned difficult job looking for someone the way it is.'

'But you came out unharmed, thank God.' Theo touched his shoulder and said goodnight.

Alex went silently to the kitchen, taking care not to disturb Sofia and the boys as he collected fruit juice and mineral water for Eleanor. Who would probably take him up on his offer to sleep in his office, now there was no danger lurking down below, or none that he'd found. Nevertheless he couldn't rid himself of the feeling of unease as he left the lift to make for his bedroom. Even though there'd been no trace of anyone lurking down below, Eleanor's account of her nightmare had been so detailed it was hard to dismiss it as nonsense. He shrugged. She'd probably seen a photograph or a painting somewhere on the Internet during her research. There'd been enough representations of the Minotaur by artists down the ages.

He knocked softly on his bedroom door. 'Alex, Eleanor.'

She flung it open, her eyes luminous with relief. 'Are you all right?'

'Dirty and thirsty, but otherwise fine.' He locked the door behind him. 'There was no sign of anyone down there, but I'd rather you stayed here with me tonight.'

So would Eleanor. She smiled gratefully as Alex put the water and juice on his dressing chest. 'You raided the kitchen, then.'

'Very stealthily, to avoid waking Sofia and the boys. Now I need a shower. I will be quick.'

Alone in the bedroom, reaction suddenly hit Eleanor in a rush of tears and chattering teeth. The strain of worrying about Alex getting injured—or worse—by the monster suddenly caught up with her. She heaved in a few deep, calming breaths as she mopped her eyes, then drank some water and curled up in the leather chair beside the bed. She smiled brightly as Alex came out of the bathroom.

'You've been crying,' he accused.

'Just a reaction. I was worried.'

He smoothed a hand over her hair. 'You are exhausted. Come to bed.'

'No thank you.' Eleanor smiled politely. 'I'll sleep here in this comfortable chair.'

His lips curved. 'I'm no threat to you tonight, *agape*

mou. You've had an exhausting day and need sleep. So do I. You may sleep undisturbed. Humour me, Eleanor.' He yawned, shrugged out of his dressing gown and slid into bed. 'I can't rest with you sitting there.'

She turned out the lamp, then took off Talia's robe and got into the near side of the bed, keeping to the edge to leave as much space as possible between them.

'You'll fall on the floor in the night if you try to sleep like that,' he commented.

'I'll take the risk.'

There was silence for a while.

'Eleanor.'

'Yes?'

'I found nothing down there, so it must have been a dream. Relax. You can sleep undisturbed by monsters or anything else—including me.'

'Thank you. Goodnight, Alex.' She turned away from him and burrowed her head in the pillows, suddenly so tired she wouldn't have stirred if the creature in the bull mask had come to tuck her in.

At some point during the night Eleanor woke to find she was alone in the bed and light coming from the bathroom. Alex opened the door and stood looking at her.

'I disturbed you.' He switched off the bathroom light and got back into bed.

Eleanor flushed in the darkness. This enforced intimacy was hard to take. Tomorrow night she would sleep in Talia's bed and sleep well with no danger of a monster lurking in her doorway. As there never had been. She felt hideously embarrassed about getting in such a state over a nightmare. Screaming her head off, sweating with fear and, top of the bill, fainting like a maiden in a Victorian novel.

'You cannot sleep?' said a drowsy voice.

'Sorry to keep you awake.' She gasped as a hard arm snaked round her waist and pulled her across the bed.

'Lie still,' Alex muttered, and settled her comfortably against him.

She obeyed, waiting motionless until he relaxed his grasp so she could escape. But Alex's arm stayed firmly in place, holding her fast as he slept. Eleanor yawned, blinking hard. Heavens she was tired...

When she woke again, heart pounding, she was held close to Alex's chest.

'You were making little cries in your sleep,' Alex told her in a tone that set all her alarm bells ringing. 'Were you dreaming?'

'Probably, but nothing scary this time. At least, not that I can remember.' She stirred restlessly, but his hold tightened. He smoothed his cheek against hers, turning her face until their lips met in a kiss so gentle it disarmed her. As it was meant to, the still-functioning part of her brain warned her. His mouth caressed hers until her lips parted to his insistent tongue as he held her so tightly she could feel him hardening against her. She stifled a moan at the touch of seducing hands which ignited her into arousal, heightened by the emotions of the night. He smothered her half-hearted protest with kisses as he dispensed with her nightgown, and sent his mouth roving lower. She choked back a groan as his mouth closed over a hard, sensitive nipple while his fingers caressed its twin and sent fire streaking through her body right down to her toes, disposing of her resistance as his free hand slid between her thighs.

When his seeking fingers found the evidence of her response, she was suddenly a wild thing in his arms. He crushed his lips to hers as he moved over her and into her, then held her tight in pulsing possession for several glorious seconds before his body urged hers into a rhythm which rapidly accelerated into a wild, gasping ascent towards a peak of pleasure he reached alone. He stiffened in the throes of his release as he left her stranded and breathless, the magnificent body heavy as lead on her bruised ribs when it collapsed on hers.

Eleanor pushed at his shoulders. 'You're squashing me,' she hissed, and with a groan he heaved himself away to look down into her flushed, none-too-happy face.

'Forgive me,' he said, surprising her.

Her eyes glittered coldly. 'If a man wakes up in the night with a woman in his arms—any woman—the result is inevitable. I should have gone back to the other room, but I was too scared.'

'The apology,' he informed her formally, 'Was for my haste.'

'Don't worry about it,' she said airily. 'The hassle of searching for the intruder obviously affected your performance.' She searched for her nightgown, her face hot as she came in contact with a bare, muscular leg. 'May I use your shower now, please?'

'You need to ask?'

'Yes!'

'You're angry.'

'Yes to that, too.'

'Because I was too rushed?'

'No!'

'Then because you feel I forced you, Eleanor?'

Eleanor shook her head. 'You know perfectly well that you didn't force me. You're so skilled at the foreplay stuff I had no chance from the start. I'm angry with myself for giving in so easily.' She pulled on the dressing gown and switched on the lamp to find Alex surveying her with narrowed, brooding eyes.

'You need have no worries, Eleanor,' he informed her.

'Splendid. None for you, either. I use birth control, so there won't be any embarrassing little outcome.'

'It would not be embarrassing for me! If there was a child, I would care for it. I was reassuring you about my sexual health.' He chuckled as she flushed. 'You are a surprising lady, Eleanor. You discuss the possibility of an illegitimate child so calmly, yet on the subject of health pitfalls you blush.'

She pushed a strand of hair behind her ear. 'I wasn't blushing. I went hot because that was a risk I hadn't thought of!'

'You need think of it no longer.'

'Splendid.' She caught her breath as Alex leaned to seize her hand, and kissed each finger very deliberately.

'Why so hostile?'

'Stop trying to distract me,' she snapped, eyes flashing like danger signals as he laughed.

'So tell me, Eleanor Markham, if the man you lusted after had returned your feelings, would you have married him?'

'Oh yes, like a shot—at the time. But that was years ago.' She smiled brightly. 'I was soon deeply grateful to him for marrying someone else. And now I'm going to shower, and then I'll spend the rest of the night in that chair.'

Alex took over the bathroom after Eleanor emerged, and frowned when he came out at the sight of her curled up in the chair with a pillow.

'Come back to bed, Eleanor. You need sleep, and so do I. And neither of us will achieve that if you sit up all night.' He smiled persuasively. 'I promise to let you sleep in peace.'

She shook her head. 'I'll keep to the chair. Pretend I'm not here.'

'As if I could possibly do that!' His eyes were sombre

as he got into bed. 'You will be leaving soon, but I think you are unlikely to forget your stay on Kyrkiros, Eleanor.'

'You're absolutely right. I actually achieved an interview with Alexei Drakos.'

He scowled. 'Is that all you will remember?'

'Of course not. I also had the great good fortune to meet your mother.'

'And had so bad a nightmare you fainted,' he reminded her, eyes darkening. 'When I found you unconscious on the floor, my heart stopped.'

She shivered a little. 'Then it's high time you got some sleep to recover.'

'In the morning I shall take you to see a little of my island,' he said, and smiled. 'I feel confident it's no longer necessary to hide you away.'

'I'll enjoy that very much. Will you let me take photographs? Not for my column. I just want souvenirs of my time here, Alex.'

'To remind you of me?'

She smiled sadly. 'I doubt I'll need reminders, Alexei.' She closed her eyes very deliberately and turned her head into the pillow.

'You can't sleep like that and neither can I.' He slid out of bed to sink to his knees in front of her. 'Come back to bed. I shall stay here like this until you do.'

Eleanor stared into the glittering dark eyes locked on hers. 'That's blackmail.'

'I know!'

'Oh—very well.' He was right, not that she was going to admit it. The chair was less comfortable than it looked.

Alex got up, holding out his hand, but Eleanor shook her head, picked up her pillow and resumed her former place on the edge. Without a word he turned out the light and got into bed on the far side, and then leaned back against his pillows, so utterly still it was impossible for her to relax because she kept expecting that arm to reach out and draw her close again. She wanted it to, she realised, heart sinking. What a fool! In a couple of days she would be home again, back in the real world, in her humdrum life. And, back in his anything but humdrum life, Alexei Drakos would forget about her the moment her plane took off.

'I shall miss you,' he said as though he'd read her mind.

She blinked. 'You haven't known me long enough to miss me.'

'Our acquaintance has not been long,' he agreed and laughed softly. 'But it has been so memorable I will never forget you, Eleanor.'

'Good to know I made such an impression.'

'While I have made a very bad impression on you.'

'Only in the beginning. You made up for that with the interview.'

'Could you forget the damned interview? I meant my love-making.'

Heat rushed, unseen, to Eleanor's face. 'Don't talk about it any more. You should sleep.'

'Hold my hand and I will.'

With a sigh Eleanor turned onto her back and stretched out her hand. He grasped it in his, then very slowly he drew her across the space between them and into his arms, holding her against his chest with her head on his shoulder.

'This is good, *ne*?'

'Yes.'

'Can you sleep like this?'

'No.'

'You want to go back to the other side?'

'No.'

His arms tightened. 'You feel almost perfect in my arms, Eleanor.'

'Almost?'

'If I tell you how to make it perfect you will go back to that chair,' he whispered into her hair.

'No I won't. You were right. I couldn't have slept there.'

'Why not?'

Oh, to hell with it, she thought, suddenly reckless. 'Because I want to be here with you.'

Alex tipped her face up to his and kissed her fiercely, and with a purring sound she kissed him back, running a caressing hand down his bare chest.

'You have changed your mind?' he said unevenly.

'Yes.'

'Why?'

'Because life is short and this will never happen again.' She smiled up into his taut face, glorying in the fact that his chest was rising and falling rapidly as she caressed it. 'Now tell me how to make it perfect. Or perhaps I can guess.' She sat up and took the nightgown over her head. 'Is that what you had in mind?'

'Exactly,' he agreed, the look in his eyes as tactile as a caress.

'Now you!'

He promptly threw his only garment away with such drama, Eleanor laughed.

'You laugh at me?' he demanded, crushing her to him.

'Not at you—with you. I do so admire a grand gesture!'

He grinned, and then sobered, looking down at her in wonder.

'What's wrong?'

'Nothing, *glykia mou*. Everything is suddenly, wonderfully right.' He kissed her, taking his time over it, nibbling at the bottom lip then licking around the edge of her lips before kissing them with a sigh which melted her completely. He raised his head to smile at her. 'I have made love to women before.'

'Really bad time to mention it,' she warned, eyes flashing.

He laughed, rubbing his cheek against hers, and then nipped at her lips with fierce, plucking kisses. 'I mention it because with you it is different.'

'I bet you say that to all the girls!'

'*Ochi*! I do not. You are different because I can laugh with you—even though I want you so much it is hard to breathe.'

Eleanor buried her face against him and held him close, glorying in the drumbeat of his heart against her as she pressed hot, open-mouthed kisses over his chest, licking at him with the tip of her tongue until he turned her face up to his and took her open mouth in a kiss of rough possession which thrilled her down to her toes.

He tore his mouth away and buried his face in her hair. 'This time,' he said huskily, 'I will not give way to greed and rush. I want—I *need*—you to share the glory I found with you earlier.'

'Is it a matter of pride to bring a woman to orgasm every time?' she asked, and he shook with laughter.

'Since you ask, clinical one, yes it is. But it is more a desire to share my pleasure than pride.' He tipped her face up to his. 'Do your lovers leave you wanting sometimes?'

She bit her lip, eyeing him under her lashes. 'I don't think of them as lovers.'

'It does not surprise me if they leave you unsatisfied!'

'None of the men in my past fitted the description, exactly.'

Alex held her closer. 'How many?'

'Hundreds!' Eleanor laughed at the look on his face. 'Only teasing, more like one or two. Since I started in my present job, relationships are hard work because I travel so much. I met my first boyfriend in school, but we were too young for the sex thing, I suppose.'

His arms tightened around her. 'Teenage boys are walking hormones, Eleanor. I speak from experience. He would have wanted sex!'

She shook her head. 'He was too wrapped up in his work. He was totally focused on doing well in exams. He never wanted sex with me.'

'I don't want sex, either,' Alex said, startling her. The evidence that he did was hard to miss.

'Let's go to sleep then.'

'Not yet. First, *glykia mou,* we make love.'

'You said you didn't want that.'

He tipped her face up to his and kissed her. 'I said I didn't want sex. That is just a mindless, mechanical meeting of bodies, *ne*? To achieve true rapture, the mind and spirit must be involved.'

But not the heart. Eleanor and ran a questing finger down his chest. 'Show me, then.'

This time Alex lingered so long over making love to every part of her Eleanor was trembling and impatient and almost reduced to tears before his body joined with hers. The blissful sensation of union was so intense they achieved instant perfect rhythm, which threatened to hurtle them towards climax far too soon. But this time Alex took her to the brink and held her there several tantalising times before she came apart in his arms at last, and with a visceral groan he surrendered to his own release, his face buried in her hair.

Eleanor was happy to have Alex stay where he was. By some strange alchemy his weight was easy to bear this time. She revelled in the feeling of the graceful, muscular body still joined with hers in the ultimate intimacy, his arms still holding her close. One of them ought to move, but since it obviously wasn't going to be her she was content to stay where she was and enjoy the experience to the full. As Alex had promised, it had been no mere mechanical process. Making love with him had transcended anything she'd experienced before. Alex raised his head and smiled down into eyes which widened in surprise as she felt him harden inside her.

'I want you again, *kardia mou*,' he said huskily in a tone which caused such a melting sensation inside her he thrust deeper to take advantage of it. 'You want me too, *ne*?'

When he kissed her she responded wildly, her body saying yes without words as he began to make love to her all over again, but this time faster and wilder, as she met him thrust for thrust until they gasped together in the throes of culmination so overwhelming it left them speechless in each other's arms. It was a long time before Alex reluctantly separated from her. He slid from the bed, holding out his hand and, feeling irrationally shy, Eleanor took it and let him draw her to her feet.

'We shall shower together and then sleep together, *ne*?'

She nodded silently, thrilled to her toes when Alex picked her up and carried her into the bathroom. He set her down very gently in the shower stall and turned on the water, waited until it warmed and drew her into his arms to stand under the spray.

'We must not stay here like this together very long or I will want you again!'

Eleanor stared at him, astonished. 'Really?'

'Really!' He soaped her with caresses which proved it was no idle threat, and she laughed and pushed him away while she rinsed.

'I would like a towel please,' she said primly.

'You Brits are so cold-blooded,' he mocked, and then

leapt away, laughing as her eyes flashed. 'Shall I help you get dry, *agapi mou*?'

She shook her head, stifling a yawn as she swathed herself in the towel. 'I'll do it so we get back to bed faster. I'm tired, *kyrie* Drakos.'

'Which is no surprise,' he said, drying off quickly. 'After enduring storms and nightmares and my love-making, it is only natural you are tired.' He took her hand and led her back into the bedroom. He tidied the bed a little then got into it and held out his arms. Eleanor gave her hair one last rub, turned out the light, slid into Alex's embrace and with a murmur of pleasure he pulled her close and drew up the covers.

'I didn't *endure* your love-making,' she said sleepily.

He rubbed his cheek against hers. 'You liked it?'

Eleanor raised her head to smile at him. 'I loved it.'

He kissed her gently and smoothed her head back down against his shoulder. 'In the morning we shall swim together, Eleanor.'

She sighed happily. 'Yes, Alex.'

'Now sleep.'

'Yes, Alex.'

He chuckled and held her close as he gazed into the darkness. Just one more day and Miss Eleanor Markham would be gone. And so would he. His stay on Kyrkiros had been longer than intended and now it was time to stop lotus-eating and get back to the real world which provided the means to go on with the work planned on the island. But, before spending time on the beach with Eleanor, he would take another look in the Kastro basement. Then after their swim he would take her on a short tour of the island and touch base with as many inhabitants as possible.

CHAPTER EIGHT

ELEANOR's interior alarm woke her early enough to let her pull on the bathrobe and unlock the door before Alex caught her in his arms.

'Where are you going?'

'Back to my room before Sofia finds I'm missing.'

He pushed the tousled curls back from his face and kissed her at such length they were both breathless when he let her go. 'Come back to bed,' he whispered, but Eleanor found the strength from somewhere to shake her head.

'The bed will be dry by now in my room.' She smiled ruefully. 'Humour me. I want to make it up with fresh linen before Sofia arrives.'

Alex laughed indulgently. 'If you must, you must, Eleanor Markham.' He glanced at his watch. 'But Sofia will not be here for half an hour yet.'

'In that case, we can sort your bed out before I go.'

And, no matter how much he laughed, Eleanor insisted on restoring Alex's bed to some semblance of order, demanding his help to plump up pillows and turn down the covers.

'Good,' she said with satisfaction afterwards and made for the door. 'Now I can do mine.'

'Shall I come and help?'

She shook her head, smiling. 'Think how shocked Sofia would be.'

Alex ruffled her hair. 'Be quick, then. I shall come for you when breakfast is ready.'

In the bright light of day Eleanor's fears seemed so silly as she hurried to her room, she bitterly regretted sending Alex off on a wild-goose chase. To her relief the mattress had dried overnight, but to be on the safe side she did some hauling and pushing and turned it over before putting the clean linen on it. When she was satisfied it looked pristine and perfect in its white covers, she got into a black one-piece swimsuit, added shorts and T-shirt and did some work on her hair and face, faintly surprised to find she looked much the same as usual. Eleanor laughed at herself in the mirror. Had she really expected a night of love to show on her face? There were one or two suspicious marks on her skin, but a touch of concealer soon remedied that. If she'd been alone she'd have left them as evidence that, although she'd dreamed about a monster, Alex's love-making had been hot, sweet reality.

When the expected knock came on her door Eleanor threw it open to find Sofia smiling at her.

'*Kalimera, kyria.*'

'*Kalimera,* Sofia, how is Yannis?'

Yannis, she was informed, was much better this morning, due to the *kyria's* medicine, and now he was eating a big breakfast. The woman patted Eleanor's hand gratefully. 'You are a very kind lady. *Kyrie* Alexei is waiting for you.'

Eleanor thanked her and walked with her to the lift, then ran to the tower room when she saw Alex in the doorway. He kissed her hand and held out a chair for her at the table.

'I'm hungry,' he informed her.

'So am I!' Eleanor surveyed the array of fruit and freshly baked rolls with anticipation.

'Love has given you an appetite?'

Love? She was proud of her steady hand as she poured coffee into his cup. 'Yes. Though it can sometimes do the reverse.'

'When this idiot friend of yours rejected you as a lover?' he said instantly and took her hand. 'He was a fool to miss the glory of making love with you.'

'Thank you.' She buttered a roll and ate half of it as she tried, and failed, to picture Dominic Hall making love to her with even a fraction of Alex's skill.

Alex eyed her accusingly. 'You are thinking of him?'

'Yes. I realised an experience like last night would never have been possible with him,' she said candidly.

'It would not have been as good as with me?' he said, reaching out a hand to touch hers.

Eleanor curled her fingers round his. 'No.'

Alex gave her the smile that made her heart turn cartwheels. 'Good. Now, eat. And then we swim.' He passed his cup over. 'More coffee, *parakolo.*'

Eleanor's eyes lingered on his sun-burnished hair, and strong, sculpted features. *You can have anything in the world you want,* she thought as she refilled his cup. Yet in two days she would be back in the UK and would never see him again. She blinked the thought away. Until she left to catch her plane, she must make the most of every moment left of this unique, never-to-be-repeated experience. Alexei Drakos, philanthropist and entrepreneur, was so far out of her league it would have been better in some ways if last night had never happened. Making love with him had been as life-altering as expected—and feared. No other man would ever compare.

'You are day-dreaming,' Alex stated, his eyes kindling. 'What were you thinking about?'

'You.'

'So honest.' He got to his feet and pulled her out of her chair and into his arms to kiss her. 'You are a new experience in my life, Eleanor Markham.'

'Ditto, Alexei Drakos!'

He held her closer. 'Stay longer.'

She shook her head regretfully. 'I need to get back to reality. And you're overdue at whatever destination you were making for after the festival.'

'They can wait for me,' he said with careless arrogance.

'But my job won't wait for me. As Ross McLean constantly informs me, there are dozens of others eager to step into my shoes.'

Alex made a chopping motion with his hand. 'If he gives you trouble, I will take care of him.'

Eleanor found Alex in this mood a big surprise. The love-making in the night might have been the most thrilling experience of *her* life but, sure it was the norm for him, she had expected him to revert to his former persona this morning. To find him behaving like a lover was delightful but unnerving.

'Thank you for the thought, but I can deal with Ross. I thought we were going for a swim,' she added.

He frowned. 'I should search the *Kastro* basement again first.'

'Surely that's unnecessary? You found nothing last night.' She looked him in the eye. 'It will take you too long. I'll be gone tomorrow, remember.'

'You think I have forgotten that?' He took her hand. 'As you wish. I will ask Theo to keep everyone away from my beach, so that I can have you all to myself. How long will you be?'

'Ten minutes.'

He laughed. 'Which means half an hour, *ne*?'

'No, it means ten minutes!'

'Let's make a wager. What will you give me if—when—you lose?'

'My apologies,' she said, laughing, and took off down the hall to her room.

After her period of virtual captivity Eleanor found it so good to be out in the sun with Alex, she felt like singing as he helped her down a steep path to a triangle of sand enclosed in complete privacy by sheltering rocks, softened by shrubs and greenery.

'You keep this entirely to yourself, Alex?'

He shook a towel out for her to sit on. 'Only when I'm here. Otherwise all are welcome to use it.'

'Ah, but do they?' Eleanor leaned back against her tote bag.

'I've never asked.' He took off his shirt and let himself down beside her with a sigh of pleasure. 'I'm happy to help you with your sun lotion.' He stroked a hand along her thigh.

'I put it on before we came out.'

'A pity. I would have enjoyed smoothing it over your skin.'

Eleanor quivered inside and cast a look at the graceful, muscular body stretched out beside her. 'I could put some on you, if you like.'

Alex laughed. 'I would like it far too much! Perhaps you could do that later when we are alone in my room.'

So he expected her to sleep with him again tonight. 'No need for sun block at night!'

'True. But I would delight in the touch of your hands on me, *glykia mou.*'

Eleanor frowned at him. 'Time to swim,' she said gruffly and got up to remove her jeans and shirt. 'Come on.'

When she took off at a run he laughed and chased after her. She waded into the waves until she was deep enough to dive under them and he dove in after her, swimming stroke for stroke with her, then disappearing to come up alongside her to splash her. She laughed in delight and retaliated, enjoying this new playful Alex so much she was sorry when he said it was time to return to the beach.

'Otherwise you will get tired,' he said as they swam back at a leisurely rate. 'And I must take a walk. Will you come with me?'

Eleanor stood up when her feet touched bottom, and pushed her wet hair back from her face. 'I'd like that very much.' She took the hand he held out. 'It's so lovely here, Alex. How old would you say the island is?'

'It was first inhabited about 3500 BC,' he informed her and laughed at her look of awe. 'Come, water nymph, we must get back to the Kastro to dress and then take our walk before it gets too hot.'

Later, in a raspberry-pink sun dress she'd packed as the only alternative to the ill-fated Breton number, Eleanor went along to knock on the office door to tell Alex she was ready.

'Will I do?' she asked.

'Oh yes,' he said, giving her a leisurely top-to-toe scrutiny. 'You will do perfectly. We will walk just up to the church and back, so that you can get an idea of how people live here.'

Eleanor decided against carrying her tote bag, which looked battered after its adventure as an assault weapon. She slung her camera over her shoulder instead, put on her sunglasses and white cotton hat and smiled up at Alex. 'I'm ready.'

They went into the kitchen on their way out and found Yannis helping his mother now his friend Markos had gone home. The youth smiled shyly at Eleanor as he thanked her for the medicine, and assured *kyrie* Alexei that he was now much better.

His mother added her thanks and complimented Eleanor on her dress, then announced that lunch was cold today and could be served at whatever time it was required.

'*Efcharisto,* Sofia,' said Alex, and told her they would not be long in case the sun was too hot for *kyria* Eleanor.

'Isn't life strange?' Eleanor remarked as they set off up the steep, *maquis*-scented road together. 'I first arrived here just a couple of days ago, yet it feels a lot longer than that.'

'Because so much has happened since.' Alex smiled down at her with a warmth Eleanor marvelled at when she remembered his original hostility.

'Stop a moment; I want some shots of the houses climbing the hill up here.' She took out her camera and focused on the small houses, some of them white, others painted ochre or sky-blue, most of them with bougainvillaea tumbling over their porches in bright cascades. A woman came out of one to greet them, and Alex smiled at her and introduced his companion as a visitor from England.

'Would you ask her permission to take a photograph?' asked Eleanor.

Alex spoke to the woman, who nodded eagerly as Eleanor posed her against the white of the house and vibrant pink of the flowers to take her shot. From then on someone came out to greet them at every house as they made their way up to the blue-crowned dome of the white church, where Eleanor took a last photograph before putting her camera away.

'I would have liked to show you the vineyards, but it would take too long,' Alex told her as they turned back. 'You must come back some day to see the rest of the island.'

Never going to happen, Eleanor thought sadly.

Alex peered under the brim of the hat as they walked down the hill. 'What are you thinking?'

'I won't be sent back to this part of the world again,' she

said with regret. 'My next assignment will be in the UK, researching places for unusual weekend country-breaks.'

'Then you must come back here on vacation, with no work involved,' he said promptly, as though it was the easiest thing in the world.

'Kyrkiros isn't a holiday destination,' she reminded him.

Alex laughed softly. 'You are always welcome to share my bed, Eleanor Markham.'

'I'll keep that in mind,' she said, her voice neutral to cover the leap in her blood at the thought. When they paused for Eleanor to record the boats drawn up on the beach, Theo Lazarides came to meet them.

'Be warned, Theo,' said Alex, grinning, 'Ms Markham probably wants your photograph to add to the hundreds she's already taken this morning.'

'May I, Mr Lazarides?' said Eleanor, and when he nodded cheerfully she took a shot quickly before he could strike a stiff pose. '*Efcharisto poli.*'

'You look warm, Eleanor,' said Alex. 'Go in and tell Sofia we're ready to lunch in fifteen minutes. I need a word with Theo.'

Eleanor went up the steps into the dark, cool interior of the *Kastro*, gave Sofia the message and then took the lift to her room. She transferred the morning's photographs to her laptop and sent an email to her parents before joining Alex in the tower room, where Sofia was setting out a traditional Greek salad to eat with bread she'd baked that morning, and fresh figs for dessert.

'Where have you been, Eleanor?' he asked.

She explained. 'My parents will meet me at the airport.'

'*Kyria* Eleanor will be leaving us tomorrow, Sofia.' Alex told the woman.

'Then I will make a special dinner tonight,' she promised and smiled sadly at Eleanor. 'It is a pity you must leave, *kyria*. You must come back soon.'

Eleanor smiled brightly. 'Perhaps for next year's festival.'

'You didn't mean that,' said Alex when they were alone.

'No. Ross was too grudging about the expenses for this trip to want something similar any time soon. Besides…' She paused and helped herself to salad.

'Besides?' he prompted.

Eleanor looked at him steadily. 'This has been the kind of unique experience that never happens twice.'

'Never is a long time,' he said, returning the look. 'Who knows what fate has in store for us?'

She smiled and went on eating, but abandoned the meal after only a few mouthfuls and drank some water.

'You are not hungry?' Alex asked.

'Not very.'

'I took you too far in the heat.' He helped her to some figs. 'Eat some of these to give you energy, then rest on your bed—alone,' he added and touched a fingertip to her bottom lip. 'This afternoon I must go out for a while to the vineyards.'

'I'd rather go up to the roof and make the most of this sunshine before I go.'

Alex patted her hand. 'You may do whatever you wish, *glykia mou*. But don't stay up there too long. If you are not back in your room when I return, I will come and fetch you.'

Eleanor's eyes sparkled. 'Is that a promise?'

For answer he stood up and snatched her out of her chair to kiss her. 'Or I could stay and not go at all,' he whispered, his breath hot against her neck.

'Never let it be said I took you away from your responsibilities,' she said primly and with effort moved out of his arms. 'You go and do your thing. I shall have my final sunbathe, and then this evening—'

'We shall go to bed after dinner to enjoy every minute of our last night together,' he said emphatically, and smiled into her eyes. 'You agree with me?'

Eleanor flushed. 'You know I do.' She began putting the remains of their meal in the trolley and smiled in approval as Alex helped. 'Well done. I'm having such a good influence on you.'

'Very true.' The dark eyes met hers with intensity that quickened her pulse. 'It was my great good fortune that your Ross McLean sent you to interview me.'

'Not *quite* your original reaction,' she retorted, her tone tart to hide her delight.

'No, *kyria* journalist, it was not! But now it is hard for me to part with you for just an hour.'

This statement pleased her so much, she reached up to kiss him.

He looked down at her in surprise. 'You kissed me.'

'You didn't like it?'

He seized her in his arms. 'Of course I liked it, but until now I have done the kissing.'

'I always kiss you back,' she said breathlessly and gave him a wry little smile. 'I can't help it. You kiss me and I'm lost—which,' she added, pulling away from him, 'Is not the cleverest thing to admit.'

'I disagree. It is exactly what a lover wants to hear,' he assured her as they went along the hall and smiled as her eyes opened wide. 'I will prove it to you later,' he assured her, then kissed her and opened the door to her room. 'I must go. Do not stay up on the roof too long.'

'Are you getting to your vineyards by boat?'

Alex shook his head. 'I keep an off-road vehicle here on the island.' He strode off to the lift and waved a hand to her as the doors opened. *'Antia, glykia mou.'*

CHAPTER NINE

ELEANOR soon settled under a parasol in the roof garden, but found it so hard to concentrate on the not very thrilling plot she put her book down, feeling tired. The last couple of days had made such demands on her stamina, a short nap was necessary since she was unlikely to get much sleep tonight. Stretching like a cat in the sun at the thought, she woke later, yawning, to find she'd been asleep for more than an hour. She put her belongings in her bag and crossed over to the balustrade to gaze at the sun glittering on the sea, turned away to take a last look at the roof garden and with a sigh went down the stairs into the relative dimness of the hall. A hard arm closed round her, and she smiled in the split second before a gag was thrust in her mouth and she found her captor wasn't Alex.

She gave smothered sounds of violent protest and fought wildly, kicking out as her hands were wrenched behind her back, but she stopped dead when a knife was brandished before her startled eyes. Afraid to move as her wrists were tied cruelly tight, she was jerked round to face a man with a pelt of close-cut black curls above a broad, low-browed face, his eyes glittering with such menace Eleanor abandoned all idea of struggling in case he set to work with his knife. He slung her bag over his shoulder, and with a torch in one hand seized her arm with the other to hurry her down the old, spiral stone stairs.

When they reached the hall level he stopped, cursing in a vicious undertone at the sound of car doors slamming and voices outside. Eleanor tried to make a break for it, but he jerked her back and hauled her down into the labyrinthine depths of the old *Kastro* at such breakneck speed she was in constant fear of spraining an ankle as she tried to undo the clasp of her bracelet without her captor noticing. Her relief was intense when the chain slipped from her wrist as her captor chivvied her on a dizzying route along passageways, down flights of steps and finally thrust her into a cave-like space with a narrow aperture which let in just enough light for her to see him heave a tall stone across the opening.

Her captor pushed her to a stone ledge, his hand heavy on her shoulder to force her to sit. Head throbbing and heart knocking against her ribs, Eleanor glared at the man furiously, hoping her eyes were giving off the sparks Alex liked so much. Alex! *Please* let him find the bracelet and come looking for her. She clenched her teeth against rising nausea, but the final bout of rough handling had been the last straw. Eleanor's stomach gave such a sickening lurch she began to heave, and in panic made smothered sounds of desperate entreaty. He scowled at her, but after a moment's indecision tore the gag from her mouth. She took in a great gulp of musty air, willing her stomach to behave as he spoke roughly to her.

'Don't understand,' she gasped, swallowing convulsively. 'I'm British.'

He gaped, thunderstruck.

She nodded feverishly. 'I'm a journalist. Here to report on the festival.'

He shook his head angrily. 'Speak slow.'

Eleanor repeated the words slowly and deliberately, but the man shook his head in sneering disbelief.

'Alexei Drakos never speak to reporters. You are lovers, *ne?'*

'No.' She tried to roll her shoulders. 'Please—could you untie my wrists? My shoulders are painful.'

He snorted derisively. 'You think me fool?'

'You can tie my hands again in front of me. *Parakolo?'*

He picked up the knife, his eyes gloating as he waved it in front of her face. 'You scream, I cut.'

Eleanor nodded mutely and sat very still as he untied the ropes, but to her shame couldn't stifle a groan as the blood rushed back into her shoulder muscles and sore wrists.

'Entaxei,' he grunted and yanked the wrists together in front of her to tie them again. He went to the doorway to move the stone a little then turned to her. 'Quiet, so I can surprise Alexei when he comes to rescue.' He slashed the knife in front of his throat in graphic illustration then slithered through the narrow opening.

Eleanor set to work to loosen her bonds, but after a fruitless interval with only her teeth as tools she gave up torturing her sore wrists to study the ancient stone block walling her in. There were depressions on it which provided natural handholds for manoeuvring, so when Alex had been searching down here in the dark it must have looked like part of a wall instead of an opening into this cave-like cell. Yet Eleanor was sure her captor was no thug. She had an idea he spoke better English than he was letting on. But he definitely wasn't the man in the bull mask. He was bigger, and there was no tattoo on his forearm. He looked—and smelt—too clean to have been hiding out in this grubby little cave; and his tension was palpable. Something had obviously gone wrong with this kidnap plan too.

Eleanor looked up at the stone ceiling and clenched her

teeth against rising panic at the thought of the weight of centuries over her head. She had to calm down. A pounding headache and sore shoulders and wrists were trouble enough without claustrophobia—another fine Greek word! She tensed as the stone was pushed aside far enough to let her captor slither back into the room.

He gave her what was obviously meant to be an intimidating glare. 'Alexei come soon. No scream before I say!'

'Oh please,' she said with disdain. 'You speak better English than that.'

He scowled, taken aback, and shook his head. 'You mistake.'

'No. The mistake is yours.' She pointed to his watch. 'If you want to keep the act, lose the Rolex and expensive clothes. So, tell me, who was the man in the bull mask?'

He thrust a hand through his dark curls, scowling. 'It was I.'

She shook her head. 'Right grammar, wrong answer. He had a tattoo.'

He leaned against the wall, looking sulky. 'He said you fainted.'

'I did. But I noted the tattoo first.' Eleanor winced as she shrugged her aching shoulders. 'I'm a journalist. It's my job to note details.'

'You have habit of annoying me, lady. Because of you, Spiro failed to kidnap *kyria* Talia.' He sneered. 'Alexei must be *so* grateful to you.'

Eleanor's eyes narrowed. 'You know him well, then.'

'Too well.' He shrugged and looked at his watch. 'I heard him talking up there. Our hero will soon rush to the rescue and I will overpower him.'

Eleanor's heart contracted. The thought of Alex off his guard and vulnerable to whatever weapons this psychopath had on hand was unbearable. 'Tell me,' she said conversationally, 'Why do you hate him so much?'

A tide of angry colour suffused his astonished face as he yanked her to her feet by her sore wrists. 'I have reasons.'

She eyed him defiantly to hide how much he'd hurt her. 'Did you actually intend to harm Alexei's mother before you exchanged her for ransom money?'

'*Ochi*, I do not hurt women of her age.' His hands tightened on her shoulders. 'Taking her was just the best way to hurt Alexei.' He took in a deep breath and then smiled with a relish that sent shivers down Eleanor's spine. 'But I will enjoy conquering *you*, *kyria*.'

She yanked herself away. 'Keep your filthy hands off me!'

He laughed reluctantly. 'You have spirit, English woman. Yet Markos said you fainted with fright when he appeared in the mask.'

Markos? Yannis' friend? Eleanor eyed the man disdainfully. 'Is he the puppet-master, giving you orders?'

Eyes blazing, he pushed her back down on the ledge. 'No man gives me orders,' he hissed in fury. 'Markos is ignorant boy, but useful because poor. I gave him money to buy costume from the dancers.'

'Why?'

'To wear it to scare you into coming down to his friend's boat to bring you to me on Karpyros. But he scared you too much. Our hero rushed to your rescue when you fainted, so Markos ran away and hid the mask.' He looked at his watch. 'Alexei knows now that you are missing. When he comes, scream for help to bring him to me. If not,' he added, fingering the knife, 'I will enjoy hurting you until you do.' His mouth twisted in a cynical sneer. 'The gods sent Talia Kazan to me on Karpyros that day. I was so kind—I brought her over here in my boat because Takis was busy.'

'Why?'

'Because when I saw her I had inspiration,' he said with satisfaction. 'I would pay someone to kidnap Alexei's beloved mother during the festival when no one would notice. Then I would hide her on my boat and demand ransom from him.' He glared at her. 'But you spoiled my plan. So now you pay. And Alexei will pay to get you back.'

'If you want money from Alexei, you won't get any by harming me,' Eleanor pointed out, her calm infuriating him. She changed tack and gave him a bright, social smile. 'My name's Eleanor Markham, by the way. What's yours?'

His thick black brows shot together in anger. 'You make fun of me?'

'Not at all. What *is* your name?'

'Marinos,' he said proudly.

Eleanor's eyebrows rose. 'Are you related to Alexei's college friend, Ari?'

His eyes narrowed. 'You know that?'

'Alexei mentioned a holiday spent on Crete with her.'

'At my family home, where everyone *love* Alexei. Christina most of all.'

Christina? Eleanor eyed him curiously. 'Who is she?'

'She was my girlfriend, but when she saw Alexei she wanted *him*.' His fists clenched. 'Christina followed him round like pet dog. She was furious when my sister would not take us with them when she went sailing with Alexei that day, but glad later when Arianna almost died because Drakos lost control of the dinghy when the weather changed. It was only by Poseidon's will that they were rescued, but then Alexei abandoned Arianna, and I swore to avenge her.'

His eyes lit with a maniacal gleam. 'When Arianna married Dion Aristides, Christina seized her chance to comfort Alexei, but when he tired of her she took revenge with the lies she told reporter about him. Now I will get mine.'

'It's taken you an amazingly long time to get round to it!' For a moment Eleanor thought she'd gone too far as he raised a hand to strike her, but his arm dropped and he cocked his head to listen to sounds she'd talked her head off to distract him from. 'I suppose Alexei is a hard man to get at with his security staff and his constant travelling—'

'Silence,' he spat at her, glaring. 'Our hero is near. So keep very quiet until I give order to scream.' He seized her wrist and brandished the knife. 'Or I cut one of your fingers off as gift for Alexei.'

Eleanor's stomach objected to the idea so much she sat motionless.

'Eleanor?' yelled Alex in the distance.

'He has a knife!' she screamed at the top of her voice and gave a choked cry as a fist back-handed her across the jaw.

'And I will use it to mark your whore,' roared Marinos in English,

'How stupid! You won't get money out of him that way,' Eleanor sneered at him in such derision, Marinos bellowed with rage and lunged at her, but she held him off with her joined hands and kneed him viciously in the place that hurt him most. She overbalanced and fell in a heap as Marinos doubled up, retching, and then the stone was wrenched aside with an axe and Alexei leapt in to pull Eleanor to her feet.

'Are you hurt?' he asked harshly.

She held up her bound hands. 'My wrists are sore— Look out!' She dodged back as Marinos staggered up, knife upraised, but Alex caught his wrist in an iron grip, twisting until the knife fell, clattering to the floor.

'Still fighting dirty, little brother?' Alex said scornfully and threw a look at Eleanor over his shoulder. 'Go outside to Theo.'

'So the—hero was—afraid to come alone,' gasped the other man.

Alex's teeth glinted in a wolf-like smile. 'The others will wait outside while you and I finish this in here.'

Marinos scrambled away, clutching himself. 'Then it is you who fight dirty. I am in big pain.'

'Are you expecting sympathy?' Alex turned on Eleanor, his eyes imperious. 'I told you to go. I need room.'

She eyed the axe. 'Are you going to kill him?'

He shrugged and turned eyes like shards of black ice on Marinos. 'You caused harm to my mother and my guest,' he said in English for Eleanor's benefit. 'Did you really expect to leave my island unpunished?'

'It was not my plan to hurt your mother.' The man glared malevolently. 'She was just best way to hurt *you*.'

'You were right. But you also enraged my father.' Marinos' face paled even more at the mention of Milo Drakos as Alex thrust out the axe and prodded him against the rough stone of the wall with its handle. 'My guest spoiled your plan, *ne*? So you hurt her. And now you pay.'

Marinos swallowed, eyes riveted on the axe blade.

Alex eyed him dispassionately. 'You paid someone to kidnap my mother, dressed up in a mask to frighten Miss Markham and then tied her up and dragged her down here, even struck her. I salute you, Paul Marinos. If I had a laurel wreath, I would crown you.'

'He wasn't the one in the mask,' Eleanor felt compelled to say. 'He doesn't do his own dirty work. He paid someone to frighten me.'

'I know. Markos went crying to Theo to confess.' Alex glared at Paul with utter contempt then turned on Eleanor. 'Go outside. Now.'

She went, outside into the dark passageway. She held

up her hands to Theo, who was waiting there with Yannis. '*Parakalo, kyrie* Lazarides.'

He exclaimed in concern and took a knife to her bonds, then handed her the bracelet and gave instructions to the excited boy. 'Yannis will take you to Sofia, *kyria*.'

Holding a large torch aloft, Yannis carefully guided a very tired Eleanor through the warren of passageways up to the hall, where Sofia was waiting anxiously. He gave a hurried explanation which brought loud exclamations of horror from his mother, but as she folded Eleanor in her arms Yannis raced away, eager to return to the excitement below.

Eleanor's grasp of Greek was less than usual as she tried to assure Sofia there was nothing much wrong with her, a statement the woman dismissed with scorn. Sofia led her into the kitchen to apply a bag of ice to the bruised jaw, and smeared something soothing on the chafed wrists, all the time heaping dramatic curses on the criminal who had injured the *kyria*, and on Markos Kosta, who had helped him.

'Now you bathe, and I will bring tea.' She sighed. 'You will be glad to leave us.'

Eleanor shook her head sadly.

Sofia patted her hand. 'I will take you up to your room so you can be clean and beautiful again.'

Eleanor smiled wryly. Clean was easy; beautiful would take longer. Limp with reaction, she was glad of Sofia's company as the woman ran a hot bath, poured bath essence into it and gave orders to lie in it and relax. She offered to stay during the process, but Eleanor declined gracefully, and Sofia hurried off, as eager as her son to get back to the excitement.

The hot water was soothing on Eleanor's various bruises and scrapes, but it was hard to relax while she fretted about what was going on in the depths of the *Kastro*. Not that she had any doubts about Alex's mastery over Paul Marinos.

She was also pretty sure there wouldn't be much pounding on an opponent who was not only physically inferior to him but who was suffering in the part of him that men value most. On the other hand, she could perfectly understand—and share—Alex's determination to punish the man who'd frightened Talia.

To pass the time, Eleanor put in some determined work on her appearance, but it seemed like hours before she finally heard the lift. She shot out of her room and ran along the hall into Alex's arms.

'I'm sorry I took so long. I had something to do after I finished with Paul. I didn't chop him in pieces,' he assured her huskily, 'Though I wanted to. I just smacked him around a little.' He grinned suddenly. 'I think you hurt him far more than I did, *glykia mou*.'

Her eyes flashed. 'Good. So where is he now?'

'I was tempted to leave him where he was, with the stone in place and guards outside,' Alex informed her grimly. 'But, because he is Arianna's brother, I told Theo to take Paul to the bathroom the security men use and afterwards lock him up in the exercise room.' His mouth twisted in disgust. 'Theo even persuaded me to let the man have coffee and brandy.'

Eleanor nodded in approval. 'He needs to be in some kind of shape for tomorrow. He looked pretty sick when you mentioned your father.'

'As well he might,' agreed Alex with relish. His eyes blazed as the late sun highlighted the bruise on Eleanor's jaw. 'But now I see your face, I regret leaving him conscious, *kardia mou*.' When they reached his room he picked her up and sat down with her in the chair, cradling her against him. 'Is that really all he did to you?'

She showed him her wrists. 'These are a bit sore, my shoulders too because he tied my hands behind my back—

and he gagged me, which was seriously unpleasant. But I managed to hurt him before he hurt me.'

'He is very fortunate that you did, otherwise I would have taken him apart,' he said with quiet violence. 'As it is, I will leave him to Dion.'

Eleanor frowned. 'Will Dion's punishment be physical?'

Alex shook his head. 'He has little love for Paul, but he will not distress Arianna that much right now. A verbal lashing will be enough. One thing is certain—Paul Marinos will not rest easy tonight.' He held her closer, rubbing his cheek against her hair. 'Not only will he be apprehensive about the morning, he will envy me the privilege of holding you in my arms all night.'

'I don't think so, Alex.'

He held her away from him. 'You don't want to sleep with me?'

'Of course I do! But I doubt that Paul Marinos will be envious. His taste runs more to the voluptuous—like the charms of his accomplice.' She hesitated. 'Did Paul tell you about Christina?'

Alex's lip curled. 'That is why I took so long to come to you. I had to go over to Karpyros for a little talk with her about aiding and abetting Paul in his revenge. He still hates me because Christina Mavros wanted me instead of him all those years ago.' His lip curled in distaste. 'For a while after Arianna married Dion, I was fool enough to console myself with her.'

'No wonder Paul hates your guts. But so, obviously, does Christina. How long were you together?'

Alex looked uncomfortable. 'For a couple of weeks only. She wanted marriage. I did not.'

'Ah!' Eleanor shook her head. 'You Greeks are a vengeful bunch. She told those lies to a reporter to get back at you. And then she colluded with Paul over his kidnap plans for the same reason. I doubt that he'd have hurt your mother, but I fancy he would have enjoyed hurting me.'

Alex crushed her close. 'If he had succeeded he would not be drinking my brandy right now, *kardia mou*.'

'He didn't succeed. I learned a bit of basic self-defence in college and got in first. I hear Sofia coming by the way,' she said into his chest.

'Then I will have a bath while you drink your tea.' He smiled as he stood her on her feet. 'But just tea, *parakolo*, because I asked Sofia to serve dinner very early tonight.'

Eleanor's face heated as she made for the door. 'What reason did you give?'

'None,' he said, surprised, with the typical hubris which half-irritated, half-delighted her.

Alex watched her go, a smile playing about his lips, and then made for the bathroom to stand under water as hot as he could bear. He needed purifying heat after the encounter with Paul Marinos, who had grown from an indulged, petulant teenager into a bored, discontented man who found a fitting partner in crime in Christina Mavros. She would have been only too delighted to help him hurt Alexei Drakos.

He smiled as he thought of her face when he found her waiting for Paul in a *taverna* on Karpyros. It had been a great pleasure to inform her that Paul's plan had gone badly wrong, and if she were wise she'd get the hell out of Karpyros and never show her face there again. And this time, he'd made it clear, there were to be no more colourful lies to the press. Otherwise Alexei would publish the facts about her involvement in kidnap and blackmail with Paul Marinos. There'd been furious protestations of innocence, but in the end Christina had taken the next ferry home to Crete. Alex's mouth curled in disgust at the thought of Paul

Marinos. Deprived of his knife, the clever swine had put up no fight against fists which had battered him in furious retaliation for the way he'd treated Eleanor. Paul had known that putting up no defence was the only way to cut short his punishment.

Alex's towelled off in a hurry, thrust his fingers through his hair by way of grooming and then anointed his sore knuckles with some of Sofia's special balm. He pulled on a white T-shirt and jeans soft with age, his mind occupied with ways to make his last night with Eleanor one she would look back on with such pleasure she would want to repeat it very soon. His eyes glinted. He would bring his trip to London forward with just that aim in mind.

Sofia was laying the table when Eleanor reached the tower room. 'I brought tea for you, *kyria*,' she said and smiled in approval. 'You look better now.'

'I feel better.' Eleanor cast an eye over the dish of pastries on the tray. 'These look gorgeous.'

'I made *kyrie* Alexei's favourites.' She gave Eleanor a woman-to-woman smile. 'He asked me to serve dinner early, which is good. You need a good sleep ready for your journey tomorrow.'

'Thank you, Sofia.'

The woman laid a hand on Eleanor's as she turned to go. 'I am ashamed that a friend of Yannis should harm you, *kyria*. Markos is not a bad boy. His parents died when he was young, and he lives with a sister who has a large family. Life is not easy for him. To earn such money for so little was too much temptation.' She rolled her large dark eyes. 'Also it was big fun to wear that stupid mask—but he did not mean to make you faint, *kyria*.'

Having understood most of this, Eleanor patted Sofia's hand. 'I understand.'

'You are a kind young lady. I am sad to see you go. Come back soon.'

Eleanor smiled, her throat too tight to answer, and with a sigh poured some tea, depressed. But when Alex came to join her the sight and scent of him pushed aside all thoughts of leaving to concentrate on the heady pleasure of now.

Sofia served grilled swordfish, and a dish of *keftedes*, the pork meatballs Eleanor had enjoyed in several eating places during her island-hopping. 'Just for you, *kyrie*,' Sofia told Alex as she left them.

'Rustic food, but my favourite,' he commented as he seated Eleanor. 'Sofia makes them for me every time I come here.'

'I've eaten them all round the Aegean. I like those bits of pork they grill on skewers, too.' She thought for a moment. '*Souvlakia*?'

He grinned. 'You're trying to impress me, but you're a journalist, *kyria* Markham. You take notes.'

Her eyes flashed. 'And pretty nasty you were when you first saw me doing it.' She tasted her fish with pleasure. 'This is so good. I don't eat enough fish at home—at least not this kind—' She stopped, flushing. 'Why are you looking at me like that?'

Alex smiled slowly, the look in his eyes hot enough to melt her bones. 'Because I hunger for you, *glykia mou,* far more than for Sofia's excellent dinner.'

With effort she tore her eyes away. 'Eat it just the same, Alex, or Sofia will be hurt.'

'I know.' His eyes darkened. 'But it does my appetite no good to know that tomorrow you are leaving. And before I can take you to the airport I must deal with Dion and Paul.'

'You have absolutely no need to come with me to Crete,' she protested. 'I'm not in any kind of danger now.'

'I will see you onto the plane, Eleanor,' he stated with such finality she gave in.

'Alex,' she said later, giving up the struggle. 'I just can't eat any more.'

'I will ring Sofia and ask her to bring coffee and leave the pastries for us to eat later.' He smiled crookedly as he got up. 'I will even help clear the food away, ready for her.'

She smiled. 'How you've changed since we first met, *kyrie* Drakos!'

'You are such a good influence!' He rang down to the kitchen to speak to Sofia, then took Eleanor by the hand and led her to the sofa. 'Sit with me here while we wait for her.'

'When will Dion get here?'

'He has a fast boat, so he will arrive early in the morning.'

Eleanor hesitated. 'Are you on good terms with him?'

'You mean even though he stole Arianna from me?'

'I suppose I meant that, yes.'

'We are in business together with the wine, and sometimes Arianna asks me to dine with them, but from a personal point of view Dion and I will never be soul-mates. His life is centred here in his beloved islands, while mine is more global in my aim to eclipse my father.' He smiled crookedly. 'I have not succeeded in that yet, but I keep striving.'

Eleanor's hand tightened on his. 'I get the feeling you're a little less hostile to him than you were. Are you thawing towards your father?'

'To a certain extent, yes,' he admitted reluctantly. 'But at one time, when I found he doubted my paternity, I wanted to kill him. Yet I owe him in one way, because my anger made me determined to make it on my own in life without any help from him.'

'He offered help?'

'Yes.'

'But you refused it, of course.'

'Of course.' His chin rose. 'I not only had money I'd made myself, I inherited a generous legacy from my grandfather. I needed no help from my father—or from anyone else. Besides, any hope of reconciliation between us died when I found his mistress staying with him on Corfu.' His eyes darkened. 'She tried to poison me to make me go away.'

Eleanor stared at the stern, beautiful face silhouetted against the fading light. 'Is that why you were ill?'

Alex nodded. 'She was clever enough to make me just sick enough to go home and leave the field clear for her.' His face hardened. 'She need not have troubled. When I found Melania there, I couldn't get away fast enough.'

'And afterwards you shut your father out of your life,' she said softly and hesitated. 'Did your mother do the same?'

'I don't know. Mother will never talk about him.' He shrugged. 'But it must have been obvious the other night that they are not indifferent to each other. Nor,' he added darkly, 'Do I think it was the only time they'd seen each other recently.'

'It seemed obvious to me that he cares for you too, Alex.'

'Only because he has no other son to carry on his name.' He smiled as Sofia came in with a tray. He spoke to her at length and she nodded and patted his hand, then came to Eleanor and patted hers.

'You were too sad to leave to eat much tonight,' she said slowly so Eleanor could understand. She turned to Alex. 'Do I give the prisoner food?'

'Yes. But *kyrie* Lazarides must take it to him, not Yannis,' he ordered, and she nodded and wished them goodnight.

Alex drew Eleanor to her feet. 'And now,' he said, kissing her hand, 'I think we should take this tray to our room and lock the world away, *ne?*'

'Oh yes,' she sighed, and smiled as she saw that Sofia had provided both tea and coffee. 'I'll miss all this when I get home.'

'Will you miss me, too?'

'Yes,' she said baldly as he hurried her along to his room.

Alex stood aside to let Eleanor through, then carried the tray to his dressing chest and turned back to lock the door. 'Is that true?' he demanded, drawing her to him.

'Of course it is. My life will be dull at home after all the excitement here.' She smiled ruefully. 'I had such a great time exploring the Greek islands for my travel series, yet I can't write about even half of the things that have happened to me on yours or you'll sue the paper and I'll lose my job.'

He shook his head. 'I will not be forced to sue, *kyria* journalist, because I trust you.'

'Thank you, *kyrie* Drakos. I'm honoured.'

'*You* should be. I trust very few people in this world.' He picked her up and placed her on the bed against the stacked pillows. '*You* have been subjected to such trauma today, I will personally serve you tea and pastries.' His eyes glinted. 'Another reason for you to feel unique. I do this for no one else.'

'Not even your mother?'

He shook his head. 'In England my mother has a house-keeper whose sole aim in life is to ensure her comfort— physical and mental. Grace is the ex-policewoman who left Mother to get married, but the marriage was short-lived. When my grandfather died, Mother decided to make England her permanent home and asked Grace to join her.' He handed Eleanor a cup of tea. 'She is not only intelligent and loyal but also a crack shot. Talia Kazan is in safe hands.' He filled his coffee cup and sat down in the big bedside chair, frowning at Eleanor. 'I wish you had someone like Grace in your life.'

She grinned. 'I don't need ordinary household help for my place, let alone a crack-shot ex-policewoman!'

Alex put their empty cups on the tray and sat on the edge of the bed, tracing a finger over the bruise on her jaw. 'When I came back to find you missing, I thought you'd persuaded someone to take you over to Karpyros to catch the ferry to Crete.'

She stared up at him blankly. 'Why on earth would I do that?'

He shrugged. 'To find you gone was so bad a shock I wasn't thinking straight. Then I looked in your room and saw nothing had been taken, and questioned Sofia, at which point Theo came rushing to say Markos had confessed his sins—so we knew where to look for you, even without the clue of your bracelet.'

'With no handy ball of string to unwind, or crumbs or pebbles to trail like Hansel and Gretel, it was the only thing I could think of to leave as a clue. My hands were tied behind me, so I managed to work the fastening open without Paul noticing in his tearing rush to get me down the stairs. It's only by good luck I got to that nasty little hidey-hole in one piece.' Eleanor smiled at him. 'But I knew you'd come for me.'

'I would have torn the place apart!' Alex drew her into his arms and held her close.

Somewhere in the back of her mind, the part that wasn't fully engaged with the sheer pleasure of contact, Eleanor was surprised. She had expected Alex to make love to her the moment they were alone, yet he seemed happy just to hold her and talk.

'What are you thinking?' His warm breath against her cheek almost made her purr.

'That it's good just to lie here like this with you and talk.'

He raised his head to smile at her. 'The other men in your life consider talk a waste of valuable time in this situation?'

Eleanor thought it over. 'There is absolutely no one in my life I could picture in this particular situation. The only men interested in actually talking to me are colleagues.'

'I take great pleasure in your conversation.' He kissed her fleetingly. 'This period on Kyrkiros has not been peaceful for *you*, Eleanor, but I will look back on it as a halcyon time when I was granted the privilege of your company.'

'That's such a lovely thing to say,' she said huskily.

'It's the simple truth.' His eyes were abruptly searching. 'Paul subjected you to a very bad experience today. Are you fully recovered?'

'No, I'm not.' Her eyes lit with a smile which tightened his embrace. 'I'm in desperate need of someone to guard me against nightmares.'

He laughed deep in his throat. 'You have him, right here in the hollow of your hand, *agape mou*.'

'How lovely!' She kissed him so ardently heat flared in his eyes, igniting a response which shot fire through her body down to her toes. 'But if you want to stop talking for a while now, it's fine by me, Alex.'

His breathing quickened. 'Are you asking me to make love to you?'

'Do I have to ask?'

'*Ochi*!' He kissed her with a hunger she responded to with such abandon he undressed her rapidly, managing to render her naked without taking his mouth from hers.

'Very clever! You've done that before,' she gasped when he stood up to take off his clothes.

Alex gave her a smile which took away what little breath she had left. 'I have,' he admitted, and returned to his place in her embrace. 'But with you it is not skill, but reluctance to stop kissing you even to—' He broke off with a smothered curse as his phone rang. With a swift apology, he listened intently and then began a conversation in Greek so fluent and rapid she couldn't understand a word of it. At last Alex closed the phone and stretched out to put it on the bedside table, then took her in his arms and rubbed his cheek against hers.

'Bad news?' she asked after a while.

'No, it was very good news.' He raised his head, smiling down at her wryly. 'Arianna has just presented Dion with a second son. He regrets that due to this he cannot come from Crete in person to collect Paul as promised. To avoid any distress for Arianna, he will send some of his men to take our prisoner to Naros. Dion begged me to tell her nothing about her brother's behaviour until she is recovered from the birth.'

'I should think not!' Eleanor eyed him with sympathy. 'Are you a little bit jealous? It would be only natural if you were. Arianna was yours before she married Dion.'

Alex shook his head. 'Arianna was never mine in the way you mean. We were loving friends at one time, and still are. But her relationship with Dion is different. He worships her.'

'Does she reciprocate?'

He smiled crookedly. 'As I told you before, once she met Dion she had eyes for no one else.'

Eleanor knew the feeling. One look at Alexei and she had fallen head over heels in love. Otherwise she wouldn't be here in his arms, taking full advantage of every fleeting moment until she flew home and crash-landed back to earth.

'What are you thinking?' whispered Alex, smoothing a caressing hand down her spine.

'I'm counting, not thinking.'

'This is a time for mathematics?' He chuckled and kissed her nose. 'What are you counting, *kardia mou*?'

'The minutes left before I go.'

'Stop!' he commanded, his face stern as his arms closed round her. 'I know you must leave tomorrow, but it does not mean goodbye. I will come to you in England very soon.'

'Let's not talk about it now,' she pleaded. 'We're wasting those minutes I mentioned.'

'I thought you liked men to talk to you!'

'I do. But right now, Alexei Drakos, I want you to—'

He smothered the rest of her sentence with a kiss which made it clear that, whatever she wanted, he wanted it even more. His mouth roved her face, gentle as it reached her bruised jaw.

'I could kill him just for this,' he growled against her parted lips.

'Never mind him,' she ordered fiercely. 'Just kiss it better. And then move on down to my other bruises too. If you like.'

He gave a delighted laugh and did as she commanded, then raised his head to look into her eyes. 'To make sure no bruises are left unattended, I must kiss you all over.'

'Lovely! Have you got any bruises in need of attention? Or shall I just kiss you all over too?' She bent her head to begin with his chest, teasing him with the tip of her tongue in open-mouthed kisses that tensed every muscle in his body.

Alex drew in a deep, shuddering breath. 'This is hard to endure.'

'Endure? You don't like it?'

'I like it so much I am ready to explode.' And with a swift move, he rolled her on her back and held himself poised above her. 'Eleanor, are you sure you want me this way tonight?'

She stared up at him in astonishment. 'How clear must I be? You want an email in confirmation?'

He laughed unsteadily. 'I thought that after your treatment at the hands of that man you might not want to make love tonight.'

'I want to make love with *you* tonight, Alex.' In sudden desperation, she caught him in a caress that put an abrupt end to all verbal communication. Their bodies joined together in such immediate urgency their loving was savagely short, but so sweet they remained entwined as they came slowly back to earth, his arms possessive around her, his bright curls tangled with her dark, tumbled hair as they lay cheek to cheek.

Alex stirred a little and kissed her. 'Are you thirsty, *kardia mou?*'

'Yes. But I don't want you to move. Stay just as you are a little longer, *parakolo*. Or even a lot longer,' she added shamelessly.

He chuckled. 'As long as you wish. Though there is risk like this, you understand.'

'I do.' She gave him a smile as old as Eve as she felt him harden and kissed him to show her appreciation.

Alex's response was immediate and impassioned, his mouth possessive as his hands moved over her in caresses that slowly turned her entire body into an entire throbbing erogenous zone. She gasped, her fingers caressing his back, delighting in the strength of his long, flat muscles as he began to move, urging her with him, slowly at first, then gradually faster in breathless, heart-pounding rhythm on the quest for completion which overtook her before him. He held her tightly as she gasped in the throes of her climax, and with super-human control waited until she relaxed before surrendering to the overwhelming pleasure of his own.

Later, Eleanor lay awake in Alex's arms, determined to savour every moment of the swiftly passing night. She could sleep when she got home. Tonight she would drain every last drop of pleasure from this once in a lifetime experience.

'You must be tired, *glykia mou*,' said Alex in her ear. 'Can you not sleep?'

'Am I disturbing you?'

'No.' He pulled her closer. 'This bed will seem very empty next time I sleep in it, though God knows when that will be.'

'Where will you go after I'm gone?'

'To Athens first. Stefan is growing very insistent. Will you go straight back to work, Eleanor?'

'I'll spend a day or so with my parents, then get back to my desk to polish my series up, ready to meet my deadline—and afterwards do whatever comes next.' A yawn overtook her and Alex chuckled as he held her closer.

'You need sleep, *kardia mou*.'

Eleanor knew it and, though she struggled to keep awake, the events of the day, followed by the passionate lovemaking of the night, finally conquered her as she fell deeply asleep in the security of Alexei Drakos' embrace.

CHAPTER TEN

ELEANOR woke late next morning to the scent of coffee and found Alex, bright-eyed and damp of hair, smiling down at her as he offered her a cup.

'*Kalimera*, sleepy-head.'

'Good morning.' She struggled upright and pushed the hair out of her eyes, wishing he'd given her time to look at least human. 'I didn't hear you in the shower.'

'I stole out for a swim so I wouldn't wake you.' He sat on the edge of the bed, watching her drink. 'How are you this morning, *glykia mou*?'

'Half-asleep.' She drained the last of the coffee and felt the caffeine start to take effect. 'I'm not a morning person.'

'So I see.' He took the cup from her and threw the covers back, laughing as her eyes sparked at him like an angry cat's. 'I brought my mother's robe, so you can shower here, ready for the breakfast Sofia will bring to the tower room in fifteen minutes.'

She shook her head as she wrapped herself in the robe to collect her discarded clothes. 'I'll just sprint along to my bathroom, thanks just the same. See you in ten.'

Alex tried to change her mind by underhanded means but she laughed and dodged away to run along the hall, determined to look as presentable as possible for their last breakfast together. After the fastest shower on record she tied her damp hair up in a pony-tail rather than attempt to dry it. In jeans and T-shirt, ready to travel, she slapped moisturiser on her glowing face, added a lick of lip gloss and made it to the tower room seconds before Sofia appeared with their breakfast.

'You were very fast, Eleanor,' said Alex, holding her chair for her.

'Years of practice,' she assured him. 'Though I don't eat a breakfast like this every day.'

'You should,' he said, looking oddly tense as he sat down. 'Does your housemate leave early also?'

'Yes. Pat is usually out of the house before me.'

'You get on well together?'

'Very well. We've known each other for years.' Eleanor looked at him anxiously. 'Have you seen Paul this morning?'

Alex nodded briefly. 'He looked ready to murder Christina when I told him she had left him to face the music alone.'

'When are Dion's men arriving to collect him?'

'He rang me while you were dressing. They are on their way. Arianna and the new baby are doing well, he reported.' Alex met her eyes. 'But someone else is arriving first, Eleanor—my father wants to confront the man who caused harm to my mother.'

'Heavens!' She took in a deep breath. 'Would you prefer me to keep out of the way until he leaves?'

Alex eyed her in surprise. '*Ochi!* My father wishes to speak to you, Eleanor.'

She bit her lip. 'Does he know I'm a journalist? If so please tell him I have no intention of writing about him.'

Alex gave a short, mirthless laugh. 'Milo Drakis would not care a damn if you did. But he would care very much if you wrote about my mother.' His eyes softened. 'But I have your word that you will not.'

Eleanor downed her coffee and stood up. 'Yes,' she said with emphasis. 'You have. I must go and pack. I'll be in my room if you want me.'

Alex got to his feet, frowning. 'Why not stay here with me?'

'I need to get my belongings together, send off a few emails and so on,' she said, evading his eyes.

'As you wish—' Alex broke off to answer his phone, then closed it and smiled wryly. 'My father is at the jetty. He is early.'

'I'll get out of your way, then,' Eleanor said hastily and made for the door, but Alex caught her before she reached it and swept her into his arms to kiss her.

'I will come for you later,' he promised and retained her hand as they hurried along the hall to the lift. He raised her hand to his lips then went inside, his eyes holding hers until the lift doors closed on him.

After nearly three weeks of constant travelling, Eleanor had packing down to a fine art. Once her clothes were put away she tucked her camera in her battered tote bag with her travel documents and wallet and a couple of paperbacks, her mind on what was happening down below with Paul Marinos. She checked that nothing was left in the bathroom and then took a last look round the room, suddenly so impatient to get the pain of departure over with, it was a relief to hear the expected knock on her door.

'My father is waiting,' Alex informed her. 'He would like to see you before he leaves.'

'What happened with Paul?' she asked as they made for the tower room.

'When he saw my father he was all grovelling apologies, but insisted that Christina should share the blame,' said Alex with disgust, and stood back for her to enter the tower room, where the imposing figure of Milo Drakos stood at the windows, gazing out at the view.

He turned as they entered and took Eleanor's hand to bow over it. 'I am glad of this opportunity to thank you for your brave help to my wife, Ms Markham—also to express my deep regrets for the hurt you suffered at the hands of Paul Marinos.'

'I'm fine now, except for a few bruises,' she assured him.

He smiled at her warmly, and looked at Alex, eyebrows raised. 'The man is not short of money, so revenge on you was obviously his sole motive.'

'And he didn't care who suffered in the process of achieving it,' agreed Alex harshly. 'He's lucky I didn't kill him yesterday.'

'I am grateful you did not,' said Milo Drakos dryly. 'I would have objected to seeing my son imprisoned—Marinos is not worth paying such a price.'

'And, even worse, I would have earned Arianna's wrath,' said Alex wryly. 'He's her brother, and blood is blood.'

'What will happen to him now?' asked Eleanor.

'I have discussed this with my son,' said Milo. 'Alexei is hot to see Marinos imprisoned for his intentions towards my wife, and the hurt he inflicted on you, Miss Markham—'

'He *struck* Eleanor, Father, and so did the man he hired to kidnap my mother!' broke in Alex. 'Eleanor has many more bruises than the one visible on her face.'

'You are embarrassing her, but I am in complete sympathy with you, Alexei, since your mother suffered bruises also,' observed Milo as Eleanor's face crimsoned. 'However, since you inflicted far more on Paul Marinos—relieved him of two teeth, and his nose will never recover its shape—you have exacted *your* revenge, *ne*?'

'Not enough,' said Alex harshly.

His father turned to Eleanor. 'To avoid publicity to my family, Ms Markham, and because Arianna Aristides has just given birth, I will not have her brother changed with the crimes he intended to commit against my family, because he was ultimately prevented from committing them. You, however, are at liberty to have charged him with bodily harm and attempted abduction.'

Eleanor shook her head. 'I'm about to leave for the UK, Mr Drakos. I'd rather forget about the whole thing.'

'And will you write about your adventure?' he said gently.

She looked him in the eye. 'No. I've given my word to Alexei that I won't mention your wife, nor what happened to me here. I will, of course, give a glowing account of the festival and the idyllic life *other* people lead here on Kyrkiros.'

Milo Drakos smiled and raised her hand to his lips. 'It has been a great privilege to meet you, Miss Markham. I hope we meet again in pleasanter circumstances.'

'It's kind of you to say so, but I doubt it.' Eleanor exchanged a look with Alex. 'This kind of experience doesn't happen twice.'

'I will leave it to Alexei to change your mind,' said Milo, eyes gleaming.

Alex closed his phone. 'Dion's men are here, Father. It's time to throw Paul Marinos off my island.'

Milo Drakos bowed over Eleanor's hand. 'Goodbye, my dear.'

She smiled. 'Goodbye, Mr Drakos.'

'Once Paul has gone, I'll see my father off, Eleanor,' said Alex. 'Wait for me here—*parakolo*,' he added at a look from his parent.

Eleanor went back to her room to look from her windows at the beach below and watched as Milo Drakos talked at length to his son and then offered him his hand. *Take it,* she said silently and, as though he'd heard her, Alex not only grasped the hand but even received the kiss his father bestowed on his cheek. Eleanor turned away rather than intrude, even from this distance, on something so intensely private. When Alex eventually joined her in the tower room, she was presiding over the coffee tray Sofia had sent up with Yannis.

'So Paul is on his way, Alex.'

'Not yet.' He turned to her, a wry look in his eyes. 'You're not going to believe this. Before he left, my father asked for my blessing. He wants to marry my mother again.'

Eleanor gazed at him, wide-eyed. 'What on earth did you say?'

'I told him it was her blessing he needed, not mine.' Alex shook his head in disbelief. 'What the hell was I supposed to say? In the end I assured my father that if she is happy about it, I won't raise any objections.' He smiled crookedly. 'He was pleased.'

From the tableau she'd witnessed Eleanor, could well believe it. 'I hope it works out for them. And for you.' She disengaged herself to pour coffee. 'I'm sorry to introduce a more mundane subject, but I must leave after lunch to catch the ferry.'

'You could leave a lot later if we went by helicopter—' He broke off as his phone rang. '*Me synchoreite*—I must answer this.'

Eleanor gazed out at the view as Alex spoke to the caller with increasing urgency, then closed his phone, his face grim.

'That was Dion again, asking for my help. He wants me to follow his men over to Naros to make sure Paul gets there. Once he is sure all is well with Arianna, he will arrive there later today himself—but in the meantime he wants to make sure little brother doesn't feed some sob story to his captors and persuade them to take him home to Crete to upset his sister.'

'Would they do that?'

'The men have known him all his life, and because his face is a mess right now they might.' Alex sighed and ran a hand through his hair. 'If you wait to go by helicopter, I can be back in time to fly you to Crete. But, if I can't make it in time, simply stay another night.' He took her in his arms, rubbing his cheek against hers. 'In fact, *kyria*, that is a very good idea, *ne?'*

'A brilliant idea.' Eleanor smiled at him and gave him a little push as he drew her to her feet. 'In the meantime, go and evict Paul Marinos from your island, *kyrie* Drakos.'

CHAPTER ELEVEN

ELEANOR stood at the window again, watching as Paul Marinos limped to the jetty between two men who helped him into a boat while Alex boarded his own. She watched both crafts roaring away across the sea then went to her room and sat down at the dressing table, to gaze into space for a while before drafting a note which took several attempts before she finally sealed it in an envelope.

This has been a wonderful, magical experience, Alex. But, rather than spoil the magic by trying to prolong it, we must both return to the real world. Since fate has stepped in to take you off with Paul, I'll ask Yannis to get me to Karpyros to catch the ferry. Please don't be angry with me. Thank you again for the interview.
Eleanor.

She knuckled tears from her eyes, wrote Alex's name on the envelope, then switched off her phone, collected her bags and carried them along to the lift to take down to the hall. Sofia objected strongly when she heard the *kyria* was leaving alone, but Eleanor explained why, as best as she could, and handed over the letter.

'Give this to *kyrie* Alexei, please. Can Yannis take me over to Karpyros right away?' she asked, suddenly so miserably unhappy, Sofia took her in her arms to pat her back soothingly before she went outside to call to her son.

Eleanor's relief was intense when the plane took off on time from Crete. Normally she was uptight at take-off until the plane reached its altitude. But after a wait at the airport, wound tight as a coiled spring in case a furious Alex appeared at any moment, she leaned back in her seat as the plane began its climb, and finally began to relax. In spite of guilt about stealing away, she was utterly certain it was the right thing to do. She'd meant every word about her magical stay on Kyrkiros but, much as she would have liked to stay another day—and night—it was time to leave. Enchantment on an island in the sun was an experience she was passionately grateful for, but only a romantic fool would expect it to survive a transfer to the reality of daily life on her home ground.

Not that Alex was likely to track her down there. Instead of working in London for one of the major newspapers, as he probably believed, her job was actually on the features section of a provincial paper in a town a long way from the capital. She loved the town, and she enjoyed her job, but a hotshot journalist she was not. At least, not yet. Her aim had always been a post with a major London broadsheet, so as a step towards it her interview with Alexei Drakos would do wonders for her CV. She blinked hard. Lord knew, she'd earned it.

Eleanor's parents were waiting for her at Birmingham airport to drive her to their retirement cottage near Cirencester. After the high drama of her stay on Kyrkiros, it was restful to do nothing much at all for the entire time she spent there, other than give descriptions of all the islands she'd visited, eat her mother's cooking and deal with the laundry she insisted on doing herself. Jane Markham was deeply impressed by Eleanor's account of Talia Kazan and studied the photographs in wonder.

'She's hardly changed at all! Fancy you meeting her by chance. What's she like?'

Eleanor was able to say, with perfect truth, that Talia Kazan's personality was as lovely as her face. 'An absolute charmer. She even managed to persuade her son to give me the interview Ross wanted.'

'I read the article in the paper,' said her father in approval. 'McLean got it in pretty sharpish—I've kept it for you to see. This Alexei Drakos is a striking chap, from his photograph.'

'Is he a charmer too?' asked Jane, smiling.

'Not quite the way I'd describe him, no, Mother. Too strong a personality.'

George Markham shot a look at her. 'You didn't like him?'

'Actually, I liked him very much.' This was such a lukewarm description of her feelings, she changed the subject by asking to see the paper, and found not only Alexei's photograph above the article but her own face in miniature under the heading.

Eleanor arrived back at her desk at the *Chronicle* to an immediate summons from Ross McLean.

'Thanks a lot, Markham!' He brandished a London tabloid in front of her and jabbed a finger at the gossip column. 'Explain this.'

To her horror Eleanor saw current photographs of Talia Kazan and Milo Drakos topping a piece headed:

ESTRANGED COUPLE REUNITED?

Talia Kazan, iconic supermodel of yesteryear, who divorced property tycoon Milo Drakos a year after she married him, has been spotted on the Aegean island owned by Alexei Drakos, their entrepreneur son. Since Milo was on hand too, maybe there's a reunion on the cards for the Greek Goddess and the Tycoon! How will Alexei, allegedly hostile to his father, feel about that?

'Well?' demanded Ross. 'You were there, so you must have seen Talia Kazan. The article you wrote was dull stuff compared to this. Did you sell the information to this rag?'

'I most certainly did not.' Eleanor's eyes flashed angrily. 'The only way I could get the "dull stuff" you were so delighted about was to promise Alexei Drakos I would make no mention of his mother.'

'So who the hell wrote this?'

'No idea. There was a festival on the island with crowds of people. Anyone could have seen Talia Kazan and Milo Drakos, though they were never together in public.'

'But you must have seen them!'

'I met Ms Kazan, who invited me to sit with her party at the festival. In fact,' she added fiercely, 'She was the one who persuaded her son to give me the interview. He agreed on condition I made no mention of her, but if they read this rubbish they'll think I broke my word.'

Calmer now, Ross eyed her speculatively. 'Which matters a lot to you.'

More than he could possibly know. 'Alexei Drakos said he'd sue the paper if his mother's name appeared, which is quite funny if you think of it!'

'Hilarious,' agreed Ross, looking happier. 'He can sue this tabloid as much as he likes. He gave me precise instructions before he would give the go-ahead on the article, not least that charming portrait of you to go with it. I've sold the piece on, of course so, when you leave me one day for the metropolis, as I know damn well you intend, your face will be familiar to the London big boys.'

She sniffed. 'You've never given me the honour before.'

'I complied with Drakos' demands. He expresses himself pretty forcibly, even by email. Good-looking bloke.' Ross showed his veneers in a sly smile. 'Did you like him?'

'Yes, I did,' said Eleanor briefly. 'So, now you know I didn't turn Judas on you, boss, when do you want the first of my travel articles?'

'Today, of course.'

'Of course.'

'With the photographs for the entire series.'

'Right.'

Eleanor was glad to get busy, but felt as though a thick black cloud hung over her desk as she worked. She was only too pleased to get away from it for lunch with fellow female journalists, who praised her for the interview with Alexei Drakos, and commiserated about the tabloid article. Back at her desk, she got the first of her Greek travel articles out on deadline with the accompanying photographs, and worked hard on the rest. Ross had decided to feature them all week, with the Kyrkiros feature in the Saturday magazine as the finale, courtesy of the shots of the bull dance, which even Ross had to admit were fairly good.

'Fairly good?' snorted Sandra Morris, the health columnist. 'They're brilliant, El. You surpassed yourself.'

'Good light in the Greek islands.'

'Oh, come on, the dancers were shot by torchlight, by the look of it. What's up? You haven't been yourself since you got back.'

'I'm a bit tired.' And the role of Damocles was a strain. She kept waiting for the sword to fall on her neck.

By the end of the day, Eleanor persuaded herself that the tabloid article had probably slipped under the radar where Alex and his family were concerned. Talia was unlikely to buy the a tabloid, and since Alex and Milo were in Greece they probably wouldn't have seen it either. Lord, she hoped not! When she got home to a warm welcome from Pat Mellor, they ate supper together and regaled each other with news of their respective holidays. Life, Eleanor felt, could now get back to normal, except for thoughts of Alex that kept her awake at night. And not just thoughts. To Eleanor's utter dismay, her body yearned for the physical bliss of their love-making.

Mike Denny, cricket correspondent, gave her a nudge as he passed her desk next day.

'Your presence is required, El.'

Eleanor looked up to see Ross beckoning from his office door, a look on his face which boded ill for someone; obviously her. She got up and joined him, smiling in polite enquiry

'You wanted me?'

'Shut the door,' he snapped and sat down behind his desk. 'Sit down.'

Ross McLean rarely invited reporters to sit unless he was firing them. Eleanor sat, resigned, waiting for the sword to fall.

'This came from Alexei Drakos just now. Instead of shooting it to your inbox, I printed it.' He pushed a sheet of paper across the desk.

I need Eleanor Markham's telephone number and home address immediately.

'He's obviously read the tabloid article,' said Eleanor when she could trust her voice.

'He doesn't say so. Imperious blighter, isn't he? Well?' added Ross. 'Do I do as he wants?'

'Not much choice, I suppose.' She sighed, depressed. 'Only make sure it's my address here in Pennington. I don't want him descending on my parents like a wolf on the fold.'

'Right. Whatever you say.' Ross eyed her with unusual kindness. 'Better make sure you're not alone when he calls to see you.'

'He won't come to *see* me. He'll just blister my ears via the phone.'

'Because he's contacted the tabloid by now and found you don't work there?'

She nodded miserably. 'I sort of gave the impression that I'm based in London, so he's going to be pretty furious when he finds I'm not.'

'What exactly *were* you up to on your trip, Markham?' he demanded. 'Anything I should know about if he comes rampaging in here?'

'I was doing the work I'm paid for,' she said flatly, and got up. 'Talking of which, I'd better get on.'

Ross got to his feet, his sharp-featured face deadly serious. 'Look, if you need back-up of any kind just shout, Eleanor. The *Chronicle* looks after its employees, so refer Drakos to me if he cuts up rough.'

She smiled, touched. 'Thank you.'

Eleanor got home late that night after hustling to meet her deadline, exhausted by the tension of expecting a phone call from Alex any minute. When Pat called as she was on her way upstairs, she was in no mood to chat.

'Hold it, El.'

She turned, forcing a smile. 'What's up?'

'I should be asking you that! You had a visitor an hour ago; a forceful gentleman who wanted to punch my lights out when I said lived here—with you.' Pat grinned. 'Had you deceived him, old thing? Told him I was a girl?'

'Sorry to puncture your ego, Mellor, but I didn't talk about you at all,' Eleanor snapped, and sat down suddenly on one of the stairs. 'What happened?'

Pat leapt up to sit beside her. 'He ordered me to tell you he will be back. Sort of like The Terminator, only *much* better looking.'

Eleanor groaned, and leaned against Pat's broad shoulder. 'He wasn't brandishing a newspaper, by any chance?'

'No. I recognised him, though. He's the Greek bloke you interviewed on your odyssey. I read the article. Did you sell your body to get the scoop or something? By the look of him it would have been no sacrifice— Oh God, El, I was joking! Don't *cry*!' Pat pulled her close and stroked her hair while she drenched his shirt with the first tears she'd shed since returning home.

After a while Pat pulled her to her feet and took her down to his kitchen. He sat her on a stool at the bar and mopped her face with kitchen towel before filling the kettle.

'Coffee, tea or whisky?'

'Better make it hemlock,' she said thickly and scrubbed at her eyes.

'No need to go overboard with the Greek thing, pet! You'll settle for a nice cup of tea while you tell Uncle Pat all about it.'

Eleanor gave the bare bones of her tale as succinctly as possible, and even managed a laugh with Pat when it came to Alexei Drakos in possible litigation with the tabloid.

'I bet your revered editor liked that bit! Though Drakos couldn't do that, could he? Was there any libel in the article?'

'No. Just speculation, really. Someone spotted Talia Kazan and her ex-husband on the island during the festival and sold the information to the highest bidder—which just happened to be the tabloid that's an infamous purveyor of celebrity gossip. Alex will never believe I'm not the culprit,' said Eleanor despondently.

'"Alex"?' said Pat, eyebrows raised.

She ignored him and took refuge in her tea.

'Do you want something with that, love?'

'Painkillers would be good.' Eleanor gave him a watery smile. 'Hope I haven't wrecked your evening. Were you going out?'

He shook his head, grinning. 'Which is damn lucky—I might have missed all the drama!'

She eyed him apprehensively. 'When Alex said he'd be back, did he specify when?'

'No—and I wasn't brave enough to ask! But, if you want some support when he does, I'm your man.'

Eleanor chuckled and slid off the stool. 'Thanks, friend, but I'm not afraid of Alexei Drakos.'

'Good to know.' Pat was suddenly serious. 'I meant it, though.'

'I know you did.' She kissed his cheek. 'Goodnight.'

For Pat's benefit, Eleanor marched upstairs like a soldier prepared for battle, but once she closed her bedroom door she leaned back against it, a hand across her eyes for a minute or two before making for the bathroom to swallow painkillers. She thought about making a meal but ran a hot bath instead. If her head hadn't ached so much, she would have screamed in frustration when her doorbell rang almost immediately and she had to get out of the bath again to answer. She snatched up the intercom receiver, knowing the identity of her visitor without asking.

'Alexei Drakos. I need to talk to you.'

'It's late.'

'It is not. Let me in,' he ordered. 'Or shall I ask your good friend Pat to do it?'

She pressed the buzzer that opened the main door, then shrugged into her dressing gown, dragged a comb through her wet hair and went out onto the landing to find Alex talking to Pat in the hall, imposing in a dark city suit. He looked up at her, one eyebrow raised.

'*Geia sas,* Eleanor.'

'Hello.' She smiled reassuringly at Pat, who looked very unhappy about leaving her alone with her visitor. 'Don't worry, I'll be fine.'

Alex scowled at him. 'You think I mean to harm her?'

Pat scowled back. 'You'd better not, mate! If you want me, just shout,' he told Eleanor.

'Come up,' she told Alex and turned to make for her sitting room, noting that it was reasonably tidy as he followed her inside. Not that she cared. 'Do sit down,' she said politely, but he shut the door and stayed standing, hot accusation in his eyes.

'You ran away!'

She nodded dumbly.

'Why?'

'Didn't you get my note?'

'Yes. It made no sense to me. Did our time together mean nothing to you? I came back from Naros to find you gone, and there was no answer from the phone I gave you. Did you lose it, Eleanor?'

'No. I switched it off and bought a new one when I got home,' she said quietly.

His face hardened. 'To cut off all contact with me? Why?'

'Because, as I said in my note, it was time to get back to

the real world and get on with my everyday life.' She coloured as her eyes fell from the penetrating black glare. 'I apologise. I deliberately gave you the wrong impression. I *am* a journalist, but not on a top London newspaper, Alex. I work on features in the *Chronicle* here in Pennington, and in between my travel articles I cover local events.'

'I knew that,' he said with scorn. 'I looked you up when I investigated Ross McLean.'

Of course he had. Eleanor sat down, feeling utterly stupid. 'Then now you can really see the difference between us. Your life revolves around Athens, London and even New York; whereas my trip to the Greek Islands was the most glamorous assignment I'd ever been given.' She looked up at him, unable to bear the suspense any longer. 'Have you come about the article?'

Alex sat beside her and took her hand. 'It was excellent, but I told you that before you sent it off.'

She looked down at their clasped hands, feeling her pulse accelerate at the contact. 'I didn't mean that one. There was a piece about your parents in another paper.'

'I have seen it.'

Eleanor raised her eyes in appeal. 'I didn't write it, Alex.'

'I know that! I knew you would not break your word, Eleanor.'

She almost fell apart with relief. 'Are you going to sue the paper?'

He smiled and raised her hand to kiss it. 'I was recently informed by a certain journalist that this would not be possible if the facts were correct. And, in this instance, they are. My parents are getting married again.'

Eleanor stared at him, astonished. 'Really? How do you feel about that?'

'My mother is so happy about it, I can only rejoice for

her.' His eyes glittered. 'But I warned my father that if he hurts her again this time I will kill him.'

She grinned. 'Am I allowed to ask about his reply?'

'That is better,' he said in approval.

'What?'

'At last—you smiled at me!'

Her smile widened. 'Now tell me the rest!'

'My father assured me that he would willingly allow me to kill him in such circumstances, but that it would never happen, because he will devote the rest of his life to making my mother happy.' Alex shrugged. 'That is fair, *ne*?'

'I think it's wonderful. I liked your father.'

'He was most taken by you also, and called me all kinds of a fool for letting you get away.' He glowered at her. 'I was furious when I found my little bird had flown, Eleanor. My mood did not improve when my lady mother, who for some reason is convinced that I am madly in love with you, also called me certain names, of which "fool" is the most polite.'

'Are you in love with me?' demanded Eleanor.

He shook his head in disbelief. 'You think I chase halfway round the world for some other reason?'

'I thought you came to give me hell for breaking my word.'

'I knew you did not.'

'You trusted me?'

Alex gave her a wry smile. 'Of course I did, but I confess that Stefan contacted that rag to learn the name of the reporter.' His lips smothered the spluttering protest on hers with a kiss which took the fight out of her as he lifted her onto his lap without taking his mouth from hers, a move so familiar and spine-tingling she was lost.

'And you are in love with me, Eleanor,' he stated when he raised his head.

Her eyes flashed. 'Shouldn't that be a question?'

'I was ordered to give you this,' he said, ignoring her, and took an envelope from his pocket. 'It is an invitation to the wedding, which is to be small and private. My mother says you may simply be an honoured guest if you prefer, but you have her permission to report on the occasion and take photographs for your *Chronicle* if you wish. Your Mr McLean will like that, *ne?*'

She smiled happily 'He certainly will—but forget Ross. Which would you prefer, Alex?'

He gave her a quick, hard kiss. 'It is your choice, *kardia mou.* See how kind I am? I demand a reward for such kindness.'

'Oh, do you? What do you want?'

The dark eyes gleamed into hers. 'You are tired. There are circles under those beautiful eyes.'

'I haven't slept much since I saw you last,' she admitted, and got to her feet, suddenly conscious that her hair was drying anyhow around a flushed face minus any make-up, and her fleece dressing-gown had been chosen for warmth rather than allure. 'As you can see, I wasn't expecting company tonight.'

'Since you are not dressed, I rejoice to hear it.' Alex got up to take her in his arms. 'I have not slept much either.' His eyes lit with familiar heat. 'I have a cure for this.'

Eleanor saw no point in coyness. 'If the cure involves a bed, I just happen to have a large one in my room. If you share it with me, perhaps we shall both get some sleep.'

Alex hugged her close. 'I can think of nothing I want more—except...'

'Except?'

'To make it clear that if we share a bed I will want more than sleep!'

She wriggled closer. 'I was rather counting on that.'

Much later, after a reunion so passionate it left them

shaken and breathless in each other's arms, Alex said very sternly. 'Now we talk, *kyria*.'

'What about?' Eleanor asked dreamily.

'The future. These lives of ours that you believe are too different to join together—to me, the solution is simple. My life involves much travelling. You enjoy this, so you travel with me. As my lover, my partner; perhaps one day I can even persuade you to be my wife.'

Right now, if he liked. Every instinct urged her to say yes to anything he wanted, but Eleanor's inner realist hauled on the brakes. 'You'd have to convince me first.'

Alex smiled. 'Tell me how and I will do it.'

She turned it over in her mind, ignoring the impatience of his tightening arms. 'For the time being it's only sensible to carry on with our lives as they are, but for you to come to see me at regular intervals, here in the real world, as opposed to the adventure we shared on Kyrkiros.'

'If that is what you wish, I will do it, but not for long.' He pulled her higher in his arms. 'The only shadow on my parents' happiness right now is regret for all the years they wasted apart. They urge me not to repeat their mistake.'

'How about a year?'

He shook his head. 'Six weeks.'

'Six months.'

'*Three* months—no longer.' Alex put a stop to further haggling by kissing her. 'Tomorrow we visit your parents, *ne*?'

'I'm working tomorrow.' And Jane Markham would need some notice before her daughter sprang Alexei Drakos on her. Eleanor bit her lip. 'I should be working this weekend too, but I'll try and sort something. When do you leave?'

'I fly back on Monday, so tell McLean you need time off. Or I can tell him for you. We shall visit your parents on Saturday then drive down to Berkshire to mine on Sunday.'

Alex smiled down into her startled face. 'This is how life will be, *glykia mou*. Does it change your mind about me?'

'Nothing could do that!'

'Then why in the name of Zeus are you making me wait so long?'

It was hard to think of a reason while Alex was kissing her again, but when he finally let her speak Eleanor told him the simple truth. 'I need to wait because this is still unreal to me, Alexei Drakos.'

'You need to be sure of your feelings before you commit yourself to me?' he demanded, frowning.

She took in a deep breath. 'No, Alex, I'm perfectly sure of my own feelings. I need to be sure of yours.'

His smile dazzled her. 'I love you, *kardia mou.*' He stopped dead, the smile suddenly crooked.

'What's wrong?'

'I have never said those words to a woman before.'

She grinned, secretly exultant. 'No wonder you looked so shocked.' She looked at him quizzically as he raised his eyebrows. 'Now what?'

'I am waiting,' he informed her.

'For what?' Though she knew.

'Tell me,' he commanded and pulled her hard against him. 'I will not let you go until you do.'

'Of course I love you, Alexei Drakos.' Eleanor smiled through sudden tears. 'But you can keep on holding me for a while, if you like.'

'For the rest of my life,' he assured her, kissed the tears away, then made her laugh by reaching for his phone. 'First ring down to your friend Pat to assure him I have not harmed you. Then we call your parents, after which we call mine, because my father is anxious for a sign that all is well between us. And then...' Alex paused, eyes glittering down into hers.

'And then?' she prompted, smiling radiantly.

'Before I go back to holding you, which will only lead to other things, I need food, *glykia mou*.' He grinned down at her. 'You shall display your cooking talents to me.'

'Ah, but what do I get in return?'

'Anything your heart desires but, with you here in my arms like this, I hope it is what my heart desires also.'

She grinned back at him. 'Or do you mean your body, Alexei Drakos?'

'Heart, soul and body,' he assured her. 'For as long as we both shall live.'

* * * * *

BABY OUT
OF THE BLUE

REBECCA WINTERS

Rebecca Winters, whose family of four children has now swelled to include five beautiful grand-children, lives in Salt Lake City, Utah, in the land of the Rocky Mountains. With canyons and high alpine meadows full of wildflowers, she never runs out of places to explore. They, plus her favourite vacation spots in Europe, often end up as backgrounds for her romance novels, because writing is her passion, along with her family and church.

Rebecca loves to hear from readers. If you wish to e-mail her, please visit her website: www.cleanromances.com

CHAPTER ONE

FRAN MYERS' GAZE fastened on the scenery unfolding at every bend along the coastal road. Against the azure blue of the Aegean, the miles of white beaches with their background of deep green pines didn't seem real. Dark, fast-moving clouds swirled overhead, adding a dramatic aspect to the landscape. The panorama of colors was quite spectacular.

"I didn't know the Greek Riviera was this beautiful, Kellie. I'm in awe. It's so unspoiled here."

"That's why my husband had built the resort where we'll be staying for the next few days. The Persephone is the latest getaway for the very wealthy who can afford to have peace and quiet in total luxury."

It was such a fabulous area, the news didn't surprise Fran. "Is that why you've brought me all the way from Athens? Because you think I need peace and quiet?"

"Exactly the opposite. Many royals come here to vacation. I'm hoping you'll meet one who's unattached and gorgeous. You two will take one look at each other and it'll be love at first sight."

"That'll never happen, not after my bad marriage."

Fran's best friend since childhood flashed her a searching glance.

"Don't look so surprised, Kellie."

"I'm not surprised. What I see is that a vacation for you is long overdue. Every time I've called since your divorce, you've been at the hospital doing your patient advocacy work all hours of the day and night, and you couldn't talk more than a few minutes. You need a passionate romance to bring you back to life!"

"You're hilarious. It's true I've buried myself in work to keep me from thinking, but it's been a year. I'm doing a lot better now."

"Liar. I don't need your mom to tell me you don't have a life and need to take a break in completely different surroundings. I intend to see you're pampered for a change. We'll laze around, swim, sail, hike, do whatever while we scope out eligible men."

"You're incorrigible, but I love you for it. You know very well that when I told you I would come, I didn't expect you to go to this kind of trouble for me. I thought we'd be staying in Athens to see the rest of the sights I missed when I flew over for your wedding. That was too busy a time to get everything in. Besides, your adoring husband couldn't be thrilled with this arrangement."

Kellie waved her hand in the air in a dismissive gesture. "July is Leandros's busiest time. He's off doing business in the Peloponnese and looking for new resort sites in other places. This is the perfect time for me to spend with the person who's been the sister I never had. That's why I called you to come now and wouldn't take no for an answer. We have a lot of catching up to do."

"Agreed."

The two women had been friends since they'd attended the same elementary school in Philadelphia. They could read each other's moods. Having gone through the good and the bad of their lives together, they'd become closer than most sisters.

When they'd been planning this trip, they'd talked about September. But Kellie had changed her mind and was insistent on Fran coming as soon as possible. Something was going on; normally her friend traveled everywhere with her husband. It sounded as though she needed to talk to Fran in person.

Two years ago Kellie had married millionaire Greek business tycoon Leandros Petralia in Athens. Fran had been the matron of honor at her wedding. Though they'd talked on the phone and emailed since then, they'd only seen each other the half a dozen times Kellie had flown home to Pennsylvania to be with her family for a few days. On those short visits Fran could tell her friend was so crazy over her exciting husband, she couldn't bear to be gone from him longer than a few nights.

But clearly that wasn't the case today. Kellie seemed wired, and her show of gaiety was somehow artificial. Physically she was thinner than the last time Fran had seen her. On their five-hour drive to the resort south of Thessolonika, Kellie's glib responses throughout their conversation weren't at all like her.

Fran decided to hold off until tomorrow to have a heart-to-heart with her golden-blonde friend. Right now she wanted Kellie to concentrate while she drove the fabulous slate-blue luxury saloon—too fast for Fran's liking. As they whizzed along, Fran's eyes darted to the stormy sky. "Have you noticed how black those clouds ahead are?"

"Yes. It's almost spooky and so windy, it's buffeting the car. That's very strange. This place is legendary for its sunshine. Wouldn't you know it would choose today to cloud up for your arrival?"

"Maybe it's a bad omen and your hubby came back to Athens early only to find you missing."

"Don't be absurd—" Kellie answered with uncharacteristic sharpness. "He's got his secretary with him. Maybe they're really somewhere in the Dodecanese Islands, a favorite place of his when he wants to relax."

With Mrs. Kostas? She was in her late forties.

Her friend's emotional outburst took Fran by surprise. "I was just having some fun with you." She'd never seen Kellie explode this way before.

"I'd rather talk about you. Has Rob called yet, wanting you two to get back together?"

"No. In fact, I've heard he's involved with someone at his work."

"He'll soon realize he's lost the best thing that could ever happen to him."

"Spoken like my best friend."

Kellie had been the maid of honor at Fran's wedding. Four years ago Fran had married Rob Myers after meeting him through mutual friends in Philadelphia. He was an upcoming estate-planning attorney working for a prestigious local law firm. On their third date she'd told Rob that she could never conceive, so if he didn't want to see her again, she'd understand.

He'd told her he didn't have a problem with adoption. It was a great option for childless couples. Besides, he was interested in *her*, and he had proven it by marrying her. After a year passed, she'd brought up the idea of putting in adoption papers, but he'd said it was too soon to think about and kept putting her off.

Eventually she realized he had issues and she suggested they go for counseling so they could talk about them in depth. But the counseling revealed that with the busy law practice thriving, he no longer had the time or the interest to enlarge their family, especially when the child couldn't be their own flesh and blood. Fran was enough for him.

But she wanted children badly. After three years of a married life no longer happy or fulfilling for either of them, they'd agreed to divorce. It was the only way to end the pain. Since then Fran had decided marriage wasn't for her. Kellie scoffed at such nonsense and told her she would find the right husband for her no matter what.

"Kellie? I don't know about you, but I'm thirsty. Let's stop at the village I can see up ahead and get ourselves a drink at one of those cute hotel bars."

"It's only twelve more miles to the Persephone," her friend responded in a clipped tone. "We'll order room service and have dinner in our suite where we can relax. But, of course, if you can't wait…"

"I hope you don't mind."

Kellie's hands tightened on the steering wheel, further proof her friend was barely holding herself in check. "Of course not."

There was no softening of her tone, or a reassuring smile. Right now, Fran was more concerned with Kellie, who'd been driving over the speed limit. She never used to drive this fast. After they stopped for a soda maybe Fran could prevail on her friend to let her drive the rest of the way. She'd use the pretext that she'd never been behind the wheel of a Mercedes before.

Fran wanted both of them to arrive at the resort in one piece. With this wind, the driving could be dan-

gerous. To her alarm, the idea came into her head that
Kellie wasn't even seeing the road. Intuition told her
the once flourishing Petralia marriage was having problems.

Not Kellie, too.

By the time they reached the village proper the wind
was so powerful there was actual debris in the air. "Stop
in front of that hotel on the corner, Kellie. It's starting
to hail. Let's make a run for it."

The small ice balls pounded down, emptying the
street of people rushing to take cover. All the shops and
cafés had taken their display items and tables inside.
When Fran entered the hotel bar with Kellie, tourists
and staff alike were huddled in groups talking and ges-
ticulating while they brushed themselves off.

"Kellie? You understand Greek. What are they saying?"

"I don't know, but I'll find out."

Fran followed her friend over to the counter where
Kellie got a waiter's attention. He rattled off an answer to her question. She turned to Fran. "Someone
in the back was listening to the radio and heard that
tornado-like winds have swept through the area. There's
no television reception right now. The police have issued a warning that everyone should stay indoors until
the danger has passed. It's a good thing you wanted to
stop here."

Considering the violence of the elements, it was
providential they'd been passing by this village. "Let's
get a drink and find a place to sit down while we wait
this out."

After being served, they carried their sodas to an

unoccupied bistro table. By now the hail had stopped and a heavy downpour had descended.

Kellie frowned. "I can't believe this weather."

"Since it made the six o'clock news, maybe you ought to call and let Leandros know you're all right."

Her jaw hardened. "He knows. Whenever I leave our apartment, my bodyguard Yannis follows me. If my husband is interested, he'll phone me." She pulled out her cell and checked everything. "Nope. No calls yet. See?" She showed her the screen. "No messages."

"Kellie—" Fran put a hand on her friend's arm. "Tell me what's going on. I'd planned to wait until morning to ask you that question, but since we won't be leaving here any time soon, I'm asking it now. I want to know what's happened to the happiest wife I've ever known. Where did she go?" The reason Kellie had wanted Fran to come to Greece was no longer a mystery.

Kellie averted her soulful brown eyes. "Maybe you should be asking Leandros that question."

"He's not here. *You* are. What's wrong?"

Kellie's face was a study in pain. "I'm losing him, Fran. In fact, I've discovered I never really had him and I can't stand it."

Her friend's emotions were so brittle they'd crack if Fran pushed too hard. Instead of arguing with her that it couldn't possibly be true, she took a deep breath before saying, "Does this have anything to do with the fact that you haven't gotten pregnant yet? You're probably putting too much pressure on yourself to give Leandros a child. These things take time."

"Since I've been diagnosed with seminal plasma hypersensitivity, that's the understatement of the year.

I've never wanted to talk about it, but you deserve an explanation.

"Our marriage took a crushing blow when I discovered that the painful itching and hives I experienced after intercourse was because my body is allergic to Leandros's sperm. When the doctor told me twenty thousand-plus women suffer from it in the U.S. alone, I couldn't believe it."

Fran shook her head. "I had no idea."

"I know. Growing up, I never knew such a problem existed. Leandros had to have been devastated, but he was wonderful about it. He's worn a condom every time, but I *know* deep down he must hate it.

"The doctor knew we wanted a baby and said we could try artificial insemination with a good hope of success. They have to wash his sperm of the proteins first before the procedure is done. We've been trying that method since last year, but unfortunately it hasn't worked for us. He said he's willing to adopt. How's that for irony after what you've lived through? At this point I'm thinking it's just as well," came the bleak admission.

Fran couldn't believe what she was hearing. "What do you mean?"

"I'm talking about Karmela Paulos. She came to work for Leandros a month ago as part of the typing pool."

Ah. Karmela. The woman couldn't get to him by other means, so she'd insinuated herself into the office. Now things were starting to make sense.

Karmela Paulos was the gorgeous, raven-haired younger sister of Leandros's first wife, Petra. Petra had been pregnant when she'd died in a helicopter crash over the Ionian Sea.

Two years later Leandros had met Kellie by accident at the Cassandra in Athens, one of the famous Petralia five-star hotels. It hadn't taken long before he'd married her, but it seemed that since his late wife's funeral, Leandros had acquired a constant companion in Karmela who was always around.

Fran had met her at the wedding and hadn't liked her proprietorial behavior with Leandros either. Though he was now a husband for the second time, it seemed Karmela had won herself a position that placed her closer to Leandros than before. This was foul play at its best. Being her brother-in-law, he could hardly turn her down.

"It was clear to me at the wedding that your marriage had thwarted her dreams to become the next Mrs. Leandros Petralia." Whatever subterfuge was going on here, Fran was positive Karmela was behind it in order to break them apart. She clearly still wanted Leandros for herself.

Too bad. Fran intended to make sure this was resolved before she went back to Pennsylvania in two weeks.

"Tell you what, Kellie. You heard the warning from the police, so I have an idea. Since we're not supposed to be out on the street, how about we get a room for tonight right here?"

"That sounds good."

"I think so, too. It'll be fun. How long has it been since we hung out in some cozy little hotel like this?"

"I don't remember."

"We'll watch the news on TV when it comes back on, and we'll get some food. Then we can talk all night if we want. I've got an idea about how to thwart Karmela without your husband realizing what's happening."

"I don't know if that's possible."

Fran smiled. "You haven't heard my plan yet." She got up from the table. "I'll talk to the proprietor and arrange a room for us. When the rain stops, we'll go out to the car for our luggage."

By now Fran figured Kellie's bodyguard would have contacted Leandros wherever he was and told him his wife was safe and sound. She hoped Leandros would call her soon. The problems in their marriage were tearing her best friend apart. No one knew what that felt like better than Fran.

Nik Angelis had just entered his Athens penthouse when one of his brothers phoned him. He clicked on. "Sandro? What's up?" They'd already spent part of the day in a board meeting at the Angelis Corporation. Nik had recently taken over for his father who'd retired.

"Turn on your television. The news about the tornado is on every station."

"I was in it, remember?" It was the only talk at Angelis headquarters. After he'd seen his sister and her family off to Thessalonika early that morning on the company jet, Nik had headed over to the international air cargo station to check on some shipments. While he was talking business with one of the staff, a funnel had dropped down from clouds descending on Athens. It had swept through in a northwest direction and headed straight for the air cargo station.

After a few minutes it dissipated, but in that amount of time, it had caused damage to the constructions in its path and left a trail of destruction. Fortunately everyone involved had escaped injury, including Nik. Before he instructed his limo driver to take him to his office, he'd made contact with his pilot.

Relief had filled him to learn they'd been at cruising speed and out of range of the severe turbulence of the weather pattern before the tornado had formed. Knowing his sister's family were safely on their way north for a vacation, he'd been able to relax.

"No, no," Sandro cried anxiously. "Not that one. I'm talking about another one that touched down near Thessalonika a few minutes ago."

Another one?

"Let's pray Melina and Stavros are safe."

Nik's heart had already received one workout this morning, but now it almost failed him. "Hold on." He raced into his den and clicked on the TV with the remote. Every station was covering the news using split screens to show the funnel clouds of both tornadoes.

...and then another tornado struck a part of the Greek Riviera at 5:13 p.m. this evening. It was reported as a T-4, and has since dissipated, but we won't know the true extent of the damage for a while. Word has already reached the station that a dozen villas and some private suites at the world-famous Persephone Resort owned by the Petralia Corporation, have been destroyed.

Nik felt as if a grenade had blown up his insides. The Persephone was where Melina, Stavros and their infant daughter were going to stay for the first two nights of their vacation. Nik's good friend, in business and socially, Leandros Petralia, was the owner of the resort.

"I called Melina on her cell, but there's no phone service." Sandro sounded frantic.

The knowledge sent ice through Nik's veins.

So far twenty people are unaccounted for. We repeat, it doesn't mean those are fatalities. Relief is pouring in from all over. We ask people to stay away from the area and let the police and search-and-rescue workers do their job. Cell phones are not working. We've posted a series of hotline numbers on the screen in case you have or need information about a loved one.

Pure terror seized his heart. "Do you think Cosimo is home from the office yet?"

"I don't know, but I'll try to reach him."

"Tell him to meet us at the airport, Sandro." He wanted both his brothers with him. "We'll fly to Thessalonika."

"I'm on my way!"

Nik clicked off, then phoned his driver and told him to bring the car around. On his way out the door he called his pilot and told him to ready the jet for another flight to Thessolonika. In a little over an hour Nik and his brothers could be there. They would need a car.

En route to the airport he phoned his parents at the family villa on Mykonos. They'd just heard the news and were in total anguish. "Our precious Melina, our Demitra," his mother half sobbed the words.

"Their suite may not have been among the ones affected, *Mana*. In any case, Stavros will have protected them. We have to have faith. Sandro and Cosimo are going to fly there with me now. You get on one of those hotlines and see what you can find out! Call me when you know anything. Let's pray phone service is restored there soon. I'll call you when I know anything."

A rap on the hotel-room door the next morning brought both girls awake. With the TV knocked out last night, they'd talked for hours about Karmela. Before falling asleep, Fran had made sure her friend was armed with a firm plan in mind for once their vacation was over.

Kellie lifted her head and checked her watch. "It's ten after ten!"

"Maybe it's one of the maids waiting to make up our room. I'm closest." Fran jumped out of bed in her plaid cotton pajamas. "Who is it?" she called through the door.

"Yannis."

"I'll talk to him," Kellie murmured. In an instant she slid out of her bed and rushed over to the door. The dark-haired bodyguard stood in the hall while they spoke in Greek. The conversation went on for a minute until Kellie groaned and closed the door again. Her face had turned ashen.

Fran thought her friend was going to faint and caught her around the shoulders. "What's wrong? Come sit down on the chair and tell me."

But Kellie just stood with tears gushing down her pale cheeks. "A tornado touched down twelve miles to the north of here last evening, killing nine people. Among them were five guests staying at the P-Persephone."

They stared at each other in disbelief. "I can't credit it," Fran whispered in shock. "If we hadn't pulled over when we did…" They could have been among the fatalities. She started to tremble.

"Yannis said Leandros heard about it on the television, but he was almost a thousand miles away in Rhodes. He flew here immediately, but even with his own jet and a police escort, he had trouble getting into the site until the middle of the night. Three of the twelve individual suites were demolished. There's nothing left of them."

Fran gasped. "On top of the human tragedy, your poor husband is having to deal with that, too."

"Leandros told Yannis it's a nightmare, and there's still no phone, internet or television service to that area. He got hold of him through the help of the police to let me know what has happened. I've been asked to stay put here until he joins us. Yannis said it shouldn't be long now." Kellie's teeth were chattering.

"Come on. We need to get ready and go downstairs. Knowing your husband, he must be absolutely devastated and is going to need you more than he's ever needed anyone in his life." Now would be the time for Kellie to draw close to Leandros and put the plan they'd talked about last night into action.

Both of them showered and dressed in a daze. Fran put on white linen pants with a spring-green-and-white-printed top. She tied her dark honey-blonde hair back at the nape with a white chiffon scarf. After slipping on white sandals, she announced she was ready. Nothing seemed real as they packed up and carried their bags downstairs to wait for Leandros.

To Fran's surprise, the main doors of the hotel were open for patrons to walk out and enjoy coffee at the tables set up in front of the building. Warm air filtered inside and a golden sun shone out of a blue sky. Up and down the street, life appeared to be going on as usual. You would never have known there'd been a natural disaster twelve miles away from here last evening.

A waiter approached them. "The tables in front are full. If you'll walk around to the patio in back, we'll serve you out there."

"Thank you," Fran said before taking Kellie aside. "Yannis is sitting outside in his car by yours. Let's stow our luggage and then tell him we'll be in back of the hotel. We need breakfast with our coffee. He can show Leandros where to come. I feel like soaking up some sun until he arrives. Don't you?"

"I guess so," Kellie answered in a wooden voice.

They walked over to their car and put their cases in the back. "This hotel seems to be a popular place. Go ahead and talk to Yannis while I get us a table before they're all taken."

"Okay."

Fran followed the stone pathway to the rear of the hotel where blue chairs and tables were set with bright blue-and-white-check cloths. There was an overhang of bougainvillea above the back door, and further on, a small garden. Too bad the wind had denuded most of the flowering plants. There were only a few red petals left.

She took a seat in the sun while she waited, thinking she was alone. But all of a sudden she heard a strange sound, like a whimper. Surprised, Fran looked around, then up. Maybe it was coming from one of the rooms on the next floor where a window was open.

Again she heard the faint cry. It didn't sound frantic and it seemed to be coming from the garden area. Maybe it was a kitten that had been injured in the storm.

Poor thing. She jumped up and walked over to investigate.

When she looked in the corner, a gasp escaped her lips. There, on its back in the bushes, lay a dirty black-haired baby with cuts from head to toe—

Fran couldn't fathom it. The child was dressed in nothing more than a torn pink undershirt. The little olive-skinned girl couldn't be more than seven months old. Where in heaven's name had she come from? A groan came out of Fran. She wondered how long the child had been out here in this condition.

Trying to be as gentle as possible, Fran lifted the limp body in her arms, petrified because the baby had to be dying of hypothermia. Her pallor was pronounced and her little lids were closed.

"Fran?" Kellie called out and ran up to her. "What on earth?"

She turned to her friend with tear-filled eyes. "Look— I found this baby in the garden."

A gasp flew from Kellie's lips. "I can see that, but I can't believe what I'm seeing."

"I know. Quick—get me a blanket and drive us to the hospital. I'm afraid she's going to die."

Kellie's eyes rounded before she dashed through the back door, calling in Greek for help. Within seconds, the staff came running out. One of them brought a blanket. Fran wrapped the baby as carefully as she could and headed around the front of the hotel. Kellie ran ahead of her to talk to Yannis.

"He'll drive us to the hospital."

He helped Fran and the baby inside the backseat of his car. She thought he looked as white-faced as Kellie, who climbed in front. She looked back at Fran. "What do you think happened?"

"Who knows? Maybe the mother was on the street around the corner when a microburst toppled the stroller or something and this dear little thing landed in the garden."

"But she's only wearing a torn shirt."

Both of them were aghast. "I agree, nothing makes sense."

"Do you think she could have been out there all night?"

"I don't know," Fran's voice trembled. "But what other explanation could there possibly be, Kellie? The baby has superficial cuts all over."

"I'm still in shock. You don't suppose the mother is lying around the hotel grounds somewhere, too? Maybe concussed?"

"It's a possibility," Fran murmured. "We know what tornadoes can do. The one in Dallas tossed truck rigs in the air like matchsticks. Sometimes I feel that's all we see on the news back home. I just have never heard about a tornado in Greece."

"They get them from time to time. Leandros told me they usually happen near coastal waters."

The baby had gone so still, it was like holding a doll. "Tell Yannis to please hurry, Kellie. She's not making any more sounds. The police need to be notified and start looking for this baby's parents."

Once they reached the emergency entrance, everything became a blur as the baby was rushed away. Fran wanted to go with her, but the emergency-room staff told her they needed information and showed her to the registration desk.

The man in charge told them them to be seated while he asked a lot of questions. He indicated that no one had contacted the hospital looking for a lost baby. Furthermore, no mother or father injured in the storm had been brought in. So far, only a young man whose car had skidded in the downpour and hit a building had come in for some stitches on his arm.

When the questioning was over he said, "One of our staff has already contacted the police. They've assured us they'll do a thorough investigation to unite the baby with her parents. An officer should be here within the hour to take your statements. Just go into the E.R. lounge to wait, or go to the cafeteria at the end of the hall."

When they walked out, Kellie touched Fran's arm. "I think we'd better eat something now."

"Agreed."

After a quick breakfast, they returned to the E.R. lounge. "If the baby lives, it will be thanks to you and your quick thinking. Had you been even a couple of minutes later arriving at the patio the baby might not have had the strength to cry and no one would have discovered her in time."

Hot tears trickled down Fran's cheeks. "She has to live, Kellie, otherwise life really doesn't make sense."

"I know. I've been thinking the same thing." They both had. Kellie had been praying to get pregnant and it had been Fran's fate not to be able to conceive. What a pair they made! She found two seats and they sat down.

"I wish Leandros would get here. After seeing this baby, I'm worried sick for what he's had to deal with. Lives were lost in that tornado. He'll take their deaths seriously."

"It's too awful to think about. I'm still having trouble believing this has happened. When I saw her lying in those bushes, I thought I was hallucinating."

Before long, two police officers came into the lounge to talk to them. There was still no word about the parents. After they went out again, Fran jumped up. "I can't sit still. Let's go into the E.R. Maybe someone at the desk can tell us if there's been any news on the baby yet."

Kellie got to her feet. "While you do that, I'm going outside to talk to Yannis. Maybe he's heard from Leandros."

Quickly, Fran hurried through the doors to the E.R. and approached one of the staff at the counter. "Could you tell me anything about the baby we brought in a little while ago?"

"You can ask Dr. Xanthis, the attending physician. He's coming through those doors now."

Fran needed no urging to rush toward the middle-aged doctor. "Excuse me—I'm Mrs. Myers. I understand you might be able to tell me something about the baby my friend and I brought to the hospital." Her heart hammered in fear. "Is she going to live?"

"We won't know for several hours," he answered in a strong Greek accent.

"Can I see her?"

He shook his head. "Only family is allowed in the infant ICU."

"But no one has located her family yet. She's all alone. I found her in the bushes in the garden behind the hotel."

"So I understand. It's most extraordinary."

"Couldn't I just be in the same room with her until her parents are found?"

The man's sharp eyes studied her for a moment. "Why would you want to do that?"

"Please?" she asked in a trembling voice.

"She's a stranger to you."

Fran bit her lip. "She's a baby. I—I feel she needs someone," her voice faltered.

All of a sudden a small smile lifted one corner of his mouth. "Come. I'll take you to her."

"Just a moment." She turned to the staff person. "If my friend Mrs. Petralia comes in asking for me, please tell her I'm with the baby, but I'll be back here in a little while."

"Very good."

The doctor led her through the far doors to an elevator that took them to the second floor. They walked through some other doors to the nursery area where he introduced her to a nurse. "I've given *Kyria* Myers permission to be with the baby until the police locate the mother and father. See that she is outfitted."

"This way," the other woman gestured as she spoke.

"Thank you so much, Dr. Xanthis."

His brows lifted. "Thank you for being willing to help out."

"It's my pleasure, believe me."

CHAPTER TWO

FRAN FOLLOWED THE NURSE to an anteroom to wash her hands. She was no stranger to a hospital, having worked in one since college to follow up on patients who needed care when they first went home.

When she'd put on a gown and mask, they left through another door that opened into the ICU. She counted three incubators with sick babies. The baby she'd found in the garden was over in one corner, hooked up to an IV. She'd been fitted with nasal prongs to deliver oxygen. A cardiopulmonary monitor on her chest tracked the heartbeat on the screen.

She was glad to see this hospital had up-to-date equipment to help the baby survive, yet the second she spied the little form lying on her back, so still and helpless, she had to stifle her cry of pain. The precious child had cuts everywhere, even into her black curls, but they'd been treated. Mercifully none of them were deep or required stitches. With the dirt washed away, they stood out clearly.

The nurse pulled a chair over so Fran could sit next to the incubator. "Everyone hopes she will wake up. You can reach in and touch her arm, talk to her. I'll be back."

Finally alone with the baby, Fran studied the beautiful features and profile. She was perfectly formed, and to all appearances had been healthy before this terrible thing had happened to her. All the cuts and hookups couldn't disguise her amazingly long black eyelashes or the sweetness of her sculpted lips.

With such exquisite coloring, she looked like a cherub from the famous painting done by the Italian artist Raphael, but this cherub's eyes were closed and there was no animation.

She put her hand through the hole and touched the baby's forearm. "Where did you come from? Did you fall out of heaven by accident? Please come back to life, little sweetheart. Open your eyes. I want to see their color."

There was no response and that broke her heart. Even if the baby could hear her, she couldn't understand English. "Of course you want your mommy and daddy. People are trying to find them, but until they do, will you mind if I stay with you?"

Fran caressed her skin with her fingers, careful not to touch any cuts. "I know you belong to someone else, but do you know how much I'd love to claim a baby like you for my own? You have no idea how wonderful you are."

Tears trickled down her cheeks. "You can't die. You just can't—" Fran's shoulders heaved, but it wouldn't do for the baby to hear her sobs. By sheer strength of will she pulled herself together and sang some lullabies to her.

After a time the nurse walked over. "I'm sure you're being a comfort to her, but you're wanted down in the E.R. Come back whenever you want."

Fran's head lifted. She'd been concentrating so hard

on the baby, she hadn't realized she'd already been up here several hours. "Thank you."

"Leave everything in the restroom on your way out."

"I will." With reluctance she removed her hand and stood up. "I'll be back, sweetheart."

A few minutes later she reached the E.R. lounge and discovered Kellie talking quietly with Leandros. Her attractive husband had arrived at last, but he looked as though he'd aged since Easter. When he'd flown to Pennsylvania with Kellie in the Petralia company jet at that time, the three of them had gone out for dinner and all had been well.

The second her friend saw her, she jumped up from the chair and ran across the room to meet her. Leandros followed. "Is the baby going to make it?" Kellie cried anxiously.

"I don't know. She's just lying there limp in the incubator, but she's still breathing and has a steady heartbeat. Have the police found her parents yet?"

"There's been no news."

Leandros reached for her. "Fran—" he whispered with a throb in his voice. It revealed the depth of his grief. They gave each other a long, hard hug.

"It's so good to see you again, Leandros, but I wish to heaven it were under different circumstances. I'm so sorry about everything," she told him. "I'm sure you feel like you've been through a war."

He nodded, eyeing his wife with pained eyes. Something told Fran the pain she saw wasn't all because of the tragedy. She could feel the negative tension between Kellie and her husband. Her friend hadn't been exaggerating. In fact, their relationship seemed to be in deeper trouble than even Fran had imagined.

"Five guests at the resort died," he muttered morosely. "We can thank God the honeymoon couple weren't in their suite when the tornado touched down or there would have been two more victims. Unfortunately the other two suites were occupied. Mr. Pappas, the retired president of the Hellenic Bank and his wife, were celebrating their sixtieth wedding anniversary."

"How terrible for everything to end that way. What about the other couple?" Fran asked because she sensed his hesitation.

Leandros looked anguished. "The sister of my friend Nikolos Angelis and her husband had only checked in a few hours earlier with their baby."

"A baby?" she blurted.

"Yes, but when the bodies were recovered, there was no sign of the child. The police have formed a net to search everywhere. You can imagine the anguish of the Angelis family. They're in total shock. People are still combing the area."

"Nik is the brilliant youngest of the Angelis brothers," Kellie informed her. "He's the new CEO of the multimillion-dollar mega corporation established by their family fifty years ago. He was out of the country when Leandros and I married, or he would have been at the wedding."

"I remember seeing some pictures of him in a couple of magazines while I was on the plane flying over." *Gorgeous* was the only word to come to mind.

Leandros nodded. "We've both put up money for volunteers to scour the region, but so far nothing. His parents are utterly devastated. They not only lost their daughter and son-in-law, but their little granddaughter."

Granddaughter?

The mention of a baby girl jolted her as she thought of the baby upstairs fighting for her life.

"How old is the baby?"

"Seven months."

"What color is her hair?"

"Black."

A cry escaped her lips.

Maybe she hadn't fallen out of heaven.

Was it possible she'd been carried in the whirlwind and dropped in the hotel garden? Stranger things had happened throughout the world during tornadoes.

"Kellie?"

"I know what you're thinking, Fran—" Kellie cried. "So am I." The two women stared at each other. "Remember the little girl in the midwest a few years ago who was found awake and sitting up ten miles away in a field after a tornado struck, killing her entire family? We both saw her picture on the news and couldn't believe it."

"Yes! She was the miracle baby who *lived*!"

"It would explain everything."

Leandros's dark brows furrowed. "What are you two talking about?"

"Quick, Kellie. While you tell him what we're thinking, I'm going back upstairs to be with the baby. Maybe she has come to by now. After hearing from Leandros that their baby is missing, I think she could be that lost child! She *has* to be! There's no other explanation. She *has* to live." Those words had become Fran's mantra.

The police had made a grid for the volunteers to follow. Nik and his brothers had been given an area to cover in the pine trees behind the resort. They'd searched for hours. Separated by several yards, they walked abreast while looking for any sign of Demi.

Debris had been scattered like confetti, but he saw nothing to identify their family's belongings. The tornado had destroyed everything in its path, including lives. Pain stabbed him over and over.

Where in the hell was the baby? How could they go home without her body and face their parents? The grief was beyond imagining.

Each of his brothers had two children, all boys. Their wives and families, along with Stavros's family had flown to Mykonos to join Nik's parents. He knew Sandro and Cosimo were thanking providence that their own children hadn't been anywhere near either tornado, but right now their hearts were so heavy with loss, none of them could talk.

Demi was the only little girl in the family, so beautiful—just like her mother. Not having married yet, Nik had a huge soft spot for his niece. She possessed a sweetness and a special appeal that had charmed him from the moment she was born.

Melina's baby was the kind of child he would love to have if he ever settled down. But that meant finding the kind of woman who could handle what he would have to tell her about himself before they could be married.

Up to now he hadn't met her yet and was forced to put up with the public's false assumption about him. Throughout the last year, various tabloids had put unauthorized pictures of him on their covers with the label Greece's New Corporate Dynamo—The Most Sought-After Playboy Bachelor of the Decade. He was sickened by the unwanted publicity. But this tragedy made the problems in his personal life fade in comparison.

Just two weeks ago he'd bought Demi a toy where you passed a ball through a tube and it came out the other end. She loved it and would wait for it to show up, then crawl on her belly after it. She could sit most of the time without help and she put everything possible in her mouth. Her smile delighted him. Never to see it—or her—again...he couldn't bear it. None of them could.

Hot tears stung his eyes at the thought that the seven-month-old was gone, along with her parents. It was a blow he didn't know whether he could ever get over. He and Melina had shared a special bond. She'd been there for him at the darkest point in his life. A grimace broke out on his face as he realized he couldn't even find her baby. He felt completely helpless.

Sandro caught his arm. "We've finished this section."

"Let's move to the next grid."

"Someone else has done it," Cosimo muttered.

"I don't care," he bit out. "Let's do it again, more thoroughly this time. Examine every tree."

They went along with him. Maybe five minutes had gone by when his cell phone rang. He checked the caller ID. "It's Petralia."

Their heads swiveled around, as they prayed for news that some volunteer had found her body.

"Leandros?" he said after clicking on. "Any word yet?"

"Maybe. If you believe in miracles."

Nik reeled. "What do you mean?"

"I'm with my wife at the hospital in Leminos village. It's twelve miles south of you. Come quickly. This morning her best friend Mrs. Myers from the States, who's staying with us for a few weeks, found a baby girl, barely alive, in a hotel garden."

Nik's hand tightened on the cell phone. "Did I just hear you right?"

"Yes. If you can believe this, she was lying in some bushes at the rear of the hotel. On their drive to the Persephone yesterday, the storm got so bad, they ended up staying in Leminos."

"You mean your wife and her friend—"

"Could have been among the casualties," he finished for him. The emotion in Leandros's voice needed no translation. "Fran went out to the back patio to get them a table for breakfast when she heard some faint cries and walked over to investigate."

"What?"

"It's an absolutely incredible story. The child is cut up and bruised. All she had on was a torn undershirt. They brought her to the hospital and Fran has been staying in the infant ICU with her in order to comfort her. So far no parents have shown up yet to claim her."

"You've *seen* her?" Nik cried out.

"Yes. She's about seven months old, with your family's coloring. She's alive, but not awake yet. So far that's good news according to the doctor who thought at first they were going to lose her. Come as fast as you can to the E.R. entrance. We'll show you to the ICU."

He eyed his brothers. "We're on our way, Leandros— My gratitude knows no bounds."

"Don't thank me yet. This child might not be your niece."

"I have to believe she is!"

Nik clicked off and he and his brothers started running through the forest. On the way he told them the fantastic story. Before long they reached the rental car at the police check point. Nik broke every speed record getting to Leminos while they all said silent prayers.

Once they reached the village, he followed the signs to the hospital. Leandros and his wife were waiting for them in the lounge of the E.R. His lovely wife, Kellie, was in tears over what had happened to Nik's family. He was deeply moved by her compassion. She, in turn, introduced them to the doctor who was taking care of the baby.

"Come with me and we'll see if she belongs to you." On the way upstairs the doctor said, "I'm happy to report that a half hour ago, the baby opened her eyes for the first time and looked around. I think that had something to do with *Kyria* Myers who's been singing to her and caressing her through the incubator. She's the one who first heard the baby cry and found her before she lost consciousness."

Nik couldn't wait to see if the baby was Demi, but he understood they had to wash their hands and put on masks and gowns. It took all his self-control not to burst into the ICU. If it wasn't their niece lying in there it would kill all three of them to have to return to Mykonos without her.

When they were ready, the nurse opened the door and beckoned them to follow her to the corner of the room. A woman gowned and masked like themselves sat next to the incubator with her hand inside the hole to touch the baby. With her back to them, he could only glimpse dark honey-blond hair tied back with a filmy scarf. She was singing to the child with the kind of love a mother might show for her own flesh and blood.

Touched by her devotion to a child she didn't even

know, Nik had a suffocating feeling in his chest as he drew closer and caught his first sight of the baby.

"Demi—"

His brothers crowded around, equally ecstatic at discovering their niece lying hooked up to machines, but squirming as if she didn't like being trapped in there. She kept turning her head. Sounds of joy and tears escaped their lips as her name echoed through the ICU. But Demi took one look at them and started crying. With their masks on, she was frightened.

The woman caressing her limbs spoke in soothing tones and soon calmed her down. Nik could hardly believe it. Those words might be spoken in English, but Melina's baby responded to the tender tone in which she'd said them.

After a minute, the woman pulled her hand through and stood up. Nik noticed she was of medium height. When she turned to them, he found himself staring into eyes a shade of violet-blue he'd only seen in the flowers that grew in certain pockets on Mykonos. They were glazed with tears.

"Mrs. Myers? I'm Nik Angelis," he spoke through the mask. "These are my brothers Sandro and Cosimo. I understand you're the person we have to thank for finding our niece before it was too late to revive her."

"I just happened to be the first guest to walk out to the back patio of the hotel to be served," came her muffled response. "When I heard her crying, I thought it was a kitten who'd been injured by the storm. I almost fainted when I saw her lying there face-up in the bushes." Her eyes searched his. "What's her name?"

"Demitra, but we call her Demi."

"That's a beautiful name." He heard her take a deep

breath. "There's no way to express how sorry I am for the loss of your sister and her husband, Mr. Angelis. But I'm thankful you've been reunited with their daughter. She's the most precious child I've ever seen," she said with a quiver in her voice. Nik happened to agree with her. "If you could remove your masks, I'm sure it would make all the difference to her."

"Demi doesn't seem to have any problem with *you* wearing one."

He saw a distinct flush creep above her mask. "That's because I've been talking to her since we brought her here. I couldn't stand it that she didn't have anyone to give her love. Babies want their mothers. Her experience had to have terrified her."

Not every woman had such a strong maternal instinct as Melina's, but being a married woman, he had to assume Mrs. Myers had children of her own. "Leandros told me you're here on vacation. For you to forget everything except taking care of Demi constitutes a generosity and unselfishness we appreciate more than you could ever know. She'll be the reason our parents can go on living."

"It's true," his brothers concurred before expressing their gratitude.

Nik moved closer. "I hope you realize our family owes you a debt we can never repay."

She shook her head. "What payment could anyone want except to see that sweet little girl reunited with her family?" Her eyes still possessed a liquid sheen as they played over him. "Anyone can see she's an Angelis from head to toe. Of course I don't know about the noses and mouths yet." Her husky voice disturbed his senses in ways that surprised him.

In spite of the horrendous grief of the past twenty-four hours, her comment made one side of his mouth lift. Until he'd entered the ICU and watched the loving way she was handling Melina's daughter, he couldn't imagine ever having a reason to smile again.

She took a step back. "Well—I'll leave you gentlemen alone to be with your niece. When you speak to her, your voices will be blessedly familiar and will reassure her."

Nik wasn't so certain Demi wouldn't start to cry the second Mrs. Myers left the room. "Where are you going?"

"Downstairs to join Kellie."

"Don't leave the hospital yet. We need to talk."

"Since I'm their guest, I'm not sure what our plans are now."

Making one of those decisions on sheer instinct in case she got away, he said, "In that case, I'll go downstairs with you. I need to call our parents and give them the kind of news that will breathe new life into them. Above all, they'll want to thank you." He turned to his brothers and told them his plans before he left for the anteroom with her.

Once inside, he removed his mask and gown while she untied hers. Though she was married, he was a man who enjoyed looking at a beautiful woman and was curious to see what she looked like unwrapped.

Once she'd discarded everything, he discovered a slender figure clothed in a stunning green-and-white-print outfit. She had classic bone structure and a face that more than lived up to the beauty of her eyes. In a word, she stole his breath.

"What's the verdict?" he asked after she'd studied him back.

Again, he saw warmth enter her cheeks, but she didn't look away. "I happened to see your picture on the cover of a magazine while I was reading on the plane." Nik's teeth snapped together at the mention of it. "If you want honesty, then let me say I'm glad your niece received all the feminine features of her parentage."

He'd been expecting her to say something about his reputation. Instead her thoughts were focused on Demi. Her surprising comment lightened his mood.

"Your sister must have been a real beauty to have produced a daughter like Demi."

Nik reached for his wallet and showed her a picture. "This was taken on Melina's thirtieth birthday two months ago. She and Stavros had been trying for four years for a baby before one came."

Kellie needed to hear that. Not every woman conceived as quickly as one hoped.

Fran studied it for a moment. "What a lovely family." Her voice shook. "I see a lot of your sister in her."

His throat swelled with raw emotion. "Yes. She'll live on through Demi." He opened the other door. "Shall we go downstairs?"

"I'll ride down with you," Dr. Xanthis said. "We'll need confirmation of your relationship to the baby with a DNA test."

"Of course. I'll ask the hospital in Athens to send my information so you can run a test."

"Excellent. I'll tell the lab to expedite the process."

Fran wondered what condition had been serious enough to put Nik in a hospital and to have provided a

DNA match, but it was none of her business. She wished she weren't so aware of him.

Though she'd always thought Leandros was a true hunk, Nikolos Angelis was in a class by himself. Despite the grief lines etched in his striking Greek countenance, he was easily the most attractive male she'd ever met in her life. The photos of him didn't do him justice.

Besides his masculine appeal, he had the aura of a man in charge of his life—one who could accomplish anything. Kellie's hope that Fran would meet some gorgeous royal on this trip and fall instantly in love was still laughable, but she had to admit Nik Angelis was a fabulous-looking man.

Standing next to him, Fran thought he must be at least six feet three of solid lean muscle. She wasn't surprised he was still wearing soiled suit trousers and a creased blue shirt with the sleeves shoved up to the elbows. All three brothers had arrived in clothes they'd worn to work when they'd heard about the tornado. Naturally they'd dropped everything to fly to Thessalonika to search for their family. None of them had slept.

He needed a shave, but if anything, his male virility was even more potent. She noticed he wore his black wavy hair medium length. It had such a healthy gloss that it made you want to run your hands through it. Before the door opened, Fran gave him another covert glance.

Brows of the same blackness framed midnight-brown eyes with indecently long black lashes like Demi's. Between his hard-boned features and compelling mouth, she had to force herself to stop staring. Until now, no men she'd worked around for the last year had made any kind of an impact.

To be singling him out when he'd just been hit with the loss of his sister and brother-in-law made her ashamed. She rushed from the elevator ahead of him. But just as she was about to turn toward the lounge, he grasped her elbow. A warm current passed through her body without her volition.

"Come outside with me where my cell phone will work better. My parents will want to ask you some questions."

"All right."

They walked through the sliding doors into the late-afternoon sun. It was quarter to five already. She watched and listened as he communicated in unintelligible Greek with his parents. During the silences, she read between the lines. Her heart went out to all of them.

After a few minutes his penetrating gaze landed on her. He handed her the phone. "They speak English and are anxious to hear anything you can tell them."

Fran took the cell phone from him and said hello.

"We are overjoyed you found our Demitra," his mother spoke first in a heavy Greek accent. In a voice full of tears she said, "Our son tells us you've been at the hospital with her the whole time."

"Yes. She's the sweetest little thing I ever saw. A cherub. And now that she's awake, she seems fine."

"Ah… That's the news we've been waiting to hear," Nik's father broke in. "We want to meet you. I told him to bring you and the Petralias to Mykonos when Demitra is released. After the funeral, you will stay on as our guests for as long as you wish. He tells me you've just started your vacation. We'd like you to spend it with us. Because of you, a miracle has happened."

"Someone else would have found her if I hadn't, Mr.

Angelis, but thank you very much for your kind words.
Here's Nik." She handed him the phone. "I'm going to
the lounge," she whispered.

"I'll be right there." His deep voice curled through
her as she walked back inside the building.

Once again she found Kellie and Leandros seated on
one of the couches. You didn't have to be a mind reader
to guess they were having an intense conversation that
wasn't going well. Judging by Kellie's taut body and
his grim countenance, they were both in agony. But
when they saw Fran, they stopped talking and stood up.

Kellie rushed over to her, as if she were glad for the
interruption. "Dr. Xanthis came to talk to us a minute
ago and said he'll release the baby tomorrow once the
DNA testing is done. I was just telling Leandros that
since she's been reunited with her family, you and I
can continue on with our vacation while he flies back
to Rhodes."

Obviously Kellie wanted Fran to fall in with her
wishes despite anything Leandros had to say. But her
comment caused his firm jaw to tighten, making Fran
uncomfortable. "My project supervisor can finish up
the work there. I have a helicopter waiting to fly the
three of us back to Athens. One of my employees will
drive the car home."

Kellie tossed her blond head. "Don't be silly, Leandros. I don't want to interfere with your work. Besides,
Fran and I want to sightsee in places where we've never
been before."

"Where exactly?" he demanded quietly. Fran had
never heard him so terse.

"We're going to do some hiking, but haven't decided

all the details yet. After dinner, we'll get out the map to plan our next destination."

Just when Fran didn't think she could stand the tension any longer, Nik entered the lounge and walked up to them. He darted her a searching glance. "Did you tell them about my father's invitation?"

The girls exchanged a private look before Fran said, "I haven't had time yet." Kellie's troubles with Leandros had weighted them down.

In the next breath Nik extended them all a personal invitation to fly to Mykonos in the morning and spend a few days with his family. "My parents insist."

"I was planning to pay them a personal visit anyway, Nik. We'd be honored to come," Leandros spoke up before Kellie could say anything. "Under the circumstances, I'll drive us back to Athens in Kellie's car. Tomorrow we'll fly to your villa."

Uh-oh. That meant a lot of hours for them to talk, but Fran decided that was a good thing. Kellie could approach him with the plan they'd talked about last night.

"Excellent." Nik shot Fran a level glance. "I realize you came here on vacation, but if it wouldn't inconvenience you too much, would you mind staying with me at the hospital overnight?

"Between the two of us taking turns, we ought to be able to comfort Demi while my brothers arrange for Melina's and Stavros's bodies to be flown home on our company plane. I'd very much like your help when we take Demi in the helicopter to Thessalonika airport in the morning. From there we'll fly on the plane to Mykonos."

Her heart thudded. Nik honestly wanted her help with his niece? He couldn't know she wasn't ready to say goodbye to the adorable child. Another night to hold her thrilled Fran to pieces.

Trying to sound in control she said, "If you feel it's necessary, I'd be glad to help." She looked at Kellie, knowing her friend didn't want to be left alone with her husband right now. The situation was precarious. "What do you think, Kellie? Would it be all right with you?"

Fran knew Kellie was stuck in a hard spot. She couldn't say no to Nik who'd already lost part of his family, but that meant she'd have to face Leandros sooner than she'd expected. It was providential they'd come up with an idea last night. *It had to work!*

"Of course. I'll see you tomorrow and we'll resume our vacation."

If Kellie worked things out with Leandros, maybe she wouldn't want to go on a trip after all. Fran was hoping for that outcome. "All right then."

The news seemed to relax Leandros a little. No doubt he was thankful for this much of a reprieve so he could talk to his wife. "Fran? I'll bring your bags in from the car."

Nik shook his head. "Don't bother, Leandros. I'll come with you and put them in my rental car." He turned to Fran. "I'll be back in a minute."

After the two men walked out of the lounge, Fran put an arm around Kellie's shoulders. "I'm sorry about this. I had no idea Nik would ask me to stay on. Frankly, I didn't know what to say."

"Neither of us had a choice. It would have been churlish to refuse him."

"If I stay overnight with the baby, are you going to be okay?"

Her friend took a shuddering breath. "I thought I'd

have two weeks to be away from Leandros, but this situation has changed things for the moment and can't be helped. Wish me luck broaching your suggestion to him," she whispered in a pain-filled voice.

"Kellie, last night we talked a lot about Karmela, but I sense there's still something you haven't told me. What is it?"

Her head was bowed. "I was afraid to tell you. N-night before last, I told him this vacation was more than that. I wanted a separation."

Fran groaned. "No wonder he looks shattered." Fran was aghast that their marriage had already broken down to that extent.

Her friend's lips tightened. "He said I wasn't thinking clearly before he stormed out of the bedroom angrier than I've ever seen him. On our drive back to Athens, I'm going to do what you said. I'll tell him that since I haven't gotten pregnant, I need something substantial to do and want to work with him in his private office. I'll remind him I was once a part of an advertising agency and am perfectly capable.

"But if he turns me down flat, and I'm afraid he will, then he needs to hear what I think about the sacred Karmela. Up until now I've been careful about saying anything negative, but no longer. I might as well get everything out in the open right now."

Fran would have told her not to plunge in with Leandros where Karmela was concerned yet. Let the idea of his wife working with him take hold first. But both men came back in the lounge, preventing further conversation.

Leandros put his arm around his wife. "It's going to be a long drive. We need to get going."

"I'll see you tomorrow." Fran hugged her. "Tell him you love him so much, you want the opportunity to work with him," she begged in a quiet whisper. "I don't see how he can turn you down."

When Kellie let her go without an answer, Leandros grasped his wife's hand and they walked out of the lounge.

She felt Nik's gaze on her. "We need a meal. Let's drive to the hotel where you stayed last night and get a couple of rooms so we can shower and have dinner. By then we'll feel much more prepared to spend the night with Demi."

"That sounds good to me." She would have said more, such as the fact that he hadn't had any sleep last night, but she'd bring it up to him later.

He walked her out to the parking lot and helped her into the rental car. His dark eyes noticed every detail, and she was glad she was wearing her linen pants. Once he got in the driver's side he said, "You'll have to guide me to the hotel."

"It's on the southern end of the village near the main highway." She gave him a few directions, not quite believing that he was taking her to the place where she'd found his niece. "There on the corner," she said. He flipped a U-turn and pulled up close to the front entrance where people were dining. "Before we go in, I'll show you the garden out in back."

"Good. I want to take pictures while there's still some light."

She got out of the car before he could help her and they walked around the side to the rear of the hotel where more customers were enjoying their evening meal. Fran kept going until she came to the garden.

"I found her right there." She pointed to the bushes in the corner. "There's no indication she lay there all those hours. It's still totally unbelievable to me. Finding her alive so far away from the Persephone is one of those inexplicable miracles."

Their eyes met. "Finding her alive in time to *save* her constituted another miracle. That's *your* doing," Nik said in a deep voice full of emotion.

He hunkered down to examine the spot, fingering the bushes. After he stood up, he pulled out his cell phone and took several pictures. Before she could stop him, he took a picture of her, then turned and snapped a few more of the back of the hotel. "When Demi is old enough to understand, I'll show her these pictures."

"Let me get one of you standing there," she said on impulse. "Demi will be thrilled to see her uncle in the very place she landed. She'll always be known as the Greek version of Dorothy Gale, the girl from Kansas in *The Wizard of Oz*. But instead of being blown to Oz, Demi was caught up in a tornado and deposited in a Grecian garden miles away. What a ride she must have had," her voice throbbed.

Something flickered in those black-brown depths. "Amen," he said before handing her the phone. His fingers overlapped hers, conveying warmth. She backed away far enough to get his tall, hard-muscled frame in the picture with the garden just behind him.

As she finished and gave the phone back to him, the proprietor approached. "You're the one who found the miracle baby!"

"Yes. And this is Nikolos Angelis, the baby's uncle. I was just showing him where I discovered her."

The owner stared at Nik. "You are the new head of

the Angelis Corporation. I saw your picture on television."

"That's right," he murmured.

Fran said, "His sister and her husband were killed in the tornado, but the baby survived and will be leaving the hospital tomorrow. I'll ask them to return the blanket to you."

"Not to worry about that. We are all very sorry about this tragedy, *Kyrie* Angelis."

Nik shook the man's hand. "Thank you."

"Can we serve you dinner? It will be our pleasure."

"We'd like that, wouldn't we, Mrs. Myers?" The way he included her as if they'd been friends a long time seemed to come out of the blue. Her pulse raced for no good reason.

"Come through to the front desk and everything will be arranged," the owner said.

"We'll need two rooms to change in. Later my brothers will be arriving to stay the night."

"Very good."

Nik ushered her inside the rear door. His touch might be impersonal, but she felt it in every atom of her body.

Once behind the desk, the owner gave them each a key. "The rooms are on the second floor."

"Thank you." Nik turned to her. "Why don't you go on up while I bring in our bags? I always keep one onboard the plane in case of an emergency. With a change of clothes and a good meal, we ought to be set to spend the night with Demi."

She nodded and hurried up the stairs. It was hot out and she was eager for another shower. He wasn't far behind with her suitcase. After walking into her bedroom, his gaze found hers. "I'll meet you in the back of the hotel in half an hour. After we eat, we'll take our bags out to the car and leave for the hospital."

"Demi must be so frightened."

He grimaced. "My brothers promised to stay with her until we get there. She knows and loves them. That ought to help."

Her eyelids stung with unshed tears. "But she'll still be looking for her mommy and daddy."

He lounged against the doorjamb. "Of course, but I wouldn't be surprised if she isn't looking for *you* too. See you shortly."

Fran averted her eyes. *He was too striking.*

Physical attraction was a powerful thing. Under other circumstances, she could be swept away. Thankfully she'd learned her lesson with Rob. Though he'd been conventionally handsome, she'd discovered good looks weren't enough to hold a relationship together, let alone a marriage.

For him to have said he'd be willing to adopt and then change his mind had inflicted indescribable pain. Fran had not only lost hope of being a mother, she'd lost the ability to trust.

CHAPTER THREE

AFTER A PHONE CALL to the hospital in Athens, Nik showered and shaved. Once they'd eaten a good meal, he felt restored and imagined Mrs. Myers did, too. He'd almost slipped and called her Fran in front of the proprietor, but realized he needed to keep thinking of her as Mrs. Myers, a married woman.

En route to the hospital, he phoned Sandro who told him the doctor had moved Demi to her own room in the pediatric wing. They didn't have to wear masks and gowns any longer and were able to hold her.

"That's wonderful," Fran declared when he'd conveyed the good news to her. "After what she's been through, she needs to be cuddled."

Nik's thoughts exactly. He parked around the side entrance to the hospital with easier access to the pediatric unit.

On the drive over he'd inhaled his companion's flowery fragrance. By the time they got out of the car and entered the hospital, he could hardly take his eyes off her stunning figure clothed in a summery print skirt and white blouse. She wore white leather sandals. With her hair flowing to her shoulders from a side part, she made an enticing vision of femininity he doubted she was aware of.

He thought about her being in Greece on her own. American women had a tendency to be independent. For her and Leandros's wife to be traveling alone shouldn't have surprised him. But he thought Fran's husband a fool to let his attractive wife vacation in a foreign country without him.

He wondered how Leandros handled being apart from his wife, but he had no right to speculate. The media had painted Nik to be the most eligible playboy in Greece, a label he was forced to wear. But it would do as a cover to hide his real reason for not being married by now. Therefore he wasn't in any position to judge what went on in another man's life or marriage.

In truth he felt shame for having any of those thoughts where Mrs. Myers and Kellie Petralia were concerned. If the two women hadn't been out together, Fran wouldn't have spotted their precious Demi. That was a miracle in and of itself. So was her desire to make sure the baby hadn't been left alone at the hospital.

Interesting that it had been Fran, not Kellie, who'd planted herself next to Demi in the ICU. He wondered why...

For a moment Nik's thoughts flew to Lena, the last woman he'd dated. After two dates she'd suggested they move in together. She was a desirable woman, but he didn't believe in living together. Because of a painful issue from his past that had prevented him from proposing to any woman yet, he didn't want to encourage her. In order not to be cruel, he'd stopped seeing her.

In truth, none of his romantic relationships had ever gotten past the point where he'd felt he could take the next step. As for Lena, he couldn't help wondering what would have happened if she'd been the one who found Demi. Would she have dropped everything and changed her plans in order to comfort the baby? Would she have shown such a strong maternal instinct?

He doubted it, yet the minute he'd posed those questions, he chastized himself. It wasn't fair to compare any of the women in his past to Fran. The moment she'd discovered Demi in that garden, she'd felt a special responsibility to care for her. The whole situation was unlike any other. She was unique, but his thoughts had to stop there. She was another man's *wife*. He needed to remember that before he got in real trouble.

What did he mean by *before?* He already was in trouble, because deep in his gut, he felt she was the kind of woman he might trust enough to reveal his painful secret to. Why her and why now?

Following his brothers' directions, he found Demi's room. When he walked inside with Fran, he saw an exhausted-looking Cosimo walking around holding the baby, but she was fussing. Sandro had passed out in an easy chair brought in for them.

Nik nodded to his brother and walked over to take the baby from him, needing to nestle her against his chest. He was still incredulous she was alive. She recognized him, but there was no accompanying smile because she wasn't herself. Her world had literally been blown apart.

"It's me, Demi, your Uncle Nikolos. I'm here." He kissed her neck and cheeks, careful not to hurt the cuts that were already healing. "Where's my little sunshine girl? Hmm?" But she still seemed restless, the way she'd been with Cosimo.

Fran walked up next to him and touched her black curls. "Hi, Demi. Do you remember me? It's Fran."

The baby heard her voice and turned her head to focus on her. All of a sudden she started to cry and held out her arms to Fran, almost leaping to get to her. Nik couldn't believe a bond had formed so fast that his niece would go to Fran with an eagerness that was astonishing. Even more amazing was the way Demi settled down and buried her face in Fran's neck, reminding him of the way she always was with Melina.

Fran rocked her and sang a little song. Nik took advantage of the time to take Cosimo aside and talk to him. "I've got rooms for you and Sandro at the hotel where Fran found the baby." He gave him the directions. "Take Sandro with you and get some sleep. Come back here tomorrow morning and we'll use the hospital helicopter to get to Thessalonika before we fly home. The bodies should be loaded on the plane by then."

Sadness filled Cosimo's eyes. "You're sure you won't need help?"

"Positive. Fran and I will take turns tonight."

"She's willing to stay?"

Nik nodded. His brother looked relieved. "But you haven't had any sleep."

"I'll get it now."

"I'm afraid Demi hasn't slept. She's looking for Melina. I've never felt so helpless in my life."

"I have a feeling she might get her rest now that Fran is here. You two go on."

Cosimo nodded and woke up their brother. Nik walked them out of the room and down the hall. After saying goodnight, he went to the desk where he asked for a cot to be brought in.

Within a few minutes, housekeeping delivered one and left. Finally he was alone with Fran and turned off the light. Though he was beyond tired, he still wanted to talk to her before he got some sleep. Heaving a deep sigh, he sank down in one of the chairs and sat back, marveling over her rapport with his niece.

"I think you've gotten her to sleep."

"Yes," she whispered. "The dear little thing must be so tired and bewildered."

"With you holding her, it's apparent she'll get the rest she needs. When you're too tired, I'll take over."

"I'm not desperate for sleep like you. Kellie and I slept in until ten this morning. Why don't you undo the cot and lie down? I'll waken you when it's your turn."

"Promise?"

She gave him a half smile. "Believe it."

In the semidarkness, her generous mouth drew his attention, spiking his guilt for having those kinds of thoughts about her. "Where did you come from?"

"Not from the whirlwind, if that's what you mean," she drawled.

He crossed his legs at the ankles. "You might as well have. Earlier today my brothers and I were combing through the pines behind the resort, dying a little with every step because there was no trace of Demi.

"Then the call came from Leandros telling us to get to the Leminos hospital as fast as possible because a miracle may have happened. Suddenly, out of nowhere, I find this American woman taking care of my niece as if she were her mother. I'm still not sure if I'm dreaming this or not."

Fran kissed Demi's curls before sitting down in the other chair. "Then we're both having the same inexplicable dream. Day before yesterday I flew from Philadelphia to Athens to spend my vacation with Kellie. Leandros had already flown to Rhodes on business.

"At six yesterday morning, she and I left the city because we knew we had a long drive ahead of us. We'd planned to drive around new areas of Greece neither of us had visited before. She wanted me to see the Petralias' latest resort, so we decided to stay a night at the Persphone before moving on.

"But by late afternoon a fierce storm arose and I suggested we pull off the highway in Leminos to find shelter. Kellie wanted to keep going because the resort was only twelve miles farther, but then the hail started, so we hurried inside the first hotel we came to.

"When we learned from the staff that a tornado had destroyed some suites at the Persephone, we both fell apart. Not only because we realized we might have been caught and lost our lives, too, but because she knew Leandros would be devastated to think such a thing had happened to the guests staying at the resort. He would take it very hard and he was so far away on business. There was no way to reach him by phone."

Nik sat foward. "For a while it was chaos. Do you know about the other tornado?"

Her beautiful eyes widened. "What are you talking about?"

"There was one at the airport yesterday morning."

"You're kidding!"

He shook his head. "I came close to being affected. After seeing my sister and her family off around 6:30 a.m., I went over to the air cargo area to do business when a funnel cloud struck. No one was injured, but it was terrifying to see how much damage it did in the space of a short time."

"Now I understand why it was so windy when we left, but we haven't had any news here."

"That's not surprising. I was just leaving my office at the end of the day when my brother phoned and told me about a second tornado."

"We get so many in the States, but I didn't realize you got them, too."

"Once in a while," he murmured, "but yesterday's phenomena probably won't happen for another couple of decades or more."

"Let's pray not."

"When I turned on the TV, what I heard was enough to make my blood run cold." Just the way he said it made her chill. "My brothers and I took off in the plane for Thessalonika. By the time we reached the resort, we learned that Melina and Stavros were two of the victims. To our horror, there was no sign of Demi."

"I don't know how any of you are holding up." The sadness in her voice touched him to the core.

"It's our parents we're worried about. That's why it's so important you come to the villa with me tomorrow. They love their grandchildren, but Demi has a special place in their hearts because she's the only girl."

"I can understand that." Fran looked down at Demi who was cuddled in her arms, fast asleep. "This little child is too precious for words. She'll always be a special joy to them."

"And to me."

A tremor rocked his body. On Melina's birthday, she'd taken Nik aside and asked him to be Demi's guardian if anything ever happened to her and Stavros.

Without hesitation he'd told her yes, but he was unable to entertain the thought of anything ever happening to his sister and her husband. Remembering her request, the hairs lifted on the back of his neck. Had she asked him because of a premonition?

"Demi's blessed to have such loving family."

Nik eyed Fran speculatively. "Since you're married and have such a close rapport with my niece, I'm wondering if you have children."

She didn't meet his eyes. "No."

No?

"How does your husband let you leave him for such a long time?" The question he'd sworn not to ask left his lips before he could stop it.

"We're divorced."

His thoughts reeled. "How long ago?"

"A year."

What husband in his right mind wouldn't have held on to a woman like her? Nik sensed he'd be wandering into forbidden territory with more questions, yet he was intrigued by her. Now that he knew those pertinent facts, he was determined to learn more and no longer felt guilty about it. With time and patience, he'd get his answers. "Are you ready to let me hold her now?"

"I'm fine. I was going to suggest you go to sleep."

"Maybe I will for a little while."

He got to his feet to undo the cot. After taking off his shoes, he stretched out. Another heavy sigh escaped him. "This feels so good, I fear I might never get up again. You're sure you don't mind?"

"Positive. Holding this angel is a joy. You need sleep or you won't be any good to your family tomorrow."

"You're right. If I haven't said it already, I'm grateful you're here for Demi."

"*I'm* the one who's grateful."

His instincts told him those weren't empty words. He needed to find out what emotions were driving them, but before he could ask, oblivion took over.

The next time he was aware of his surroundings, it was morning.

Nik sat up and got to his feet, removing the blanket Fran must have thrown over him. His gaze shot to her. She was asleep in the easy chair while Demi slept in the hospital crib.

He had no idea how long Fran had stayed awake, but she'd chosen not to disturb him for any reason. Unable to help himself, he looked down, studying her facial features. With no makeup and her dark blond hair somewhat disheveled, she was lovelier than most women who worked at it all day.

Since Demi was still asleep, he tiptoed out to the hall to phone his brothers. They were on their way over with a new outfit for the baby. As he talked with them, the doctor slipped inside the room. By the time Nik hung up and returned, he discovered Fran standing by the crib talking to the doctor. She'd brushed her hair and applied lipstick, looking amazingly fresh for someone who'd probably been up most of the night.

The doctor turned to him with a smile. "The lab has confirmed she's your niece. I'm happy to say her cuts are starting to heal. She's doing fine in every regard and can be released. Keep her hydrated. What she needs now is the love of her family which I can see isn't going to be a problem. Just so you know, the media has been inundating the hospital for information.

"In order to make them go away, I gave a statement that I hope will satisfy them and give your family a chance to breathe before they descend on you. When you're ready to leave, come to the desk and someone will escort you to the roof where the helicopter is waiting."

Nik shook his hand. "Thank you for everything you've done, doctor. The Angelis family is indebted to you."

The older man's eyes flashed. "And no doubt to *Kyria* Myers who made the baby feel safe and loved until you arrived. We could use more like her around the ICU." He eyed Fran. "Are you a nurse?"

"No. But I work in a hospital for patients' rights and make certain they get the follow up care they need after they go home."

"You wouldn't like a job with us, would you?" he threw out.

"I've already got a position in mind for her," Nik inserted, flashing her a glance. She looked at him in confusion. "Of course I haven't discussed it with her yet."

The thought had been percolating in his mind since yesterday, but until he knew she was divorced, he'd kept it at bay. Before he could explain more, the doctor said, "I'll be at the desk. When you're ready to leave, I'll escort you to the private elevator that will take you to the roof." He left as Nik's brothers arrived with a new quilt and stretchy suit they'd purchased.

All the talking woke up Demi who turned to the bars and tried to get up. She babbled and looked longingly at Fran, asking to be rescued. Everyone chuckled as Fran leaned over and plucked her from her prison. Giving her a kiss on both cheeks she was rewarded with a smile on Demi's face that had been missing until now. That happy countenance cemented the idea Nik planned to propose to Fran when the time was right.

She spoke to the baby. "Look who's here—your favorite uncles!"

He was witnessing another kind of miracle, one of communication despite the fact that Fran didn't understand Greek, nor did the baby comprehend English.

Nik and his brothers took turns kissing her, but the baby clung to Fran. The nurse came in with a bag of diapers and enough formula to satisfy the baby until they reached home. Fran changed her and put on the new pink outfit, then looked around. "Who wants to feed her?"

Sandro took Demi from her arms, but the baby wanted none of it. "Well, that settles it." He kissed her curls before returning her to Fran's arms. "I'm afraid you're stuck, *Kyria* Myers."

"Call me Fran, and I don't mind at all."

The nurse handed her a bottle. Soon Demi had settled down to drink, content for the moment. She eventually burped a couple of times, announcing she'd drained it. More chuckles ensued from everyone. Despite the sadness ahead when they returned to Mykonos, Demi was the bright light that kept them all from sinking right now.

Nik walked over to Fran. "We're ready to go. I'll carry Demi to the helicopter. After we're onboard the plane, we'll eat breakfast." He relieved her of the baby and wrapped her in the quilt.

"Come on, *Demitza*. We're going for a ride."

Fran followed him from the room with his brothers. Once they rode the elevator to the roof, they helped her into the helicopter while he climbed in with Demi. He handed her over to Cosimo who strapped her in the infant seat next to Fran. His brothers sat on the opposite side.

When everyone was settled in, Nik noticed Fran reach for Demi's little hand before he took his place in the copilot's seat. The gesture touched him and told him even more about the compassionate woman who'd put her vacation plans aside to make Demi secure. Again he wondered how many other women he'd known would have done that.

In a few minutes they lifted off and made a beeline for the airport. He heard his brothers talking to Fran. "We want to thank you again for all your help so far. Demi hasn't been around other people besides family, so it's a real surprise that she's taken to you."

"I'm sure it's because I was the one who found her in the garden. She'd been lying there helpless all night."

"I think it's more than that," Sandro confided. "You have a loving way with her like our sister."

"Well, thank you. It's been my pleasure to stay with her, believe me."

"How long will you be in Greece?"

"I fly home in less than two weeks."

Maybe not, Nik mused. Before he introduced Fran to his parents, he needed to have a private talk with her. The best place to do that would be aboard the jet in the compartment he used for his office.

"I guess you know our parents would like you to stay with us on Mykonos for part of the time."

"That's kind of them, Cosimo, but it's really up to

my friend Kellie Petralia who invited me here. She'd
planned this time for us to be together."

"She and her husband are welcome to stay with us,
too," Sandro chimed in.

"Your parents told me as much on the phone."

"That's because we're all grateful to you."

Grateful didn't exactly cover Fran's deepest feelings.
She'd been empty for too long. To suddenly be taking
care of a baby who was content to be in her arms made
her feel whole for the first time in years. Even though
she would have to relinquish Demi tomorrow, she would
savor this sweet time with her today and tonight.

In her teens she'd been told she couldn't have children. It had been like a light going out, but over the
years she'd come around to the idea of adoption.

During the short flight to Thessalonika, Fran looked
out the helicopter window at the sparkling blue Aegean
below, wishing she could concentrate on the spectacular panorama. Instead she found herself reliving the
painful moment when Rob had shattered her dreams
of being a mother.

Even if it were possible to love another man again,
the idea of meeting one who said he'd be willing to
adopt wasn't an option for her. Maybe one day she might
meet and fall in love with a widower who had a child or
children. At least then she could take over the mother
role to help fill that empty space in her heart.

She simply couldn't see it happening, but Kellie
wouldn't let her think that way. Dear Kellie... Her
friend was in turmoil right now.

Her eyes strayed to Demi who was wide awake for
the trip. She made sounds and was growing restless at

being confined. In order to placate her, Fran got out another bottle of formula to keep her happy. Demi held it and mostly played with it, only sucking on the nipple without absorbing a lot of liquid. Her two bottom teeth had come in, helping her to tug on it.

Fran was amused to see the funny behavior coming from this child who could win the most beautiful baby of the year award. That was because she had the classic features of her mother and glossy black hair like Nik's... and his brothers, Fran hastened to remind herself.

But Nik possessed an unconscious sensuality and sophistication that stood out from his siblings. She put her head back for a minute and closed her eyes so she wouldn't keep staring at the back of his head where a few tendrils of black hair lay curled against his neck. Once in a while he turned to say something to his brothers and she glimpsed his striking male profile and chiseled jaw.

Dressed in the light brown sport shirt and dark trousers he'd changed into at the hotel last night, there was no man to match him. The celebrated bachelor's appeal went far beyond the physical. He was warm and generous. She doubted he had a selfish bone in his body. Nik was so different from Rob....

Before long the helicopter landed, and they were driven to the Angelis Corporation jet, the size of a 727, waiting on the tarmac. While Sandro and Cosimo helped her and Demi onboard, Nik excused himself to talk to the people who'd taken care of putting his family's bodies in the cargo area.

A few minutes later he walked down the aisle toward her. After speaking to his brothers on the way, he came to sit on the other side of her and Demi. His half smile turned her heart over.

"The flight to Mykonos won't take too long. Then it's just another short helicopter ride to the villa. After we reach cruising speed, we'll eat breakfast, then I'd like to have a private talk with you in the compartment behind the galley. My brothers will entertain Demi."

She nodded, but couldn't help but wonder what was on his mind. He'd said something about a position in front of the doctor. What exactly had he meant?

She strapped herself in, and the jet took off. Like clockwork, the minute the Fasten Seat Belt light went off, the steward started serving their food. Fran needed a good meal, if only to brace herself for their talk.

Once the steward removed their trays, she undid Demi long enough to change her diaper. Nik got up from his seat and reached for another bottle in the hospital diaper bag. Once Demi was strapped in again, he kissed her and gave her the bottle to keep her occupied.

Touching Fran's elbow he whispered, "Follow me."

She did his bidding, but it was but a few seconds before they could hear Demi cry. Fran felt like the biggest meanie on earth, but she kept going. Once inside the compartment set up as a den with a computer, Nik closed the door and invited her to sit in one of the club seats opposite him. They could still hear Demi's cries though they sounded fainter. Fran knew the baby's uncles would take care of her, but the sound of her distress tugged at her.

Nik sat back in his club chair with that unconscious aura of a CEO at home in his world. His dark eyes seemed to scrutinize her as if he were looking for secrets she might be hiding. Her pulse quickened in response.

"Before we reach Mykonos, I wonder if you'd answer some personal questions for me."

Personal? "If I can."

"Are you a full-time employee at the hospital?"

"Yes."

He cocked his head. "What would happen if you needed more time off? Would they give it to you without it causing you problems?"

"I think so, but it would have to be because of an emergency."

"Of course. One more question. Are you involved with another man right now?"

She blinked. He obviously had a reason for all this probing. "No."

"And your friend Kellie. Would it disappoint her terribly if you didn't spend your vacation with her?"

"Yes," Fran answered honestly. "Why?"

Her question caused him to lean forward with his hands clasped. His intelligent dark eyes fused with hers. "Because I have a great favor to ask of you. I know I don't have the right, but Demi's needs are going to be top priority for my family in the days ahead."

"I can understand that."

"Judging by her behavior around you in the hospital, and including the fact that she started crying the minute we walked away from her a few moments ago, it's clear Demi has formed a strong attachment to you. I dread what things are going to be like when you leave on your vacation with Kellie. She'll not only be looking for her parents, but for you. That's what's got me worried."

Fran had been worried about it, too, but she would

never have brought it up. "Surely when she's surrounded by your family again, she'll get through the transition."

He inhaled sharply. "I would have thought her seeing me and my brothers would have been all she needed. We're a close family and get together often. But this experience has traumatized her in some way we don't understand. If she isn't clinging to us, then I don't expect she'll want anyone else, not even the staff who are familiar to her."

"What about your parents? Your mother? Does she look like Melina?"

"They shared certain traits." His eyes stared into Fran's. "But I don't know if Demi would cling to them the way she does to you. I'm very interested to see what happens when she's with them again. Something tells me it won't be enough to make the baby feel secure."

"You'll have to give Demi time."

"That goes without saying. Nevertheless, I plan to consult a child psychiatrist after the funeral is over. Depending on what he or she says, I'll go from there. But for the time being, I'd like to hire you to take care of Demi until you have to get back to Philadelphia. By then I'll have some idea of how to proceed."

Fran stirred in the chair. While trembling with excitement at the prospect of loving that little girl for a while longer, she knew how painful it would be when she had to say a final goodbye. She'd known a lot of pain in her life. First the death of her brother, then the death of a dream that had ended in divorce. She might not have lost Rob in death, but it felt like one.

No brother, no husband, no child of her own after three years of marriage. Fran knew herself too well. Another twenty-four hours taking care of that precious baby would be hard enough. But ten more days? She couldn't risk the inevitable pain. It would come and she wouldn't be able to stop it.

"When she's been with your parents, or one of your brothers' families, she'll eventually adapt."

One black brow dipped. "I don't know. It's too soon to work all that out and I want a doctor's opinion first. The one thing I do know is that Demi wants *you*. If you could bring yourself to help us out here, you'll be handsomely compensated. Anything you want."

She shook her head. "That's very generous, Nik, but I wouldn't do it for the money."

He sat back again. "If Kellie doesn't mind a change in your plans, would you consider it? You'll stay in an apartment at the villa. There's a guest room and another smaller room we'll set up as a nursery. Kellie is welcome to be with you any time you want. But I guess I haven't asked the most important question. Is this something you wouldn't mind doing?"

Mind? If he had any idea... Demi had climbed into her heart where she would always stay. Discovering the baby in that garden was as if providence had set the baby down in those bushes at the precise moment for Fran to find her.

But the flags had gone up, warning her that if she told him she wouldn't mind at all, she could plan for rivers of anguish down the road when she had to tear herself away from that baby. It was a trauma she'd never get over.

"Fran?" he prodded. His smoky-sounding tone defeated her.

Although the youngest, Nik clearly carried the weight of the Angelis family on his shoulders. She had noticed how his brothers looked to him. This was a problem none of them had faced before. At the moment she recognized he needed a different kind of help and wanted Fran's.

But for her own self-preservation, she needed to remain firm. "It isn't a case of minding. It's just that I know what Kellie's answer will be when I ask her. We've been planning this trip for a long time. It will upset her too much and I can't disappoint her. I'm sorry. But until the funeral is over, I'll be happy to help out."

"Then I'm grateful for that much." He got to his feet. "Shall we get back to Demi before my frantic brothers come bursting in here with her?"

Fran had hated disappointing him, but her first priority had to be to herself.

CHAPTER FOUR

AT THREE THE NEXT afternoon, Nik left Fran holding the baby while he walked out to meet Leandros and his wife at the helicopter pad behind the villa. They'd been paying their respects to the other family, the ones who had lost their parents in the tornado and who couldn't get away before now.

"Fran will be relieved you're here now. It's all that matters." He led them out to the patio of the Angelis family villa where everyone had congregated to talk and eat. More tears ensued while Leandros and Kellie commiserated with his family.

Incredibly, the pain of losing Melina and Stavros was softened by the joy of having found Demi alive, a blessing no one had expected. Nik was heartened to see his family's spirits had lifted despite their loss.

"It's all over the news," Sandro spoke up. "Demi is known as the Miracle Baby. Did you know the hotel in Leminos has become famous overnight?"

"So has the hospital," Cosimo declared. "They even interviewed Demi's doctor on the noon news."

Though the whole family was eager to hold her, Demi clung to Fran just as Nik had suspected she would. The only time she didn't cry was when his parents held her.

But after a few minutes, Demi was looking for Fran and making sounds that indicated she didn't want to be with anyone else.

Nik knew his parents were hurt, but they hid it well. When they had issued her an invitation over the phone to be their guest for as long as she wanted, they had had no idea they would need her on hand to keep Demi happy. He smiled to himself. Though Fran had turned him down about staying on, she didn't know this story wasn't over yet.

His father eyed Fran who was holding Demi against her shoulder. The baby looked around chewing on her teething ring. "Tell us what you thought when you found her. We want details," he beseeched her.

Fran broke into a tender smile. Once more she repeated her amazing tale. "The hotel is situated on a corner of the street. My first thought was that her mother or father had been walking her in a stroller on the other side of the hotel when those gale-force winds drove Kellie and me to run inside for shelter.

"It seemed more than possible she'd been blown into the garden at the rear of the building. But if that were true, then where were her parents? I was in shock to think she'd been exposed to the elements all night. Honestly, she looked like she'd been dropped from the sky."

Nik's sisters-in-law made moaning sounds to think such a thing had happened.

Kellie sat forward. "I came around back and saw Fran holding a limp baby who was wearing only a torn shirt. I thought I was hallucinating."

"You weren't the only one," Fran added. "When neither the police or the hospital staff had heard of anyone looking for their baby, I began to think that's exactly what had happened, that she'd been carried by the wind and deposited in a cushion of bushes."

"But twelve miles—" Nik's mother cried out and put her hands to her mouth. "God wanted her to live." His father nodded his silver head and wept.

"Nik?" Fran eyed him from her place on the swing. "Has your family seen the pictures you took with your camera?"

He'd been planning to show them later. "Let's do it right now," he said, but he had difficulty talking because of the lump in his throat. After pulling out his phone, he clicked on to the picture gallery and handed it to his parents. "Slide your thumb across to see all of them. I took a few pictures in the hospital, too." He'd made certain he'd gotten some shots of Fran.

For the next little while his family and the Petralias took turns viewing them. Nik's six- and seven-year-old nephews were eager to look at them, too. The younger three- and four-year-olds had no idea what was going on and played with their toys. In the quiet, Fran's eyes met his. They were both remembering that surreal moment when she'd showed him the now-famous spot.

While everyone was talking, he walked over to her. "Do you think she's ready for something besides a bottle?"

"I hope so. She needs the nourishment."

"That's what I'm thinking. I'll tell cook to get out a jar of her favorite fruit and meat."

Fran hugged the baby. "You'd like some food, wouldn't you, sweetheart?"

Whether she wanted it or not, she needed it. Having made up his mind, Nik left the patio and headed for the kitchen. In a minute he returned with the food and the high chair that had been in use for several years.

He put it in front of Fran, then plucked the baby from her arms and set her inside it. The cook had given him a bib that he tied around her neck. Both Fran and Demi looked up at him in surprise.

Nik shot them an amused glance. "We'll both feed her," he explained and sat down on the swing next to her. "You take the turkey." He handed her the jar and a spoon. "I'll give her some plums."

"Coward," she whispered. Her chuckle filled him with warmth.

To his relief the baby began to eat, which meant her initial trauma had passed and she was relaxed enough to want her semi-solid food again. Once she'd been put in a private room at the hospital, the nurse hadn't been able to get her to eat anything. Fran had to see the transformation and think twice about turning him down when he asked her again.

"Well, look at you," she said to Demi with a big smile. "I didn't know you were such a good eater."

Demi beamed back at both of them. Nik had never actually fed Demi before. Aided and abetted by Fran, he found himself having more fun than he could remember. Some turkey clung to the baby's upper lip, making her look adorable. Both he and Fran chuckled in delight to see her behaving normally.

Soon she finished her food while the family looked on in varying degrees of interest and curiosity. They weren't used to seeing Nik feed her. But most of all, they were shocked at the way Demi responded to Fran. The hurt in his parents' eyes had intensified. It didn't surprise him when Nik's father eventually got up from his chair and walked over to give his granddaughter a kiss on the cheek.

"One would never know what you lived through, Demi," he spoke in Greek. "Come to your grandpa." He wiped her mouth with the bib, then untied it and picked her up to take her over to Nik's mother.

Demi adored her grandfather, but the further he took her from Fran, the more she squirmed and kept turning her head to find her. Nik's mother got to her feet and held out her hands to Demi, but the baby started to cry.

"What's wrong, darling?" his mother talked to her in their native tongue, attempting to cuddle her. "Tell me what's the matter."

Nik knew the answer to that. She wanted Fran. It really was astonishing to see that even with the entire family surrounding her, Demi wanted a stranger if she couldn't have her own mother and father. He eyed Fran covertly, daring her to close her mind and heart to what was going on here.

His stomach muscles tightened as he watched the looks of surprise and confusion from everyone, but especially at the pain on his parents' faces when Demi started crying in earnest.

They'd lost Melina, but it had never occurred to anyone that Demi wouldn't soak up the love they were ready to heap on her. Nik believed it was a passing phenomenon. It *had* to be. But right now something needed to be done to calm the baby down.

"You know what I think?" he said in English. "Demi's barely out of the hospital and needs to go to bed." So did his parents who needed to rest to get through this ordeal.

"Of course," his mother concurred.

"Fran and I will take her and put her down, then we'll be back."

He clutched the baby to him and started for the villa. Fran got up from the swing and followed him to the apartment. Earlier he'd asked the housekeeper to get it prepared. With the help of the staff, they'd moved the crib and other things from the nursery in Melina's apartment to the spare room. For now it would serve as a nursery while Fran took care of Demi.

Together they got the baby ready for her afternoon nap with a fresh diaper and a white sleeper with feet.

"You look so cute in this," Fran said, kissing her cheeks several times. Once again Nik marveled how natural she was with Demi, almost as if the baby were hers. Neither of them were bilingual, but it didn't matter. They spoke a special language of love that managed to transcend. Watching Demi, you'd think Fran was her mother. How could that be? Unless...

Was it possible that the baby's head had suffered an injury when she hit the earth and she'd developed *amnesia*?

Were there cases of such a thing happening to an infant? Amnesia might explain her connection to Fran. She'd been the first person Demi saw when she'd awakened in the hospital.

But if that were true, then why did she respond to the family, to Nik? Though it was half-hearted, she did recognize everyone. He was baffled and anxious to talk to a doctor first thing in the morning.

Nik drew a bottle of premixed formula from the bag. When Fran put the baby in the crib, he handed Demi her bottle. Speaking Greek to her, he told her he loved her and wanted her to go to sleep.

Before she started drinking, the baby made sounds and stared up at the two of them with those dark brown eyes that could have been Melina's.

"Come on, Fran," he whispered. "Let's go."

"See you later, sweetheart." Fran patted her cheek, then started to follow Nik out of the room. They'd no sooner reached the door than Demi burst into tears.

Fran looked at him with pleading eyes. "I can't leave her yet."

Nik had been counting on that. "She loves you."

Again Fran averted her eyes because she knew what he'd just said was true. "You go on and be with your family, Nik. I'm sure you have things to discuss before the funeral tomorrow. Tell Kellie to come and keep me company while Demi falls asleep."

"I will. Maybe when she sees how much the baby wants you, she'll tell you the vacation can wait a few more days."

"I—I don't think so." Her little stammer indicated she wasn't quite as confident as she'd been on the plane.

"We'll see," he murmured.

She gripped the bars of the crib. "The baby's worn-out from all the excitement, but still needs time to settle down and get sleepy. I'll join you on the patio later."

This extraordinary woman was right on all counts, but if the truth be told, Nik would rather stay in here with her. "All right, but I'll be back soon to relieve you if she proves too restless."

He strode swiftly through the villa to the patio and sought out Kellie. "Fran wants to talk to you. I'll show you to the nursery."

She spoke to Leandros who nodded his head, then she followed Nik through the house. Before they entered the apartment he said, "I'm not sure there wouldn't have been a catastrophe tonight if Fran weren't here to take charge of Demi."

Kellie smiled at him. "After college she went into hospital administration, but they soon found out she's a remarkable people person for the young and the old. That's why they put her in the position she holds now. I wager she's sorely missed already. I'm lucky she could take off these two weeks for our vacation."

Having seen her in action with Demi, Nik agreed. He also got the message from Kellie not to count on Fran's generosity beyond tonight. In fact, he was sure he'd been warned off, in the nicest way possible. While cogitating on that thought, he was more determined than ever to prevail on Fran to remain longer.

They reached the door to the apartment. "Come find the family after my niece has fallen asleep."

A half hour later Fran tiptoed out of the nursery with Kellie and they went into the bedroom. "I think she'll stay asleep now. Tell me what's happened with Leandros?"

"If anything, things are worse. But before we get into that, tell me what's going on with Nik."

"What do you mean?"

Kellie sat down on the side of the king-size bed. "He has you ensconced in this fabulous apartment with the baby in the adjoining room, almost like you're a permanent fixture."

"I told him I'd help out until after the funeral tomorrow."

"But he'd like it to be longer, right?"

Nothing got past Kellie. Fran nodded. "On the flight

to Mykonos, Nik asked me if I would stay on to tend Demi until she's comfortable with the family again. He hopes I'll remain here until I have to go back to Philadelphia. I told him no because you and I were on vacation."

"Are you hoping I won't hold you to it?"

She shook her head. "No, Kellie. I only told him that as an excuse. This has nothing to do with you or our trip. I need to leave tomorrow before I find myself wishing I could take her back home with me. If it were possible, I'd like to adopt her."

"Adopt an Angelis?"

"I know how outrageous that sounds. That's why I'm glad we're leaving tomorrow."

Looking haunted, Kellie got up from the bed. "I know how attached you are to the baby already and would love to say yes to him."

"Actually, I wouldn't."

"You must think I'm being difficult, but it's because I'm afraid to see you get hurt again. When I think what you went through with Rob…"

Fran sucked in her breath. "Believe me, I don't want that kind of pain again either. When I found Demi in that garden, I felt like I'd been handed a gift. I wanted her to be mine. But she isn't! If I stayed here ten more days, it would kill me to have to walk away from her, traumatizing her once again. I refuse to put myself or her in that position. I've had too many losses in my life."

"Oh, Fran—" Kellie gave her a commiserating hug.

She wiped her eyes. "I'm glad we're leaving after the funeral. I need to put this experience behind me and forget Demi exists. It has dredged up too many painful memories. I need to move on."

By now Kellie's eyes were wet. "That makes two of us. Leandros doesn't want me working in his office."

"He wouldn't even consider it?"

"No. He says he wants to be able to come home to me after a hard day's work, but the reason is crystal-clear. Though he hasn't come right out and said it, our love life has never been satisfactory to him.

"How could it have been with a bride who was in terrible pain the first time he made love to her? His marriage to Petra was nothing like ours. They were expecting a baby when—when—" She couldn't go on. "That's why I have to put some real distance between us. Karmela can supply him what's missing. Our marriage is over."

"I can't bear it, Kellie."

"It's for the best. Like you, I refuse to wallow in any more pain. As for the Angelis family, they need to hire a nanny as soon as tomorrow after the funeral and get her installed right away."

"Agreed. I know Demi will miss me, but she'll get over it. She'll *have* to. I made that clear to Nik."

"For your sake, I'm glad." They eyed each other for a long moment. "Even though I'm nursing a horrendous headache, what do you say we put on our best smiles and go out to the patio as if nothing in the world is wrong? After we've mingled for a while, I plan to have an early night."

"So do I. Demi will be needing another bottle before sleeping through the night."

They reached the door. "Leandros will cover for me until he's ready for bed. It's what he's good at. You might as well know we haven't slept together for the last month."

Fran understood her pain. She hadn't slept with Rob for the three months leading up to their separation. It had been the beginning of the end.

The day was winding down. Nik's mother and sisters-in-law spoke together while he talked with the men. But they all stopped long enough to admire the two American beauties who'd just stepped out onto the patio.

At the first sight of Fran, Nik felt an unwanted quickening in his body. The same thing had happened at the hospital when they'd been removing their masks and gowns. In a very short time she'd grown on him despite the pain he was in.

Most of the Greek women he'd known and dated were more chatty and conscious of themselves, famous for drama on occasion. His sisters-in-law were like that. Fiery at times—beautiful—and they knew it. Melina hadn't been quite so theatrical. That's probably why she'd appealed to the quietly spoken Stavros.

Fran was an entirely different kind of woman. She seemed comfortable in her attractive skin, reminding Nik of still waters that ran deep. Did her calm aura hide unknown fires within? He felt in his gut this woman could become of vital importance to him.

After some soul-searching, he recognized his motivation to keep Fran in Athens wasn't driven exclusively by Demi's best interests. Already he was trying to find a way to persuade her to stay on for his own personal reasons. But he feared that if he lowered the bars to let her inside his soul and she couldn't take what he would be forced to tell her, blackness would envelop his world. He faced a dilemma he'd never experienced before.

Should he run from what he feared most? Or did he

reach out for the one thing that might bring him the greatest joy?

On impulse he turned to the others. "If you'll excuse me, I need to talk to *Kyria* Myers."

By now Kellie had joined her husband, leaving Fran alone. He watched her wander to the wall at the edge of the patio and look out over the water. Her violet-blue eyes flicked to his when she saw him approach. "I can't imagine gazing out on this idyllic view every night of your life. All the stories about the Greek Islands are true. You live in a paradise, especially here on Mykonos."

"I agree there's no place on earth quite like it. On the weekends, I look forward to leaving the office in Athens and coming home. The temperature of the air and the sea turns us into water babies around here."

She smiled. "There's an American artist who has done some serigraphs of Mykonos. He's captured the white cubic style of a villa like your family's to perfection."

"I know the artist you mean. I'm fond of his artwork, too, particularly several of his Italian masterpieces."

"Aren't they wonderful?"

He nodded, enjoying their conversation, but was impatient to get down to business. "How long did it take Demi to finally fall asleep?"

"Um, maybe ten songs," she quipped. Her gentle laugh found its way beneath his skin.

"Let's go for a walk along the beach." He took off his shoes. "Be sure to remove your sandals. You can leave them here by mine."

"All right." Together they walked down the steps

to the sand. From there it was only a few yards to the water. "Oh. Lovely. It warms my toes."

Nik chuckled. "Twilight is my favorite time to swim. If you wait a while, the moon will come up. Then everything is magical."

"It already is."

They walked in companionable silence for a long time. Unlike most women he knew, she felt no need to fill it in with conversation. That was a quality he liked very much, except for tonight. At the moment he had the perverse wish she would speak her mind. Fran knew he was waiting to hear she'd changed her mind.

Taking the initiative, he said, "Are you and Kellie still intent on leaving tomorrow?"

She slowed to a stop. In the dying light, she looked straight at him. "Yes. Much as I'd like to help you out, I'm afraid I can't. But I'll have you know it has been my privilege to take care of Demi over the last few days. If it's your wish, I'll stay with her until the funeral services are over. Then I'll fly back to Athens with Kellie and Leandros."

His heart clapped to a stop. She'd turned him down flat. Over his years in business, he'd made a study of people to find out what made them tick. Before Kellie Petralia had spent time alone with her in the bedroom, he could have sworn Fran was considering his proposition. He rubbed the back of his neck. Leandros's wife had a definite agenda and Nik's appeal to Fran had gotten in the way.

Trying a different tack he said, "Could you possibly wait another day? With the funeral tomorrow, I won't be able to do anything about Demi's care until the next day.

What I'd like to do is interview some nannies for the position. It would be a big help if you were there, too.

"Your hospital work makes you somewhat of an expert in reading people. If we both come up with our own questions, I'm sure we'll be able to pick the right nanny for her."

"I'm sorry, Nik, but I promised Kellie we'd leave as soon as you all came back from the interment. Surely your own mother and sisters-in-law would be the perfect ones to help out?"

Disappointed by her noncapitulation, he bit down hard on his teeth. "They would if Demi would let them hold her. I'm afraid a hysterical baby could put off a potential nanny."

"If that's the case, then you need to keep looking for one who can handle the situation, no matter how difficult."

Damn if beneath that ultra-feminine exterior she didn't think like a man....

He felt a grudging respect for her, but this battle was far from over and he was determined to win. "What if I offered you the job of permanent nanny? It's what I'd been thinking about all along after I saw how you cared for her in the hospital. No one could have been more like a mother. That's why she responded to you."

"Thank you for the compliment, but I already have a career," she came back without blinking an eye. "As much as I love that little girl—and who wouldn't?—it's a job, and the last one I'd want."

Nik was dumbfounded. "Are you so enamored of your hospital work, you can't imagine yourself leaving it for a position that could pay you an income to set you up for life in surroundings like this?"

"Actually, I can't, and I don't want that kind of money."

Then she belonged to a dying breed.

"Let me ask you the same question, Nik. Do you love what you do to make a living?"

His eyes narrowed on her appealing features, particularly her generous mouth. "What does one have to do with the other?"

"I was just thinking of a way to solve your problem. In the hospital, you treated Demi like a father would. Maybe you ought to become her nanny and give your brothers more responsibility for running the Angelis Corporation. Your sister Melina and Stavros would look down from heaven and love you forever for making such a great sacrifice."

Fran didn't know he'd agreed to be Demi's guardian if anything happened to them. Her comment found his vulnerable spot and pierced the jugular. He could feel his blood pressure climbing.

"Then again," she said softly, "you could find a wife who would love Demi and make a beautiful home for the three of you. That would take care of every problem. Your parents must be worried sick you haven't settled down yet."

Adrenaline pushed his anger through the roof. "Now we come to the crunch. After reading the tabloids on the plane, is it possible you're offering to become my bride and bring an end to my wicked ways? Is that what this verbal exercise has all been about?"

Her gentle laughter rang out in the night air. "Heavens, no. You're no more wicked than the next man."

While he digested that surprising comment she said, "I've been through marriage once and have no desire to be locked in that unhappy prison again. I was only teasing you, Nik, but it was wrong of me to try to lighten your mood on the eve of the funeral. Forgive me for that. I can see why you're such a powerhouse in business. You make it impossible to say no."

"Yet you've just said no to me." The nerve at his temple throbbed. This woman was twisting him in knots.

She eyed him critically. "You've told me you value what I've learned from my hospital work. If that's true, then listen to me. Demi's going to be all right. I promise. For a while we know she'll grieve for her parents, but in time she'll respond to your loving family.

"They're wonderful and they're all here willing to do anything. Let them help. Don't take it all on by yourself or you'll burn out."

"What are you talking about?" he growled with impatience.

"I'm talking about *you*. Leandros sings your praises as the new brains and power behind the Angelis Corporation. But you can't be everything to everyone every minute of the day and night the way you've been doing since you heard about the tornado. You remind me of Atlas carrying the world on your shoulders."

Atlas?

"I've seen it happen in families once a patient goes home from the hospital. There's always one person like you who carries the whole load, whether because of a greater capacity to feel compassion or a stronger need to give service. Who knows all the reasons? But the point is, this develops into a habit, and you're too young for this to happen to you."

Without question Fran Myers was the most unique

individual he'd ever met. No woman had ever confounded him so much before.

He sucked in his breath. "Let's go back, shall we? On the way, I want to hear about the reason why your marriage failed you to the point that you no longer believe in it."

Slowly they retraced their footsteps. "In a couple of sentences, I can tell you why it didn't work. He was the live wire at his law firm trying to make it to the top. Furthermore, he didn't feel he had the time to be a family man. He was too consumed by his work."

"What vital ingredient have you left out?"

When Fran almost stumbled, he knew he'd hit a nerve. "I'm afraid we both fell out of love. It happens all the time to millions of people."

"But not to someone like you. If he didn't have an affair, then what's the real reason it failed?"

"I'd rather not discuss it."

"Since you pretty well laid me out to the bare bones a little while ago, how about some honesty from you in return?"

"I suppose that would only be fair." She tossed her head back, causing the dark blond mass of gleaming hair to resettle on her shoulders. "You could say that when he didn't live up to the bargain we'd made before we married, there was nothing to hold us together any longer."

"Then he lied to you."

"I wouldn't say it was a lie… More of a human failing. When faced with the reality of what he'd committed to while we were dating, he couldn't go through with it. I didn't blame him for it, but my disappointment was so profound, my heart shut down."

"I'm sorry. How long were you married?"

"Three years."

And no children.

He wanted to know more. "Was he your first love?"

"No. Over the years I met and dated several men I thought might be the one. I'm sure the same experiences have happened to you."

"It's true I've enjoyed my share of women and still do. All of them have traits I admire."

"But so far none of them has delivered the whole package. At least that's what the tabloids infer," she added in a playful tone. "It was the same for me until Rob came along. He had everything that appealed to me and I didn't hesitate when he asked me to marry him."

Nik's dark brows lifted. "And once you'd each said I do, the one essential element to make your marriage work wasn't there after all, and it drove you apart."

"Precisely."

She was good at maintaining her cool, but every so often when their arms or legs brushed while they were walking, he could feel her trembling because she was holding back critical information. Her friend Kellie could enlighten him, but he knew deep down that wasn't the route to go. He'd find Leandros.

As if thinking about him conjured him up, they discovered him taking a swim. Like Nik, he'd been born on an island in the Aegean and found the water the ideal place to wind down at the end of the day. But Nik had to admit surprise his wife hadn't joined him.

"Hey, Leandros—" Fran called to him. "Where's Kellie?"

When he saw them, Leandros swam to shore. After picking up a towel he walked toward them while he dried himself off. "She had a headache and went to bed."

"After the horror of the last few days, I'm not surprised," she said in a quiet tone. "I'm ready to turn in myself." She glanced at Nik. "Thank you for your hospitality and the privilege of taking care of Demi one more night. I'll see you and your family in the morning before the funeral. Goodnight."

She gave Leandros a hug before she started for the steps leading up to the patio. Once at the top, she waved to them before disappearing inside the villa.

"Would you mind leveling with me about something?"

Leandros's gaze switched to Nik. "Not at all."

"I asked Fran if she'd be willing to stay on for another week to help while our family tries to find the right nanny. Because she looked after Demi from the moment she found her, I thought she might be willing. But when I asked her this evening, she indicated she's planning to travel with your wife and can't change her plans."

A grimace broke out on his face. "My wife's mind is made up."

There was a lot Leandros wasn't saying, but it was none of Nik's business until his friend chose to tell him.

"Then that relieves my fear. I thought maybe she'd said no to me as an excuse because of something I may have said or done to offend her. In my attempt to compliment her for the way she took care of Demi by asking her to stay on for a while longer, I may have accomplished the opposite result.

"As you saw earlier, my little niece clings to her and is unhappy with anyone else. When I told Fran she'd be well paid for her sacrifice, I think she took it as the final insult, which was the last thing I meant to do."

Leandros shook his head. "Not Fran. She stayed with your niece at the hospital because she wanted to. I'm sure she would have agreed to help you if Kellie weren't so insistent on their taking this trip."

"Where are they going?"

"On a driving trip to see other parts of Greece and do some hiking."

"I see."

"Fran's first marriage didn't work and Kellie has worried about her ever since. Just between us, my wife is determined to find Fran a husband."

That was an interesting piece of news. "Does she have someone particular in mind?"

"I doubt it. I think she's hoping they'll meet some unattached American over here on holiday with the right credentials who will sweep Fran off her feet. In the meantime, rest assured Fran's decision has nothing to do with you or the baby. I happen to know she's as crazy about kids as Kellie is."

Finally Nik had his answer though he already had proof how much she loved children by her attachment to Demi.

He patted Leandros's shoulder. "Thanks for the talk. You've relieved my mind in more ways than you know. See you in the morning. If I haven't told you yet, my family and I are honored that you'll be here for us."

"It's the least I can do for a good friend," Leandros's voice grated. "I plan to attend the services for the other family this weekend."

But Leandros's wife wouldn't be with him. Something was wrong and it gave him an idea.

"Leandros? Before you go to bed, there's something else I'd like to talk to you about it if you don't mind. I've been trying to think of a way to reward Fran for all she's done and would like to run it by you."

"Go ahead. I'm not ready for bed yet."

CHAPTER FIVE

THE ANGELIS FAMILY lived on a private part of the island overlooking a brilliant blue sea. Fran found the dazzling white villa with the main patio as the focal point for the family to congregate, an architectural wonder. She could see why the Cyclades was the desired vacation spot in Greece, especially this portion of the renowned Kalo Livadi Beach where she'd walked with Nik last night.

Their conversation had created a tension that had still gripped her after she'd gone to bed, making her sleep fitful. She'd never been so outspoken in her life with anyone, but fear of being in pain again had driven her to say those things to him.

While some of the staff came out to get things ready for the meal to be served when the family got back, Fran's gaze lit on the beautiful child whom she'd put in the high chair to feed her a midafternoon snack. She'd placed Demi beneath the shade of the umbrella while Fran sat in the sun to soak up what she could. Pretty soon everyone would return. After that, she and Kellie would leave for Athens.

Out of deference to his family, she'd dressed more formally in a light blue summer suit and white high heeled sandals. Beneath the short-sleeved jacket she wore a white T-shirt. After applying her lipstick, she'd fastened her hair back with a tortoise shell clip. She often wore it this way to work.

Rob had said he preferred it back because it made her look more sophisticated. For him, the right look was everything. But Fran had chosen to wear it this way today because Demi liked to pull on it and she was strong.

"Do you know you're the best eater?" Though the seven-month-old couldn't possibly understand her, she smiled and opened her mouth for more peaches. "You like these better than plums, don't you. Two more bites and you're all finished." She moved the spoon around to bait her before putting it in her mouth. Demi laughed, encouraging Fran to do it again.

As the baby laughed harder, a shadow fell over her. It couldn't be a cloud. She turned her head in time to see a somber-faced Nik staring down at her from those dark eyes she couldn't read. Standing there so tall and hard-muscled, he looked incredibly handsome in the midnight-blue mourning suit and tie he'd worn to the funeral.

"There's nothing like Demi's laughter to dissolve the gloom, is there?" he murmured before bending down to kiss his niece on both cheeks. "Sorry we're late, but there was a huge crowd at the burial and many people who wanted to express their sympathy."

Fran nodded, feeling his pain. Demi's parents had been laid to rest. She would never know them. The enormity of raising this little girl who would need the Angelis family from here on out settled on Fran like a mantle.

She could only imagine Nik's feelings of love mixed with inadequacy right now. Their whole family had to be weighted by the new responsibility thrust upon them. Moved with compassion, Fran got to her feet and wiped Demi's mouth with her bib. Driven by her own heart-felt emotions, she picked up the baby and handed her to Nik, who must be feeling empty inside.

"Demi's going to need all of you now. If you'll excuse me, I have to go finish the last of my packing."

She practically ran inside the villa so she wouldn't hear the baby start to cry. Nik was a big boy now. He would deal with this crisis in the expert way he handled all of his business transactions.

Fran had done her packing early, but she'd needed the excuse to tear herself away from Demi. To be sure she hadn't left anything behind, she made one more trip into the bathroom.

"Fran? Are you about ready?"

"Whenever you are." She came back out to find Kellie who'd changed from her black dress to white pleated pants and a watermelon-colored top.

"I asked Leandros to tell the family the three of us couldn't stay to eat. We've already said our goodbyes to them. I'll help carry your cases out to the helicopter pad." She took the big one while Fran reached for the smaller bag.

Halfway down the hall they met Leandros, whose drawn features aged him. He gave Fran a hug. "You look beautiful."

"Thank you," she whispered.

There was an ominous quiet as he took the suitcase from Kellie and they walked through the villa to the rear entrance. Neither of them had another word to say. Fran was so uncomfortable, she could scream.

When they stepped into the sunlight, Fran could see

the helicopter waiting for them in the distance. She almost ran toward it, but as she drew closer, she saw a tall figure talking to the pilot. It was Nik!

Her heart missed a beat because she'd thought she'd seen the last of him. When she'd handed Demi to him on the patio, she'd intended that to be her own form of goodbye.

"Here. Let me take your bag while you climb inside."

Fran had no choice but to give it to Nik before he helped her up. The touch of his hand sent fire through her body. No sooner had she found a seat than he joined her in the one next to her. Behind him came Kellie. Apparently their luggage had been put onboard ahead of time. Then Leandros climbed in next to the pilot and shut the door.

She turned to Nik in shock. "You're not staying with your family?" But her question came too late because the rotors whirred and they lifted off.

He gave her a ghost of a smile. "Last night after I went to bed, I thought about our conversation and decided to take your advice. Everyone who loves Demi is there to take care of her. I'm going to let them, and give myself a vacation. In another week they'll have sorted out what's best for her without my taking charge."

Guilt smote her for having been so outspoken. "You're joking...aren't you?" she blurted in consternation.

"Not at all. You made perfect sense. I'm afraid I have a tendency to do everything myself. Thanks to you, that's a flaw I'm going to work on. A vacation from my problems is exactly what I need. I haven't had a real one in over a year."

She blinked. "Where will you go?"

"Well, I was hoping you'd let me and Leandros drive you and Kellie around. I talked to him about it last night. I never drive anywhere anymore. Believe it or not, driving used to be one of my great passions. Not only would it be a great pleasure, but it would make me feel like I'd paid all of you back for everything you did for Demi and my family."

Kellie looked even paler than she had earlier in the morning. She shot Fran a private message before she looked at Nik. "That's very thoughtful of you, but Fran and I have decided to fly back to the States in the morning and vacation in California."

Uh-oh. For Kellie to have made a decision like that, the situation between her and her husband had reached flashpoint.

Nik's piercing gaze shot to Fran. "I haven't been there in years. How would you feel about having a third party along?"

Fran had no choice but to back up her friend. "I had no idea you could be such a joker."

"It turns out we make a good pair." His comment was meant to remind her of the way she'd talked to him last night. "But if you're not going to take me seriously, at least agree to have dinner with me this evening. I refuse to let you leave the country without enjoying a night out in the Plaka. I owe you a great deal for all you've done."

Afraid he would be unstoppable until she gave in, she decided to capitulate to that extent. "Your invitation sounds delightful, but if I say yes, it will have to be an early night."

"Good. In that case I'll ask Leandros to drop us off at my apartment. You can change clothes there. We'll go casual and play tourist while we walk around and eat what we want."

In the next instant he spoke to Leandros who nodded and gave instructions to the pilot. Soon Fran saw the glory of Athens spread before them in the late afternoon sun. The magnificent Parthenon, one of the most famous landmarks in the world, sat atop the Acropolis.

Seeing this sight from the air with Nik gave it special meaning. Just when she thought she'd figured him out, he did something unexpected that illuminated other appealing facets of his intriguing personality. She had to admit she wanted to spend the rest of the day and evening with him.

Right now his spontaneity thrilled her down to her toenails. With Rob every move had been calculated and planned out. She didn't want to compare the two men, but she couldn't help it. Rob wasn't unkind, but he'd expected her to conform. When she didn't, he went into a private sulk until she ended up being the one to apologize.

Nik, on the other hand, wouldn't know how to pout. He had hidden depths. Already she'd learned that his way was to zoom in and change the game plan if necessary to achieve the desired outcome. If he ever settled down, it would have to be with a woman who was even more unpredictable than himself. His psyche required a challenge.

Unfortunately Nik occupied too many of her thoughts and was becoming important to her. Any woman who became involved with him would know joy for a time, but in the end she'd pay for it. Wasn't that what Kellie had been saying about Leandros? The thought was terrifying.

Her mind was still full of him when the helicopter set down on the helipad atop his apartment building. She had to look away so she wouldn't get dizzy. This form of transportation was as natural as breathing to businessmen like him and Leandros, but for Fran it would have to become an acquired taste.

She turned to Kellie. Close to her ear she said, "I'll see you later tonight."

"Be back before the clock strikes twelve," her friend responded without mirth. Something dark was on Kellie's mind, leaving Fran troubled.

"I promise."

Nik grabbed Fran's bags. As they started for the stairs, the helicopter lifted off, creating wind that molded her skirt to her shapely legs. She caught at it with her hands, but she was too late. When they entered the elevator, he could see the flush that had crept into her cheeks. How nice to be with a truly modest woman. It made her more enticing to him.

"Here we are." The doors opened on his glassed-in penthouse.

She stepped into the entrance hall. For a full minute she appraised his fully modern apartment. "If I didn't know better, I'd think I was in the control tower at the airport."

He burst into laughter. Fran Myers was a breath of fresh air. "I pretend Athens is the sea I miss when I'm working in the city."

"The view is spectacular." She darted him a mischievous glance. "I'd say Atlas has it pretty good splitting his time between here and Mykonos."

"There's no Atlas here today. Haven't you noticed I'm not carrying the world on my shoulders?"

She studied him rather intently. "How does it feel to have all that weight removed for a little while?"

"I'll let you know later. First I'm sure you'd like to freshen up and change. The guest bedroom is down this hall." He set her bags inside the room. "Come into the living room when you're ready."

After closing the door, he walked to his bedroom for a shower. The idea of mingling with the crowds like any foreigner visiting Athens appealed to him. In deference to the heat, he changed into a well-worn pair of jeans and a linen sport shirt. Once he'd slipped on his sandals, he was ready to go.

The funeral had robbed him of an appetite, but the thought of being with Fran for the rest of the evening had brought it back. In fact, he was starving, and he wagered she was hungry, too.

More pleasant surprises greeted him to discover she was waiting for him at the window overlooking Stygmata Square. She'd put on a pair of jeans and a short-sleeved cotton top in a raspberry color. Her skin absorbed some of its hue. With her luscious honey-blond hair worn up, she presented a prim, cool look, making him long to put his lips to the curve of her neck.

He wandered over to her, once again aware of her wildflower fragrance. "We'll be walking in that area beyond the square," he pointed out. "I know a taverna that serves flaming sausages and grilled trout to die for. But if that doesn't appeal, there are dozens of restaurants offering what you would consider traditional Greek cooking."

Purplish-blue sparks lit up her eyes. "I'm one tourist who doesn't want traditional fare."

"Then be prepared for a gastronomical adventure. Let's go."

They rode the elevator and set off for the Plaka, the oldest part of the city. The place swarmed with visitors buying everything from furniture to jewelry in the shops lining the streets.

Hunger drove them to eat before they did anything else. She ate the trout and sausage right along with him. While they sat watching people and making up outrageous stories about who they were and where they'd come from, a girl selling flowers came up to their table.

"Isn't she sweet, Nik?"

"I agree." He bought a gardenia and put it in Fran's hair. The flower gave him an excuse to touch her. He wanted to touch her and the desire was growing.

Filled with good food and wine, he ushered her through the streets so they were constantly brushing against each other. While she marveled over all the souvenir shops, he marveled over her. She didn't want to buy anything, just look.

They ended up on top of the roof at the outdoor theater. With the Acropolis lit up in the background, they watched a local film with English subtitles. "The tragic story was ridiculous, but I loved it," she confided after they left to explore another street. Nik had been so aware of her, he hadn't been able to concentrate on the story line.

"Around the next corner is a taverna famous for its ouzo. Would you like to try some?"

"I experimented the last time I was in Athens and didn't care for it, but please don't let that stop you."

He smiled. "I don't like it either."

His comment prompted laughter from her. "How unpatriotic! I promise I won't tell anyone. Let's go down this narrow little alley and see what goodies could be hiding there."

Nik guided her along, amused at the way she expressed herself.

One of the shops sold every type of cheap figurine, both religious and mythological. He thought she'd just look and keep going. Suddenly she stopped and picked up a small metal figure of Atlas holding up the world. She asked the owner how much. He named a price and she paid for it with euros.

"Shall I wrap it?"

"No. I'd like to take it just as it is."

When they'd walked a little ways further, she turned to Nik. "It's getting late and I have to go to Kellie's. Before we leave, please accept this as my gift for showing me your world today. If you dare to keep it on your office desk, it will remind you about the necessity of taking a breather once in a while."

"The table by my bed will be an even better place for it," he fired back. "Each night it will be the last thing I see before I fall asleep. What greater way to help me keep my priorities in order."

They eyed each other for a moment. "Thank you for tonight, Nik. I've never had a better time."

Neither had he. The realization had made a different man of him.

He reached for the simple gift. It meant more to him than she could imagine. Instead of her begging him to buy her something the way one of his girlfriends would have done, she'd turned the tables. Her generosity of spirit ranged from saving a baby in the aftermath of a tornado, to presenting him a keepsake he'd always treasure.

"On our way back to the apartment, there's one more place you have to visit."

"Will I like it?"

"I'll let you be the judge."

Nik had been saving this stop until the end. He needed to get closer to her. The Psara taverna was housed in two old mansions with a roof garden. You could dance while you enjoyed a view of the Plaka. Getting her in his arms had been all he could think about.

He asked her to keep the figurine in her purse until later. After they'd consumed an ice cream dessert, he led her out on the floor. The band played the kind of rock whose appeal was fairly universal. At last he was able to clasp her to him while they moved to the music.

"You're a terrific dancer," he whispered against the side of her neck. "I could stay like this all night."

"I'm enjoying it, too."

"Have you dated much since your divorce?"

"There've been a few men, but if you're fishing for compliments, I can tell you now they don't dance like you."

"It's my Greek blood, but please continue. Flattery will get you everywhere, *Kyria* Myers."

Her body shook with silent laughter.

He relished the feel of her, pulling her even closer. "Don't fly back to the States tomorrow."

"I have to, Nik."

He pressed a kiss to her temple. "You do realize Kellie is running away from her husband."

The second he spoke, she stopped dancing and looked

up at him. "Did Leandros confide in you?" She sounded anxious.

"He's told me nothing, but it's clear they're having problems. I felt something was wrong from the start. Leandros isn't the same man I've known in the past."

"Neither is Kellie," she said in a tremulous voice.

Unfortunately it was Nik's fault the mood had been altered. "It's eleven-thirty. I heard her warn you not to be late. Let's go back for your cases. My driver will run us to their apartment. Are your bags packed?"

"Yes. I put them outside the bedroom door."

"Then I'll have them brought down."

As they moved through the crowds, he pulled out his phone to make the arrangements. When they reached his apartment building, the limo was waiting for them. He helped her in the back. Once he'd told his driver where to take them, he got in across from her so he could look at her. She had a glow about her he'd noticed while they were dancing.

"You're not really going to California."

She put the flat of her hands against the seat. "I don't honestly know."

"So if I flew over to the States, too, would I find you home tomorrow evening, or not?"

"Are you pursuing me?" she asked with refreshing bluntness.

"Isn't that obvious? I know you're not indifferent to me."

She stirred in place. "No woman could be indifferent to you, Nik, and you know it."

"So you're already branding me as a Romeo with no staying power."

Fran looked away. "You said it, I didn't."

"The tabloids never print the truth, but the public will consume it."

She rolled her eyes. "Give me a little credit for not believing everything I read. As long as you're still single, I guess it's your lot to be labeled. But I haven't done that."

"If this isn't about me, then it's personal where *you're* concerned."

"Not at all. But we both know you won't be making any trips to Pennsylvania."

"If you knew the real me, you wouldn't make such a careless statement."

In the silence that followed, her cell phone rang. He checked his watch. "It's five to twelve, Cinderella."

She eyed him almost guiltily before pulling it from her purse to check the caller ID. "It's Leandros—" Her voice sounded shaky before she clicked on. Once she'd said hello, the color drained out of her face. She only said a few more words before hanging up.

"What's happened?"

"It's Kellie. This evening at the apartment she became ill and fainted. They're in the E.R. at the Athens regional medical center. Will you please ask your driver to take us there?"

Nik alerted him, then moved across to sit next to her. Without conscious thought he drew her into his arms. Whispering into her hair he said, "I'm sure whatever it is, she's going to be all right."

If Nik just hadn't joined her on the seat...

If he hadn't held her like some cherished possession...

While they'd been dancing earlier, the contact had been wildly disturbing. But this comforting tenderness was too unexpected and welcome for her to move away from him. She'd been worried sick about Kellie. Now her worst fears were confirmed and he knew it.

"Do you have any idea what could have brought on her fainting spell?" His lips grazed the side of her forehead before she buried her face in her hands.

"You might as well know the truth. She's going to file for a legal separation after she's back in Philadelphia. They probably quarreled tonight. Kellie's emotions have been so fragile, I was afraid the stress might be too much."

"I didn't realize their problems had reached such a serious state. Otherwise I wouldn't have suggested the four of us take a trip together."

His sincerity reached her. "Don't feel guilty. In truth, I didn't suspect anything was wrong until she called me several weeks ago and insisted I take my two-week vacation right now. She said Leandros would be away on business and it would be the perfect time.

"They've been so happy, I couldn't believe she didn't want to travel with him the way she always does. That was my first warning all wasn't well."

"I'm sorry for them—and you." The limo pulled up near the doors of the E.R. "Let's find Leandros."

To Fran it was déjà vu as they entered the emergency room. Nik must have been having similar thoughts because his hand tightened on her arm. "Hard to believe it was only a few days ago I was rushing into the hospital to find out if the baby you'd rescued was our little Demi."

"Thank heaven it was!"

An ashen-faced Leandros came forward and put an arm around her. "Thanks for coming."

"As if I wouldn't. Do you know why she fainted?"

"The doctor couldn't find anything wrong, but he's still waiting for the blood-test results. Kellie doesn't want me in there and is asking to see you. Maybe if you talk to her, she'll settle down."

She'd never seen Leandros this frantic. "I'll go to her now. Where is she?"

"In the last cubicle."

"Try not to worry." She turned to Nik. "I'll be back out in a few minutes."

His compassion-filled eyes played over her features. "Take as long as she needs. I'll keep Leandros company."

"Thank you." She had an urge to kiss his cheek for being so understanding, but she held back. Without a minute to lose, she hurried through the E.R. and pulled the blue curtain aside.

"*Fran*—I thought you'd never get here."

"I'm so sorry, Kellie." She pulled up a chair. "How are you feeling right now?"

"Foolish. The doctor just came in and said nothing showed up on the tests. He says I fainted because I hadn't eaten all day. They gave me something to eat so I'm fine now. I'd like to get out of here and check into a hotel. The last thing I want is to go home with Leandros."

"He won't allow you to go anywhere without him. At least not tonight. Kellie? What else aren't you telling me? This is truth time. I can't do anything to help you if I don't know what's going on."

She sat up. "Not ten minutes after we arrived back, Karmela let herself in the apartment carrying a stack of work for Leandros to look over. She looked positively shocked to find me there."

Fran's eyebrows knitted together. "If she had plans to be alone with him, *she* should have been the one who fainted to realize you weren't on vacation with me yet."

"She's not the type to faint. That woman is as cool as the proverbial cucumber, treating me like I was the interloper and not his wife. No doubt she was allowed to use the security hand code to get in while her sister was alive and Leandros never deleted it.

"Leandros disappeared into the study with her for a few minutes. When she came out again, she flashed me this satisfied smile and bade me a safe flight in the morning. Fran—how could she have known my plans if Leandros hadn't discussed them with her? I don't want her knowing my business. I tell you, that was the last straw."

She groaned. "It would have been for me, too."

"When he came to find me, I was in the kitchen getting some juice and didn't say anything to him about her. He hovered around me until it drove me positively crazy, so I said goodnight and went to bed in the guest bedroom. It wasn't long before he came in and found me on the phone with Aunt Sybil. He told me to hang up because he wanted to have a serious talk with me."

"Did you?"

"Yes. I've never seen him in a rage before. He swore he didn't know Karmela would be by. The more he tried to explain his way out of it, the more I couldn't listen to him. Suddenly I felt so sick I passed out."

"I'm not surprised. Under the circumstances it's a good thing we're flying home tomorrow."

"Please forgive me, Fran. I'm ashamed to have to

confess I got you to Athens on my terms, not yours. It was horribly selfish of me when you wanted to wait until September."

"None of that matters. You need help."

"So do you," came Kellie's cryptic comment. She stared hard at Fran. "You're back late. I don't need to ask if you had a good time with Nik tonight."

"I did." It was a night she'd always remember.

"With that droopy gardenia in your hair, I can just imagine. Did he put it there before or after he kissed you?"

"There was no kiss." Except on her forehead.

"Not yet maybe, but it's coming. It's the Angelis charm working like clockwork. Just be careful you don't get completely sucked in."

"Why do you say that?"

"He already wants to go on vacation with you!"

"Kellie—he was only flirting."

"No. Nik Angelis is a compelling force in the corporate world, and he's an even more compelling sensual force when it comes to women. One of the secretaries in Leandros's office says he's had a string of them over the years. Leandros claims that when Nik wants something, he's relentless until he gets it. I can see where his persuasion tactics are leading where you're concerned."

"In what way?"

"He wouldn't think twice about asking you to quit your job at the hospital and move to Greece in order to become his niece's nanny."

Fran swallowed hard. "He already has. I turned him down. When the doctor at the hospital in Leminos mentioned he'd like to hire someone like me, Nik said something about having other plans in mind for me."

"I knew it!" Kellie muttered. "He's going to use every trick in the book to get you to take care of Demi. His plan is to make the moves on *you* to ensure victory. He's counting on a beautiful, vulnerable divorcée like you to cave. Have you told him you can't have children?"

"No, of course not."

"Then don't! That piece of information would be all he needed to get you to say yes. You can't do it, Fran, or you'll be facing even greater heartache than with Rob. He's got enough money to buy anyone he wants, but not you—" Her eyes pooled with moisture. "I say this because you're the best person I've ever known and you're *beyond* price."

"Oh, Kellie—" She gave her friend a long, hard hug.

"Promise me you won't let him get to you. If you do, it will mean you've given up on marriage altogether. You and I have talked about you falling in love again with a widower who has small children. Isn't that what you said?"

She pulled away from Kellie and wiped her eyes. "Yes, and you know it's what I'd like to happen."

"Then if you really mean that, don't get any more involved with Nik. I promise that if you do, you'll end up being stuck in the Angelis household as nothing more than a glorified servant. I don't care how strong your maternal feelings are for Demi. The years pass quickly. Think, Fran! One day she'll grow up and won't need you anymore. *Then* what will you do? You'll be too old for what you really want, and you'll live the rest of your life with a broken heart! After we're home I'll concentrate on helping you meet a terrific guy. There are hundreds of widowers looking for a wife online through a dating service."

"Ugh. That sounds horrible."

"Maybe not. You deserve to meet someone fantastic and fall in love with him. It happens to lucky couples all the time. Second marriages can be wonderful if you're not desperate, and if you take the time to meet that one person you can't live without."

"I know."

"Then remember something else. One of these days Nik's parents will bring pressure to bear and he'll have to get married, thus joining the ranks of his married brothers. They'll all have families except for you. So, what then? When Demi goes to college, will you go back to the States and get another job at another hospital, only to keep taking care of other people?"

The words stung, but she knew Kellie was saying them partly from her own pain and partly to help Fran think straight.

"You need to take charge of your life and live for *you*. I think you should have gotten out of your marriage the first time Rob said he didn't want to adopt. That was a year into your marriage. Look at the time you've wasted! I never said anything to you about it, but I wanted to."

Fran eyed her friend in surprise. "I had no idea you felt this strongly about it."

She bit her lip. "You don't know half of the things I thought about Rob and his utter selfishness where you were concerned. Your situation has made me take stock of my marriage. That's why I'm planning to separate from Leandros. I refuse to hang around another year or two while he and Karmela are involved. I don't know if they're actual pillow friends yet, but don't think she isn't lying in wait for the opportunity.

"On our drive back to Athens yesterday, it was like talking to a wall. He's in denial over her infatuation with him, but all the signs are there. After he tires of her, he'll want someone else yet expect me to look the other way. I knew it was too good to be true that he fell in love with me, but idiot that I am, I was so crazy about him, I left the blinders on."

She grabbed Fran's arms. "Don't do what I did— don't be charmed by Nik and his Greek-god looks. Don't let him get to you. Above all, don't sleep with him. He can pour it on like Leandros. It's their gift and their curse."

"*Kellie*—I've never seen you like this before."

"That's because I realize my marriage was a mistake. Karmela was in the picture from the first time I met Leandros. The warning signs were there, but I didn't pay any heed to them."

Fran was shaken because, despite her friend's bitterness, she was making sense.

"When I get back home, I'm filing for a divorce through my uncle's attorney. I'll stay with them until I figure out what I'm going to do."

"Do they know your marriage is in trouble?"

"Not yet."

Fran folded her arms against her waist. She threw her head back. "Out of all the marriages I've seen, I thought yours was the most solid. I have to tell you I'm devastated over this."

"I've been in agony since I realized Karmela was never going to go away. So don't let Nik talk you into something that will be difficult for you to get out of.

No matter how much that little girl tugs at your heart, she's not yours! She belongs to the Angelis family. They circle their own and you won't be an integral part of anything."

Fran shot to her feet, not needing to hear any more. "Do you want me to come back to the apartment tonight?"

"No. That would be the last straw for Leandros. I need to show him I'm in control and can handle life on my own. He thinks I'm a pushover. Well, no longer! He should have married Karmela. I can't imagine why he didn't."

She let out an anguished cry. "Tell Nik to drive you to the Cassandra. I've already made arrangements for you to stay there in our private suite. We'll pick you up in the morning on our way to the airport."

"I'll be ready." She leaned down to give her a hug. Her eyes misted over. "You have to know my heart's breaking for you and Leandros."

"Now you have some idea of how I felt when you told me Rob didn't want to adopt after all. But you got through that terrible ordeal. Given time, I will, too."

Fran blew her friend a kiss, then slipped past the curtain and headed for the E.R. lounge. Both men got up when they saw her. Leandros's grave countenance haunted her. "How is she?"

"She's surprisingly good and ready for us to fly home in the morning. I'll watch out for her, Leandros. I'm so sorry this has happened. Obviously she needs her space. Once back in Philadelphia, time will have a way of making her see things more clearly. One thing I do know. She loves you with every fiber of her being. Don't ever forget that." Her voice shook.

His lips tightened. "I've forgotten nothing," he rapped out. "If she still wants to fly home in the morning, I'll fly her there in my jet. We have things to discuss. As you know, we've made arrangements for you to stay at the Cassandra tonight. Tomorrow morning my driver will be there to take you to the airport. I've booked you first class on a flight leaving at eight."

CHAPTER SIX

THIS WAS LEANDROS at his most intimidating. The situation was out of Fran's hands. She gave him a last kiss on the cheek. Nik grasped her elbow and led them out to the limo where he sat next to her.

"You're staying with me tonight. It's late, and it would be absurd for you to go anywhere else when I have a perfectly good apartment going to waste. Tomorrow will be a new day. After a solid night's sleep you can make decisions. Who knows, you might even decide to finish your vacation here."

The fight seemed to have gone out of her. "You've talked me into it. Thank you," she half sighed the words. "I'm drained, as I'm sure you are. I can't tell you how much I appreciate your generosity."

He flashed her a white smile that melted her bones. "At last I can do something for you."

"How many times do I have to remind you that taking care of Demi was a joy?" All of a sudden her voice caught. "Have you had any word from your family yet?"

"Yes. My father called."

"They must miss you terribly."

"I didn't get that impression. He phoned to thank me for bringing Demi home to them. He said my mother is a different person now that she has the baby to worry about. Demi fussed and cried all day, but the girls helped her and by bedtime she'd calmed down."

"I miss her, Nik."

"She's never off my mind either. My father says having Demi there has chased away the darkness and spirits are improving. He also admitted he envies me for being able to look forward to work. I told him he retired too soon and should come back in the office for half days, or at least for several times a week."

Nik was a wonderful son. Though Kellie had spoken the truth about Nik's determined nature, there was a noble side to him she couldn't dismiss. "That must have thrilled him."

"He said he'd think about it, which tells me he wants to keep his hand in things. I told him something else."

"What was that?"

"I've gone on vacation for a week and have left all the worry to my assistants. I suggested to Father he might want to check up on things while I'm gone."

"And?" she prodded because his eyes were smiling.

"He didn't say no."

"If he's anything like you, I bet he can't wait to dig back in."

"I'm sure you're right. So you see, taking your advice is already paying dividends. If you hadn't convinced me to let go, I wouldn't have realized my father is still struggling with his retirement. I owe a great deal of what's going on at the villa to you, Fran."

Before she could think, he pressed a light kiss to her lips. It only lasted for a breathless moment, but the aftershocks traveling through her nervous system were as powerful as Kellie's warning. *Don't do what I did—*

don't be charmed by Nik and his Greek-god looks. Don't let him get to you.

He grasped her hand. "Speaking of vacations, you could use a break from worry about Kellie. Left alone with Leandros who plans to stay in Philadelphia with her for a while, she'll have time to consider everything and rethink her decision to leave him. Why don't you stay on in Greece for a few more days? If you're not there then Kellie and Leandros will be forced to confront their feelings. I know that Leandros won't want a divorce."

That sounded encouraging. Maybe Kellie had gotten through to him after all....

"To my knowledge, there's no finer man. I get the impression Kellie is his whole world."

"She worships the ground he walks on, too. I liked him the first time I met him and that has never changed. But I'm not married to him. Their personal problems are none of my business."

Except Fran knew what was tearing her friend apart. It wasn't just about Karmela. Sometimes Fran got the feeling Kellie was using Karmela as an excuse to cover her own insecurities. She'd married a powerful man whose first marriage had been happy. Kellie needed to talk to someone professional about her problems.

"In that case, let's concentrate on enjoying our vacation," Nik suggested.

Fran chuckled to cover the sudden spike of her pulse. "*Our* vacation? I didn't know we were going on one."

"Leandros wants time alone with his wife and you're still here in Greece, ostensibly to travel. Does the thought of hanging out together frighten you?"

A small tremor rocked her body.

"I'll ask you again. Are you afraid at the thought of being alone with me?"

Adrenaline spilled into her veins. "Why would I be?"

"Liar," he whispered.

His response made her laugh before she removed her hand.

"Admit you're afraid you'll like it too much."

He knew her too well. "Oh, I can admit to that already. It's what happens when the vacation is over that bothers me."

"Forget about the over part. When you're on vacation, you're not entitled to think, only to accept everything that comes as a special gift."

Her lips curved. "Your spin on the subject is without equal."

"I take it you can't wait for us to embark on our journey. Where would you like to go?"

"That's easy. How about a hike to the top of Mount Olympus?" she teased.

"The home of the gods."

"It's so famous, I want to climb it. Though I might be out of shape, Kellie and I planned to do it before a tornado swept through Greece and changed all our lives." She hated the throb in her voice.

"I can't think of anything I'd like more. We'll not only hike, we'll camp out. It's my favorite thing to do besides water sports."

"And driving," she added.

He grinned. "Your mind is a steel trap. This trip will be an experience to remember. I'll throw all my camping gear in the helicopter and we'll take off for Pironia tomorrow after breakfast. That's the start of the trailhead."

"You've climbed it, of course."

"Twice. Once with my brothers and another time with my friends."

She darted him a glance. "Is there anything you haven't done?"

"I haven't climbed all our Greek mountains yet, and I've never gone camping with a woman."

"That's probably the best idea you've ever had."

Once again he broke into the kind of deep masculine belly laughter that shook the back of the limo and warmed her insides, neutralizing Kellie's concerns for her for the moment.

Nik drew Fran to the side of the forest trail to allow a team of donkeys carrying packs to the refuge to go on ahead of them. This was a good place to stop for a drink of water. They'd been hiking for over an hour, passing and being passed by other hikers.

In another hour they would reach the refuge where everyone would spend the night. Nik had another place in mind where he would set up camp for them in total privacy. Tomorrow they'd climb to the top of Mytikas, the highest peak.

He hadn't known what to expect, but so far Fran had kept up with him, carrying her own backpack without complaint. She'd worn her hair up again to keep it out of her face. In jeans and a layered cream-colored top that her figure did amazing things for, he was hard-pressed to look at anything else.

"Are you ready to move on? We'll ascend a gorge and then you'll see the red top of the refuge."

"How high up is it?"

"Two thousand meters."

"Are we going to stay there tonight?"

"No. We'll set up our own camp above it. You don't know how lucky we are to see the mountain today. Usually it's covered with clouds. That means we'll see stars tonight."

"I can't wait!"

Neither could he.

She started off without him. He paced himself to stay alongside her as they headed for the spot he had in mind to spend the night. They'd bed down in the pines where the air would be fresh and cool.

Along the way she used his field glasses in the hope of spotting the wildlife that flourished on the mountain. After ten minutes of hiking she cried, "Oh, Nik—look at that huge bird!"

He understood her excitement. "I can see it without the binoculars. It's a bearded vulture."

"Bearded?"

"It has a mustache." She giggled like a girl. "That one probably weighs ten pounds.

"I can see why. Its wingspan is enormous."

"Three to four feet across. This is a protected eco-system with multiple climate regions. Some plants and animals here aren't found anywhere else in the world."

Her face lit up. "I'm so glad we came here. I wouldn't have missed a sight like this for the world."

As far as he was concerned, the sight staring up at him had no equal. If there weren't other hikers moving back and forth on the trail, he would have taken her in his arms and kissed the daylights out of her. "This is only the beginning," he murmured. "Come on. Let's get to our destination. I'm hungry. How about you?"

She laughed. "Do you even need to ask?" They

headed out for the tougher part of the climb, but she proved herself equal to the task. Before long they reached the refuge where the climbers could have a meal and a bed for the night.

"One more drink of water will sustain us until we reach the sacred spot."

Her lips curved upward. "Sacred?"

"It *will* be after we've christened it."

"That's an interesting choice of words," she said with a half chuckle before draining the rest of her water bottle.

Nik watched her throat work. Her natural beauty caused every male in the vicinity to take a second and third look. One of the male hikers passing by muttered in Greek to his buddy that Nik had it made for tonight with the dark blonde goddess. Nik ignored him.

For one thing, if he'd been the hiker who'd seen Fran standing there with another guy, he would have wished he'd found her first. For another, he was too happy being with her to take offense at anything.

Again he marveled that despite the tragedy that had struck their family, despite Demi's parentless state, despite the headaches of becoming the new head of the Angelis Corporation, being with Fran felt right and filled the gaping hole inside him. She brought a new sense of purpose to his life that had been missing.

Last night he'd fallen asleep holding the small Atlas in his hands, enchanted by her inimitable charisma and her extraordinary insight. He could wish he'd met her before she'd ever known her husband. But there was no use wandering down that pointless road.

The past needed to stay in the past. She was here now. That's what was important, and she was with Nik.

If she hadn't felt the connection to him growing stronger every minute they were together, she would have flown to the United States today. For now he'd shoved his deepest fear to the back of his mind.

"It's getting dark. Ten more minutes and we can call it a night. Let's go."

She followed him up the trail that had grown even steeper. "I'm surprised we're the only ones not staying there."

He smiled to himself. "They don't have your sense of adventure."

"Too bad we can't climb Mount Athos next."

Nik chuckled. "You mean the Greek mountain forbidden to women?"

"Yes, but it didn't stop the French author Maryse Choisy. Kellie and I read the paperback she wrote."

"Un mois avec les hommes?"

"That's it! *A Month with the Men*. She sneaked into one of the monasteries on the mountain undercover to see how the monks lived. In her words, she turned one of them down. Kellie and I decided she broke his heart."

"More like his pride," Nik theorized.

"To find a woman there, he must have thought he was having a vision."

Nik couldn't resist adding a comment. "She must have found him unappealing, otherwise she might have spent a much longer time there and no book would have been produced."

Suddenly the air was filled with the delightful sound of her laughter. It startled some squirrels who scrambled into the higher branches of a pine tree.

"Let's be thankful we're on Mount Olympus, where

Zeus allowed both male and female gods to romp together in the Elysian fields."

"That must have been something," she quipped. "I always pictured those fields to be white."

"When we're up on top slipping and sliding on the barren summit covered in rocks, you'll learn the truth. I'm afraid mythology has a lot to answer for," he drawled.

"I guess I like reality better."

"Good, because we've arrived at our reality." He headed through the trees, far enough away from the trail so no one would spot them. Soon he came to a small clearing surrounded by pines. Excited to be here, he removed his pack. "In a few minutes I'll have the tent erected and we can eat." He pulled out the big flashlight and turned it on.

"Let me help." After taking off her pack, she pitched right in. They worked together in companionable silence.

"I can tell you've done this before. You're the perfect person to bring on a hike like this."

"Coming from you, I'm flattered. The truth is, I used to camp with my parents and my younger brother, Craig. We usually took Kellie with us. She's a great camper, too. Fearless. We'd go on lots of trips with some of our extended families who loved the outdoors."

Nik digested everything before glancing at her. "I didn't know you had a sibling."

"He died at fifteen of leukemia. I didn't think I'd recover from the loss, but time took the worst of the pain away. One day your pain over losing your sister will fade, too."

The news sobered him. "Tell me about your parents."

"Dad works for a newspaper and has his own political column. My mother still works as an administrator at the school district. I have a lot of aunts and uncles and cousins on both sides. It makes for a big family like yours."

She'd experienced more than her lot of suffering. The death of a loved brother followed by an agonizing divorce… No wonder she had so much depth of character.

"Where have you lived since you've been on your own?"

"In a small condo."

"Not with your parents?"

"No, but it's near my parents' home where I grew up."

"You're more independent than most of the women I know. I admire you for that."

"I could have gone back home, but I need my own space. So do my parents."

They moved inside the tent to lay out their sleeping bags. He reached in another part of his pack for the picnic food they'd purchased before leaving Athens. Salad, fruit, sandwiches and a half dozen pastries.

Nik positioned the light so they could see while they sat across from each other to eat.

"Mmm, this tastes fabulous."

He flicked her a glance. "Have I told you how fabulous you've been today?"

She had to finish chewing before she could talk. "I was just thinking the same thing about you. You're so easygoing. After Rob, I—" She paused for a minute. "I'm sorry. I can't believe I bring up his name so often. Forgive me."

"What is there to forgive? You were married what, three years? It's normal."

"Maybe, but it's rude to you and disrespectful to him."

"A woman with a strong conscience. It's one of the many things I like about you." He popped some grapes in his mouth. "I'm curious about something. Did your parents name you Fran at birth?"

She reached for a morsel of baklava. "No. My legal name is Francesca, but I got kidded about it at school, so I went by Fran."

He frowned. "You were kidded because of it?"

"It sounds too pretentious. I was named for my grandmother on my mother's side."

"How would you feel if I called you Francesca?"

"Why would you do that?"

"Because it appeals to me."

"My parents only called me that when I was in trouble with them."

One eyebrow lifted. "Did that happen often?"

"More than I'd like to admit. In the seventh grade I signed up for a dance class at a local studio with Kellie without thinking about it. When my parents got the bill, they couldn't believe what I'd done. They didn't get mad exactly. Dad said it showed ingenuity, but I was still in trouble for a while."

Nik chuckled.

"And then there was the time we decided to skip our last year of high school and go to a finishing school in France. We wrote to this *pensionnat* as a lark, not thinking we'd get accepted because we applied to the school so late. Wouldn't you know my parents got another letter in the mail, this time from Paris? The directrice informed them she was happy to enroll me in the school and would they please send $2,000 to secure my place.

"Once again I got called to my parents' bedroom and they showed me the letter. I honestly couldn't believe it and told them Kellie and I had just been fooling around."

"But your parents recognized that indomitable spirit in you and they let you go," Nik divined.

"Yes. They felt the experience would be good for me."

"And was it?"

"Yes, after I got over a fierce, two-week bout of homesickness. We had the most awesome adventures of our lives and came back speaking adequate French."

Intrigued, he said, "Did you inherit your candor from your mother or your father?"

"Both my parents, actually." She wiped her fingers on the napkins they'd brought. Now that she'd finished eating, she settled back on the sleeping bag, propping up her head with her hand. "Since you've never married, tell me something. Have you ever lived with a woman?"

"No."

"That sounded final. Then tell me about the latest love interest in the life of the famous Nikolos Angelis. Don't scoff. Your legendary reputation precedes you."

He laughed instead.

"Why didn't you take her camping? I can't think of a better way to get to know someone than on a trip like this."

"Agreed." After putting the leftover food in the bag, he stretched out on his back and put his hands behind his head. "Lena would have pretended to enjoy it for my sake."

"So-o?" She strung the word out.

He turned his head to look at her. "So, I didn't feel like getting to know her better. Does that answer your question?"

Fran sat up looking shocked. "How long did you date her?"

"Twice."

"Does this happen with every woman after you've dated her twice?"

"Sometimes three, but most of the time it happens after one experience."

"You're not kidding me, are you?" she said in a quiet voice.

"No."

"If that's true, then why did you agree to bring *me* camping?"

He turned on his side and moved closer. "You're an intelligent woman. You figure it out."

"You're starting to scare me, Nik."

"Good. It's time you began to take me seriously. Surely it hasn't escaped your notice I'm attracted to you? I did everything I could to prevent you from leaving Athens. No woman has ever caused me to walk out on my family and my job to make sure she didn't get away from me. You must know how much I want you."

"You shouldn't say things like that to me. Our relationship isn't like any other."

"I'm glad you've noticed."

"Please don't come any closer. We'll both regret it if you do."

He cupped the side of her face with his free hand. "Don't pretend you don't want the same thing," he whispered against her lips. "I see it in your eyes. Right now that little pulse in your throat is beckoning me to kiss it."

"No, Nik—"

But he couldn't stop. Consumed by a desire so much greater than he'd known before, he covered her pulse with his mouth, relishing the sweet taste of her velvety skin. When it wasn't enough, his lips roamed her features, covering every centimeter of her face until he found her quivering mouth. Slowly he coaxed her lips apart until she began to respond with a hunger she couldn't hide.

Their low moans of satisfaction mingled as their kisses grew deeper and longer. Like water spilling over a dam, there was no holding back. Time lost meaning while they brought pleasure to each other. He couldn't get enough. Neither could she. When had he ever felt like this in his life? Never.

"You're so beautiful," he murmured, undoing her hair so he could run his fingers through it. "Do you have any idea how long I've been aching to do this?" Nik buried his face in her honey-blond tresses. He couldn't stop kissing her.

When he felt her hands slide into his hair, thrilling chills raced through his body. "Admit you want me, too," he said, out of breath.

"You don't need me to admit to anything," she came back.

"But I want to hear the words." He plundered her mouth once more.

"I'm afraid to get close to you."

"Because your ex-husband hurt you?"

"It's hard to build trust again."

"So I'm condemned without a trial?"

"If that were the case, I would have flown home this morning."

Nik sat up. "Don't you know I would never hurt you?"

"I want to believe that," she said in a tremulous voice.

Her husband had done a lot of damage. He could see this was going to take time. In frustration, he got to his feet. "I have to go outside, but I won't be gone long." He picked up the flashlight and unzipped the front of the tent.

"Nik—"

He swung around. "What is it?"

"Nothing. Just be careful."

Fran's heart thudded sickeningly for fear she'd offended him. She gave Nik five minutes before she left the tent to find him. Though the sky was full of stars, there was only a thumbnail moon. The darkness gave the surroundings a savage look. She walked around trying to get her bearings. "Nik? Where are you?"

"I'm right behind you," came his deep male voice.

She whirled around and almost lost her balance. His hands shot to her shoulders to steady her, but he kept their bodies apart. "Explain to me what went on in your marriage that has made you afraid to be with a man again. To be with me," his voice rasped.

"I—I lost my belief in him," she stammered. "When you give marriage your all, and it fails, the fear that another experience could turn out the same way is immobilizing. It's better not to get one started."

Fran heard his sharp intake of breath. "You're the most honest woman I've ever known, but you haven't told me everything. I want to know what he did to kill your love." His hands tightened on her shoulders. She knew he didn't realize how strong he was.

"I can't."

With a withering sound, he let her go. She had to brace her legs not to fall down. After such a beautiful day, Fran couldn't bear for there to be trouble now, but she was standing on the edge of a precipice. If she caved, she'd plunge headlong into a world where the risk of falling in love with this man would be too great.

She'd been playing with fire since agreeing to spend an evening out with him in the Plaka. Now she'd gotten burned around the edges. Better to escape him with a few scars than stay in Greece to see her whole life destroyed. This situation was no longer solely about Demi.

"Since I suggested this hike, I take full responsibility for our being here, Nik. I'd like us to enjoy the rest of the climb tomorrow. You've been so wonderful to me, I'd be a wretch if I didn't thank you for everything. Do you think it's possible for us to be friends from here on out?"

"No," his voice grated. "The situation is murkier than ever and I don't feel the least friendly toward you. But to honor my indebtedness to you for finding Demi and taking care of her, I'll be your guide until we're off the mountain. If you can't open up to me, then so be it. I'm going to bed."

"Nik—"

"Plan to be up by six. Early morning is the best time to reach the summit." He thrust the flashlight in her hands before he disappeared inside the tent.

She bit her knuckle, hating herself for bringing on this impasse. Out of a sense of self-preservation, she'd stopped things before they'd made love. He'd get over this without a problem. Fran wished she could say the same.

Tonight she'd been shaken by the most overwhelming passion she'd ever known. She'd come close to paying the price to know his possession. It didn't seem possible that after just a short time she was on the verge of giving him whatever he wanted.

After pulling herself together she entered the tent, careful not to shine the light near him. He'd climbed in his bag with his long, hard body turned away from her. Once she'd removed her hiking boots, she got inside hers.

He'd opened the screened window at the top of the tent. She could see the stars he'd promised, but they grew blurry with her tears and she knew nothing more.

"It's time to get going," Nik called to her. She let out a groan because it was still dark. "I'll have breakfast waiting for you when you come out of the tent. We'll leave everything here and pack it up after our descent."

The next two hours proved to be a grueling hike with a taciturn Nik only feeding her vital information when necessary. The trail left the sparse pines and vegetation behind. From there they followed it up a ridgeline all the way to the top. He told her this section was called the Kaki Scala. The narrow path was nothing more than scree and shale, rising straight up.

They finally stopped to drink water. She was panting, but Nik didn't seem the least out of breath. He stayed too fit to be winded by a climb like this.

The peak of Mount Mytikas was still forty-five minutes away. Fran's muscles were clearly aching so badly,

Nik declared they'd opt for Mount Scolio, the second-highest peak. It was only twenty minutes further.

When they arrived, clouds had started to form, blocking out the view of the Aegean. Maybe the elements were delivering an omen. They took some pictures with their cell phones. When she was back home, she'd have them made up so she could pore over them and feast her eyes.

"Thank you for bringing me up here, Nik."

"You're welcome."

He might be civil, but there was no softening him up. Before last night, he would have told her some fascinating tale about the gods who played here and worked their intrigues on each other. She missed that exciting man who'd brought her alive in a way she would never know again. Already she was in mourning for him.

After they signed their names in the register, he suggested they head back. Now that he'd done his duty, she sensed he was anxious to get down the mountain and fly home.

She followed him, but the descent was far from easy. Fran had to be careful where to place her feet on the slippery shale. You could twist an ankle if you weren't careful. She had a feeling that for the next few days, she'd suffer from sore knees more than anything else.

By the time they reached the tent, it looked so welcoming, she went inside and crashed on top of her bag. He paused in the entry to look down at her. She eyed him warily. "I'm worn out. Can we stay here for a half hour to rest before starting back?"

His lips thinned. "You do it at your own risk."

"Nik—please— I can't bear for us to have trouble."

He stood there and drained his water bottle, staring at her the whole time through narrowed eyes. "Has this morning's hike worn you down enough that you're ready to tell me what I want to know?"

She sat up, circling her knees with her arms. "This is so hard for me," she whispered.

"Why?"

The air crackled with tension. He hunkered down to pull some rolls and dried fruit from his pack. Being the decent man he was, he shared them with her.

"Because I want things I don't have and probably never will."

Nik squinted at her. "What kinds of things?"

"You'll mock me when I tell you."

"Try me."

"I ache for the one thing that has eluded me. Mainly, a good marriage and children. I need to put myself in a position where I can meet a man who wants the same thing. When you asked me if I'd consider becoming Demi's permanent nanny, I thought seriously about it before I told you no. Demi is precious and I already love her, but being a nanny would put me out of circulation."

"Fran—"

"I know what I'm talking about," she interrupted him. "You'd have to be a woman to understand. To be the bridesmaid for the rest of my life is too ghastly to contemplate. I still have some good years ahead of me and—"

"Just how old are you?" he broke in, sounding upset. A scowl marred his handsome features.

"Twenty-eight. I know it's not old, but having been married, I feel much older. And let's face it, I'm out of the loop. Since you've never been married, you wouldn't know about those feelings, but they're real, believe me."

He handed her some sugared almonds. "Since you're not an unmarried male, you don't have any concept of what my life is like either. Everyone sees the bachelor who can sleep with any woman he wants with no strings. My life is constantly portrayed as something it isn't and no amount of protests on my part will change it. By that blush on your cheeks, I can see you've had those same thoughts about me."

There was no point in her denying it. "After reading about you in a magazine, I might have entertained certain ideas at first, but no longer."

"Even after I came close to ravishing you last night?"

"Nik—nothing happened that we didn't both want."

"Your honesty continues to confound me."

"Why? Have most of the women you've known been deceitful?"

He put the sack of nuts back in the pack before moving closer to her. "No. The fault lies with me for never giving any of them a chance."

Fran cocked her head. "Tell me what your life has really been like, the one no one knows about."

CHAPTER SEVEN

NIK'S EYES WANDERED over her features. "Like you, I was physically adventurous and logged more than my share of visits to the E.R. for stitches and concussions from water and climbing accidents. My parents drummed it into my head that I had to get top grades or they would forbid me from doing the activities I loved.

"Since I couldn't bear the thought of that, I made deals with them. I would study hard and put in my hours at the company, then I'd be given a reward. As a result, when it came time to play, I played harder than my brothers and enjoyed my girlfriends. I went through a phase of wanting to be Greece's greatest soccer player, then that fantasy faded and I decided I wanted to be a famous race-car driver."

"You believed yourself invincible," she said with a grin.

"With top grades came other rewards. I'd been saving the money I earned, and I traveled to the States and South America. While I was climbing in the Andes I met a guy who was putting an expedition together to climb Mount Everest. When I got back from my trip, I put in for a permit to go with him. That climb changed my life."

"In what way?"

"We got caught in a blizzard and lost two of the men. When they fell, I was pulled away from the ledge. The rope saved me, but I was flung back against the rock wall and ended up with internal damage. At first everyone thought I was dead."

"Nik—"

"I was in the hospital for over two months for a series of surgeries. It took me a year to fully recover and I realized I was lucky to be alive. Like you, I did things sometimes without really thinking of the impact on the family. They'd always given me a wide berth because they knew I couldn't be stopped. It took a force of nature to bring me to my senses."

"So that's the reason you haven't climbed *all* the mountains of your country."

He winked at her. "It's one of them. When I saw the toll my accident took on my parents, I decided I'd better get serious about work. The day I joined my brothers in the upper echelons of our company's business, a lot of my playing ended.

"Despite the gossip, my experiences with women have been sporadic of necessity. I found I liked the work. The stimulating challenge of increasing profits and cutting costs appealed to me in a brand-new way. I dug in to make up for lost time. No doubt that's when I developed my Atlas complex."

"Ah. Now I'm beginning to understand."

"That was five years ago."

"How old are you now?"

"Thirty-four."

"And in that short amount of time you surpassed everyone's expectations to the point that you earned your place at the head of the company. You're young to have so much responsibility, but you've obviously earned it. I'm proud of you and so sorry you lost your sister. The pain must be excruciating."

"You've known that kind of pain, too."

"Yes. But in your case, you have that adorable little Demi who'll always bring joy to you and your family. She's so fun to play with. I'd love to see her again."

In a lightning move he grasped her hands. Slowly, he kissed her palms, sending erotic sensations through her hands to the other parts of her body. "Whenever you talk about her, I can feel this deep wound inside of you. Maybe if you talked about it, you could eventually get over it."

Oh, Nik... She lowered her head, not having counted on his exquisite tenderness.

"Tell me," he urged.

"In my later teens I developed a disease called endometriosis. A lot of women suffer from it. My case was so severe, it prevents me from ever having a child. I'd grown up hoping that one day I'd get married and have a cute little boy like my baby brother, but—"

"Francesca—"

Before she knew it, she was lying in his arms. His embrace opened the floodgates. For a few minutes she sobbed quietly against his shoulder, breathing in the wonderful male scent of him. "I'm sorry," she said at last. "Rob knew about my condition before we married. He told me he was fine with the idea of adoption. I believed him.

"Yet a year later he said he still wasn't ready. Eventually I asked him to go to counseling with me because I wanted a baby. In the first session he blurted that he

wanted his own flesh and blood or no children at all.
I was enough for him. His admission shattered me."

"Agape mou," Nik whispered, covering her face with
featherlight kisses. Fran didn't know what the words
meant, but his tone was so piercingly sweet, she nestled deeper in his arms, never wanting to move again.

Nik awakened while Fran was still asleep. Both of them
were already emotionally exhausted. The fatigue after
their hike had done the rest. They'd slept all afternoon.
She was still curled into him with her arm flung across
his chest, almost possessively, he thought.

Much as he didn't want to leave her for a second, he
knew she'd be stirring before long and they needed dinner. Extricating himself carefully from her arms, he left
the tent and hurried down to the refuge. The staff fixed
him up with some boxed lunches and drinks.

On the way back, he phoned his helicopter pilot.
Nik told him to meet them at the dropoff point at seven
the next morning. After hanging up, he checked his
phone messages. His father had let him know Demi
was doing better.

That was a great relief. Under the circumstances,
there was no reason to call him back. Nik was on vacation. Since Fran had pointed out to him that he did his
work and everyone else's without thinking about it, he
knew she was right.

When he entered the tent, he found Fran on her feet
brushing her glorious hair. It flowed around her shoulders. Her smoky-blue eyes lit up when she saw him.
"Food—" she cried. "I'm starving. Bless you."

Nik put everything down between their sleeping

bags. "Let's eat and then walk over to the stream for a bath."

Her eyes rounded. "Is it deep enough?"

"Probably not for a full submersion."

"That's just as well because I don't have a bathing suit."

They both sat down to eat. "Don't let that stop you."

She sent him an impish smile. "So you're saying you wouldn't be scandalized if I waded in without it?"

His pulse accelerated. "I would be so overjoyed, I'd probably expire on the spot of a massive heart attack."

"I love the things you say, Nik." Ditto. "Do you suppose the gods wore clothes during their picnics up on top?"

Laughter rumbled out of him. "I never thought about it. I find I'm dazzled by the sight before my eyes right here." Upon that remark, he tucked into his sandwich.

"Kellie thinks you look like a Greek god."

"Then it's a good thing she couldn't see the scars on my midsection when I was holding up the world."

Her smile warmed him in all the hidden places. "I'm sure she was talking about the whole picture. American women, and probably all the other women in existence, have a certain penchant for the authentic Greek-god look. Like I told you in the hospital, it's a good thing Demi inherited her mother's features. As for everything else, she's almost too beautiful to be real. Her black hair and olive skin are still a wonder to me."

"Just as your northern-European blond locks and violet eyes stop traffic over here."

"Just once I'd like to see that happen."

She never took him seriously. "It already did on the hike yesterday."

"What do you mean?"

"There were two guys watching you all the way to the refuge. At one point they stopped. In my hearing they commented I had it made to be with a goddess like you."

"They really called me a goddess?" She laughed in patent disbelief. "Thank you for telling me that. You've made my day." She drank her soda.

"Leandros confided that Kellie was going to find you a husband while you were here. I must say she knew what she was doing when she asked you to take this trip. My helicopter pilot Keiko wasn't able to keep his eyes off of you. As for my brothers..."

"Oh, stop—" She put down her can. "Let's get serious for a moment. Don't you think we should break up camp and head down before it gets dark?"

Without looking at her he said, "Plans have changed. Because we took such a long nap, I phoned my pilot. He'll be waiting for us at the dropoff point in the morning at seven."

He heard her take an extra breath. "In that case I'm going to the stream to take a little sponge bath."

"Do you want any help?"

"I'll call out if I need it."

Nik looked up in time to see the blood flow into her cheeks. She reached for her backpack and stepped outside like a demure maiden who sensed the hunter.

While she was gone, he cleaned up their tent. When she returned, smelling of scented soap and toothpaste and wearing a new blouse, he grabbed his pack and took off. After following the stream to a pool, he stripped and took a real bath.

Half an hour later he rejoined her in a clean T-shirt

and jeans, and found her inside her bag, reading a book with the flashlight. She'd braided her hair. It lay over her shoulder like a shiny pelt, just begging him to undo it. The woman had no idea what she did to him.

Darkness had crept over the forest, sealing them inside. All that was left to do was tuck them in for a summer's night he could wish would go on forever.

He lay down on top of his bag and turned to her. "What are you reading?"

"*The Memphremegog Massacre*. It's about a gruesome murder that takes place in a monastery. But after a day like today, I can't seem to get into it." She put the book down and turned off the light. "You were gone for a while. Any news from home?"

"Yes. My father left a message."

"Problems?" she asked a trifle anxiously

"No. Demi seems to be doing fine."

"Oh, thank goodness. Did you talk to him?"

"No. I took your advice and didn't call him back. I'm on vacation with the first woman I've ever taken on a trip and want to enjoy it."

After a silence, "Are you? Enjoying it I mean?"

"What if I told you that despite everything, I've never been happier?"

"Nik—"

"What about you? Are you having a good time?"

He heard her bag rustle. The next thing he knew she wrapped her arm around his neck and kissed him on the lips. "Despite everything, I'm in heaven." She kissed him again all over his face, brows, eyes and nose, as if she really meant it. "I've decided I've been in a dream all this time because no man could be as wonderful as you. Goodnight."

"Don't go to sleep yet," he begged after she let go of him and moved back to her bag. "I need to talk to you."

Something in his voice must have alerted her he was serious because she lifted her head to look at him. "What is it?"

"After you've been so open and honest with me I want you to know the truth about me. Before I was released from the hospital after my climbing accident, the doctor told me I would never be able to give a woman a child."

A minute must have passed, then, "Oh, Nik—" Tears immediately filled her eyes. "If anyone understands what that news did to you, I do. It explains so much," she cried.

He kissed her sensuous mouth. "My injuries were such that I had impaired sperm production. In a flash, any dreams I had of generating my own offspring died. Like you, I had time to come to grips with it.

"But there was a bad side effect. I found myself not getting into serious romantic relationships. If I gave myself to a woman who couldn't handle it, then I feared *I* wouldn't be able to handle it. In a sense I was emotionally crippled."

"I went through the same thing. You've been suffering all this time."

"Though it's true I hadn't found the woman I was looking for up to the point of my accident, the situation was changed after I was released to go home."

"Does anyone else know?"

"Only my doctor, and now you."

She tried to sit up, but he put his hands on her shoulders. "Let me finish. Out of the refiner's fire after losing my sister and her husband, you suddenly appeared in my life, loving my niece. Two miracles happened that day. Demi was found alive and there you were."

"Nik—"

"I don't want you to leave Greece."

"I know."

He jackknifed into a sitting position. "I'm being serious."

"Nik—I thought we were going to forget our cares and enjoy our vacation? You were the one who told me not to think about when it was over, and just take each day as a special gift."

"I can't stop thinking. The idea of you flying back to the States is ruining the trip for me."

A throaty laugh poured out of her. "You're impossible, do you know that?"

"But you still think I'm wonderful."

"Yes. That will never change."

Keep it up, Fran. "How do you know?"

She sighed. "I just do."

"You sound very sure."

"What's this all about? If I didn't know better, I'd think you were worried about something."

"I didn't know I was until you mentioned it."

"Then let's talk about it now."

"Maybe tomorrow."

"That's not fair!" she cried. "So what's going to happen tomorrow?"

"A surprise I can guarantee you'll love."

"And then you'll tell me after?"

"We'll see."

"Will this surprise be hard on the knees?"

He chuckled. "You won't have to lift a finger, let alone a foot."

"Really?"

"Trust me."

"We're going to lie on a beach all day."

"That'll come the next day."

"How about a hint?"

He inched closer to play with her hair. "It has to do with one of your obsessions."

"I don't have any."

"Yes, you do. They come with your spirit of adventure. But now I find I don't want to talk anymore. It's my turn to kiss *you* goodnight."

"I don't think I could handle that right now."

"Good. I like you best when you're a little off kilter. Give me your mouth, Francesca. With or without your capitulation, I need to taste it again."

Her back was still to him as he began kissing her neck, working his way around until he was on the other side of her. He tangled his legs with hers, crushing her to him the way he'd been longing to do. Her mouth seduced him, thrilled him beyond belief. After thirty-four years it was happening.

"I don't think you have any idea what you're doing to me," he murmured feverishly, "but I never want you to stop."

Fran's body gave a voluptuous shudder. "I don't want to stop either. I love the way you make me feel, but this is all happening way too fast and we can't always have what we want."

"Give me one good reason why."

"Because I'll be leaving Greece shortly. I don't want to be in so much pain I can't function after I get home. I don't know about other women, but I'm not able to have a romantic fling and then move on to the next one without giving it a thought.

"You and I met under the most unique of circumstances. I'll never forget you and I'll cherish every moment we've had together, but this isn't right. I take full blame for everything. Your Angelis charm worked its magic on me, but now you have to help me be strong."

Shaken by her words, Nik raised up. "Will you at least agree to see what I've planned for tomorrow before we fly back to Athens?"

"Of course."

Afraid if he kissed her again, he wouldn't be able to stop, he moved as far away as he could. Without her in his arms, the night was going to be endless.

The helicopter was waiting for them in Pironia. With Nik's assistance, Fran climbed on board, having eaten a substantial breakfast at the refuge before their final descent. The sun was already hot, portending one of the sunny days for which Greece was famous this time of year.

She felt the pilot's gaze on her as she took a seat behind him and strapped herself in. He was attractive and wore a wedding ring. Because of Nik's remarks last night she was more aware of him, of everything.

Nik handed her the field glasses. "We're going sightseeing. You'll want those." As soon as he'd fastened himself in the copilot's seat, the rotors whipped the air and they lifted off.

Her stomach lurched. She was okay in the air, but feared she could never get used to the takeoffs and landings. Then she chastised herself for thinking the thought because she'd probably never travel in a helicopter again once she left Athens for home.

Home. Strange how it sounded so remote. Her Grecian adventure with Kellie had turned out to be so much more, she felt as if she'd become a part of the landscape. It seemed as though her world started and ended with him and little Demi. What would life be like when there was no more Nik and that sweet little girl? She couldn't bear to think about it. Couldn't wait to see her and hold her again.

When they'd been flying for a while she leaned forward to ask him a question. "Where are we going? Is it still a secret?"

He turned on the speaker. "We're coming up on a long peninsula on your left. The whole thing is called Mount Athos."

"You're kidding! I mean, you're really taking us there? But women aren't allowed!"

"True, but since you're dying to see it, I'll show it to you from the air."

"Oh, Nik—this is the most exciting thing that's ever happened to me!"

The two men smiled at her enthusiasm, but she didn't care.

"The place is a national treasure, but you already know that after reading about it. Still, to see it like this will give you a greater understanding of why it's called the Holy Mountain. I think it's one of the most beautiful places on earth."

"Have you spent time here?"

"When I turned eighteen, my father brought me and my brothers. To me, it was like a fantasy. The various monasteries dot the landscape. As you will see, some of them are as enormous as castles. My favorite is the Monastery of Saint Docheiariouthe, situated right on the Aegean. The beach is pristine because the monks don't often swim."

"I'm envious of your experience."

"It was something I'll never forget. We walked everywhere, discovering caves that still house religious hermits. Do you know some of the churches have more gold than many countries keep in their vaults? The beauty of their architecture and the icons are something to behold."

"Are the monks all Greek?"

"No. They come from every country in the Orthodox world and even some from non-orthodox countries. You'll notice gardens tended with meticulous care. There's a spiritual atmosphere to the whole place."

"Mountains seem to have that essence, even without monasteries. I felt it yesterday on top of Mount Olympus. During your travels, did you ever climb Mount Sinai?"

"Not yet. Maybe one day. I hear it has monasteries, too."

Her heart ached at the thought of him going there without her.

The pilot dipped down so she could get a bird's-eye view. For the next twenty minutes she feasted her eyes on the marvels passing beneath them. She knew her oohs and aahs amused the men, but she couldn't hold back. The sights were incredible. Nik pointed out his favorite monastery.

"I can see why. The setting against the water is indescribably beautiful." He loved the water.

"If you've had enough, we'll head for Thessalonika."

"I don't think you could ever get enough of this place. Thank you so much for this privilege. Thank you for flying us here in perfect safety, Keiko. I'm in awe of your expertise."

"He's the best at what he does," Nik interjected, while the pilot just smiled.

Before long they landed at the airport's helipad where a dashing black sports car was waiting. Nik walked her over and helped her inside. "I asked my driver to bring my favorite car here so we could drive it back to Athens at our leisure. Keiko will fly our camping gear back." After stowing their packs, he got behind the wheel.

In the next moment he put a hand on her thigh, squeezing gently. It caused her to gasp. "Since the car is carrying precious cargo, I promise I'll keep the speed down."

"How fast can it go?"

"One hundred and ninety-nine miles per hour." After a pause he said, "If you'd rather I rented a car, I'll do it. The decision is yours."

She saw the heightened excitement in his dark eyes and wouldn't have deprived him of this for the world. Besides, she'd never been in a sports car. With Nik, everything was a first, but he didn't need things to add to his remarkable persona. The man himself was the most captivating male on the planet and had a stranglehold on her.

"Well now, darlin'," she drawled with an exaggerated Texas accent. "Why don't y'all show me what a famous race-car driver you really are?"

An explosion of laughter resounded in the car.

She'd said the magic words. He was in his element, and she'd given him permission to enjoy himself. That was one of the things she loved about him. Nik considered her feelings before he did anything. The fact that he always put her first put him in a special class of human beings.

He wasn't a show-off in any sense of the word, which was the reason why she wanted to see him discard his cares and have fun. A second later they wound around to the main road. After the coast was clear, they literally flew down the highway. He flashed her a smile that said he didn't have a worry in the world. It was wonderful to see him this happy after the pain he'd just lived through.

The man seemed to be in heaven, driving with the expertise of any race-car driver she'd ever watched on TV. He infected her with his excitement.

Eventually he had to come to a stop at the intersection for the next town. She turned in his direction. "I'm convinced you could have made it big in the racing world."

Nik eyed her back. "I was tempted, but some newer thrill came along."

"You're like me, always wanting to see what's around the next corner in case I missed out."

"That describes us, Fran. Since you mentioned Mount Sinai, how would you like to climb it with me?"

She blinked. "You mean before I fly home?"

"Why not? Neither of us has ever been there. It'll be a first-time adventure we can experience together."

Fran shook her head. "I couldn't take advantage of you or your generosity like that."

"I think you're afraid I'll take advantage of *you*, so I'll make you a promise. Earlier you asked if we could just be friends and finish our hike to the top of Mount Olympus. I was too frustrated at the time to reassure you. But if you'll give me a second chance, I'd like to spend more time with you. We'll travel there as two friends, nothing more."

Oh, Nik...

"Being with you has made me forget my troubles for a while. I love this feeling of freedom. You're easy to talk to, easy to be with when we don't talk. I'm enjoying your companionship. Can you honestly tell me you don't feel the same way?"

He already knew the answer to that question. How could she say no to him when she knew in her heart he was being totally sincere with her? Since coming away with him, she'd seen and felt how the years had fallen away from him. She'd been given a glimpse of the younger, responsibility-free Nik who had existed before his mountain-climbing accident. With him she felt carefree, too.

They *were* good together. Good for each other. They'd confided in each other and she felt she could trust him. After what she'd told him about trust the other night, that was saying a lot.

"Tell you what. You've convinced me to live dangerously for a little longer."

For an answer, the car shot ahead, leaving her dizzy and reeling. It took zipping along for ten minutes before she could speak. "I hate to tell you this, but you're running high on adrenaline right now."

"But you don't mind," he said with a confidence that seemed part of him.

"No." *I don't mind.* She turned her head to look out the passenger window. Her heart was palpitating so hard in her throat, she couldn't make a sound.

They drove on to the next village where he turned

off the road into the parking lot of a café. After shutting down the motor, he undid his seat belt and turned to her. "I'm going to run inside and get us some food we can eat in the car. Now that we have new plans, I can't get us back to Athens fast enough. You like lamb?"

"I adore it." Her response corresponded with the vibrating sound of his cell phone. "Are you going to answer it?"

He checked the caller ID. "It's from Sandro. That's odd."

"Maybe you'd better get it."

He flashed her another heartstopping smile. "Is that *Mrs. Atlas* talking now?" he teased.

Her soft laughter filled the car as he pulled the phone from his pocket. It was a text message. In the subject line Sandro had put *Emergency.* Nik clicked on to read the message.

Demi started a fever during the night and cries incessantly. Mother hasn't been able to get it down and called the doctor. He told her to bring her to the hospital in Mykonos. We're here now. We don't know if she's come down with a cold, or if she's still suffering from her trauma. She won't eat or drink. I promised Mother I'd keep you informed. She wants everyone here.

Nik pressed Reply.

I'm in my car approximately 160 miles from Mykonos. Should be there within two hours. Have a helicopter standing by at the dock for me. Make sure my driver is there to take care of my car. Keep me posted.

Fran stared at him after he'd pocketed his phone. "Something serious has put those frown lines on your face. Tell me what's wrong."

"Your instincts were right. Demi's back in the hospital."

"Oh, no—" Tears sprang from her eyes. "Not that little darling—"

"She's feverish and won't settle down. I'm afraid Mother's falling apart. Wait here for me. I'll be right back with the food. Sandro will keep us informed if she gets worse."

Fran watched his long, powerful legs eat up the distance and disappear inside. She feared any plans he'd had to take her to Mount Sinai would have to be put on permanent hold. Neither of them could think with little Demi in the hospital again.

Nik was back before she knew it. "I'm glad we're in this car. We ought to make it to the port under two hours. The helicopter will ferry us to the hospital."

She opened the sacks and they helped themselves to food and drink. "Your brothers told me Melina had never had other people tend Demi, so I'm not surprised she's having trouble. Of course she's comfortable around your family, but it was her parents she was bonded to. Obviously this transition is going to take more time than I thought."

"I agree. When we get to the hospital, I'm going to follow through and call a child psychiatrist for consultation. I want another opinion besides the pediatrician's. And there's another possibility. Maybe she has internal injuries like I received on my climb of Everest. Landing on her back like that could have damaged a vital organ and she's in pain."

"Just remember she was all right when you took her home."

"Sometimes internal injuries show up later."

"If that's true, then the doctor will find out. She's going to be all right, Nik. That child survived a tornado. She'll survive this. You're all doing everything possible for her."

He grimaced. "What if it's not enough? If our family lost her…"

She touched his arm. "Don't even think it!" But deep inside, Fran was worried about it, too. She adored that baby. This was new territory for all of them. His love for his niece had never been more evident. "I wish I could help you."

"You already have simply by being with me." He grasped her hand, twining his fingers through hers while he drove with his left. But soon he had to let her go to answer another text. They kept coming, feeding them information until they reached the helipad near the ferries.

Nik's driver jumped down and hurried around to the driver's seat while they climbed in the helicopter once more. Nik stowed their backpacks onboard. "We're flying to the hospital in Mykonos."

She sat in her usual spot and buckled up. Her emotions were so up and down, she was hardly cognizant of the takeoff. Fran found herself repeating a new mantra. *Demi can't have anything seriously wrong with her. She just can't.*

It seemed to take forever to reach the island. The pilot set them down on the pad outside the E.R. area of the hospital in the town of Mykonos. Nik helped Fran out, then gathered their backpacks before hurrying inside with her.

"Cosimo said they've got her in a bigger private room for the moment to accommodate the family. It's down this wing."

The second they opened the door, their family descended on Nik as though he was their savior. He was the force they gravitated to because he had that intangible aura that made everyone feel better.

Fran felt terrible she'd said anything to take him away from them. Yet, on the other hand, she'd seen him freed of responsibility for a few days, and he'd become a different man who'd been revitalized.

He turned to Fran. After the others greeted her, he led her over to the crib. Demi lay on her side. An IV had been inserted in her foot. She looked and felt feverish.

"Evidently she's been like this all day," Nik whispered. "Her temp is still too high."

Fran looked at his mother. She was an elegant woman with silvery wings overlaying her short black hair. "Have they done all the tests on her?"

Mrs. Angelis nodded, clutching the railing of the crib. "They can't find anything wrong. The doctor's perplexed."

"Is she asleep?"

"No, but they gave her something to help her rest in order to bring the fever down."

Nik put an arm around his mother's shoulders. "She has to be missing Melina."

His mother's eyes filled with tears. "She was the best mother in the world. It's wicked that she was taken away from us. I feel so helpless. My dearest little Demitra."

"She'll get past this, Mrs. Angelis," Fran assured her, but deep down she was weeping inside to see Demi lying there, limp. It reminded her of the way she'd found her in the bushes. "Homesickness can bring on all her symptoms, but it won't last forever," she said, if only to try and convince herself.

Nik's father, whose salt-and-pepper hair was thinning on top, had come to stand on the other side of the crib. "Of course it won't."

Unable to resist, Fran leaned down and smoothed the black curls with her fingers. "Demi, sweetheart? It's Fran. What's the matter?"

Nik slid his arm around her waist. "Sing to her. Maybe your voice will rouse her."

Fran tried several lullabies, but there was no response. She thought her heart would break and started with another one. All of a sudden Demi's eyes opened and she looked up at Fran. Then she made whimpering sounds and stretched an arm out.

There was a hushed silence in the room. All eyes were on the drastic change in the baby.

"Go ahead and pick her up," Nik murmured.

At his urging, Fran bent over and gathered the baby in her arms. "Well, hi, little sweetheart. Did you just wake up?" She had to be careful because the IV was still attached to her foot.

Demi snuggled in her arms. It was almost as if she was saying she'd missed Fran. The demonstration of affection was too much for Fran who hid her face in the baby's curls for a minute. She kissed her forehead and cheeks. "I've missed you, too. So has your uncle Nik."

She would have handed Demi to him, but he shook his head. "She wants you."

In the periphery she noticed his family. They appeared pretty well dumbstruck. "Let's see if she wants a bottle and will take it from you." He turned to his mother. "Did you bring one?"

"Oh— Yes. There are several in the diaper bag over there on the table."

Nik got one out and brought it to Fran. After pulling a chair over to the crib, he told her to sit and see if Demi wanted any milk.

Fran subsided in the chair and cradled the baby. "Are you hungry, you cute little thing? Would a bottle taste good?" She put the nipple in her mouth, not knowing what would happen.

Gasps of surprise escaped everyone when Demi stared up at Fran with those beautiful brown eyes and started drinking. Nik's exhausted-looking parents smiled at her with tears in their eyes. The relief on their faces spoke volumes. His brothers were so joyful, they squeezed Nik's shoulder.

Fran was tongue-tied and glanced up at Nik. "I honestly don't know why Demi responds to me."

His dark eyes were suspiciously bright. "You rescued her from the garden and were the first person to show her love when she came back to life. I don't think we need to look for any other answer than that. Do you?" He stared first at her, then around at his family.

His father wiped the wetness off his cheeks. "Our only problem now, *Kyria* Myers, is to convince you to stay with us a while until Demi feels comfortable again with everyone."

"She went downhill after you and Nik left the island," his mother volunteered. "Please stay." Her heart was in her voice.

Conflicted by her fear of what was happening here, Fran couldn't look at them.

"What do you say?" Nik was still leaving it up to her. She loved him for that.

CHAPTER EIGHT

"OF COURSE I'LL STAY."

As if Fran needed to be convinced...

Demi had caught at her heart the second she'd seen her lying in the bushes. She might be Nik's flesh and blood, but Fran loved her, too. "It'll be no penance to help out."

He squeezed her shoulder, filling her with a new kind of warmth. "I'll tell the doctor. As soon as he releases her, we'll all drive home together." Near her ear he whispered, "We'll do the Sinai climb later."

No. They wouldn't. But it was a beautiful thought she'd cherish forever.

Within fifteen minutes they were able to leave the hospital. It was decided Fran would be wheeled outside holding Demi so there was no chance the baby would revert back to hysterics.

The family had come in two cars. Nik helped her into the back of his parents' car before sliding in next to her. His brothers followed in one of their cars. The whole scene was so surreal, Fran had to pinch herself.

Anyone seeing her would think she was a new mother, except that Demi was too big and her coloring was the opposite of Fran's. Still, she imagined this was how a new mother felt taking her baby home for the first time. How she wished Demi were really hers! Babies were miracles, and this one happened to be the miracle baby everyone in Greece was talking about.

When they reached the villa, Nik carried their backpacks to the suite where she'd stayed before. "Let's bathe her."

"I was just going to suggest it."

They worked in harmony. He got everything out she would need to bathe the baby in the tub. Nik filled it. Together they washed her hair and played with her. Demi loved it and kicked her legs.

"That's it, Demi. Kick harder." With his encouragement, she splashed water in her face, but she didn't cry. They both burst into laughter.

"Aren't you a brave girl!"

After wrapping her up in a towel, Nik carried her into the bedroom and laid her down on the bed. Fran sprinkled some powder, then put on her diaper and a summery sleeper. Nik dried her hair and brushed the curls.

"It's time to take her temperature. I'll get the thermometer." Fran hurried over to the dresser. "Here—" She handed it to Nik.

"This isn't going to hurt, Demi." Fran held her breath while he checked it. A few more seconds and he glanced up. "Ninety-nine degrees."

"Wonderful! You're almost back to normal." She kissed the baby's tummy, producing gurgle-like laughter.

"Let's take her out to the patio. When everyone sees how happy she is, they'll all stop worrying and get a good night's sleep." Nik picked Demi up and they walked through the villa and out the doors. Twilight was upon them, the mystical time of evening that gave the island a special glow.

This time the family didn't reach for Demi. They let Nik take charge. He sat down on the swing holding the baby on his lap and patted the spot next to him for Fran. "Her temperature is down. She's had her bath and is ready for bed. You'll be glad to know Fran has agreed to stay here for a few days to help out. Hopefully it won't take long for life to get back to a new normal."

"Demitra isn't the same baby we drove to the hospital this morning," his mother remarked. She eyed Fran. "It's absolutely uncanny how she responds to you. We're thankful you didn't leave Athens yet."

Fran felt it incumbent to explain. "Before the tornado touched down, Kellie and I were on our way to hike Mount Olympus."

"Ah—you like to climb? So does our Nikolos."

"I found that out. Since Kellie wasn't well, he took me to the top. And this morning we flew in the helicopter over Mount Athos."

"An intriguing place," Nik's father interjected.

"For you men," Fran teased. Everyone chuckled.

Nik flicked her a glance with the private message that he looked forward to their climb of Sinai. She got a fluttery sensation in her chest.

"We were up early and then had a long drive back. If you'll forgive us, we're going to put Demi down and we'll see you in the morning."

His father nodded, but Fran saw the speculative gleam in his eyes as they got up to leave. Their family knew Nik never spent this much time with a woman. She could tell his brothers were equally curious about what was going on, though they made no comment. They'd be even more surprised if they learned she and Nik had been on the verge of flying to Egypt.

"Nik? I can tell your parents want to talk to you. Why don't you let me take over from here and give her a bottle?" She drew the baby out of his arms.

"Don't count on me being long."

"Take all the time you need."

Fran was glad to escape to her suite. She disappeared down the hall to the nursery and sat in the chair next to the bed to feed Demi a bottle. Once she'd sung a few songs, the baby fell asleep much faster than Fran would have thought. Maybe there was still a little of the sedative in her system. Between that and her exhaustion, she'd no doubt sleep through the night.

Fran tiptoed out of the nursery and checked her own phone. She found two text messages. One from her mom who wondered how she was doing. Fran hadn't had a chance to tell her anything yet. The other one came from Kellie.

I've been trying to reach you for two days. What's going on? Why haven't you phoned?

Fran checked her watch. It would still be early afternoon in Philadelphia. While she waited for Nik to come, she decided to phone her friend.

"Kellie?"

"Thank goodness it's you, Fran. I was beginning to worry."

"I'm sorry. So much has happened since you left Athens, I hardly know where to start. But before I talk about me, I have to know how you're doing. By now your aunt and uncle have been told everything."

"Yes, and they're being so wonderful to me." Fran heard tears in her voice.

"What about Leandros? Is he still there?"

"No. I told him to leave, but I promised to call him when I was ready to talk. He finally gave up and flew back to Athens."

Fran sank down on the side of the bed. She was sick for both of them. "Are you feeling all right physically? No more fainting spells?"

"No. My aunt says she's going to fatten me up."

"You *have* lost a few pounds since Easter."

"Enough about me. How soon are you coming home?"

Fran took a deep breath. "Not for a while."

"How come?"

Her hand tightened on the phone. "The baby was in the hospital again with a high fever."

"You're not serious."

"I wish I weren't. She's missing her parents and the family has been at their wit's end."

"Does Demi still reach out to you?"

Fran wasn't about to lie to her. "I'm afraid so. Their family is really hurt by it. None of us can figure it out. Since we brought her back to the villa, her temp is already down. It's uncanny."

"Has Nik—"

"No, Kellie," Fran broke in, reading her thoughts. "He's never mentioned the word *nanny* again. Tomorrow he's going to consult with a psychiatrist to find out what could be going on with Demi. I've promised to stay that long."

"Oh, Fran... Why didn't you come home on the flight Leandros arranged for you?"

Good question. "Because Nik volunteered to take me up on the top of Mount Olympus before I went home."

After a pregnant silence, "Did you go?"

"Yes. On the descent he got a call that Demi was back in the hospital." A little lie that could be forgiven.

"She's his number one priority. I was there before, during and after the funeral. It's clear he put Melina on a pedestal and would do anything for her. I learned he was instrumental in getting her and Stavros together. Did you know Nik was in a bad mountain-climbing accident?"

"He told me."

"Did he also tell you Melina took it upon herself to be at his bedside both in and out of the hospital? Her devotion to him was praised at the funeral."

Fran's eyes closed tightly. She didn't know that.

"If you stay any longer, you'll end up taking care of the baby. It's his way of paying back Melina."

Fran didn't believe Nik had a hidden agenda, not after the rapturous few days together when they'd both opened up their hearts. But she couldn't dismiss the nagging possibility Kellie was right in one regard. Fran was still in Greece of her own free will with no date set to go home yet. Demi's tug on her was growing stronger. *So was Nik's.*

"Are you still there? Are you listening?"

"Yes." She'd been listening to Kellie spill out her broken heart since coming to Greece. Her friend's agony went fathoms deep and colored her thoughts where Fran's relationship with Nik was concerned.

"Remember that old cliché about blood being thicker

than water? It happens to be true. Believe me, I know. After marrying Leandros, I have proof."

In Kellie's mind, Karmela had turned her marriage into a threesome. Maybe there was some truth in it, but Fran knew there had to be a lot more going on. Kellie had a hard time talking about her deepest fears. Fran doubted she'd talked to Leandros about them.

"Do you hear what I'm saying, Fran?"

"Yes." She would have said more, but she heard a noise. Nik had entered the bedroom and shut the door. Turning her back to him she said, "Forgive me, Kellie, but something has come up and I'll have to call you later. I promise."

She hung up and turned around. "I was just returning Kellie's call."

Nik stood at the end of the bed with his hands resting on his hips in a totally male stance. "Is she all right now that she's with her aunt and uncle? She was raised by them, right?"

"Yes. Physically she's fine, but emotionally, I've never seen her so completely devastated. Leandros is back in Athens."

He rubbed his chest absently. "I'm sorry to hear that, especially when it appears her pain has rubbed off on you."

Fran was gutted by her conversation with Kellie. "I have to admit I'm worried about them."

"I'm sorry. Under the circumstances I'll say goodnight and see you in the morning. After breakfast we'll take Demi out in the sailboat. She loves it. Hopefully while we're enjoying ourselves, the doctor will get back to me with some ideas, and we'll go from there."

"I'd like that. Good night, Nik."

Much to her chagrin she wanted him to grab her and kiss her senseless, but he was a man of his word and made no move toward her. Instead, he tiptoed into the nursery. She watched from the doorway as he leaned over the crib to touch Demi's hair. The sweet moment moved her to tears before he came back out.

His eyes looked like glistening black pools in the semidarkness. "*Kalinitha*, Fran."

A light breeze filled the sail. With the surface of the blue Aegean shimmering like diamonds, Fran felt she'd come close to heaven. "Where are we headed, Nik?"

He manned the rudder with the same expertise he did everything else. In bathing trunks and a T-shirt that revealed his hard-muscled body, he looked spectacular.

"Delos. It's that tiny, barren island you can see from here, only three miles away. The Ionians colonized it in 1000 BC and made it their religious capital. There's a specific reason I'm taking us there."

Fran had been holding Demi since they'd climbed onboard. They were both dressed in sun suits and hats. Fran wore her bathing suit underneath. When it got too hot, she'd take the baby below for a nap. "Is there a statue of Atlas? If so, I want to take a picture."

He grinned, dissolving her insides. "Sorry to disappoint you. He resides far away in North Africa."

"Of course. The Atlas Mountains. I'd forgotten. That explains your affinity for them."

"Maybe," he teased. "I'm afraid Delos is the birthplace of Apollo and Artemis, but that's not what's so interesting."

She kissed Demi's cheek. "We're all ears, aren't we, sweetheart?"

"At one point, the island was so sacred, no one was allowed to be born there or die there."

"You're kidding!"

"Those who were about to leave this world, or get ushered in, were rushed off to the nearby islet of Rinia."

She laughed. "Sometimes you just can't stop either one from happening."

"Somehow they managed."

"Sounds like shades of the rules on Mount Athos."

"I was waiting for you to make that connection. At least here on Delos, males and females can go ashore and walk around the ancient ruins."

"What about children? Are they permitted?"

"Yes, but Demi will have to wait until she's six or seven. This afternoon we'll just circle the island. While all the other tourists from Mykonos scramble around, we'll be able to sit back and see many of the remains from the deck."

"It's a glorious day out for sightseeing."

"With this light breeze, my favorite kind."

She felt his gaze linger on her, overheating her in a hurry. "What's the name of your boat? I can't read Greek."

"The *Phorcys*."

"A mythological creature?"

"To be sure. I was raised on the myths. When I was a boy I made up my mind that when I was old enough to buy my own boat, I'd name it for the ancient sea god who presides over the hidden dangers of the deep."

"That sounds exactly like something the protective Atlas would do."

Laughter rumbled out of his chest.

"Does he look like you?"

"Tell you what. One day I'll bring you to Delos alone." *Don't say things like that, Nik. In a few days I'll fly home and never come back here again.* "We'll walk up to the highest point on the island where I'll show you an ancient mosaic of him. He's a gray-haired, fish-tailed god with spiky crab-like skin and forelegs who carries a torch."

"Oh dear. He must have done an excellent job of keeping everyone away." They were getting closer to the island now.

"He did better than that," Nik quipped. "With his wife, Ceto, they created a host of monstrous children collectively known as the Phorcydes."

"That's terrible! How sad they never had a child as beautiful as Demi." Fran shifted the baby to her shoulder and hugged her. "If the gods did exist, they'd be jealous of Melina's daughter. Even without them, she'll need to be guarded well."

And Nik would see to that.

She lifted the binoculars he'd given her to examine the various archaeological sites studded with temples and pillars. Demi reached out to touch them, of course. The action pulled off Fran's hat, which in turn pulled her hair loose from its knot. "You little monkey." She kissed her cheeks and neck, giving up on the binoculars for the moment.

For the next hour they slowly circled the island, but most of the time Fran simply played with the baby who stood up with her help and bounced when Nik talked to her. The baby babbled a lot, causing both of them to laugh.

"She's happy and says she wants to go ashore."

"I know you do, *Demitza*, but you can't have everything you want." Fran loved the way he talked to her.

"I think it's getting too hot for her, Nik. I'd better take her below."

"Go ahead while I drop anchor in this little cove, then I'll join you and we'll have an early dinner."

Fran carried Demi down the steps to the bedroom and changed her diaper. Once she'd put her in a little stretchy suit, she walked her into the galley to feed her. Nik had brought her swing along. It worked as a high chair.

"I bet you're thirsty. I'll fix you a bottle of water first." The baby drank some eagerly. "What would my little princess like for lunch? How about lamb and peaches?"

She grabbed some bottled water for herself and sat down to feed Demi. After a minute Nik appeared. With his olive skin, it didn't take much exposure from the sun to turn him into a bronzed god.

"There's nothing wrong with her appetite," he observed, reaching for a water, too. He sat down next to the baby and watched the two of them. In such close quarters, Fran could hardly breathe because of his nearness. She felt his warmth and smelled the soap he'd used in the shower earlier.

"If you want to finish feeding her, I'll get the food out of the fridge." Anything to keep busy so she wouldn't concentrate on him to the exclusion of all else.

Demi obviously adored Nik and thrived on his attention. Between his smiles and laughter, she couldn't help but be charmed by her uncle. Nik would make a wonderful father one day. Demi was lucky to have him in her life. Just how lucky, she had no idea.

Fran put their meal on the table—salad and rolls, fresh fruit, pastries and juice. A feast.

"This is delicious." She smiled at him. "I see there's nothing wrong with your appetite either." He'd eaten everything in sight.

"That's because you're with Demi and me. We thrive under the right conditions."

"If you'll notice, I ate all my food, too," she admitted.

He flashed her a penetrating glance. "I noticed." After wiping the corner of his mouth with a napkin, he got up from the table. "Come on, little one. It's time to sleep." He picked up the swing with her in it and carried it into the bedroom.

Fran followed with a bottle of formula. Once he'd turned on the mechanism that started it swinging, she handed her the bottle. Demi looked up at them and smiled the sweetest smile Fran had ever seen before she started drinking.

Nik moved Fran over to the bed a few feet away. "We'll have to stay here until she goes to sleep, so we might as well make ourselves comfortable."

She lay down on her side, facing the baby. Nik moved behind her and put his arm around her waist. His sigh filtered through her hair splayed over the pillow. "This is what I call heaven."

They stayed that way without moving. Fran was so content in his arms, and the sound of the swing had a hypnotizing effect on her. When she looked at Demi, the little darling had fallen asleep.

Fran suspected the gentle rocking of the boat had put Nik to sleep, too. But in that regard she was mistaken. In an unexpected motion he rolled her over so she was half lying on him. "Sh-h," he said against her lips before his hungry mouth covered them in a long, languid kiss that went on and on, setting her on fire.

Her need of him was so all-consuming, she couldn't hold back her desire. For a time she felt transported.

"I know I promised I'd treat you like a friend," he whispered in a husky voice, "but it won't work. I can't stop what I'm feeling." He was actually trembling. "I've never wanted any woman in my life the way I want you." His fingers tightened in her hair. "Before I forget all my good intentions, you'd better hurry up on deck while you can. I'm giving you this one chance before all bets are off for good."

Something in his ragged tone told her he meant what he said. If she stayed here a second longer, there'd be no going back and it would be her fault, not his. It shocked her that he had more control than she did.

But when she finally found the strength to move off the bed and get to her feet, she heard him groan. It almost sent her back into his arms until she saw Demi lying there in the swing. Fran's gaze took in both of them.

Neither of them will ever be yours. Go upstairs now, Fran.

She didn't remember her feet touching the ground. When she reached the deck, she threw off her sundress and dove into the water. It was late afternoon now, when the sun was its warmest near the shore. Delightful. But the wonder of it was wasted on Fran who swam around while she struggled with the war going on inside of her.

Should she engage in one mad moment of passion at the age of twenty-eight, then have to live out the rest of her life tortured by the memory? Or should she do the smart thing and avoid the fire? It meant she'd never know joy. Either option was untenable. Thank goodness for the water that hid her tears.

When she finally started back to the boat, she discovered Nik on deck holding Demi. She swam over to the side. "Demi?" she called out and waved her arm. "Can you see me?"

"She's squirming to jump in with you."

A different man had emerged from the bedroom. This one was calm and collected, her urbane host until she left Greece. She died inside, knowing the other one wouldn't make a second appearance. As he'd said, he'd give her one chance. Fran hadn't taken it in order to avoid sabotaging her own happiness. Now she had to pay the consequences.

"The water's wonderful. I'll come onboard so you can cool off."

Nik would never cool off. He'd come down with a fever when he'd first met Fran. With each passing day it had climbed higher until he was burning up. He'd already taken a big swim that morning in cooler water before anyone was up. It had done nothing to bring down his temperature. There was only one antidote, but the thought of it not working terrified him.

Afraid to touch her, he let her climb onboard by herself. She put on her sundress over her yellow bikini. Her movements were quick, but not quick enough. At the sight of her beautiful body, he practically had a heart attack. With Demi in her swing, he could unfurl the sail and raise the anchor.

She hunkered down next to the baby and kissed her, then looked in his direction. "Don't you want to swim?"

"Maybe tonight. I'd prefer to take advantage of the

evening breeze on the way back. Mother will be missing Demi by now."

"Of course. How long did she sleep?"

"Until five minutes ago."

"She doesn't act like she's hungry yet. I think I'll hold her for a while."

Fran couldn't keep her hands off the baby. She walked her over to the bench and sat down with her, giving her kisses on her tummy that made Demi laugh. While she was preoccupied, Nik set sail for Mykonos and guided them toward the villa. By seven-thirty, he brought the boat around and it glided gently to the dock.

In a few minutes he helped her out of the boat with Demi and followed with the swing. No one was on the patio yet. That was good. At the top of the steps he put the swing down and they entered the villa without passing any family members who might pick up on the tension between them.

"I'll start Demi's bath," Fran called over her shoulder. "When she's dressed, you can take her to your mother."

"Good. I'll pick out an outfit." He opened the cupboard and reached for a sundress. In the drawer he found some white stockings and little matching shoes. He put everything on the bed. When he peered in the bathroom, Fran had just finished washing the baby's hair.

She looked up. "Demi's such an easy baby, she's a joy."

"She has Melina's nature."

When Fran lifted the baby from the water, he grabbed a towel and wrapped her in it before carrying her into the bedroom. For just a moment it hit him that his sister really was gone. Tears stung his eyelids. He hugged the baby to him while he fought to regain his composure.

"It's all right to cry, Nik," Fran murmured gently. "Even Atlas has do it once in a while. The problem is, emotion catches up with you when you least expect it. I know what that's like. Even if it's a horrible adage, the pain will ease with time."

He lifted his head. "I'll keep that in mind." Nik lay the baby on the bed and dried her hair.

"Oh—what a darling outfit!"

"I bought it for her several months ago, but it was too big at the time."

"Now it's the perfect size! With her skin she'd look beautiful in any color, but I dare say peppermint pink trumps them all." She held it up in front of Demi. "Don't you love it, sweetheart? Your uncle picked this one out especially for you."

The baby got all excited and touched the hem. Warmed by Demi's reaction, Nik's crushing sense of loss faded. He got busy powdering and diapering her. Fran's eyes shimmered a violet blue as she handed the dress to him. "You do the honors."

"When I bought this, I never dreamed I'd be the one putting it on her." His fingers fumbled with the two buttons in the back. Fran helped the baby to sit up so he could fasten it. Then she put the stockings and shoes on her tiny feet.

"One more minute while we comb her hair." Fran dashed over to the dresser for it. "She has a head of natural curl. What a lucky girl." Nik watched her style it to perfection. "There you go." She kissed her on both cheeks. "Now you're all ready to go see your *yiayia* and *papou*."

"How did you know those words?" She continually surprised him in wonderful ways.

"I've been listening to the children talk. In France I used to walk through the park near our school and practice my French with them. They make terrific teachers, *Kyrie* Angelis."

To hear her speak any Greek excited him no end. "I'm impressed."

"Why don't you take Demi to find your folks? I'll hurry and shower so I'll be available if you need me. But I'm hoping she had such a good time with us, she'll be able to enjoy her grandparents without me before she has to go to bed."

Nik left the room carrying Demi and found his parents in the living room talking with Stavros's parents. He'd been so focused on his own pain, he'd forgotten they mourned their son and needed Demi's love, too. Four pairs of eyes lit up when they saw their granddaughter decked out like a little princess. For the next few minutes he sat with them while the baby was passed around. Dinner was about to be served. They gravitated to the patio where the rest of the family had congregated.

He put Demi in her swing with a fresh bottle of formula and told them he'd be back. On the way to his apartment he swung by Fran's. There was something he had to say to her, and he couldn't put it off any longer.

"Fran?" He knocked on her door.

His breath caught when she opened it wearing a pair of pleated tan pants and a white blouse. Fresh from the shower, she'd fastened her damp hair at the back of her head with a clip. She'd picked up some sun and wore no makeup, except a frosted pink lipstick, because she didn't need any.

"I take it Demi's all right so far."

"I left her on the patio with the family. We'll see how she does. Before I shower and change, I need to talk to you. It's important. May I come in?"

"Of course."

He shut the door with his back and lounged against it. "What happened on the boat made me realize I can't go on this way any longer."

Fran stood a few feet away from him, rubbing her hips with her palms in a nervous gesture. "Neither can I. While I was showering I came to the decision that I have to leave in the morning, no matter what."

"I have another solution."

"There's isn't another one."

"There is, but I've hesitated to mention it because we've only known each other a week. I want you to marry me."

"Marry?"

The world spun. She turned clumsily and sank down on the side of the bed before she fell. Kellie's warning rang in her ears. *He'll do anything to get you to take care of Demi.*

"You don't want to marry me," she whispered.

"You're terrified again."

She looked away from him. The nerve palpitating at the base of her throat almost choked her. "You know the thrill will wear off."

"I've never been married, but you have. That's your bad experience talking."

"Be serious, Nik."

"I don't know how to get any more serious. I just asked you to be my wife and am waiting for an answer."

She kneaded her hands. "You're not thinking clearly. For one thing, I can't give you children."

"That goes for both of us. We'll adopt."

"That's what Rob said."

"Don't you dare compare me to your ex-husband," he ground out. "To prove it to you, we'll get the adoption papers ready in my attorney's office before the wedding ceremony. The second it's over, he'll get the process moving with the quickest speed possible."

She shook her head. "You don't know what you're saying."

"But I do because I've found the right woman for me." He cupped her face in his hands. "I'm in love with you, Francesca Myers. I can't honestly tell you when it happened, but the point is, it's finally happened to me. I believe it's happened to you, too, but you're too frightened to admit it yet."

Before she could take a breath, he lowered his head and closed his mouth over hers, giving her a kiss that was hot with desire. *A husband's kiss with the intent to possess.* When he finally let her up for air, he pressed his head to her forehead while he tangled his fingers in her hair. "I can't let you leave Greece. We belong together. You know it, and I know it."

Tears ran down her cheeks. "You say this now, but you might not always feel this way."

"I'm not Rob," he bit out. "Your ex-husband did a lot of damage to you, but he's not representative of most males I know, and certainly not of me."

She wiped away the moisture with her fingers. "You've overwhelmed me, Nik."

"Sorry, but it's the way I'm made. Up on Mount Olympus, you told me I was wonderful and you'd never change your mind about me. Was that a lie?"

A ring of white circled his lips, revealing his vulnerability. It was a revelation to her. "You know it wasn't."

"Then prove it and tell me what I want to hear."

She bit her lip. "I need to think about it, Nik."

His jaw hardened. "You still don't trust me?"

"It's not that. I can hardly trust the situation. As I told you in the tent, this is all happening too fast."

"How long did it take your father before he knew he wanted to marry your mother?"

She half laughed through her tears. "Mother rear-ended him in a parking lot at the college. When he got out of the car, pretty furious about it, she ran up to him full of apologies. He said one look in her eyes and he was a goner."

Nik kissed her lips. "My parents had a similar experience when they first met. It happens to lots of couples. Why not us?"

"But our circumstances are different. I've been married, and you haven't. You deserve to start out with a single woman who has no past. I'm a has-been."

"So am I. Don't forget my legion of women I've left in the dust."

"How could I possibly forget them?" she croaked.

He hugged her to him. "I'm madly in love with *you* and everything that formed you into who you are. That includes warts, Rob and Kellie, who won't want me for her best friend's husband."

"I'm afraid she won't while her marriage is in trouble. Oh, Nik—" She flung her arms around his neck and sobbed.

"Am I getting my answer yet?" he whispered into her hair.

She eventually lifted her head and stared at him without flinching. While she had the courage, she needed to ask him something. Her whole life's happiness depended on his answer.

"Nik— Try to be baldly honest with me because I'm going to ask you a hypothetical question."

"Go on."

"If we'd met under different circumstances and there'd been no Demi, do you think you would have asked me to marry you?"

An eerie silence crept into the room. He didn't move a muscle, but she sensed his body go rigid. Instead of the look of desire she'd always seen in his eyes when he was around her, he scrutinized her as though she were an unknown species of insect under a microscope. The longer he didn't say anything, the more fractured she felt.

"What kind of a hold does Kellie have on you that she could turn you into someone I don't know?"

"This has nothing to do with Kellie."

"The hell it doesn't." His wintry voice hit her like an arctic blast, prompting her to fold her arms to her waist. "Tell me what she said to you."

"She's been worried you'd do anything to get me to take care of Demi."

His face morphed into an expressionless mask. "I guess we'll never know if she spoke the truth or not, will we?"

Following his delivery to its ultimate conclusion, a gasp escaped her lips.

"Your advice to let my family come up with solutions has produced fruit. Ever since the funeral they've been in the process of looking for a nanny and expect to interview some candidates as early as tomorrow. For that, I thank you.

"However, you won't be among the prospects because you'll be on a plane flying out of Mykonos airport in the morning to join your best friend in the States where you came from. I hope you'll both be very happy together. Since I don't expect to see you again, I'll say goodbye now."

He was out the door so fast, she was incredulous.

What have I done?

Absolutely panicked, Fran wanted to run after him, but she didn't know where to go to find him. Doing the only thing she could do under the circumstances, she picked up the house phone. Nik had told her the house-keeper would answer.

When she did, Fran asked her if she could find either Sandro or Cosimo and tell them to come to the phone. In a few minutes, Cosimo came on the line.

Without preamble she said, "I hate to disturb you, but I—I'm afraid Nik and I just had words," she stammered. "I *have* to find him."

"I just saw him leave the villa."

Her heart plunged to her feet. "Do you know where he was going? I have to talk to him, Cosimo. It's a matter of life and death to me."

After a distinct pause he said, "He was headed for the marina. When he's stressed, he spends the night on his sailboat away from everyone, but don't tell him I told you that."

"I swear I won't. Bless you."

CHAPTER NINE

NIK RAN TO THE BEACH. After tossing his T-shirt on the sand, he plunged into the water and swam out to his boat moored on the other side of the dock. It was a good distance away, but it was the workout he needed.

He'd never been one to turn to alcohol, but he'd never been this gutted. When he reached the boat, he'd drink until he passed into forgetfulness. If the gods were kind, he wouldn't wake up.

The same stars that had lighted the sky above their tent on Mount Olympus now mocked him as he torpedoed through the water to his destination. When he rounded the pier, he heaved himself over the side of his boat.

A moonlight sail in calm seas sounded perfect. When he was far away from shore, he'd drop anchor and stretch out on the banquette with a bottle of Scotch. With the canopy of the heavens to keep him company, he'd drink himself into oblivion. Always one for adventure, who knew if it wouldn't be his last...

He went down the steps to the galley and rummaged in the cupboard till he found the bottle he was looking for. No glass was needed. Back up on top, he undid the ropes, then walked toward the outboard motor. It would take the boat beyond the buoy. If the wind didn't pick up, it didn't matter.

As he leaned over to turn it on, he thought he heard a voice call out, but the sound coincided with the noise from the motor. It was probably a gull. He put the throttle at a wakeless speed. The boat inched away from the dock. When he was young, he used to pretend he was a thief on the boat, sneaking away into the night.

That's what he felt like right now. Sneaking to a place where he could get away from the pain.

There went that cry again, stronger this time. That wasn't a bird. It was human! He cut the motor.

"Nik—"

It sounded like Fran. Was he hallucinating when he hadn't tasted a drop of Scotch yet? His head shot around behind him. He saw a form doing the breast stroke, trying to catch up.

"Wait for me!" she cried.

Galvanized into action, he slipped over the boat and swam to her. She practically collapsed in his arms while he trod water with her. "Put your head back and take deep breaths."

Her arms tightened around his neck. "I'm all right." Her lips grazed his cheek. "I was afraid you'd l-leave. I couldn't let that happen before t-talking to you first."

"Come on. Let's get you onboard and into some dry clothes. Your teeth are chattering. Let me do the work."

In no time he'd helped her up over the side. She'd plunged in the water wearing the same pants and blouse she'd had on earlier. With her hair streaming down, she looked like a shipwreck victim plucked out of the sea, albeit one more beautiful than he could begin to describe.

He gritted his teeth. "You could have broken your neck."

"But I didn't."

Nik helped her down to the galley and pushed her into the shower. "Take off everything. I'll leave a towel and robe hanging close by."

"Th-thank you."

After he'd found the desired articles for her, he went back up to weigh anchor, then he headed down to his bedroom. Luckily he kept a pair of sweats and a T-shirt onboard. He removed his swimsuit and got dressed.

While he waited for her, he made coffee for both of them. Having a sweet tooth, he added an extra amount of sugar to both mugs. She'd need it after her workout.

Right now he chose not to think about why she'd come. The fact that she'd put herself in jeopardy to catch up to him would do for starters. The rest could come after she was fully revived.

A few minutes later she appeared in the tiny kitchen in his blue toweling bathrobe. Her freshly shampooed hair had been formed into a braid. She smelled delicious. He handed her the coffee which she drank with obvious pleasure.

"Oh, that tastes good."

He lounged against the counter sipping his. "How did you know I was out here?"

"I ran after you. Cosimo saw me and volunteered to stay by Demi. I raced as fast as I could, but you move like the wind. Kind of like the way you drive your car. That was a thrill of a lifetime for me."

"I was in a hurry," he muttered.

"I know. It was all my fault. Every bit of it. Forgive me. Kellie never used to be like this, but the problems in her marriage have made her so unhappy, she doesn't see anything working out for herself, or me."

"Their situation isn't ours."

"You think I don't know that?" She put the mug down and grasped both his arms. "She jumped to all the wrong conclusions from an outsider's perspective, but she lost sight of one thing. I love you, Nik. You have no idea how much." She slid her arms around his neck. "Help me, darling. I can't reach your mouth and I need it more than I need life."

Not immune to her pleading, he picked her up and carried her to his bedroom. But after laying her down, he sat beside her. She tried to pull him down. "Nik—you have to forgive me," she implored him.

His eyes smarted. "I'm the one who needs forgiveness. I fell in love with you the moment we met, then panicked because you were leaving on a trip with Kellie. I had to think of a way to keep you in Greece so we could get to know each other. I used Demi shamefully as my excuse."

"I can't believe it!" she cried for happiness.

"On our camping trip, I was building up the courage to tell you about my medical problem when you told me about yours. After that I couldn't hold back. On our drive home, I would have asked you to marry me, but then we got that call about Demi."

"But I almost ruined everything with that awful question." She broke down in tears. "Please forgive me, Nik."

"I think I like this ending better. To watch you swim toward my boat as if your life depended on it told me I hadn't been wrong about you. I couldn't swim out to you fast enough."

Her face glistened with moisture. "Are we through talking now?"

He chuckled. "Not yet, but soon. Let's get back to the house and relieve Cosimo. He deserves a break if Demi has fallen apart again. They all do."

A half hour later, Nik grasped her hand and they tiptoed into the nursery. Cosimo had dealt with a miserable Demi until they got there. Now they were finally alone with the baby, who'd fallen asleep.

He pulled Fran close. "Since the hospital in Leminos, I've had this dream we'd get married and adopt her. I honestly believe Melina made sure she was dropped literally at your feet so you'd become her new mother. That's why Demi reached out to you."

Fran hugged him with all the strength in her. "It felt like heaven had delivered her expressly to me."

"Then let's adopt her as our own miracle daughter and give her all the love we can. Later on we'll adopt another baby and another after that."

"You're making me too happy, Nik." She sobbed against his shoulder.

"We need to get married soon so she'll become bilingual in a hurry."

"I've got to learn Greek fast! Oh—I'll have to resign from my job at the hospital."

"We'll tell my parents in the morning." He rocked her in his arms for a long time. "I'm going to enjoy seeing the look in their eyes. They're not going to believe their youngest upstart son is finally going to settle down."

"They've had to wait a long time." She laughed through the tears. "Mine won't believe it either. They're going to adore you."

"You've already got my family wrapped around your little finger."

"It's you I'm worried about. Let's go in the bedroom so we won't wake up Demi."

He pulled her into the other room before cupping her face. "I want to spend the rest of the night with you, but I'm old-fashioned and would like your father's permission to marry you before I work my wicked ways with you. My bachelor days have come to an end. You're going to be my precious wife and I want to do everything right."

"You *do* do everything right. So right, I don't know how I was ever lucky enough to have found you. Just be with me for a little while. We'll stay dressed on top of the covers," she begged.

His lips twitched. "Once I start touching you, I'll never stop. I want you to be able to tell Kellie that I didn't coerce you into marrying me."

Her eyes filled again. "I wish I'd never told you anything about our conversation."

"Hush. I'm glad you did. Now we don't have any secrets. That's the way it should be. When you think Kellie's ready, you can tell her about our mutual problem."

"She'll be mortified when she learns what happened to you on that climb."

He smoothed the hair off her forehead. "But you'll know how to comfort her. She needs a lot of that right now while her marriage is suffering. That's one of your special gifts. Now kiss me like you mean it, then let me go for tonight. Tomorrow, and all the tomorrows after that, will be a different story."

"Nik—"

CHAPTER TEN

Three weeks later...

"TIME FOR YOUR NAP, sweetheart." Demi had finished her lunch. Fran took her from the high chair and carried her through the penthouse to the bedroom they'd turned into a nursery filled with adorable baby furniture and curtains.

After changing her diaper, Fran put her down in the crib. She sang her one song. "Now be a good girl for Mommy and go to sleep. I've got a lot to do before your daddy gets home tonight."

Her watch said one-thirty. There was still the table to set in the dining area and the kitchen to clean up, not to mention making the bed and getting herself ready later. She'd bought a new black dress with spaghetti straps in the hope of wowing her new husband.

Today marked their first-week anniversary as man and wife. She was making some of Nik's favorite foods for a special dinner she wanted to be perfect. Fran had gotten the recipes from his mother and had already been on the phone with her twice to make sure she was doing the moussaka right.

The traditional recipe called for eggplant and meat

filling. "But the trick," his mother said, "is to layer in potatoes and zucchini to make it even richer before you top it with the bechamel sauce. Use heavy cream. My Nikki will love it."

Fran loved her new mother-in-law and smiled as she hurried back through the rooms to the kitchen. She hardly recognized Nik's elegant bachelor domicile anymore. The penthouse was still filled with light and open, but a family lived here now, complete with a baby. It contained the kind of clutter that turned a house into a home. She was so happy it was scary.

Today Nik had gone to the office for the first time. She'd missed him horribly.

Because of the baby, they hadn't taken an official honeymoon yet. In another month they hoped Demi would be able to handle a few days away from them, but none of it mattered. Once they'd said their vows at the chapel in Mykonos with their families looking on, they'd become insatiable lovers.

The only thing to mar the event was Kellie's absence. After she'd learned there was going to be a wedding, and had been told the true facts, she was desolate for all the things she'd said. But Nik had gotten on the phone and put her mind at ease. Just when Fran thought she couldn't love the man more, he did something to win her heart all over again.

Unfortunately, Kellie hadn't been feeling well and decided not to make the flight over.

Fran believed her, but she also knew she was afraid to come to Greece. Leandros kept an eye on her even when they were apart. He would know if she returned to attend the wedding. Fran promised to stay in close touch with her.

Nik had taken another week off in order to be home. When they weren't playing with the baby or eating, they found joy in each other's arms. Fran was existing on an entirely different level of happiness. It transcended what she'd known before.

The thought of tonight after they'd put the baby down and could concentrate on each other sent heat surging through her body. It was embarrassing how eager she was, but she loved her husband so much, she couldn't hide it if she tried.

She hurried into their bedroom barefooted to get busy and was just smoothing the duvet when she was grasped at the waist from behind and spun around.

"Nik!" she squealed in shock and joy. No one looked more gorgeous than he did, especially in his tan suit and tie. "You're not supposed to be home until tonight! You've caught me looking terrible."

His dark eyes devoured her. "Every husband should be so lucky to come home and find his wife in a pair of shorts like yours. I have to admit my T-shirt adds an allure, but I think we'll dispense with it."

"Darling," she half giggled the words as he put actions to his words and followed her down on top of the bed she'd just made.

"There's no help for you now," he growled the words into her neck. "I peeked in on Demi and she's out for the count."

"But today's your first day back."

"It was." He plundered her mouth until she was breathless. "Sandro told me I was worthless and sent me home."

"He didn't—"

Nik rolled her over so she was lying on top of him.

"No, he didn't. Actually, I sat at my desk and didn't hear a word my assistant said to me. My bros came in to eat lunch with me. When I couldn't carry on a coherent conversation with them, I knew what I had to do."

He turned her on her back once more. "Something smelled good when I walked in."

"It's my surprise dinner for you."

That heartbreaking smile broke out on his handsome face before he pulled a necklace out of his pocket. "This is a choker of gemstones the color of your eyes. It's for seven days of bliss," he murmured as he fastened it around her neck. "Happy anniversary, you beautiful creature. If a man could die from too much happiness, I'd have expired a week ago."

"I love you, Nik. I love you," she cried as rapture took over. She forgot everything until they heard Demi start to fuss much later.

Nik groaned and slowly relinquished her mouth with a smile. "We're going to have to do something about this. While I was in my office, the thought came to me that you could work with me. We'd bring in a playpen for Demi."

Laughter bubbled out of Fran. "That would be a novelty for about ten minutes before it turned into a disaster, but I love the idea of it. Maybe if your father put in two days a week, you and I would have more time together and could sail around the Aegean with our little girl. What do you think?"

He planted a long, hard kiss on her mouth. "I love the way you think. I'll call him later."

"Go ahead and do it right now. Think how happy it will make him."

Nik frowned. "What's the matter? Are you tired of me already?"

"Darling—" She leaned over him, kissing every centimeter of his face. "You know better than that. I just thought if you do this now, my Atlas will stop worrying about him. I'm afraid I'm very selfish and want all your thoughts centered on me."

"Don't you know they are?" he asked in a husky voice. "Why do you think I came home early today?"

She pressed a kiss to his lips. "Then humor me."

He groaned again. "Hand me your phone. Mine is on the floor with my clothes."

"Where they *should* be."

Laughter escaped his throat. "Whoever dreamed I'd be married to such a 'wicked' wife?"

"There's still a lot you don't know about me." With a chuckle, she took her phone from the bedside table.

As he pressed the digits, she whispered in his ear. "Tell him we need him to start work as soon as possible. I want you all to myself for as long as you can stand me. When the tornado brought Demi to me, it also brought her uncle. *It was written in the whirlwind.*"

* * * * *

MILLS & BOON®

Mills & Boon have been at the heart of romance since 1908... and while the fashions may have changed, one thing remains the same: from pulse-pounding passion to the gentlest caress, we're always known how to bring romance alive.

Now, we're delighted to present you with these irresistible illustrations, inspired by the vintage glamour of our covers. So indulge your wildest dreams and unleash your imagination as we present the most iconic Mills & Boon moments of the last century.

Visit **www.millsandboon.co.uk/ArtofRomance** to order yours!

MILLS & BOON®

Why shop at millsandboon.co.uk?

Each year, thousands of romance readers find their perfect read at millsandboon.co.uk. That's because we're passionate about bringing you the very best romantic fiction. Here are some of the advantages of shopping at www.millsandboon.co.uk:

* **Get new books first**—you'll be able to buy your favourite books one month before they hit the shops

* **Get exclusive discounts**—you'll also be able to buy our specially created monthly collections, with up to 50% off the RRP

* **Find your favourite authors**—latest news, interviews and new releases for all your favourite authors and series on our website, plus ideas for what to try next

* **Join in**—once you've bought your favourite books, don't forget to register with us to rate, review and join in the discussions

Visit **www.millsandboon.co.uk**
for all this and more today!